praise for

No Place Like Home

"Sweet entertaining story! *No Place Like Home* by Betsy St. Amant brings us back to Magnolia Bay and her entertaining cast of characters. A captivating, page-turning story of friendship and second chances. Honesty, overcoming misperceptions about their families, humor, friendship, funny banter, and a sweet romance kept me turning pages late into the night.."

—JEANNE, GOODREADS

"Another fantastic read. *No Place Like Home* involves former school rivals, a circus, and secrets. The storyline was engaging, heartwarming, and captivating."

—ALLYSON, GOODREADS

"Magnolia Bay is a place that I would like to visit not only for the food but also for the wonderful people there! I love that we get to see characters from the previous book and learn more about characters, especially Cade this time. Reading about an aerialist and a circus was so interesting!"

—LAURA, GOODREADS

No Place
Like Home

· MAGNOLIA BAY ·
BOOK 2

Do Place Like Home

BETSY ST. AMANT

sunrise
PUBLISHING

No Place Like Home
Magnolia Bay, Book 2
Published by Sunrise Media Group LLC
Copyright © 2025 Betsy St. Amant Haddox
Print ISBN: 978-1-963372-50-2
Ebook ISBN: 978-1-963372-51-9

This book is a work of fiction. Names, characters, places, and incidents are either products of the author's imagination or used fictitiously. Any similarity to actual people, organizations, and/or events is purely coincidental.

Scriptures taken from the Holy Bible, New International Version®, NIV®. Copyright © 1973, 1978, 1984, 2011 by Biblica, Inc.™ Used by permission of Zondervan. All rights reserved worldwide. www.zondervan.com The "NIV" and "New International Version" are trademarks registered in the United States Patent and Trademark Office by Biblica, Inc.™

For more information about Betsy St. Amant please access the author's website at the following address: www.betsystamant.com.

Published in the United States of America.
Cover Illustration and Design: Raya Decker

· MAGNOLIA BAY ·

Where I Found You
No Place Like Home
Meant for Me

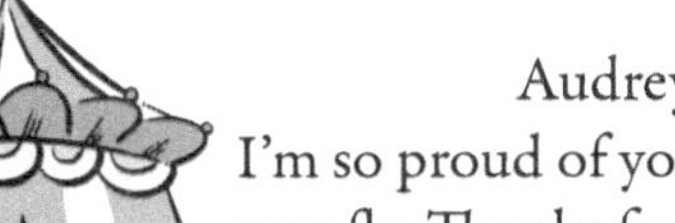

Audrey -
I'm so proud of you and the way
you fly. Thanks for asking me to
write a book starring an aerialist.
This one is for you.

One

IF A GUY HAD TO EAT A FEW FROG LEGS to save the family legacy, Cade Landry better find a bib.

Still . . . "Frog leg food truck, you say?" Cade leaned back in his desk chair in the mayor's office building in downtown Magnolia Bay and propped his brown Sperrys on the desk. The phone cord snagged against the overflowing bin of papers awaiting his attention, knocking half the stack onto a red folder that teetered before dropping. More papers fluttered to their freedom.

He closed his eyes—would that make the mess go away?—as the Cajun drawl continued in his ear.

"That's right. I heard about that Magnolia Days festival you got going on end of the month, thought we could snag a spot." The man, who'd introduced himself as Bruno and who Cade imagined *ha*d to be tanned and burly, cleared his throat. "Best in Louisiana, we are."

"Uh-huh." Was that a flex though? How many frog leg restaurants could there even be on the mainland?

Then again . . . Cade squinted at the open spreadsheet of vendors thus far committed to Magnolia Days—and at the multiple empty rows that had been full just two years ago. Before the hurricane. Before the annual festival had taken a nosedive and, with it, the much-needed funding for his beloved city still undergoing storm restoration.

Could he afford to be picky? His secret weapon for the festival had ghosted his emails. Two months and still no answer. Cade reached over and clicked refresh on his computer, hoping for a miracle.

Nope.

And now he was going to be late to meet with the balloon arch lady. "Listen, Mr. . . ."

"Guidry. Bruno Guidry, at your service." *Clang.*

That sounded like a stockpot lid. Was he cooking the legs as they spoke? Cade grimaced, fighting the irrational urge to pinch his nose shut. "Look, I'm sure they're great—as far as frog legs go—but I'm looking for crawfish meat pies. Shrimp tacos. Cajun biscuits. Beignets."

"Tell you what," Bruno said. *Clang-clang.* "Why don't you come up to New Orleans for a tastin'?"

Cade swallowed, smoothed the front of his fitted button-down. "Um . . ."

His office door, cracked as usual so it didn't jam when summer heat swelled the wood, swung all the way open to reveal his father's secretary, Pearl. She fanned herself with an envelope as she clutched the neck of her floral blouse with her free hand. "Miley is here."

Without waiting for an invitation, Miley Mitchell, the twenty-something barista from Chug a Mug, pressed past Cade's overheated receptionist and plopped into the chair adjacent his desk. She wore fishnet leggings under denim shorts, an oversized men's button-down with the sleeves rolled up, and a sullen expression. He jotted the word *latte* on a notepad—the coffee would be good today.

But probably not the pending conversation.

He raised his eyebrows at her as he leaned back in his chair. "What now?"

Clang. "No, you don't have to come now. Anytime next week works."

"Oh, sorry. Not you, Bruno." Cade held up a finger at Miley as Pearl slipped back into the hallway. "I'm actually not sure I can get to New Orleans at all—"

"He can't. He's busy." Miley cupped her hands and talked loudly toward the receiver. "Fixing potholes."

"No, we don't sell tadpoles." Bruno sounded confused. "Frog legs don't work that way."

Oh, for Pete's sake. Cade's feet hit the floor as he lurched forward. "Just a second, Bruno. I'm putting you on a brief *hold*." Not pole. Or hole. He jabbed the red button on the phone base and gave Miley his full attention. "You were saying?"

A second line rang. His cell buzzed. Cade ignored both.

Miley gestured, black nail polish contrasting her white skin. "I sent in a request to meet with you."

He looked at his chaotic desk. "When?"

She hiked a dark eyebrow. "This mess is organized by date?"

Fair point. He rummaged a little, carefully. Miley leaned over and rescued the red folder from the floor. "Man. You need an assistant."

He snorted as he continued to fruitlessly dig. "I *am* the assistant." The framed diploma on the wall behind Miley taunted him—Yale Law. Ha. And look at him now. Working for Dad, being the face of Magnolia Bay. He'd probably shaken more hands and kissed more babies than his mayor father.

"I can't find it." Giving up, Cade reached in the top desk drawer and rustled around for the bag of M&Ms he'd stashed. At least he knew where those were. "I don't know why my father thought making me town director was a good idea."

Miley thumbed through the folder's contents. "It *was* a good idea—three years ago. Maybe you've outgrown the job." She narrowed her eyes. "Sort of like your workload has outgrown your desk."

"I like my job." Besides, the only place to go in small-town politics was *up*. And he certainly wouldn't be taking on the role of mayor anytime soon. He ripped the bag of candy and palmed a cluster into his mouth. "The festival is just . . . a lot. More pressure this year."

"Found it." Miley tossed the folder toward him. It landed on his desk calendar, which still showed last month. "There's a chocolate stain on the corner."

That was probably from the Twix he'd inhaled last week while crunching numbers—more red than black. He picked up the meeting request. "What's the big deal? We've always had potholes." The phone blinked, indicating Frog Legs still waited for an answer. And he'd never gotten a quote for the extra festival chairs. Had he confirmed the porta-potties?

Miley snapped her fingers in front of her own face. "Hey, right here. Focus."

He zeroed in, though the blinking red light of the phone still teased his peripheral. So many things to do. The festival was in less than a month. He fisted another bite of candy, chewed fast.

"Have you seriously not noticed the potholes have gotten worse?" Miley crossed her arms over her chest. "Take a walk and check them out sometime. That storm last month apparently finished what the hurricane started. And let's just say my dad's not happy about the crater in front of Chug a Mug. He says it's deterring customers."

Miley's mood swings were more likely the cause of that. Still, Mr. Mitchell, the wayfaring owner of the coffee shop who occasionally swooped into the Bay to see Miley, was not someone you wanted to disappoint. Cade sighed. "You know what's ironic?"

Miley lifted one shoulder. "A duck that can't swim?"

"Well, sure." He pointed at her with the bag of candy. "But more so, the fact that everyone seems to need something that costs money, but asking for it is taking me away from planning the event that is going to bring in that money." He squinted at her. "Are you too young to know Alanis Morissette?"

She squinted back. "I feel like this is a trick question."

"Forget it. She has song about irony." Cade reached up and loosened his tie. "I am that song right now."

Miley rolled her eyes. "Regardless, Dad wants it handled. He keeps saying 'Tell whoever's in charge down there to make it top priority.'" She walked two fingers up the air on an invisible ladder.

Cade shrugged. "I'll see what I can do, but as you pointed out, there are a lot of potholes in Magnolia Bay."

"That could comfortably house a family of four?"

"I'm just saying I can't guarantee yours will be fixed first—or any of them right now. We're trying to *earn* money, not spend more of it."

"You really think people are going to come to Magnolia Days this year?" Miley's nose ring glistened, mocking him as much as her tone. But the girl had never been cruel, just brutally honest.

He eyed the phone, the frantic flashing starting to match his heart rate. "I have a plan."

"Hope it's not buried on your desk."

It might be the only thing that wasn't. Cade threw the empty candy bag into the trashcan full of gum wrappers and crinkled chip bags. "We're having a special event this year to go along with all the food trucks and face-painting and vendors. A big draw to get people's attention, put Magnolia Bay back on the map."

The intercom on the phone released a burst of static, then Pearl's voice squawked. "Cade, some exotic animal sanctuary is on line two."

Miley slid her hand down her face. "Is that your plan? Monkeys and bearded dragons?"

"*No.*" Cade mashed the intercom button. "Pearl, I told that guy he couldn't come—too much liability. Get rid of him."

"Get rid of who?" An offended Australian accent sounded from the speaker. "*Me?*"

Oh brother. "One moment." Cade jabbed the mute button. "Look, Miley. I'll fix it, I promise." He'd fix the hole. He'd fix the town budget. He'd fix *everything*.

"How exactly are you going to fix . . . this?" She waved one hand toward his desk that now strongly resembled what he'd imagine an office supply store would look like if a bomb went off.

"Easy. We're going to host a Cajun Circus." He smiled, waiting for Miley's grin of approval.

He only got a blank stare. "A what?"

Okay, not what he had hoped. It would work . . . right? Cade stood. "Cajun Circus. You know—clowns. Juggling. Aerial acts. Hoops of fire." He spread his arms wide like a game show host. "All with a Southern flair."

She frowned. "What's aerial?"

"Like Cirque de Soleil. Where they perform those flips and elaborate moves on strips of colored fabric hanging from the ceiling?"

"Sounds dangerous."

"I'm sure it is. But it's also impressive. You probably don't remember Rosalyn Dupree—you're younger than us. She and I went to school together. We kind of had a back-and-forth rivalry thing." Cade waved one hand in the air, as if it was no big deal. As if Rosalyn wasn't a combination of his best and worst memories. As if she wasn't the one ghosting his emails. "She's made a pretty big name for herself in the industry—even internationally."

Miley crossed her arms again. "That's your plan to save Magnolia Bay? Your old high school rival and clowns?"

"To save *Magnolia Days*," he corrected. "And hopefully Magnolia Days will help save the town."

"There won't be a town to save if the potholes get much bigger."

Miley tossed the comment like a grenade, then left with a stomp of ankle boots.

Oh well. At least she'd left annoyed, which meant Cade was still on for his latte later.

He took his seat, picked up the desk phone, and noticed the exotic animal sanctuary had hung up. Oops. Though now he wouldn't have to try to tell him no. He clicked the line for Frog Legs, instead. "Sorry about that hold, Bruno."

Even the man's laugh held a Cajun accent. "No problem. Already fried up another batch."

Cade winced. "Perfect."

"So you're coming, then?"

"I . . . well." Why was it so hard to say no? Cade didn't want frog legs. He didn't want to even *try* frog legs. And he doubted the rest of the Bay felt any differently. But they needed vendors. "I'll think about it."

Clang. "Trust me, boy, you can't just think about my unique Cajun seasoning blend. You must *taste* it."

This guy wasn't giving up. Cade ran a hand over his face, his five o'clock shadow coming in early. Did stress grow hair faster? "Okay, yes. I'll be there sometime next week."

As Cade hung up, his cell buzzed with an incoming text—another food truck vendor canceling. Ugh. He winced, then scrolled up to the texts he'd ignored during Miley's visit. A form response to his dancing poodle inquiry, another from his father asking if he'd finished his third quarter projections yet. Also one containing Mama D's Wordle score.

Buzz. Great. Now Miley, sending several emojis in a row of a family of four, a house . . . and a knife.

How had he ended up here, again? Cade's gaze landed once more on the diploma on the wall, highlighted by the afternoon sun streaming through the window, and his chest tightened. Oh yeah. That was how. Was he going to be able to pull this off? The festival, the circus. Without Rosalyn or a special act—*something impressive*—he'd just end up with his fishing buddy Owen walking on stilts. Hardly marketing worthy.

His heartbeat accelerated. He couldn't fail.

Pearl sounded on the intercom. "Cade, there's a visitor for you."

"Not *now*!" Oh, he hadn't meant to snap. But breathing was still difficult, and who had decided to squeeze his head between their hands? His vision blurred.

A blonde head poked into his office. "Bad time?"

He looked up with a start. Rosalyn Dupree.

Rosalyn?

Cade blinked rapidly, but the golden-haired woman, dressed in a white linen top and paper bag shorts leaning one slim shoulder against his doorframe, didn't dissipate. She'd showed up. Here. Back in Magnolia Bay.

He opened his mouth, then shut it.

"Guess so." Rosalyn winced, green eyes crinkling as she tucked wavy tresses behind her ears. "Sorry."

"Wait!" Cade leaped to his feet, finally finding his tongue. His manners.

But the door had already shut behind her.

She shouldn't have come. Her mother was wrong.

Rosalyn rushed past the secretary—Pearl, she'd said?—and kept her head ducked, hair curtaining the side of her face as she hurried to the elevator. *Don't talk to me, don't talk to me . . .*

"Where are you going, honey?"

Shoot. She couldn't be rude.

She forced a smile, turned to see the kind older woman posed with a stapler in hand, brow wrinkled. A desk fan hummed atop a tower of file folders next to a Chug a Mug coffee cup.

Where *was* Rosalyn going? Wasn't that the million-dollar question. "Just . . . away." She punched the elevator button with a shaky hand. Away . . . backward . . . in circles. Pick one.

Down the hall, the door to Cade's office rattled. Despite her mother's assurance, he had *not* been happy to see her—and why would he be, after she'd ignored his email asking her to perform at Magnolia Days. She hadn't *meant* to ignore it, of course. It'd simply fallen off her radar after a skim-read a few months ago. Before . . . well, before a lot of things.

Her gaze darted to the bandage wrapped around her knee. She'd have hidden it under yoga pants, but after so many years touring abroad, she'd forgotten how hot it got here in the Bay. Plus, she'd come home to heal. Physically and mentally.

Emotionally might be asking for too much.

The AC hummed and she tapped her sandaled foot, willing the elevator door to open. She'd been back in town several days now, and her mom had kept not-so-subtly leaving a flyer advertising "Magnolia Days' First Ever Cajun Circus—Details to Come" strategically around the house until she'd taken the bait.

"What's this?" Rosalyn had asked earlier that morning, watching her mother blend a smoothie.

Elegant as always, Mom wore a high-necked blouse patterned with a swirl of emerald that brought out her eyes. "The town's fundraiser effort could use a little help." Mom scooped in a handful of berries, poured a measuring cup of milk. "And how convenient to have such a talented performer back at home—right on time."

"But I don't even know how long I'm staying." The excuse sounded as weak as it felt. But what was she supposed to say—that she couldn't risk media attention right now? She'd just sound like a diva. She crossed her arms over her workout top, going for the stronger excuse. "I have to take it easy on my knee."

Mom's all-knowing gaze dropped to Rosalyn's bandage, then back to the bowl of blueberries. "I thought you'd been given the all-clear."

"That doctor didn't know what he was talking about."

"Ah, I see. Well, it's a good thing second opinions exist in Magnolia Bay." The whir of the blender cut off Rosalyn's protest, and the urge to see Cade again—to participate in something bigger than her that wasn't *about* her—nudged until she couldn't resist. The next thing she knew, she'd changed clothes and driven to the mayor's office to find Cade exactly where her mother claimed he'd be.

Just not apparently where Rosalyn needed to be.

Down the hall, Cade's office door rattled again. *Where* was the elevator? Rosalyn jabbed the lit button one more time, despite logic proving it made no difference. She hadn't seen him since that Harvard-Yale football game five years ago, when they'd had a . . . whatever you call it. Near-moment? Maybe that's why he'd been so annoyed to see her. Or maybe he'd somehow heard about—

"Rosalyn!" Cade hurried down the hall, all sandy brown hair and pressed clothing and . . . smiles?

Oh. She frowned, hesitant. So, not annoyed, then? "Hey . . ."

He passed Pearl's desk, clearly not noticing the way the woman's eyebrow hiked. Then again, Rosalyn sure hadn't noticed the cut of Cade's designer button-down, or the way it hugged his biceps, when she'd glimpsed him from his doorway a moment ago.

Someone had started working out since college.

"Sorry about that. The door sticks." Slightly winded from his battle, Cade's smile shifted from brilliant to sheepish. Five o'clock shadow graced his cut jaw line, his brown eyes sparking with the charm that had always kept him popular in high school. "It's a little low on the priority list of fixes around here."

"I'm sorry I interrupted. I should've made an appointment." Rosalyn shoved her hands into her shorts pockets, hating she wasn't sure where else to put them. Normally, poise and grace came easy for her—she was a performer. No one wanted to watch clunky and awkward ten feet in the air. But since coming home, she seemed to have slid back into the role of nerdy, unsure teenager.

The girl Cade used to have no problem ignoring until it was time to compete.

"Oh, that had nothing to do with you—just work." He waved one hand in the air, the movement as confident as he'd always been. "I'm really glad you're here."

A bit of tension eased out of her shoulders. Not that she ever cared *too* much what he thought. Not since that one time in sixth grade when he'd added too much vinegar—make that too much *arrogance*—to their volcano experiment and ruined going to regionals in the science fair competition for them both.

She shifted her weight off her knee. Tested a smile. "It's been a long time."

"Too long."

"I'm sorry I didn't email you back." She winced. "I was traveling, and I'll be honest—it fell through the cracks." For good reason, but that wasn't a story for an old rival and a delayed elevator. Where *was* that thing?

Though maybe she wasn't in quite as big a hurry as before.

Cade nodded. "I saw you were on a European tour earlier this year."

And Saudi Arabia. She fought the shudder that crept up her back, fought the urge to look over her shoulder despite the fact the only person behind her was a sixty-something-year-old woman playing solitaire.

Definitely not a mob boss.

"But hey, you're here now." Cade slid his own hands into his pockets, mirroring her. "You have no idea how relieved I am."

He might not be as relieved if he realized she hadn't committed to the circus. She was just here to get info. Get her mother off her back. Get . . . something. "About that. I'm not in town for too long."

"Long enough for the circus, hopefully. Name your terms." He held up both hands, that same charismatic smile tugging his lips. "If they're not within our budget, I'll make it happen."

"It's not about the money." Well, that was a partial lie. The fact she desperately needed money in the first place was still foreign. Rosalyn hesitated. So much she could tell him, and so much she shouldn't. She took the easy way out again and extended her leg. "I'm still on light duty."

His gaze dropped to her knee, to the flesh tone bandage that he clearly hadn't noticed before that moment. "*Oh*. Are you okay?"

She nodded. "It's healing. I just haven't performed since I fell."

"You *fell*?" His eyes bugged from his head, his mouth open. "From your . . . fabric thingies?"

"Silks." She pressed her fingers to her lips to hide her laugh but was too late.

"Sorry. I'm a Muggle." He matched her grin, and more of the tension she'd worn for the last several months lifted off her weary shoulders. "You'll have to teach me the terminology."

There was that charm that had landed him two prom dates. Though she hadn't been either of them. "I might." The words left her lips and hovered between them, seemingly surprising him as much as her.

"I mean, at this point, you have to stay for a while, right?" Cade rocked back on his heels. "Teach me about this aerial thing. It's not often you know something I don't, Ace."

His old nickname for her lit a spark in her chest she hadn't felt in ages. "Ace. Now *that's* been a while. When did you first call me that?"

He looked up at the tiled ceiling, lips twisted. "Probably fifth grade, when I read more books than you for that class Reading Railroad Train."

"You most certainly did not." She crossed her arms over her chest, feeling lighter than she had in weeks. Months. Her knee didn't even throb. "I read thirty-one."

He nodded seriously. "I read thirty-two."

"Liar!" It was hard to pretend to be mad when you were smiling.

He harrumphed, eyes sparkling. "Prove it."

"Find me a yearbook."

Pearl's stapler smacked against a stack of paper. "He's got one in his office." She pointed down the hall.

"Now Pearl, that is not helpful." Cade took Rosalyn's elbow, steered her away from the receptionist and closer to a potted fern. "What do you say, Ace? Want to go talk terms?" He tilted his head. "*Not* in my office, near the yearbook that absolutely doesn't prove anything?"

Rosalyn hesitated, his touch warm on her bare arm. *Ding.* The elevator doors finally slid open, beckoning her back to her car. To her childhood home.

To the distressing memories of the past few months and the new urge to watch her back, even tucked away in Magnolia Bay. Could she risk the circus? Though honestly, how much media attention could it really get nationwide? It should be safe in that regard.

Not in others. Was she ready to try again?

"We could start with a post-hurricane tour of town. Show you why we're doing the circus in the first place." Cade let go, took a short step back—clearly giving her space to make the decision.

Huh. That was new. High school Cade barreled ahead, expecting whatever he wanted to be handed to him if he couldn't nab it for himself.

She sort of wanted to know a little more about this Cade.

"I'll throw in a latte." He gestured toward her with one finger. "Or a vegan matcha almond foam tea, or whatever it is you probably drink now."

Her laugh escaped, and there was no shoving it back in. "Fine. A tour it is." It couldn't hurt. Maybe the company would be nice.

Behind them, Pearl hummed in approval. Cade seemed to ignore her. "Let me grab my keys. Wait here?" The concern in his eyes that maybe she wouldn't was sweet.

She nodded. "I'm not going anywhere."

For now.

CADE HAD PLANNED TO CHECK AT LEAST four things off his endless Magnolia Days to-do list, but giving Rosalyn a post-hurricane tour of Magnolia Bay could still count as productive, right? Maybe it'd make her say yes.

He watched the afternoon sun reflect off her golden hair and decided yes, yes it could.

"Your chariot." He pulled the used golf cart he'd convinced his father to buy last year up to the curb in front of his office building, where Rosalyn waited next to a clump of bushes that had recently been trimmed back. The wind stirred her hair, wafting citrus toward him as she settled into the seat beside him.

"Wow. Such service." She smoothed one hand over the dash, slightly buckled from the heat. "Do you treat all the ladies in the Bay like this?"

"Just the gimpy ones." He pointed to her knee. "Do you remember Delia? She had hip surgery a while back and already called dibs for Magnolia Days if she's still using a cane by then."

"Of course I remember Mama D." Rosalyn grabbed the handle overhead as Cade released the brake and pressed the gas. "I'm sorry she needed surgery though."

"It was a good thing. She'll be getting around a lot better soon, and the whole ordeal led to Elisa taking over the Magnolia Blossom diner." Cade slowed at the approaching stop sign. Sun glinted and he pulled his sunglasses from the neck of his button-down and slid them on. Maybe Rosalyn wouldn't notice him noticing her emerald-green eyes. "You'll have to check out her new recipes."

She nodded. "I remember Elisa. We probably haven't seen each other since graduation."

Cade steered them onto Village Lane. A warm breeze ruffled the loose hem of Rosalyn's top and stirred her hair into her eyes.

She tugged a tie from her wrist and scooped her long tresses into a high ponytail, sending more citrus his way. "Everything is the same but different, isn't it?"

"I guess it would seem that way, coming back here after so long." He risked another glance her direction. The same could be said of her. Same ol' Rosalyn . . . though maybe a little more graceful, elegant, poised than in school. But always capable. Whether it was writing a thesis, working through pages of trigonometry, or hanging upside down from multicolored silks, the girl—*woman*—had always been able to handle herself.

But the way Cade's eyes kept gravitating to the curve of her jaw and to how her top lip dipped in the middle, well, that was certainly different. Reminded him of that night in the alley at the Lazy Spoon, after the Harvard versus Yale football—

Thunk.

His left tire dipped into a crater in the pavement, jarring them back onto the road with a force that shook his teeth. "That's one more thing I need to get fixed from the hurricane."

"Ah." Rosalyn's elbow swung as she gripped the overhead handle. "Hence the circus?"

"Yep. One of many *hences*. It's hard to believe it's almost been a year since the storm." He attempted to see Magnolia Bay's main drag through Rosalyn's eyes. At the rows of colorful shops lining Village Lane, the tulip beds with petals turning crisp in the summer heat. "I know what you mean, though, about everything being the same yet different. There are these pockets of town that look like nothing ever happened, and then you turn a corner and realize there's still plenty of damage lingering around the edges."

Missing fence planks. Torn awnings. Mismatched, patched roofs awaiting their final restoration—restoration many couldn't afford, given their various insurance situations. Not to mention the potholes now creeping up like extras in a zombie movie.

The knot of pressure that frequently aggravated Cade's stomach pulled tighter as they drove around the caving concrete in front of Chug a Mug. "Man, this one *has* gotten bad." He gestured to the pothole, half-expecting to see Joseph standing in a coat of many colors. "Miley wasn't exaggerating."

"Miley?" Rosalyn asked.

"The Chug a Mug manager. Her dad is the owner, but she runs the place while he's overseas on business." He shot Rosalyn a sidelong glance. "Be sure to ask for weather reports before you order any coffee."

"That's a new one." Rosalyn smiled. "I've heard of the weather affecting baked goods, but never coffee."

"Not that kind of weather." Cade chuckled. "You'll see." *Ask her for coffee.* The words stuck inside his mouth. But it wasn't a date—he'd promised her a drink for the tour, right? "Do you want that coffee now? Or tea?"

"I'm actually okay—should probably lay off caffeine the rest of the day." She smiled. "Thank you, though."

See? That hadn't been so hard.

Though technically he *had* gotten turned down.

A jaunty ringtone filled the sudden silence, and Rosalyn pulled her cell from her purse. Her brow pinched as she stared at the display. Then, she quickly hit the reject button and slid it back into the bag.

"So, the circus is to help get revenue for Magnolia Days?" Rosalyn folded her hands in her lap as they continued driving. Farmer Branson exited Chug a Mug juggling a pastry bag and a to-go cup, pausing to hold the door open with his overall-clad leg for Trish, one of the waitresses at the Magnolia Blossom.

Cade lifted one hand from the wheel to wave. "Yeah, we need Magnolia Days to be lucrative this year." To put it mildly.

Rosalyn tilted her chin toward him. "Okay, I recognize that frown. It's the same one you had senior year when they were tallying our GPAs." She lightly elbowed his side. "You're stressed." She could tell that? He touched the brake as they pulled up in front of the fenced-in community park. "It's stressful, sure. The city budget is tight, and there are so many things that haven't received attention yet. Like the gazebo." He pointed to the half-repaired structure. "It's been tall and proud as long as I can remember—the most popular summer wedding spot, but it's not safe right now to hold a ceremony."

Rosalyn's brow pinched. "I guess until lately, I've never realized how little things add up and get expensive."

"And give an impression." Cade nodded. "We need the rest of Louisiana and our neighboring states to recognize Magnolia Bay as a place still worthy of tourism dollars. But when everything is in a different state of repair, it doesn't really scream 'Southern getaway,' does it?"

Rosalyn was too polite to agree, but he could see it in her expression. "You sound like you know your stuff."

"I hope so. The town is counting on me."

They drove past Magnolia Bank & Trust, where his buddy Owen Dubois worked—the same bank where Cade had sweet-talked the branch manager into sponsoring Magnolia Days. Their contribution would help pull off the event.

But the circus and surrounding events weren't going to be enough by themselves. Even if he could add Rosalyn's name to the roster. Which she hadn't technically agreed to yet.

Maybe he needed to tell Owen to start practicing his stilts after all.

"You get that a lot, don't you? People counting on you?" Rosalyn asked.

Astute as always. He dipped his head, flashed a smile to hide the weight of it all. "It's not so bad. I assume out there somewhere, minstrels are writing songs about a gallant town director in coastal Louisiana."

Rosalyn let out a little sigh. "I guess I only have one other question, then."

"Shoot."

Her emerald eyes locked on him. "Is there a theme I need to know about? Any particular music you want me to perform to?"

He sucked in a breath, looking at the road and then back to her, half afraid to hope. "Are you saying you'll do it?"

"I'll do it." She hesitated. "I don't know how long I'll be in town, but I can at least get past the circus before leaving."

"And your knee . . ." He glanced at her bandage.

She patted the wrapping. "I can scale, if I need to." She worried her bottom lip. "It sounds like Magnolia Bay needs me."

He exhaled a dozen concerns. "You're a lifesaver, truly."

"But no pressure." She grinned—or was that a wince?

"I'm sure whatever routine you do will be amazing." He started to tell her about the one time he'd seen her perform, then stopped. Might seem stalkerish? Still, he didn't want her to feel the same pressure he carried.

"Oh, Second Story looks good." Rosalyn gestured toward Sadie's two-story, used-book shop, making the decision for him. "That was one of my favorite spots to study in high school. She had the best bean bag chairs."

"Yeah, still does. Sadie gave the place a paintjob a few months ago." The eggshell blue store front looked welcoming and charming. Next door, the Spin Shop held its own with a fresh coat of coral. "Both of these escaped a lot of damage compared to other shops on the strip."

"I'm glad." Rosalyn worked her lower lip, her brow furrowing.

Cade matched her frown. What was she thinking about? Probably not Sadie's choice of paint colors.

And why was he suddenly so curious about Rosalyn's flavor of lip gloss?

He glanced back at the road just in time to swerve and miss another pothole. Not in time, however, to prevent Rosalyn from sliding into him, her side brushing his driving arm. "Oops. So sorry."

She grabbed the overhead bar. "Someone actually gave you a license to drive this thing?"

"Sure." He winked. "The town director."

"How convenient."

"You'll come to realize a lot of jobs around Magnolia Bay default to me." Like—all of them, lately.

"So why aren't you mayor, then?" She tilted her head toward him.

He tightened his grip on the wheel. "Maybe one day. When I've earned it."

"Seems inevitable. You've always been the face of Magnolia Bay." Rosalyn's ponytail flipped over her shoulder as she twisted toward him. "Small-town boy."

"And you were always destined for bigger and better things."

She stared straight ahead, the wind funneling through their cart, carrying the scent of lilacs and stirring loose tendrils by her cheeks. "I don't know about better."

"Don't tell me the world-famous aerialist has regrets?" Cade missed the next pothole with room to spare, thankfully.

But Rosalyn seemed to sink right into his verbal one. Her profile tightened. "I guess we all have a few, huh?"

"I've got one." He took a chance, hurled a dumb question into the air. "Like why weren't we ever actually friends?"

That snapped her out of it. She snorted. "Because you were always trying beat me?"

"And yet you somehow managed to always beat *me*."

Rosalyn shook her head with a grin, the shadows on her face retreating. "Not always. There was that one mathletes competition, remember?"

He remembered. "Eh. I got lucky." He'd also studied harder than he ever had before. Wanted to impress her—which had always been impossible. She was too smart. Too perfect.

She continued. "And you always beat my team at trivia when we had history questions."

Cade shrugged as he slowed the cart at the upcoming intersection. "But you always got the English and science questions right. I still have no idea what elements do what to who."

She shot him a sideways look. "Whom."

"Oh, don't even start, Ace." He chuckled, loving the sound of hers when she laughed in return.

And maybe *that* was why they'd never been friends. Rosalyn would've burrowed under his skin much too quickly, camped out there. She'd been too busy with her girl group anyway, the ones who'd spouted man-hate and turned their nerdy noses up at Cade for four years because he liked to date cheerleaders and got along with the jocks and still managed to make good grades.

See? He hadn't depended on Dad for *everything*.

"You aren't lying about not knowing elements, by the way." She squinted at him. "Or compounds, rather. Like how much vinegar is needed for a volcano."

Ha. "I swear, you're going to engrave that on my tombstone one day, aren't you? It was *one* project." *One* mistake.

But all his mistakes seemed to hover over him, didn't they? Like the mist over the bay in the morning.

"Being forced to work together in sixth grade didn't go very well, did it?" Rosalyn winced, her dimpled cheeks providing apology. "But hey, look at us now."

"Yep. The small-town boy and the aerialist." Two people who couldn't have any more different goals.

They'd always been rivals. And even if they'd had a near-moment years ago in an alley, or even if her laughter felt like the best possible remedy for his stress, and even if she could give Blake Lively a run for her money in the beauty department . . .

That's clearly all they were destined to be. She'd always seen him as a spoiled extension of his father. Besides, she'd be off and running to the next big performance out of town—probably out of the country—once her knee allowed her.

"The small-town boy and the aerialist?" Rosalyn repeated, tilting her head as Cade turned onto Bayou Boulevard. "Sounds like a book title."

Cade snorted. "Maybe so."

Just not a romance novel.

Maybe she'd agreed too quickly. But the small-town boy and the aerialist had a ring to it, didn't it? Hard not to let the idea linger a little, the more they rode around town together. Unfortunately, staying to explore the idea wasn't an option.

Her life didn't have very many of those at the moment.

Cade parked on Bayou Boulevard, and nostalgia slammed Rosalyn harder than that pothole. "My old dance studio!"

The charming little brick building didn't look like it'd taken a big hit from Hurricane Anastasia, save for a missing awning. Unless it'd been one of the lucky ones already repaired. She rushed past Cade and pulled on the handle of the heavy wooden door. It swung open with the same extended creak it always had, and she shot Cade an excited look over her shoulder.

Cade peered through the beveled window. "Are they open?"

"The door sure is." Rosalyn stepped inside, eyes struggling to adjust to the shadows. "Come on. Madame Paulette won't care."

"Sheriff Rubart might," Cade muttered. But he followed anyway, his presence behind her providing warmth that had nothing to do with her sunbaked skin.

The studio, though encased in silence, pulsed with life and memory. Shafts of sunlight shone through the wall of narrow vertical windows, sending tiny dust fairies dancing through the beams. The hardwood floor had been redone since she'd left and now offered a polished gleam.

Rosalyn drew a deep breath of the familiar air, filling her entire diaphragm like Madame Paulette had taught her. As if on autopilot, she gravitated toward the wooden barre lining the far wall of mirrors and rested her hand on the polished wood. Her feet slid into first position, then second, and she lifted on her toes.

Cade shoved his hands in his pockets, staying on the perimeter of the room. She felt his eyes on her, which she didn't mind at all. Until her secret tapped the edges of her memory, a permanent sidekick these days. She lowered herself back to the floor.

"I didn't know you took ballet." Cade paused in front of a wall of framed photos, showing various group classes over the decades. He pointed to one of the pictures. "Blue tutu?"

"That's me." Rosalyn left the barre to join him, memories practically leaping in grand jetes from the frames. "Once a week for years, until I discovered aerial in the sixth grade."

Cade tilted his head, his hands back in his pockets. "But there's not an aerial studio in Magnolia Bay."

"Trust me, I know."

"So how did you train?" Cade genuinely seemed interested in the answer.

"See that hook up there?" She pointed toward the metal claw still protruding from the structural beam in the center of the high ceiling. "That's there because of me."

His gaze drifted upward. "Oh yeah?"

"Yeah. Mom drove me to New Orleans for classes." Reluctantly. "Until I got my license and took myself. But even after I quit ballet, Lettie allowed me to hang a practice rig in here for my silks, so I could train more often."

Cade's eyes met hers once again. "Lettie?"

"Madame Paulette. Only select people can call her that and live to tell about it." Rosalyn smirked. "I'm certain you're not one of them."

Cade's gaze roamed back to the photos. "I bet you were a star pupil."

"I actually wasn't that great." She tapped the framed image of herself, snaggle-toothed and bun-headed. "Can't you tell?"

"I don't believe it." He clicked his tongue. "You're annoyingly good at anything you try, remember?"

"Oh, come on." She squared off with him, her heart jumping with another jolt of pleasure. Why had their rivalry in high school never been this fun?

Probably because of Amber's voice always in her head back then, reminding her that men were bad news.

Though in hindsight, maybe her jaded friend hadn't been all wrong.

Cade faced her, his sculpted chin lifted in challenge. "Name one thing—other than this alleged ballet attempt—that you're not good at."

"I can't cook. But I like trying new vegetarian recipes."

"Which I'm sure taste amazing." His eyes danced now, despite the faux resentment in his tone.

She planted her hands on her hips, noting how he'd inched a

little closer to her. Or maybe she'd moved closer to him. "Do I have to invite you over for dinner and burn something to hush you up?"

"Sounds fun." He was definitely standing closer, holding her gaze. The sunlight bathed his profile in gold, adding to the boy-next-door looks he had now fully grown into.

Her mouth went dry. Goodness, but he made her feel like an awkward freshman again. The gangly, not-quite-grown-into-her-height nerd in awe of *the* Cade Landry, trying to hide her crush on Mr. Popular by shoving her nose in yet another book. Trying to impress him with yet another A or with pushing the tabletop buzzer in debate first.

Funny how she always had all the answers until he was around.

He leaned in, so close the smell of cedar drifted lazily into her senses. Someone needed to tell his cologne's marketing team they had a winner. In fact, they could put Cade himself on the ad and sell out.

His voice dipped an octave, husky and warm. "Do you want to know a secret?"

She had a doozy of her own. But yes. Anything he wanted to tell her. "What?" The word caught on her lips, finally escaping to hover in the ever-decreasing space between them. Her skin flushed on high alert.

His face drew down to hers. She swallowed, waiting for the inevitable whisper. Cade Landry, telling *her* secrets?

His words tickled her ear. "I really did read more books than you in fifth grade."

She recoiled as if drenched in cold water, adrenaline soaking her veins. "Cade Landry!"

He offered a cheeky grin as he backed up a step, dodging her playful slap and looking more like the schoolboy she'd easily recognize. "I'm just saying."

"Well, *I'm just saying* you should learn to count." Her heart raced and she straightened her shoulders. "I beat you fair and square."

"Why you so worked up, Ace?" His teasing gaze arrested hers. "You don't have to compete with me anymore, you know."

"I know." She crossed her arms, hoping it hid the way her hands still shook. "No point anyway—you already think you won everything."

A shadow flickered across his face, dimming his smile. He paused a heartbeat. "Not everything."

Her shaking stilled. He didn't mean . . . her? No. This small-town nostalgia had gone to her head, that was all. She was home for the first time in years, and vulnerable, and—

A door banged open. "Rosalyn, darling!" Madame Paulette's deep, raspy voice echoed through the studio. "I thought that was you." She swept toward Rosalyn in a tidal wave of patchouli oil and earth-toned scarves.

Rosalyn returned her hug, losing sight of Cade as her face was buried in the woman's bottle-red hair. "Yep, it's me, Lettie." She fought the urge to cough against the hint of cigarette smoke hidden behind the essential oils and smiled. Some things never changed. The woman could stop a train on its tracks, but she also knew the world of dance—and show business in general.

"Back to save the day, are we?" Madame pulled free, turning her attention toward Cade. "I've heard about this circus fundraiser. The show must go on!" She pumped one plump fist into the air. Gold bracelets jangled down her arm.

"Something like that." His easy smile was back now, no evidence of that passing regret. Cade had had his entire life to ask Rosalyn out and never tried—why would he now? She'd never been good enough for him. Too nerdy compared to the cheerleaders he usually ran around with, too invested in aerial to waste time trying to befriend the jock circles. Plus, Amber would've killed her if she'd ever tried.

"I don't believe we've formerly met." Cade extended his palm to Madame Paulette, who clamped it eagerly in both hands. "Cade Landry."

"Oh I know who you are, honey. Charmed, I'm sure." She shot him a wink. "I tried to get your mother to put you in my dance classes when you were younger. She humored me a little but your father never would go for it."

Cade shot Rosalyn a wide-eyed look. She hid a smile behind her hand, then realized Cade's were still clamped in Madame Paulette's.

She tugged on Madame's arm, redirecting her attention. "Since I'm going to be in the Cajun Circus, could I possibly hang a rig in here to practice? For old times' sake."

"I'm only as old as I feel, honey—which is roughly thirty-two these days." She winked at Cade, who had subtly maneuvered a safe distance away. "But yes, of course." She raised one ring-filled hand and patted Rosalyn's cheek. "My little insurance nightmare."

Rosalyn concealed her smile. "Thanks, Lettie."

With a dramatic swirl of her scarf, Madame Paulette drifted toward Cade. "I let her hang her silks in here back in those days, despite not being insured for it." Her smoky eyes widened. "Oh, I probably shouldn't tell the mayor's son that." She let out a deep belly-laugh.

Cade dipped his head. "Your secret's safe with me, ma'am."

"Call me Lettie, Cade." Madame jerked one thumb toward Rosalyn, missing Cade's triumphant grin. "I always wished the dancing bug had bitten this one a little harder. That potential! Those *legs*!"

Cade rocked back and forth on his heels, not even attempting to mask his smirk. "I agree, ma'am. I mean, Lettie."

Rosalyn narrowed her eyes at him.

"But you found your calling, dear. Look at you!" Madame raised

Rosalyn's arm high over her head and spun her in a quick pirouette. "You were born to fly."

She'd always thought so. Honestly, the fact her mother let her take aerial lessons after she failed so miserably at ballet, well . . . God had to have been involved in that miracle.

But lately? He'd seemed absent for a while.

And who could blame Him?

Madame continued to gush over her while Cade continued to listen, so Rosalyn tugged her performance smile in place. The one she wore when the show really did have to go on—despite heartache or menstrual cramps or any other interruption life threw at her.

Born to fly? Once upon a time, sure.

Now, after Saudi Arabia, she seemed much more destined to crash and burn.

Three

*Y*OU KNOW WHAT I REALIZED TODAY?" Cade hoisted his end of the antique bed frame that he and Linc were helping Noah move into a renovated suite at the Blue Pirogue Inn.

"What's that?" Noah inched another step up the refinished staircase. A hint of lacquer still hung in the air.

Cade followed, trying to at least give the appearance that he was carrying his fair share of the bed's solid bulk. But they all knew Linc was doing the heavy lifting. "I've never fully appreciated country music before."

Noah let out a huff. "Think you could save this deep revelation for when we're not hauling three hundred pounds up a flight of stairs?"

Linc grunted from his end of the frame. "If you'd been up-front about the second-floor bit, you might not have been nominated for walking-backward duty."

Noah set his side of the bed down on the steps with a groan. "If I'd been up-front, you wouldn't have come."

Linc pursed his lips. "Fair." He lowered his end, forcing Cade to do the same.

Cade cast a glance around as he stretched his back. The inn

looked like an entirely different place under Noah's headship. Crazy to think a few months ago, Noah had been worried about black mold and losing the inn altogether, which was part of his inheritance from his grandfather. Now the Blue Pirogue was back in top shape and ready for a steady stream of summer tourists . . . which would hopefully arrive for Magnolia Days.

Yet another reason Cade had to come through.

He almost brushed his hands on his pants, then noticed his dust-coated palms. He was getting a blister too, but he liked the physical labor. It got his mind off everything with Rosalyn that morning—and the weight bearing down on him regarding his town. "This bed isn't that bad, guys."

"Say the two men walking forward." Noah shook back his hair, sweat beading on his forehead. He kept one hand on the frame to keep it from toppling into the banister. "Fine. Enlighten us. What's changed your mind about country music?"

"Keep listening to your instincts, Cade. They were right to avoid the genre altogether." Linc used the neck of his T-shirt to wipe the sweat from his face. "Can we get this over with, please?"

"What? Cade's announcement or moving the bed?" Noah smirked.

Linc grunted again. "Both."

On three, they all grabbed their designated corners and heaved.

"I always thought country lyrics were dumb. You know, all the stuff about short shorts and drinking in a hayfield." Cade shook his head as they cleared the top of the staircase and started a slow shuffle across the hallway. "But after spending most of the morning with Rosalyn today, well . . ."

Noah craned his neck to see Cade around the massive piece of furniture. "Well?"

Cade adjusted his grip. "Now I kind of understand why there are so many songs about long tanned legs."

The bed wobbled as Linc shook with silent laughter.

"They're hard to forget, that's all." Nothing about Rosalyn had ever been immodest. But she had that performance air about her, the kind of beauty that held people rapt.

And he'd only seen her perform live that one time.

"Dude." Noah scoffed as they scooted into the guest room, minding the newly painted doorframe. "You're just now realizing Rosalyn is beautiful?"

"Beautiful?" Linc's eyes narrowed. "*Oy*. I've been accused of living under a rock, and even I realize *beautiful* is not the word you're looking for here."

"Hey, I'm taken. I'm being respectful." Noah shot him a look. "Besides, even if Rosalyn does have red-carpet vibes, she's classy about it. *Beautiful* fits."

"Wait a second." Cade narrowed his eyes back at Linc as they set the bed down. "How do you even know what she looks like? You were a few grades ahead of us in school, and you"—he switched his glare to Noah—"haven't seen her since before you moved to Shreveport in high school."

"We looked her up." Noah offered a sheepish grin. "Social media, her website, newspaper articles. Her name got a lot of hits."

"With photos." Linc raised his eyebrows pointedly.

Cade's phone burned a hole in his pocket. But he didn't need to google Rosalyn. He had plenty of memories, both from a lifetime ago as well as from a few hours ago.

"I remembered her from school, before I moved." Noah rested his hands on his hips.

"What was she like back then?" Linc asked.

"Smart." Noah and Cade answered as one.

"She gave Cade a run for his money." Noah grinned.

"She gave everyone a run for their money." Cade shook his head. "But she wasn't just a brain. She had her fun moments too—when that Amber girl let her, anyway."

"Oh, I remember her." Noah grimaced. "She hated every male in the school—maybe Cade the most."

"Definitely the most." Still didn't know why. "Anyway, one night, Rosalyn and a group of us snuck out after midnight for senior prank."

Rosalyn had tucked her blonde hair up into a beanie, like this elegant ninja in a black leotard and leggings. Again, probably not a detail the guys needed to hear.

He cleared his throat. "We met up with our group of upperclassmen on the front lawn, but she and I both changed our minds last minute." He smirked. "Well, she did because she realized it wasn't worth risking valedictorian status, and I did because I didn't need my father to bail me out of something *else*."

"So what happened?" Noah asked.

Cade shrugged. "We did what any self-respecting senior would do with their parents' money." He grinned. "Got ice cream and spent an hour debating whether audiobooks counted as reading."

Linc nodded. "They count."

"They definitely *don't*," Noah said.

They glared at each other.

"I know." Noah snapped his fingers. "You should tell her you've been in a movie."

"Are you kidding?" Linc scoffed. "Don't you remember how incorrigible this guy was as an 'actor'?" He jerked his thumb toward Cade. "Don't encourage him."

"What are you talking about?" Cade lifted his chin. "I *made* that movie."

"Sure. Crowd Scene Bro Number Three—five stars." Linc hesitated. "But yeah. You could tell her—chicks like that."

Noah rolled his eyes. "How do *you* have any idea what chicks like? You've never even had a girlfriend."

Linc's face darkened. "You don't know—"

"Can we not say *chicks*? Women aren't poultry." Cade held up both hands. "Also, I'm not trying to impress Rosalyn."

"*This* time." Noah's grin took a knowing quality.

"What do you mean?" Linc asked.

"It means he literally blew up a science project in sixth grade trying to impress her." Noah grinned.

Cade reached to pick up the bed again. "So *that* part you remember."

"Dude, it's a core memory." Noah grabbed his end of the frame and began back-stepping across the room. "The look on Mr. Thompson's face when volcano goo hit the ceiling."

More like the look on Rosalyn's face when she'd laid into him for showing off. Leaving her to do all the work and coming in last minute to ruin it. *You always get away with everything because of your dad. Because you're a Landry.*

Cade winced. "Yeah, we never really got along in school. I think that senior-prank-turned-ice-cream night was a fluke."

Until the Harvard-Yale game, anyway.

Linc set his side of the bed on the rug by the window. "So why aren't you trying to impress her now?"

Cade released his end of the frame, took a step back. "She's not even staying in town. What does it matter?"

"Maybe you're afraid to try."

Cade glared at Linc.

He lifted both hands. "I'm just saying . . . women aren't poultry, but someone here seems like a chicken."

"She *just* agreed to do the circus. Hardly the right time to ask the woman out." He'd thought about it though, hadn't he?

Noah scooted the end of the bed to align with the window. "If you're not going to try, why were you whining about Rosalyn being beautiful?"

"I thought we'd already established this whole *beautiful* thing."

Linc ran one hand down his scruffy face. "I'm buying you both dictionaries for Christmas."

Cade lifted his chin. "Careful calling other women attractive. Zoey might get jealous."

A thundercloud formed in Linc's expression. "Now why would she do something stupid like that?"

Cade fought the urge to back up a step.

Noah wiped his face with the hem of his flannel, but not before Cade caught the smirk spreading across his lips.

It boosted Cade's courage. "Now *I'm* just saying."

Either Linc missed, or ignored, the tossing back of his own words against him. "Zoey and I are friends."

Were his eyes growing darker? Cade went ahead and took that step away. "Of course."

Linc moved forward. "*Just* friends." His long hair, piled on his head in his usual tangled knot, also seemed to be growing blacker.

"I was kidding." Linc wouldn't hit him. He didn't think so, anyway.

Linc grunted as he turned back to the window. "Why don't you focus on a real problem? Like getting this circus pulled off."

"How's that going, by the way? The festival plans?" Noah straightened. "No pressure, but I hope your answer is 'fabulous.' The inn needs customers."

Cade corrected the folded over corner of the rug with the toe of his shoe. "First of all, I would never say *fabulous*."

"Sorry. I don't know what the cool kids are saying these days." Noah hiked an eyebrow. "Probably because I'm busy with my girlfriend."

"Low blow." Cade snorted. "But you know I'm happy for you and Elisa."

Noah's jaw twitched. "Even though you flirted with her that one time."

"Force of habit." Cade shrugged. "She's cute."

"Beautiful, you mean." Linc snorted.

"Okay, I'm uncomfortable with where this conversation is heading." Noah pulled a rag from his back pocket and wiped sweat off his forehead.

"You mean, where you and Elisa are heading?" Linc grinned, a genuine one for once.

Noah threw the rag at Linc, who easily caught it. "Can we get back to the Magnolia Days conversation?"

"Everything's going exactly as planned, especially now that my secret weapon agreed to participate." Cade checked his palms for dust, shoved his hands into his pockets. Hopefully that would hide the telltale shaking that always seemed to strike when he was nervous and didn't have a snack. "Hey, you guys hungry?"

"Is it *really* going fine?" Noah headed toward the stairs. "Or are you doing that thing where you change the subject because you're trying to deny reality?"

"You know me being hungry is always a reality." Cade followed Linc out of the room. They took the stairs down much faster than they'd come up.

At the bottom, Noah paused. "Seriously, what do you need? We're here to help. This is a town affair."

"Yeah, we can bring the muscle." Linc turned on the stairwell and arched a pointed brow at Cade. "Some of us more than others."

"I'll remember that." Cade shuffled after them. "But I got it." He would find a way to pull this off and show Dad he had what it took to represent the Landry name.

But he also couldn't lie.

Cade hesitated on the last stair. He couldn't mention he still had to finish lining up the booths, create more promo materials, and confirm about a dozen other details like porta-potties and dancing poodles. But he had to give them *something*. "I'm worried Magnolia Days, even with the circus, might not be enough to bring in the revenue we need."

His friends turned to face him on the bottom floor. "What do you mean?" Noah's brow furrowed.

"Well, for starters, it seems like for every dollar I anticipate getting, another pothole pops up on Village Lane."

"Say what?" Linc crossed his corded arms over his chest. Did the guy ever skip arm day?

"Long story." Cade shook his head. "My point is, the fundraiser is set to be a hit, but I'm wondering if we need a second hit at the same time." Or a third. Or a tenth.

"You're only one person." Noah's gaze sobered. "Don't forget that."

"I also only have *one* job, and it's this." Cade straightened his shoulders. "I'm a Landry—it'll work out. I'm glad Rosalyn came to help, because that expands our reach."

They headed across the lobby, the faint hint of woodsy air freshener lingering in the air. Rosalyn was a life saver. There was the one hitch with her knee, but she'd assured him it'd be okay to perform in three weeks.

And he had no other choice than to believe her.

"I know we were joking about the movie thing earlier, but seriously—what about getting the crew to come back?" Noah rested one arm on the front desk, where a tiny potted plant struggled to bloom in mid-summer heat. "Consider Magnolia Bay for another movie? That would get tourist attention for a long time to come."

"Not a bad idea." Cade tilted his head. "I still know the producer. We send each other social media reels sometimes."

"There's a solid relationship for your generation," Linc muttered.

Noah raised his eyebrows. "Might be worth asking them to scout post-hurricane and see."

The idea wilted like the plant next to Noah's elbow. "But Magnolia Bay is still sort of a disaster."

Noah shrugged. "Then ask them to come during the circus."

The idea blossomed again.

"That'll be a fun distraction—a way to show them what decor and the right lighting can do." Noah grinned. "And wouldn't hurt to remind the guy that Louisiana still offers big tax breaks for movies."

Valid points.

Linc and Noah began arguing about the merits of communication via messenger apps as they headed across the gravel walk to their vehicles, but Cade was only half listening. Maybe he'd go set up at Chug a Mug and work a few hours—and make that call to remind the film studio about Magnolia Bay. Maybe Noah was right. Maybe the crew was scouting a location already and this could be perfect timing. Maybe Cade could put Magnolia Bay back on the map.

Maybe he wouldn't have to fail again.

Four

HAD SHE MADE A MISTAKE? Kneeling on the hard floor of Lettie's studio, Rosalyn watched the evening shadows cross the familiar space. Maybe she'd been too hasty in agreeing to do the circus.

Or maybe she'd been too hasty in coming home.

If this even was home anymore.

Drawing a deep breath, Rosalyn ran her hands over the red silks that had taken up a large portion of her suitcase, trying to conjure the peace the fabric usually brought. A dozen memories flitted through her mind. Once upon a time, she'd been at home in the air, her happy place. A shooting star.

But ever since she woke up in that hospital bed in Saudi Arabia, she felt more like a caged bird.

"Knock, knock." A female voice sounded from behind.

Rosalyn glanced back. Elisa Bergeron. "Hey. Wow, it's been a while."

"I heard you were in town." Elisa slipped in, catching the door so it shut softly behind her. She tucked her blonde hair behind her ears, her grin contagious. She hadn't changed much from senior year, her trim figure clad in a tank and jeans boasting some sort of sauce-looking stain on the legs. "Haven't seen you since graduation—in person, anyway." She hunched her shoulders, sheepish. "I follow you on social media."

"So I have at least one fan, then." Rosalyn grinned back as she stood. "Madame Paulette isn't here. She's just letting me rig my silks to train." Weird she brought them, honestly. Wasn't she supposed to be resting? Healing?

Hiding?

"You're doing the circus, then?" Elisa raised her eyebrows.

"That's the rumor."

"It'll mean a lot to Cade."

Now it was Rosalyn's turn to raise her eyebrows.

Elisa shook her head. "I mean, for Magnolia Days in general. He's been working hard to make this year profitable. Help out the town."

Was that all it was? Cade had seemed almost flirty in the golf cart. Which was ridiculous, because he was Cade. Her old rival.

Even if he did look really good all grown up and responsible. Driving a golf cart and planning fundraisers and wearing a button-down.

"Anyway, I was going to talk to Madame about a catering order, but I'll catch her later. I'm glad you're here—I've always found this stuff so fascinating." Elisa gestured with her chin toward the silks. "I can't even turn a cartwheel without getting dizzy."

"Me neither," Rosalyn joked. "I could use a second pair of hands, if you have a minute." She stooped to pull her fabric away from the ladder propped in the middle of the room, taking a moment for a deep breath. No more distracting thoughts of Cade, or the fundraiser. Rigging demanded her full concentration, or she could get hurt.

Again.

Elisa set her purse on the floor under the barre. "Tell me what to do."

"Grab that carabiner, please." She gestured to the black clip lying next to the hook on the floor. "I've already tied the fabric to the figure eight. Just need to get this in the air, and the silks are heavier than you'd think."

She started up the ladder, fabric bundled under her arm, and gingerly tested her knee while Elisa hovered near the bottom. Usually she could do this exact rigging process in her sleep. But usually, she wasn't in a bandage.

Elisa cleared her throat from below. "I heard Cade gave you a tour this afternoon."

So much for no distractions. Rosalyn focused on the fabric in her arms, hoping her expression didn't give her away. Sometimes she forgot how small this town really was. All the more reason to keep her secrets close.

Elisa didn't seem the nosy type though, and it was obvious she and Cade were friends. Rosalyn smoothed the silks draped over her arm, filtering her words. "Yeah, it was sad seeing so many businesses not fully restored. But thankfully, some are in good shape, like the studio here—and your diner."

"Well, that's another story." Elisa looked up, amusement flickering across her face. "Magnolia Blossom has been through it the last few months, not even counting the hurricane. But I know what you mean."

Rosalyn shifted positions on the ladder. "I'm just grateful Madame Paulette is letting me practice here like the good ol' days." Funny. She used to be so ready to hit the big time, she could hardly stand it. Now, she'd give anything to go back to those carefree days spinning on the silks a few inches off the ground.

Where it was safe.

"Did you and Cade keep in touch all these years?" Elisa's overly casual tone sounded anything but subtle.

Rosalyn accepted the carabiner Elisa passed to her. "Not really. We ran into each other a few years into college, at a football game." That night played through her dreams more than she wanted to admit. Usually when she was tossing and turning in yet another hotel room alone, city lights bright outside her window. What-ifs swirling. She shrugged. "We lost touch after that, besides the occasional social media message."

"I love the type of friendships that pick up like nothing ever happened." Elisa kept one steadying hand on the ladder.

"Cade and I were more like friendly rivals." Though he *had* started using that nickname for her again, and there *had* been that banter about who beat who at what competition.

"I've known Cade a long time, and he and Noah have gotten closer the past year, which has been good for Noah." Elisa's voice warmed like a woman in love.

Rosalyn clipped the carabiner onto the swivel. "I'm sure it's been good for Cade too. Not that he ever seemed to have trouble making friends." Or having girlfriends. She leaned forward to attach it all to the reinforced beam on the ceiling. "He always fit into every clique in the school with ease." Especially the cheerleaders—a fact that annoyed Amber to no end.

And when Amber was annoyed, everyone in her friend group had to be annoyed. Rosalyn still wasn't sure why she'd hated Cade *so* much back then.

"Maybe the four of us could go out together while you're in town."

Rosalyn jerked, her leg wobbling on the upper rung.

Elisa grabbed the ladder with both hands. "Careful!"

"Sorry. I'm usually much steadier up here."

"I'll quit talking until you finish." Elisa mimed zipping her lips shut.

Rosalyn double-checked the setup as her mind raced. A date with Cade was definitely not penciled into her calendar for this brief stay in town. But the thought did send a little happy skitter up her spine.

Still, she couldn't even entertain the thought right now. Not while she had to watch her back. Not while her future was a giant question mark.

"Speaking of Cade . . ." Elisa's voice trailed off and Rosalyn glanced down in time to see her point toward the front window of the studio.

Cade paced the sidewalk in the dying evening light, a leather laptop bag tucked on his shoulder, a cell phone glued to his ear as he gestured with his freehand. Even with his sleeves rolled up and top collar unbuttoned, he still looked professional. Put together. Confident.

Yeah, she better get off this ladder before her knee went from achy to swoony.

Elisa stepped back, out of Rosalyn's way. "I swear that man can talk anyone into anything. You should've seen him with the police a few months ago when Noah and I broke into the courthouse."

"I believe it." If Rosalyn hadn't witnessed Cade talking the school cafeteria cooks into double portions of mystery meat and single-handedly convincing the principal to install a second vending machine, she would've believed it simply for the dimple crowding his jaw.

Cade Landry was hard to turn down.

Then the rest of Elisa's statement registered. "Wait. Did you say the police?" Rosalyn joined Elisa near the window, crossing her arms over her chest and hoping the other woman couldn't hear her suddenly erratic heartbeat. "I'll have to hear that story sometime."

"He still gets a little paranoid about Sheriff Rubart." Elisa chuckled. "Which is fair."

They watched as Cade continued to pace and gesture. Rosalyn tilted her head. "So who is he sweet-talking now, you think? Another vendor for Magnolia Days?"

"Rumor has it—and by rumor, I mean Noah called me an hour ago—Cade is looking to get a movie crew back in these parts." Elisa tucked her hair behind her ears. "It's not a bad idea."

"Back?" Rosalyn watched Cade pace. "They've been here before?"

"Cade didn't tell you?" Elisa snorted. "I assumed he told everyone he met he was an extra in a 'major motion picture.'" She air-tagged with her fingers.

Rosalyn raised an eyebrow. "And by major motion picture you mean . . ."

"Decently successful low-budget, high-quality indie film."

"I see." Her admiration for Cade inched a notch higher. The man was a go-getter—the only one who'd ever truly given her competition. On the ground, anyway. He made everything look easy.

The thought of sitting across from him on a double date suddenly felt . . . appealing. She shook her head. No. No sense going there. Cade had every chance to ask her out in high school and chose to spend time—and dates—with other girls, instead. She'd never even been invited to the parties he'd thrown. He could go months without acknowledging her in school.

She'd not been his type . . . which made her wonder if that moment at the Lazy Spoon had been embellished in her memory all these years.

"We should probably stop spying." Elisa turned to face Rosalyn and clasped her hands. "Are you practicing tonight? I'd love to watch, if you want someone to cheer you on."

Rosalyn rolled her lower lip, eyeing the silks now secured above them. She was tired, but it was more than that lately. Stress felt heavier ten feet in the air. And *that* probably wasn't going to go away anytime soon. "Sure. That'd be great."

Elisa moved the ladder to the corner of the room while Rosalyn separated her silks into two poles. Then she wrapped her feet to provide a foothold and climbed upward.

"You make that look easy," Elisa called.

"Wasn't at first." Once Rosalyn reached six feet or so, she unwrapped her ankles, holding the silks with both hands, and flipped backward into an inversion.

Elisa gasped.

"It's not as bad as it looks." Rosalyn chuckled as she came right side up, continuing to weave the fabric around her legs and hips. Then she flipped again, rolling out of the silks sideways, legs extended, in a short wheel down.

Elisa clapped. Which was nice.

But not as nice as the view Rosalyn's inverted position granted her of Cade, watching through the studio window, a big smile on his face as he munched through a bag of chips. He tucked the bag under one arm and provided an exaggerated slow clap, as if she'd performed an Olympic-worthy move.

So maybe the Lazy Spoon memory hadn't been embellished after all.

Flustered, Rosalyn scrambled to lower herself as he shot her a wink. Her chest burned.

Elisa caught the exchange as she glanced back and forth between Rosalyn and Cade.

"Don't even think about it." Rosalyn bit back a groan as her feet landed on the mat, providing her with stable ground again. Though arguably, coming down from the silks had done nothing to get her head out of the clouds.

"I didn't say anything." Elisa held up both hands. "Your face is red though."

"I was upside down!" Rosalyn protested.

"Don't worry. Cade makes a lot of women blush." Elisa stood with a grin. "It's not just you."

And there it was. The reality check that doused Rosalyn's flush with a bucket of cold water. Cade Landry had been—and would always be—Mr. Popular. The mayor's son. And maybe Rosalyn had made a name for herself in recent years, but did she even want to flirt with someone she'd never been good enough for?

As much as she hated to admit it, her friend Amber had been right that evening on the phone, when Rosalyn got stood up for a dance. *Men are destined to hurt you, Rosalyn. They're not emotionally evolved enough. Look at guys like Cade Landry and you'll see everything you need to know.* And hadn't Blaine proven that men lied enough for the entire male species?

She watched Cade head around the corner of the studio toward the door. Maybe Cade wasn't like that. Maybe he was an overall good guy.

But it didn't matter. Her secrets owned her right now, and there was only room for friendship.

It was safer for everyone—and her heart—that way.

Elisa had vanished like a blonde Houdini, muttering something about it being past her bedtime—not that Cade was complaining about impromptu alone time with Rosalyn.

He stood in the shadowed doorway of the dance studio, Elisa's perfume hovering despite her abrupt departure, and shook his head as he watched Rosalyn gather her things inside. "She's subtle."

"So was her suggestion of the four of us getting dinner while I'm in town." Rosalyn tugged her blue athletic top down over the waistband of her leggings and laughed, though it sounded a bit forced.

He held the door open for her as she flicked off the lights. Everything about the stiffness in Rosalyn's back suggested a double date would *not* be a good thing to request.

What else had Elisa said to her?

"Thanks for walking me to my car." Rosalyn pulled the door shut behind them. "I didn't mean to stay past dark, but Elisa wanted a demonstration once we got my silks rigged. I lost track of time."

"No problem. I'm sure you'd be safe here in the Bay—it's not like the big cities you're used to now." Cade stepped back to give her room to lock up.

"Well, never hurts to be careful." Rosalyn checked the handle to make sure the door was locked, then slipped the key into her purse. She was on edge . . . maybe it didn't have anything to do with him personally?

Overcome with the urge to make her smile, reclaim their banter from the golf cart that day, Cade nodded his head back toward the studio as they headed for the sidewalk. "Ever going to give me a lesson on those things?"

She shot him a sidelong look, illuminated by the streetlamp above, and his heart stammered . . . And not from that espresso he'd thrown back in Chug a Mug a few hours ago.

Then a grin emerged on her lips and he internally pumped a victory fist. "You wouldn't be able to handle it."

"*Me*?" He pressed a hand against his chest.

"I didn't stutter."

"I can do anything."

"Except beat me for valedictorian."

Yes. The banter was back. He shook his head in mock chagrin. "You flirting with me, Ace?"

"Right. I wouldn't even know what that looked like." She snorted.

So the idea was too far-fetched to imagine?

She slowed her pace, clearly favoring her knee. "Elisa and I saw you on the phone. Seemed like an animated conversation."

And there was the subject change. He'd much prefer the flirting. "The call didn't go great, honestly."

Rosalyn met his gaze as they continued down the street to her car. She was definitely limping, so he slowed their pace another notch. "You're so convincing. I remember that whole vending machine campaign at school like it was yesterday."

He remembered a lot of things like they were yesterday, especially back alley near-kisses. But he knew better than to bring that up with the guard she had locked and loaded. "I guess I should switch my goal away from production crews and back to packaged junk food, then."

"What happened?" A gentle summer wind teased Rosalyn's loosely tied-back hair, sending strands fluttering against her cheeks. "Were you talking to the production company, like Elisa guessed?"

Speaking of the movies. If anyone had star potential, it was Rosalyn. She'd clearly made a name for herself in the aerial arts industry, but she would light up a film like a firefly on a dark night. Even more reason to convince the crew to come back during Magnolia Days and check out the circus. They didn't realize what they'd be missing.

He looked back down at the sidewalk so he wouldn't trip in the increasing darkness. "Yeah, I was trying to walk off my espresso after working at the coffee shop, and the assistant to the producer I connected with a few years ago called me back mid-lap around the block."

How had he looked, pacing the sidewalk as he pleaded with Janie to convince her boss—his social media "friend" who apparently didn't want to take his call—to send a scout to the Bay?

It'd come to that—begging.

"And?" Rosalyn pressed.

"I worked my magic but only got a halfhearted commitment for a return phone call from him tomorrow." He shrugged, as if it didn't matter. But it did—a lot. "Not very promising."

She squinted at him. "But it wasn't a no."

He nodded slowly. "It wasn't a no." That was one way to look at it—the hopeful way, which was something he'd been losing track of lately in the throes of fundraising. It was hard to keep his normally positive outlook with this much pressure riding on his success.

They walked the rest of the way toward her car in companionable silence, as if talk of his failure had somehow lowered Rosalyn's guard.

It was too overcast and early in the evening tonight for stars, but the crickets provided a full chorus from the shadowed bushes along the sidewalk. He thought of that boat scene in *The Little Mermaid*, where all the wildlife banded together to urge the prince to kiss Ariel.

Not that he needed a singing crab to give him that idea.

"The Cade Landry I remember never took no for an answer."

He stumbled as Rosalyn elbowed him in the ribs, lighting his torso on fire, and he had to remind himself she hadn't read his mind. She wasn't talking about a kiss.

"Except, of course, when he realized he'd been beat for valedictorian." She winked.

Rival days. Right. "I still think that poor, underpaid staff member made a tally error."

"Underpaid staff?" Rosalyn snorted, eyes lighting as they neared Chug a Mug. "They used computers to compare our GPAs."

He pretended to concede. "Well, there you go. You can't trust machines these days."

Rosalyn scoffed. "People aren't much more reliable." Then she pressed her lips together, as if she hadn't meant for the words to escape.

"Touché." He paused by the door of her car and studied her a moment, noting the angle of her cheekbones, the way her delicate nose dipped in the middle. The slight furrow between her professionally drawn brows. "I guess I didn't think that through, did I?" He gave her a window to reveal more of what she meant, if she wanted.

He hoped she did.

But instead, she lifted her chin and smiled before she slid into the driver's seat, clearly trying to cover the rare moment of vulnerability. "Always be prepared, Landry."

"Hey, that's easy. Prepared is my middle name."

"Is your car still at Chug a Mug?"

He nodded.

"Hop in." She gestured toward the passenger seat. "I can drive you."

"It's only a block." But why was he protesting? Didn't he want to go?

She insisted, so he walked around and slid in—just in time for her to tug that scrunchie from her tresses and release a wave of citrus-scented temptation through the interior.

Okay, maybe his name wasn't Prepared, after all.

He closed his eyes against the scent, against her proximity. Against the wave of regret flooding his heart at not making a move when he'd had the chance years ago.

That night in Cambridge, after the Yale rival game. He'd run into her and her group of friends—ugh, and that awful Amber girl—at a sports pub, the first time he'd seen Rosalyn since graduation. She'd been wearing a flowing top in Harvard crimson, and skinny jeans paired with heels that made her legs go on forever and a day. She'd been laughing, until that one beef-head in a jersey had—

"You okay?"

He opened his eyes, half startled to realize he wasn't surrounded by face-painted fans and cheese fries. "Oh, yeah, of course. Long day."

But what he really wanted to say was—*do you wanna get out of here?*

The question fairly begged to leave his lips—just like it had roughly nine years ago in the alley behind the Lazy Spoon.

But just like then, he swallowed it. Rosalyn hadn't given him signals that anything had changed from their glory days of competing. That she thought any differently of him than she had then, the entitled mayor's son who got bailed out. Now, though—she was back.

And maybe this time he could figure out how to say what he wanted.

Stay.

Five

S HE HADN'T BROUGHT ANY OF HER PER-
formance leotards home. What would she wear in this circus?
Still in bed, the late morning sun peeking through the
blinds in her childhood room, Rosalyn opened her go-to shopping
app and started scrolling through the options. Not that the leo
was top priority right now. But stressing over glittery fabric felt a
lot better than allowing herself to replay last night's walk and car
ride with Cade.

Purple with feathers. She wrinkled her nose. *Flick.*

Red sequins. She squinted. Maybe. *Flick.*

Cade's smile as he'd grinned at her through the studio window.
She swallowed. *Flick.*

Funny how being home somehow turned her right back into the
schoolgirl she'd always been—telling herself she wasn't crushing on
her number one rival, Cade Landry. Back then, Amber would've
disowned her from their group. Well . . . not that it mattered. Cade
never gave her the time of day unless he was trying to beat her.

And being in this particular room—the one where Rosalyn
used to sit in front of the full-length mirror and check for runs
in her ballet tights—brought back the overwhelming feeling of

imperfection. Of being not *quite* enough for Mom to be proud of. For having traded her tutu for silks, her bun for glittery braids.

You mean, you're really going to run away and join the circus? Mom's reaction to Rosalyn announcing she'd been accepted into her dream aerial college her junior year at Harvard.

Rosalyn swallowed, the images on her phone blurring. Ironic that Mom tried to talk her into joining Cade's circus. Mom acted proud, but it felt so . . . obligating. Like maybe she had no choice and was on board because it was the proper thing to do.

If she had been proud, wouldn't Rosalyn's trophies and medals still be on display? Wouldn't she have saved some of her old competition costumes and local newspaper clippings, the way most parents saved baby blankets and cheerleading trophies?

But when Rosalyn had come home from Harvard that first time her freshman year, her mom had removed all the embarrassing pieces, leaving behind only freshly painted baseboards and a clean slate.

Rosalyn's phone buzzed with an incoming call, and she jerked, her head rolling against the pillow. She clutched the phone to her cheek and braced before checking the number, hoping she was wrong despite every instinct shouting she wasn't.

She risked a peek.

Blaine.

Ugh. She silenced the call, then tossed the phone to her nightstand and pulled the fluffy white duvet over her head. Heart racing, she tried to pray, but the words froze on her lips. It was her fault—she couldn't exactly expect God to bail her out of her own bad decisions, could she?

Did good intentions count?

Her fingers twitched with the urge to return the call to her manager. To see if Blaine finally had good news—*the* news she'd been waiting for.

But if he didn't, well—she didn't want to talk to him, tell him she was performing without him for the first time since her injury. Besides, she didn't owe him anything—he'd lied to her. *He* was the reason she had to stay alert, had to get an escort to walk her to her car parked one block away in her own hometown.

And to think mere weeks ago, she thought he'd saved her.

Had she brought danger to her parents' doorstep?

Frustrated, she threw back the duvet and stared at the ceiling fan whirring overhead. The metal chain clacked in the created draft, white noise that had finally lulled her to sleep sometime after one a.m. Some big star she'd turned out to be. She was a grown woman, back in her parents' house, fighting insomnia, nursing an injury, and carrying a pack of secrets no one could discover.

Or else.

A knock sounded on her door and she nearly fell out of the bed.

"Honey? You awake?"

She gulped. Only Mom—still a little scary, in a different way.

Rosalyn untangled from the blanket and opened the door, willing her heartbeat to slow. Mom was already dressed for the day in pressed slacks and a silk blouse, lipstick securely in place and a mildly concerned frown pinching her brow.

"I'm up." Barely, but she couldn't let her mother know how tired she was or she'd be pumped full of vitamin smoothies and herbal tea before she'd even brushed her teeth. Rosalyn stifled a yawn. "Was online shopping for a leo for the Cajun Circus."

Mom gasped. "So you're going to do it?" Her delighted smile hid the age lines attempting to peek through her designer makeup. "That's wonderful news!"

She mutely nodded. Would Mom still smile at Rosalyn that way if she knew what happened in Saudi Arabia? Knew what Blaine had done?

Knew Rosalyn's secret?

"How's your knee?" Mom's gaze dropped expectantly to Rosalyn's leg, still clad in pink knit pajama pants, and frowned. "Would you like a heating pad?"

Rosalyn shrugged. "It's okay. A little sore from practice yesterday, but manageable."

Though she wondered if she'd made the right decision. Hadn't she come home to heal and *hide*? Not that a small-town circus would raise the type of media attention that would draw an unwanted spotlight to her. And Blaine *had* said he was buying her some time.

Still . . . he'd lied before.

Her chest tightened. Regardless, she needed the money.

And that was *not* a lie.

"I'm so glad you agreed to help out, sweetie. Your participation really brings this fundraiser to a new level for Cade. For the whole town!" Mom clapped her hands together, gold rings sparkling. "This is going to be great."

Butterflies threatened Rosalyn's empty stomach. "Yes, great."

"You don't seem convinced." Mom frowned again.

"I haven't performed since my fall." Rosalyn shrugged like it didn't matter. Like she wasn't constantly trying to figure out what to do next with her career. Like Blaine wasn't pressuring her to return to performing ASAP to pay off her growing debt.

Like she wasn't in so far over her head, she couldn't find the light.

"Oh, you'll be fine. It's normal to have stage fright after something like that." Mom's frown eased and she offered an encouraging smile.

Stage fright was for people nervous about stuttering or forgetting their lines. What was the term for "scanning the audience for sleek, dark-haired men in expensive suits looking to hurt her?"

Maybe Mom had been right all along and Rosalyn should've stuck with ballet. Somehow, she doubted she'd be in this giant mess if she'd kept to pliés and pirouettes at Lettie's.

"Thanks." Rosalyn started to shut the door. "I was about to change and head over to Madame Paulette's to do some stretching, so . . ."

"You know, while you're out, you might see if Cade could use any help with Magnolia Days planning." Mom touched the door, stopping her from shutting it completely. "He's doing such a good job as town director, but I'm sure it's overwhelming for him."

It'd certainly seemed that way yesterday. But she had her own problems, didn't she? Rosalyn nudged the door another inch, forcing a smile. "I might."

Being around Cade wouldn't be a horrible way to spend the day, but keeping her guard up after their connection last night would be tricky. Still, that defeated look in his eyes when he'd shared about the disappointing phone call wasn't one she'd ever seen on a Landry before. Cade Landry, affected by . . . anything?

"Helping him out with some tasks might keep your mind off your nerves." A knowing smile spread across her mother's signature pink lipstick. "And besides . . . you could do worse than Cade, you know."

Wait. Did Mom think *she* thought she was too good for Cade? More like the opposite. Regardless, she had no business trusting anyone right now—including herself.

But she couldn't say all that, so she dragged in a breath and simply nodded. "I know."

Mom took the hint and backed away from the door. "Anyway, you'll do great at the circus, hon. Your father and I can't wait to see you perform again." Then she strode down the hall, leaving a trail of confusion and flowery *Dior* in her wake.

Rosalyn hesitated, clutching the doorknob. She *sounded* like she meant it. But . . . she'd always been good at saying the right thing at the right time. Having grown up in a low-income family, she'd literally taken etiquette classes after marrying Rosalyn's father—a successful businessman with a degree in accounting and an eye for a deal—and made Rosalyn do the same as a pre-teen. Rosalyn knew exactly which fork went where on the table, how to discreetly fold a napkin in your lap to hide food stains . . .

Could Mom finally be genuinely proud of her? Or was this another fork to place?

"Oh, that reminds me." Mom turned back and snapped her fingers. "You might want to check your closet."

Rosalyn frowned. "What do you mean?"

But she was gone, taking *Dior* into the kitchen.

Rosalyn slowly moved to the walk-in closet, where she'd stowed her clothes when she arrived in town days ago. She flipped on the light and haphazardly rifled through the hangers containing work-out tops, sundresses, tanks, and leggings. A few stuffed animals, too big to box up, perched on the top shelf next to a cardboard container marked BEDDING in bold Sharpie, along with an antique lamp and packaged tea set.

She reached farther, toward the back, where Mom's wedding dress had hung ever since Rosalyn moved to Harvard, and pushed the heavy garment bag aside.

And there, sparkling up at her—as if winking to prove a point—were all her old performance leotards.

"You had a big day yesterday." Dad set his coffee mug on his desk and turned an expectant gaze on Cade.

Cade leaned one shoulder against the doorjamb to his father's office, next to his own, and scrubbed a hand down his chin. "Yeah, it was pretty wild seeing Rosalyn again."

He'd watched her drive safely away from his parked car at Chug a Mug, then gone home and spent a good three hours remembering her smile before he finally dozed off.

Dad's graying eyebrows shot toward his receding hairline.

Oops. Obviously, Rosalyn wasn't what he'd been referring to.

Cade straightened. "I mean, you know—it was busy, trying to meet with Rosalyn about the circus on top of all the community issues that popped up and the Magnolia Days planning."

"Right, right." Dad's all-seeing eyes narrowed, but he was too good at reading a room to push further. He knew when to keep his cards close—a fact Cade had never been more grateful for.

Cade cleared his throat. "Turns out the pothole in front of Chug a Mug is legit. Miley wasn't exaggerating." He gestured in the general direction of the paperwork he'd dropped off before leaving the office yesterday. "I told her we'd make it a top priority."

"Did you, now? Sounds like politician talk to me." Dad chuckled as he shuffled through his inbox. How did that thick tower of papers not stress him? Cade could feel his blood pressure spiking and he wasn't even in charge of that particular pile.

"Speaking of politics . . ." Dad pointed to the chair across from him. "Got a minute?"

No—his overwhelming responsibilities awaited him in his office down the hall—but it was most likely a rhetorical question.

Cade sat.

The clock on the wall ticked a steady rhythm. "You know I don't like to beat around the bush." Dad leaned forward, resting his forearms on the desk. "So I'm just going to say it."

Oh boy.

Cade mentally ran through his list of recent potential failures as he hooked one ankle over his knee and kept his smile projecting confidence. Had some other disgruntled community member filed a complaint about him? Had he overbudgeted for Magnolia Days? Honestly, Rosalyn was the most expensive piece of that puzzle, even at what he knew was a heavy discount. If it had been a single performance, she might've done it for free. But three performances, during the last three nights of Magnolia Days, required a lot more energy and time away from her big-money gigs at wherever she'd been the last several months.

"—the past few years, as I'm sure you've noticed."

Oops again. He hadn't been listening. Cade tried to focus on his father's words and not thoughts of Rosalyn. Of the way her eyes crinkled at the corners when she called him "Landry," or how cute she was when she pretended to be mad and how graceful she looked even while dangling upside down from a bunch of fabric—

"—don't you agree?" Dad lifted his chin.

On what? Though regardless, it was probably best if he did. Cade hesitated and then nodded. He needed context clues, quick.

Dad reclined back in his chair, looking . . . relieved. Okay, so agreement had been a good thing. At least he'd guessed right.

"It'll be a long transition, don't worry. And of course you'll have to officially run. We can't get around that."

Run? Cade squinted. He hadn't run since his failed track attempts in high school, when the coach had busted him for hiding Snickers in his gym shorts pockets. Which was crazy. Everyone knew runners needed to refuel.

"But running should only be a formality. After all, no one has challenged my race the past several terms." Dad smiled as he tapped his knuckles on the desk. "I'm sure the same will go for you."

Run. Race. The context clues became all too clear—and there weren't enough Snickers in the world.

Dad wanted him to run for mayor.

"You're retiring?" Cade's voice cracked. But wait. He was supposed to have known that at this stage of the conversation. He sucked in a breath. "It's going to be weird to see you retire, I mean." Which was true. Dad had been mayor since Cade was a kid. But *now*—in the midst of the hurricane recovery crisis?

He shifted positions in his chair. "Dad, this is great. But I'm a little worried about the timing." The timing . . . the people . . . everyone loved Cade, sure. He practically *was* Magnolia Bay.

But did they see him as capable of leading their town rather than simply marketing it? He tugged at his suddenly tight collar. Or worse . . . would they only vote for him *because* of his dad?

"Your mother and I have been discussing it since my last term. I hung in there longer than I intended, which turned out to be a good thing because of Hurricane Anastasia. But it'll be good to take a step back. Play more golf." He smiled. "I'm sure you'll be a shoo-in."

Maybe. But to start a campaign—even as a formality—the same time as Magnolia Days? Who was going to do *his* job if he transitioned into his father's?

His thoughts raced with the same intensity as the pulse in his ears. He still hadn't confirmed the porta-potties. The food truck vendor battle raged, potholes were popping up all over the city like an endless game of Whack-a-Mole, and he was still waiting to hear back from the animal trainer up north about dancing poodles. Not to mention the permit paperwork that hadn't fully cleared his desk and the advertising graphics he'd started but not finished creating . . .

A knot formed in Cade's stomach, rising into the center of his chest until he couldn't breathe. He hadn't had an anxiety attack in years, not since attempting the bar.

He forced oxygen into his lungs, but his vision blurred.

Dad tossed a stray paper clip into the wire holder near his monitor. "I know this puts a little extra load on your shoulders with all the fundraising going on."

No kidding.

What was that grounding technique Cade used to do? List something he could smell, something he could see, and something he could hear. He desperately scanned the room.

Dad continued. "I know you're up for the task . . ."

Lemon-scented air freshener.

The unwrapped, multicolored pack of sticky notes near the desk lamp.

Birds chirping outside the office window.

"But I think it best to keep our plan a secret a while longer." Dad gestured between himself and Cade, seemingly still oblivious to the bomb he'd tossed. "Your mother knows, of course, but let's keep it to that."

Wait.

Cade sucked in a full breath. "So, no campaign?" His vision cleared.

"Not yet. Re-election isn't until November, so there's plenty of time to get past Magnolia Days first."

He could breathe again. Cade tried to school his features into a casual expression, as he fished in his pocket for Tic Tacs.

His father steepled his fingers atop his desk calendar. "I wanted you to be prepared to shift in that direction the moment the fundraiser is over. Besides, even if we don't start campaigning until mid-July, it seems prudent to start training you as soon as possible."

"Right." Cade dumped several mints into his hand and popped them into his mouth.

Dad's eyes shone. "I'm so glad you're on board with this."

And Cade was so glad his father got that impression from the past two minutes. Apparently Cade's acting skills were better than he realized. He popped another mint and mumbled around it. "Of course."

What was he going to do? His own job was overwhelming enough—his father had a huge responsibility to the people that Cade didn't want. All these years, Dad had managed to be charismatic *and* capable with the town. Firm *and* kind. Authoritative *and* approachable.

Cade wasn't a mixture of those things. Cade was the good guy, the friendly face, the fundraiser. The go-between. When his father didn't approve something, Cade didn't take the heat for it. He could pass the buck upward and still be liked. He didn't want to be the ultimate decision maker.

He just wanted to help the town he loved and have everyone love him back.

"You know something?" Dad offered a wide smile. "I think this is finally what you've been working toward since leaving Yale."

A mint lodged in Cade's throat. He coughed, nodding, even as his eyes welled. His father believed Cade had simply changed his mind about law to come home and pursue a career in small-town politics.

He didn't know Cade had failed the bar. Failed the family name. Now he was expected to take this on? Carry the Landry legacy into another generation of glory?

What if he failed again?

No pressure.

"Here." Dad tossed a bottle of water over the desk. "You okay?"

Cade managed to nod as he caught the bottle. He drank, chugging even after the mint had long left his throat. He needed to think. Why hadn't he seen this coming?

"I have to say, I'm relieved." Dad relaxed in his chair. "It's much easier making this change when I know who is filling my shoes. I think you're tailor-made for this position, son."

Oh no. The approval in his eyes had shifted into pride.

Cade closed his own and went back to downing the water. How could he say no to the man who'd supported him when he least deserved it? Who'd protected the family name despite all of Cade's immature hijinks over the years, who'd taught the value of a solid legacy? *You're a Landry,* Dad had said in disappointment, scribbling a check to cover the cost of repainting Mr. Thompson's shed Cade vandalized in seventh grade. *You're a Landry,* when Cade had nearly gotten suspended in high school for allegedly fighting. Without Dad bailing him out, he'd never have gotten the good grades or gone to Yale.

Though, in hindsight, maybe Yale hadn't been such a great thing.

Still, Cade owed him. He lowered the empty water bottle. Maybe this didn't matter right now. The campaign wouldn't start for several weeks, and no one was going to know until then. He still had time to figure out his life.

On top of everything he was trying to figure out for the town.

"Thanks, Dad." Cade channeled his best smile, the one that had gotten him a lot of what he'd wanted over the years. He'd learned from the best, after all. He tossed the bottle into the nearby wastebasket. "Don't worry, I'm a Landry. I won't let you down."

Though he was certainly not making any such promises to himself.

Time to find out about the weather report.

Rosalyn stood in line at Chug a Mug, eyes roving the chalkboard menu, inhaling the scent of fresh ground beans. She didn't drink coffee often, preferred tea, but she loved the way it smelled. Reminded her of Saturday mornings with her father, back when life was a little more simple.

Would it be again?

The black, silver, and brass decor of Chug a Mug offered the illusion of cool, despite the climbing temps outside. Rosalyn fanned her face with one hand. The customer in line ahead of her hunched over his phone, the chimes of incoming texts ringing one after the other. Good grief, he should put that on silent.

Wait.

It was Cade.

She appreciated the opportunity to study him—the trim line of his back, the cut of his button-down shirt, the tailored pants cuffed above polished shoes. He was much broader than he'd been in high school, and still just as handsome.

Enough staring. She cleared her throat. "Great minds think alike, I suppose."

He lifted his head and turned, a slow smile spreading across his face. "Well, aren't you a sight for sore eyes?"

"Am I?" She crossed her arms over her tee, heart spiking at being the center of his focus. Also much like high school. But unlike his polished professionalism, she wore cutoffs, her hair swept up and looped in a bun—hardly worth his admiration. "And . . . didn't you always have twenty-twenty vision?"

"You know, the term *sore eyes* doesn't necessarily refer to one's vision." He moved up in the line, his grin widening.

"Idioms, am I right?" She snorted.

He held up both hands. "I should have just said 'Fancy meeting you here.'"

"Well, that depends."

Cade matched her stance, crossing his arms. "On?"

"Are you looking for a come-on line?" Oh, what was she doing?

"Well, now *that* definitely depends."

She held his gaze, accepting the challenge. "On?" Oh man. Was she flirting?

He seemed up for it, his eyes shining like when he'd turn from the white board in geometry, confident of his dry-erase answer. "On whether you want one."

She pulled in her lower lip, appreciating and regretting their easy banter all at once. *Danger, danger.* And yet—

"Couldn't hurt to try."

Goodness, she didn't even need caffeine anymore, the way he spiked her pulse looking at her like that.

But this was Cade Landry. He knew how to flirt with women. "I've got plenty of lines. Trust me."

See?

"I don't doubt it." She raised a brow. "Didn't you end up with two dates for the senior prom?" Oops. Hadn't meant to go there.

He cocked an eyebrow, lowered his voice to a sobering tone as if ashamed. "Don't hate the player, Ace. Hate the game."

Her laugh burst free, the tension between them dissipated. Time for a subject change. She gestured toward the cell in his hand. "Heard your phone blowing up, Mr. Popular."

Cade shook his head, turning the screen to show her a group text marked "Gone Fishing." "It's all the guys. We meet up every other week or so, fish from the same pier by the Blue Pirogue. They're in rare form."

She squinted, reading the texts.

Noah

Cade, you still coming tonight? 🎣

Linc

Ten bucks says he bails.

Noah

You used to say that about me.

Linc

In a weird twist of fate, you've become more re-liable.

Ha. Rosalyn grinned up at Cade. "Do you bail a lot?"

"Been busy with Magnolia Days. They keep asking if I need to delegate anything to them, but . . ." Cade shrugged.

"Well, do you?" They moved up again in line. Almost Cade's turn.

"See for yourself." He held out his phone again with a smirk.

Cade

Why does everyone keep asking me that?

Linc
Because you're literally putting on a circus by
yourself.

Owen
🌀 Is it true about the poodles???

Cade
You'll have to buy a ticket and find out.

Owen
Have you decided about the stilts yet?

Cade
Can you walk on stilts?

Owen
Yes.

Cade
Without falling?

Owen
. . .

She laughed. "I'd like to meet this Owen. Funny."

"They're good guys. Except when they dog me like this, of course." Cade's gaze drifted over Rosalyn's shoulder to the bar. "Uh-oh."

She turned. The dark-haired barista, wearing over-the-head earphones and a hoop nose ring, shimmied her hips and shoulders as she worked the milk frother.

"I'm assuming the weather report is . . . undesirable?" Rosalyn winced. She needed the pick-me-up if she was going to train today at Madame Paulette's. "Bad mood equals good coffee, right?"

"Correct." Cade lowered his voice. "Though lately, Miley seems to be in better moods more often than usual."

Rosalyn leaned in close to whisper back. Kinda fun, being one of the locals again. "Maybe she got a boyfriend."

Cade's gaze held hers, a teasing spark lighting his eyes. "Is that all it takes to make a gal happy?"

That depended. Rosalyn's throat went dry.

"Next!" The barista chirped.

Saved, she quickly ordered an iced matcha latte—decided to risk it anyway—while Cade ordered only a scone and gallantly paid for both their orders. They stepped to the side as Miley whipped up Rosalyn's drink.

Cade leaned one hip against the counter. "Big plans today?"

A boring question after their flirting, but definitely safer. She remembered the text messages and shook her head. "I was going to warm up on my silks, but now I think I'm going to come help you."

"Help me?" He frowned. "Why?"

"With the fundraiser."

Cade stiffened. "That's nice of you to offer, but like I told the guys, I can handle it."

"Oh, come on." Rosalyn leveled him with a stare, probably the same one she'd given him freshman year when he claimed he could be the first to solve the bonus points algebra problem. "There's got to be *something* you can take off your plate and dump on mine. I've got room."

She could see the battle in his eyes, but then he hesitated. "Maybe you could make some of my confirmation calls. Like for the porta-potties and poodles."

"Pretty sure that sentence has never been uttered in the history of language, but sure. I can make calls." She grinned at him. "See? That wasn't so hard."

"Here you go!" Miley reached over the counter and handed Cade a pastry bag with a curtsy, which seem to confirm his decision to pass on coffee.

She handed Rosalyn her latte next, then danced back toward

the cash register. Rosalyn tried to hide her smile. Maybe she had found love.

Must be nice.

"Here goes nothing." Rosalyn took a cautious sip as they moved toward the napkin station. She licked her lower lip to catch the foam. "Not bad."

"You missed a spot." Before she could process what he meant, Cade reached over and gently wiped her cheek with a napkin.

Her skin tingled under his touch. The grinding of espresso beans and the chatter of fellow patrons faded to the background as she stilled.

Cade took a breath.

She might not be breathing at all.

Their gazes remained locked until a warning signal flashed through the haze. Danger, again. This was still *Cade*, after all. Apparently, a few days in Magnolia Bay could make her a teenager again, secretly giddy over Cade Landry.

He must have gotten the same radar blip. "Sorry." He quickly backed up a step. "I should've asked—"

"No, it's okay. I didn't want to be walking around town with a mustache." She grinned, though her shaky hand belied the breeziness she infused in her tone.

He crumbled the napkin and moved to throw it in a trashcan. "Remember that time you had spinach in your teeth for Mrs. Swanson's entire fourth hour class?"

On the other hand, maybe she'd imagined the whole chemistry thing. He was just strolling down memory lane now. "Oh, I remember." She swatted playfully at his arm, knocking his aim askew as he went to toss the napkin. "Everyone said that's why Justin Davies said no to being my date for the 'Girls Ask Guys' spring fling."

"Actually, that's not why."

"What do you mean?" She took another sip of latte—which

really wasn't great—and frowned at him over the lid. What did he know?

Cade drew a breath. Did he regret bringing it up? "Justin Davies said no because I'd threatened him."

She lowered her cup. "*What*?" Just in time, she remembered to swipe her own face with her wrist for leftover foam.

"I overheard him in the locker room during gym. Justin had heard you were going to ask him and he was bragging about plans for *after* the dance." Cade shrugged, a bit of red flushing the base of his throat. "So I made sure he understood that accepting an invitation from you would be . . . let's say, painful."

Her chest warmed. He had tried to protect her?

Avoiding her eyes, Cade started to pick up the wadded paper on the ground, but Rosalyn stopped him with a touch on his arm.

"Let me get this straight." She let her hand fall. "You threatened to beat up Justin Davies if he came on to me?"

Cade rocked back on his heels. "Well, technically, I had Simon LeMoine ready to beat Justin up." He smirked. "Simon was a linebacker. It made more sense."

Rosalyn released an incredulous laugh. "You went to all that trouble? For me?"

The red at his throat deepened as he fiddled with his pastry bag. "It was nothing."

But she couldn't let it go that easily. "It was definitely something. I thought you barely tolerated me."

"Only when you beat me." He winked.

She lifted her chin. "Well, that was all the time, so . . ."

"Ha, ha." He rolled his eyes. "You weren't so bad—when you weren't listening to Amber's all-men-stink speeches, anyway."

She opened her mouth, then closed it. He had a point. And still . . . "She was right about a few things."

"Maybe. Regardless—" Cade picked up the napkin and took

aim once more. This time, it landed easily. "Let's just say I'll always have your back, Ace."

Rosalyn swallowed, trying not to be affected by the secret he'd kept, by the chivalrous way Cade opened the shop door, ushered her through first as they filed outside.

He'd have a lot more than her back if she weren't careful.

It'd be way too easy for him to have her heart.

ROSALYN SHOOK THE DWINDLING ICE in her cup, then swiped a yellow highlighter across the next line on the spreadsheet. "Has the film company called you back yet?"

"Not yet." Cade set down his iPad and leaned back in his chair. Was it her imagination, or did his eyes linger on her a moment? She looked away before she could decide.

The afternoon sun that seemed to have wilted the potted plant in its path warmed her legs. She'd acquired a barefoot, crisscross-apple-sauce position in the chair opposite Cade's desk, papers strewn across her lap. The AC from the vent above blew across her cheeks. It felt right being here—like they'd been a team for much longer than a few hours. They'd grudgingly worked together at various times over their years at school, but always toward individual goals.

The collaboration was nice. And a good distraction from the consuming question marks about her future.

"I'll bug them in a few hours if I don't hear from them." Cade fiddled with a pencil on his desk. "Like Dad always says, the squeaky wheel gets the grease."

"You're hardly squeaky or greasy, Landry." More like smooth and charming. But she wouldn't say that, wouldn't let his head get any bigger or risk more unnecessary chemistry revealing on her part.

This time she didn't have to look up to feel his grin.

"So you don't see me as a hamster. That's good to know."

His pencil tapped a rhythm. "How's that cross-checking coming along?"

Rosalyn marked another line. "Everything matches up so far." She was making sure all the registered vendors for the Magnolia Days had paid their deposit. "But this one for Big Al's Porta-Potties has an asterisk?"

"Yeah, the city is paying for those. Just need to confirm the dates with Al." Cade rocked forward, his feet thumping on the floor under his desk. "I'll do that now, actually. I keep forgetting." Then he hesitated, one hand resting on the landline receiver. "Thanks for doing this, by the way. I hate that I'm keeping you from your workout."

"It's no problem. I'll get to it later." The idea of practicing completely alone in Lettie's studio didn't hold the appeal it would've even a year ago. Laughing at Cade's candy wrapper trash and quirky organizational tactics, however, held plenty.

Or maybe, like she suspected of Cade, she didn't want to admit the inevitable—they were *both* in over their heads.

"The last time I saw you surrounded by colored pens and highlighters was senior year study group." Cade unwrapped a package of Twizzlers.

"Man, I haven't thought about that study group in a while."

Cade offered her one of the red roped candies, and she shook her head. He pinched off a bite. "You bet me you'd win valedictorian."

"What were our stakes, again?"

She remembered. But wanted to see if he did.

"If you lost, you said you'd sticky-note bomb the principal's office." Cade wrinkled his nose. "Still lame."

"It was the most daring thing I could imagine myself actually doing in that situation." Rosalyn laughed. Even now, she wasn't sure if she could've actually gone through with it. She'd been on the Principal's List all four years of school, and while a lot of the kids didn't like Principal Davies, she'd respected him.

Which was why she couldn't go through with the senior prank either.

Cade pointed his Twizzler at her. "I think you only agreed to the bet because you were confident you'd win."

"That too." She returned his smile. "You know, that reminds me . . ."

"That I lost?" He took another bite of licorice.

She shrugged, turning her attention back to her paperwork. "You never paid your penalty." Her heartbeat accelerated. Oh, this was a bad idea. Had she learned nothing from the coffee shop?

"I didn't, did I?"

His casual tone was either a massive put-on, or he hadn't thought about it over the years like she had. She wasn't sure she wanted to know which. After all, Cade was Cade, which meant all flirt and no follow through. Hadn't she seen him break the hearts of half the cheerleading squad and most of the dance line?

She might've added herself to that list, if not for Amber and Gabby and the rest of her group reminding her men weren't worth it. *Grades before guys.* Or, as Amber said in sixth grade—*college before cooties.*

Rosalyn tossed back her hair and slid the highlighter across the next line, trying to match Cade's breezy tone as he went back to tapping a pencil. "Only Cade Landry would've bet kissing the winner if he lost."

He paused mid-tap. "Maybe because that would've made me a winner too."

Rosalyn's stomach flipped and her hand trembled. Wait. He'd *wanted* to kiss her? She'd always taken it as a joking insult—it was a penalty for losing. Yet another way to tease her in their competitive dynamic. He'd never brought up the bet again after their scores were announced, and neither had she. She'd been updating college resumes and writing her speech for graduation.

She cleared her throat. "Prince Charming called. He'd like his lines back."

Cade laughed. "Mine are way better."

Were they only lines?

"I heard *everything* and came as fast as I could."

Rosalyn twisted around at the sudden female voice behind her, in time to see a woman carrying a white bakery box breeze across the office.

She tossed the package on Cade's desk. "Not to be dramatic."

Cade's face lit like a New York City skyline. "I don't know what you heard, Zoey, but I hope whoever told you tells you again tomorrow." He eagerly reached for the box marked Bayou Beignets, stamped with a black and sage green fleur-de-lis logo.

"Flattery will get you everywhere." The woman dropped into the desk chair beside Rosalyn with a flourish and extended her hand. "Zoey Lakewood, resident baker."

"Rosalyn Dupree." They shook. Then Rosalyn pointed to the box. "Is that your shop?"

"It is." Zoey lifted her delicate chin and beamed. "I opened it about a year and a half ago."

"Already award-winning too. Best dessert on the island." Cade made a show of deciding which beignet to choose from the carton.

Zoey wore a loose black tank front-tucked into jeans. She seemed pretty familiar with Cade. Another old friend of his? Or . . .

Zoey squinted at her beneath thick, dark bangs. "Wait . . . Rosalyn. I think I saw you around school." She snapped her fingers. "You were valedictorian, weren't you?"

"Ugh. You *had* to remind her." Cade dug into the bakery box.

Zoey ignored him. "I was a few grades behind you, but you were in the same class as my best friend, Elisa." Her cornflower blue eyes widened. "Aren't you famous now?"

Rosalyn shifted in her chair. "Not ex—"

"Yes." Cade gestured with the pastry in his hand, sending a sprinkling of white dust across his desk. "She is. And she's here for the circus."

"Ah. So you're going to save Magnolia Bay." Zoey pulled her legs up in her chair to match Rosalyn's crisscross position. "Awesome."

Again, with the pressure. "I don't know about—"

"*These* are what's awesome, Zoey." Cade interrupted again. "And you threw in Cajun kolaches! You do love me."

A strange sensation lit in Rosalyn's stomach, a mix between a squeezing vise and a jabbing thorn.

Zoey grinned. "You're my best customer—especially when you're stressed."

Cade brushed his hands together over his trashcan, ridding himself of excess powdered sugar. "So what did you mean by *you heard*?"

Zoey folded her arms over her stomach. Her thin frame and short stature gave Rosalyn the impression of a dark-haired woodland fairy perched on oversized furniture. "That you needed help."

Cade spun from the trashcan to face them. "Let me guess. Noah and Linc?"

Zoey made a noncommittal noise in the back of her throat. "I thought a sugar rush might help you be more productive."

"You're right. But why is everyone so suddenly concerned over my to-do list?" Cade sat back in his desk chair. "I'm not standing in Linc's boat telling him how to crawfish."

Zoey scoffed. "Well, of course not. That'd be ridiculous."

"Exactly."

"You have no idea how." Zoey laughed.

Okay, maybe she liked Zoey. Rosalyn hid her smile behind her hand.

Cade picked up a kolache. "That's not what I meant."

"Don't bite the hand that fed you."

"That's the only thing keeping me from kicking you out right now." He set the kolache on a napkin. "Pearl will let anyone in here, won't she?"

"Linc said you're being stubborn. And I know for a fact you've already turned down two of Sadie's ideas and filled half the volunteer slots with your own name." Zoey leaned forward in her chair. "Magnolia Days is a community event—let the community help."

Good point. Rosalyn locked her own gaze on Cade and raised her eyebrows.

His eyes darted between her and Zoey, and he slowed his speech to emphasize. "I don't need help."

"She's helping." Zoey nodded pointedly toward the spreadsheets in Rosalyn's lap.

Cade bristled. "Rosalyn's different."

Her heart stuttered. And heat crawled up her neck, the thorn faded, leaving behind an even more uncomfortable realization—Rosalyn had been jealous.

She held up the paper. "I'm only marking paid vendors. It's not a big task."

"Really, Cade? Highlighting?" Zoey's voice dipped. "There's *so* much more that's got to be dealt with."

"I know, trust me. I got it." A brittle edge coated his voice.

Suddenly, another figure landed in the doorway—Miley. She crossed her arms over her band tee and glowered. "That family of four just signed a lease."

Cade palmed his face. "Is Pearl even *out* there?"

"They're moving furniture into the pothole, Cade." Miley stabbed her hands into her hair. "I face-timed my dad, and he's losing it. He threw out the L-word."

Great time for coffee. Zoey mouthed the words to Rosalyn as she jerked her head toward Miley. Rosalyn grinned again.

"L-word?" Cade frowned. "What? Loser?"

"Lawsuit."

Cade's face paled, then he stood, hands extended. His charming smile reappeared. "Look, Miley, I told you I'd handle—"

The landline rang. Cade sighed loud enough to compete with the AC unit. "Hold that thought."

He held up one finger as his cell buzzed from atop his desk. He glanced at the display, one hand still hovering in the air. Then his eyes widened and locked on Rosalyn's as the landline jangled a second time. "It's the assistant director."

"Get it." Rosalyn tossed the spreadsheets on the desk and sprang to her feet. Cade couldn't miss this. "The rest can wait."

"I'll grab the other phone." Zoey leaned over the desk and scooped up the black receiver before Cade could protest. "Buddy the Elf, what's your favorite color?"

Miley snorted.

Cade's face turned purple but all he could do was answer his cell. "Hey, Janie. Thanks for getting back with me." He swept out of the room, his voice trailing behind him down the hall. "Yeah, it's a great time, no worries."

Rosalyn shook her head.

"That boy needs serious prayer."

Miley was right. Rosalyn was already asking God to help Cade. But would He hear her?

The quiet inside Magnolia Library hurt his ears. Or maybe because outside the cacophony of his office, Cade could finally hear his own looping, incessant thoughts.

"I figured you'd be more excited." Rosalyn leaned against the high front desk of the library, currently unmanned save for a stack of bookmarks, a bell with a sign that read Ring for Assistance, and coupons for discount ice cream cones. A cutout banner of books, obviously colored by local children, strung cheerfully across the front of the counter, swirls of color escaping thin black borders.

"About the Friends of the Library booth? Oh yeah, I'm stoked." They'd walked over to the library after Cade had returned from his call with Janie—and after he'd placated Miley with more promises about the pothole, thanked Zoey for the beignets and kicked her out, and agreed to come see Mrs. Peters, the head librarian, about her vendor booth.

After that chaotic last hour at work, he'd become a man on a mission to accomplish something, *anything*—which apparently, started with appeasing Mrs. Peters, who didn't sound happy on the phone. With the mayoral campaign looming in his near future, he couldn't afford another disgruntled town member. The stakes were higher now.

He had to prove himself trustworthy to lead.

"Not about the library booth, silly." Rosalyn elbowed him in the side. "I meant about the film crew. That the scout is coming."

"Oh, right. Well, nothing is a done deal yet." He'd had to talk *fast* to convince Janie to even make that happen. The weary assistant had finally secured permission from her boss to send a scout the week of the circus, but only after Cade had name-dropped Rosalyn as a feature act.

But he didn't want to admit that to her. He'd seen the way she blanched when Zoey talked about her saving Magnolia Bay. Rosalyn had never been the type to back down under pressure, but Cade didn't want to risk overloading her. She seemed to have enough going on that she didn't want to talk about.

Something else they had in common.

"Hey, it's a start. And the town will be at its best during Magnolia Days." Rosalyn straightened a stack of bookmarks on the counter so they aligned neatly with the pencil holder next to it. "I'm sure it'll be an easy sell."

"We'll see." Cade drummed his fingers on the counter. "I don't want to count chickens." That reminded him, he still hadn't connected with the dancing poodles guy. He glanced at his watch. The more everyone tried to help him or worried about him doing everything alone, the more unorganized and forgetful he became. If people would trust him to be capable, maybe he could actually get something done.

Where was Mrs. Peters?

Cade double-tapped the bell right as the white-haired woman rounded the corner from the overflowing shelves behind the counter. Oops.

"Well, young Landry. I'm glad to see you're in one piece." Mrs. Peters smoothed the front of her 1990s burgundy pantsuit.

"You are?" Cade asked with a frown. "I mean . . . was there a doubt?" *He* doubted it at this point, after everything Dad dumped on him, but why would the librarian?

Mrs. Peters sniffed. "Apparently, the mayor's office has been taken over by elves."

Right. Cade fought to keep his expression neutral. Of all the people in town, of course she'd been the one on the phone when Zoey had jokingly answered his landline. "That was . . . my, ah, friend earlier." No sense in ratting Zoey out.

Mrs. Peters sniffed again. "Highly unprofessional."

"It was a joke, ma'am. Have you seen the movie *Elf*?" Cade tapped the high desk between them with one finger. "No? Great film."

She blinked at him through her glasses, unimpressed. "Television is for people who don't read."

"I actually do both." Cade waggled his eyebrows, hoping for a grin, but her stoic expression never shifted. He sobered. "Reading is superior, of course."

"Because the books are always better than the movies." Rosalyn smiled at Mrs. Peters, who appeared to have noticed her for the first time.

"Rosalyn Dupree, is that you?" A sudden grin broke across the older woman's face, taking several wrinkles and about ten years off her age.

Rosalyn dipped her head. "Yes ma'am. Been awhile."

"*Rosalyn?*" A younger woman appeared behind Mrs. Peters, toting an armful of hardback books. Cade recognized her from high school but couldn't place her name. She'd been one of Amber's friends, hadn't she? "That *is* you!"

"Harper!" Rosalyn confirmed Cade's suspicion. "I didn't know you were working here."

"About six months now." Harper set the overflowing pile of books on the return rack and smiled, smoothing back her wavy red hair. "Planning on taking over one day." She winked.

"*Hmph.*" Mrs. Peters pursed her lips, then smiled as her gaze landed back on Rosalyn. She gestured proudly. "This girl here was one of my star readers."

"I read." Harper feigned offense as she motioned around the library. "Obviously."

"Me too," Cade added. "Thirty-two books, that one year." He grinned.

Now it was Rosalyn's turn to purse her lips at him.

Mrs. Peters prattled on. "Rosalyn was always in here checking out the classics and reminiscing about her favorite young adult novels." The white-haired woman pointed down to the brightly decorated children's section. "My goodness, but you must have read *If You Give a Mouse a Cookie* a hundred times."

"So *that's* why it was always checked out," Cade joked.

Mrs. Peters frowned at him. "Harper will be handling our

Friends of the Library booth for Magnolia Days. You'll have to get with her about the story hour times, the used-book sale, and the like. I wanted to make sure you two were properly introduced and on the same page."

Ha. "Same page." Cade snorted. "Get it?"

Mrs. Peters's eyebrows furrowed so deep, it appeared a caterpillar had roosted above her eyes.

Yep. She got it. Cade sobered again. "Harper and I go way back." He nodded at the petite redhead, who had the decency to smile sheepishly from behind the counter. Maybe she, too, was remembering all the sexist quips she'd spouted at him in front of Amber a decade plus ago. "I didn't realize you worked here either."

"Probably because you're not a frequent patron." Mrs. Peters lifted her chin. "Too busy with the television, I'd imagine."

What on earth had he done to this woman? Cade scanned back through his years of juvenile pranks, but couldn't think of any that had—

Oh, yeah.

He winced as images of a freshman-year dare filled his mind. The football team. Running under the moonlight. Balloons full of shaving cream dotting the library courtyard. They'd assumed the security guard, one of the players' good-natured uncles, would stumble upon them on duty, but apparently, Mrs. Peters liked being early to work even back then.

Something else Dad had to bail Cade out of.

He sucked in a breath. "You know, Mrs. Peters, I really am sorry about that prank we—"

"Well, look who it is!" Delia Boudreaux shuffled through the automatic doors of the library. Her short hair was freshly curled, her bright pink lipstick only slightly smeared. "Cade Landry, you never texted me back."

"Mama D! Look who graduated from a walker to her cane." Cade leaned in for a hug, grateful for a friendly face to balance the pursed lips still pointed in his direction. "I apologize for not spamming you back with a dozen flamingo emojis." He should have. Mama D was a local favorite, and her surgery had been a long time coming. It was good to see her out and about.

"My Wordle score has improved too. I've averaging three guesses now." She shook the cane at him. "As for this old thing, I keep reminding myself it's better than the wheelchair I was in before my surgery."

Cade stepped back to give her room. "Much better. You'll be running the Magnolia 5k in no time."

"I don't know about all that, but I've got to be ready to dance at Noah and Elisa's wedding." Delia wiggled her hips. "Of course, he hasn't proposed yet, but we all know it's coming."

Cade choked back a laugh. He couldn't wait to tell Noah about this one.

Delia turned to Rosalyn. "And speaking of weddings, you must be Cade's friend."

Now he just choked. "Mama D, you know Rosalyn. We went to school together."

"Rosalyn Dupree. Yes, now I see it." Delia tilted her head back, her eyes gleaming. She'd known who Rosalyn was the whole time, the old bat. "You haven't been home in a while, have you dear?"

"In longer than I would have liked." Rosalyn accepted the hand Delia held out. "But it's good to be back for a while."

"You be sure to come by the diner. I'll have Elisa give you some dessert on the house." Delia grinned, still clutching Rosalyn's hand. "Or maybe Cade could take you . . ."

Oh no. "You need to call that surgeon, Mama D." Cade wrapped an arm around the woman's stooped shoulders, freeing Rosalyn from her grip. "I think they accidentally took your social filter when they fixed your hip."

Rosalyn covered her mouth with her hand and looked away.

Harper ducked her head, but her shoulders silently shook behind a curtain of red hair.

"We can't wait to watch you perform." Mama D beamed. "I heard the rumors. You're bringing our little circus up to an entirely different level."

Rosalyn's eyes darted to Cade, but her expression remained composed. "I'll do my best."

Mama D nodded. "You've got a real gift. I've seen you perform on the internet—I wasn't as lucky as Cade here to get to see you in person."

Uh-oh. Rosalyn didn't know about that time he'd come to see her. How did Mama D know? The only person he'd ever told was Elisa . . . oh. He sighed.

Delia pointed to the computer in front of Mrs. Peters, completely unaware of the gun she'd fired. "Can you be a dear and let me know if you have a certain title in stock?"

"Probably not *If You Give a Mouse a Cookie*." Cade looked hopefully at Mrs. Peters.

Nope. Zero reaction.

"I'll find it, Delia." Harper eased over to the keyboard, sending Cade a sympathetic smile. Well, that was something. "Which title was it?"

Rosalyn turned curious eyes to Cade as the chatting continued, lowering her voice. "You've been to my performances?"

"One." He couldn't lie to her. Even though it wasn't a memory he'd ever hoped to relay.

"Why didn't you say anything?" Confusion pinched her brow. "Which show?"

Cade opened his mouth, then closed it. There was no un-mortifying way to admit he couldn't stop thinking about that night at the Lazy Spoon, couldn't silence all the what-ifs that had mocked him ever since. So about three months ago, he'd found a ticket to a show in Dallas, drove through the night, bought her flowers, and hung around backstage afterward . . . only to see her run into the eager arms of another guy. After that, Cade had done what any decent man would do.

Ditched the flowers, bolted for his Audi, and pretended like it never happened.

He met Rosalyn's eyes, wide and still waiting for an answer. "It was a while ago . . ." Awkward. And why did the memory burn his cheeks as if it'd been last week instead of months ago? Of course, seeing her perform was what had given him the idea to host the circus in the first place, so maybe it hadn't been a total flub.

Mrs. Peters slid a black and white flyer across the desk to Cade. "Here's the list of requirements our booth *must* have. Harper knows the rest."

Saved. "Yes, ma'am." He scooped up the piece of paper and backed away from the counter. "Thank you, Mrs. Peters. And I really do like *If You Give a Mouse a Cookie*, for the record. If that helps."

She squinted at him over her glasses. "Well, it doesn't help as much as prime booth placement at the festival . . ."

Well played. He nodded. "Yes ma'am." Then he took a deep breath and looked back at Rosalyn, fighting the rush of anxiety creeping up his chest "I'm going to head to the office—got those calls to make." So many calls. So many things to do. "You coming back?"

She tilted her head, debating. Not that he wanted her to re-ask the question he'd avoided, but he did enjoy her company while she highlighted spreadsheets. Laughed at his jokes. Made him forget how hectic his life was.

But why did it seem like she was trying to decide something more than afternoon plans?

"Why don't you hang out here?" Harper scooted a book out of the way to brace both arms on the counter. She smiled at Rosalyn. "My break is soon. We can catch up."

Rosalyn's gaze lingered slightly on Cade before she returned Harper's smile. "That sounds good. Then I probably should get to Madame Paulette's and test my knee further on the silks." She raised an eyebrow at him. "That doesn't throw off your plans, does it?"

Yes. "No, of course not." After all, hopes were not plans. Cade ignored the disappointment coursing through his chest and found his movie star smile. "You girls have fun." Same story as always—Rosalyn's "friends" telling her what to do, what to think.

Who to date.

Who *not* to date.

Amber's voice rang in his ears as he backstepped toward the automatic doors. *Guys are losers, Rosalyn. Especially Cade Landry. He's a spoiled brat—only as good as his father's reputation and money.* Had Harper been present for Amber's declaration that afternoon in study hall too? He couldn't remember.

Now both women stared at him from the counter, like twin ghosts from the past.

Time to get out of there. "I'll—uh, see you later, then?" He shot Rosalyn an awkward thumbs-up as he continued walking backward. Oh man. That was lame.

Harper winced. Mrs. Peters shook her head with a *tsk*, and even Delia turned away as if she couldn't bear to watch. Rosalyn returned his thumbs-up with an overly dramatic one of her own. "Uh, sure."

"Great." He bumped into the door frame as the door whooshed open. "Oops. Okay, bye."

"Poor kid. He's got it bad." Delia's whisper carried.

He almost tripped on a crack in the sidewalk and caught himself. *Was* that why? He couldn't out-walk the thought as the doors shut behind him, blocking the rush of AC and what had to be more whispering.

What was wrong with him? He squared his shoulders as he continued across the library courtyard, pausing a beat to straighten the cuff of his sleeve. He was a Landry. Charming. Likable. Smooth.

In front of everyone but Rosalyn, apparently.

Maybe Mama D had a point.

He swallowed. Maybe Amber did too.

Seven

ORKING WITH THIS KNEE LIMITATION was almost like having to learn aerial all over again. Sweat beaded on Rosalyn's forehead and dripped down her temples.

As the late afternoon sun crept across the dance studio floor, she carefully lowered herself into a fist to angel drop, an upside-down move she'd flown into without hesitation hundreds of times. But discovering which moves pulled her knee was slow going. She'd have to design her circus routine around the skills she could do confidently—which meant she'd be offering a lower caliber than her typical performance.

All the more reason why she didn't need Cade or anyone else in town talking her up and setting unrealistic expectations.

How could she save the town if she couldn't even save herself?

Rosalyn swallowed as she repositioned herself into a French climb, wrapping one foot around the fabric and then releasing and repeating as she gained air. The earlier conversations spun through her mind, also gaining traction.

Why hadn't Cade wanted her to know he'd seen her perform? He'd changed subjects faster than—well, as Lettie used to say— "faster than a stage mom braiding a ponytail."

And then the discussion about the old bet he'd never followed through with. Her cheeks heated. They'd definitely been flirting, which wasn't fair to either of them. Harper's invitation to stay at the library a while had been a rescue. The more Rosalyn hung out with Cade, the more she forgot all her reasons *not* to flirt with him.

But he wasn't safe, and she wasn't free.

Rosalyn twisted her hands into the silks, pausing to rest her knee. She and Harper had chatted for half an hour, filling each other in on the last decade. Apparently, Amber and the other girl in their group, Gabby, had gone separate ways after graduating and never returned to Magnolia Bay. Harper, who'd moved back after graduating, kept up with them on social media, unlike Rosalyn.

"We comment on each other's posts now and then," Harper had said. "That's about it. Amber is single. Has several degrees and a *lot* of cats. Works remotely for a big firm out of New York."

"What about Gabby?" Rosalyn almost hated to ask. Gabby had been sweet, if not a little ditzy, blindly following Amber's lead. But hadn't they all, to some extent?

"She's divorced, two kids." Harper's lips twisted to the side. "Works in marketing in New Orleans and has become something of a social media influencer."

Of the four of them, only Rosalyn and Harper were living their original high school dreams—Harper as an aspiring novelist, working around books all day, and Rosalyn as an international performer.

Yet had any of them actually found happiness?

"Careful up there darlin'. You don't actually have wings, you know."

Rosalyn looked down at Lettie standing underneath her, hands propped on her ample hips. "Oh, I know, trust me." Her knee twinged on cue, as if reminding her of her fall. Not that she ever forgot. She slid down the silks to the ground, fireman-style, and was met with a wave of patchouli.

Lettie wrapped her in a hug as soon as Rosalyn's feet touched the mats. "I'm just too glad you're home." Before Rosalyn could respond, the older woman abruptly released her and held her at arm's length. "Even if your legs would make Carrie Underwood jealous."

"You've got pretty great gams yourself, Lettie." Rosalyn winked as she stepped back toward her fabric.

"Tell that to my ex-husband." Lettie crossed her arms over her flowing tent-dress. "Not that'd he ever admit it. He can't agree with any woman, mind you."

Rosalyn tried to hide her smile as she wrapped her wrists into the silks. "His loss."

"Indeed." Lettie lifted her chin. "Any secret lovers in your life, hon?"

She snorted. Secrets, yes. Lovers? Not quite . . . She inverted into a candlestick position. "Now, Madame, you know I'm married to my career." Literally, at this point.

Lettie let out a loud burst of laughter. "Pity. You'll have to make room for someone eventually, darlin'. The stage won't keep you content forever." She released a dramatic sigh. "Ask me how I know."

Rosalyn's smile faded as she split her legs into a straddle. Her knee held steady, and she breathed a sigh of relief. "You're a gem. Any man—or the stage—would be lucky to have you."

Lettie cackled. "You always were my favorite. Any chance of you sticking around this time? Maybe teaching aerial?"

That would've been her dream retirement, back in the day. To come home and open her own studio or take over for Madame Paulette? But now . . . She swallowed, gripping the silks tighter and splitting her legs the other direction. "Not this time, Lettie."

Breathe in. Split. *Breathe out*. She used to hate conditioning skills when she was younger. She'd wanted to perform. Wanted to prove herself to her mom, wanted to show that leaving ballet had been the right decision. Now Rosalyn would give anything to avoid the spotlight.

Funny how life worked out.

Lettie watched her with crossed arms. "The good news is, unlike me, you've got time on your side, dear. *And* prospects."

Breathe in. Split. "Prospects?"

"A certain young town development director seemed quite taken with you yesterday." Lettie dramatically bounced her hips like Ursula in *The Little Mermaid.*

"Cade?" Rosalyn sputtered. Her grip slipped and she caught the fabric in a fresh hold. "We're old friends."

"He wants to be more, trust me." Lettie moved toward the supply closet near the mirrored wall and slid out a box of exercise bands. "And no, I was never a psychic. I get asked that a lot, though, when I go to the French Quarter." She straightened and stared at her scarf-layered, bejeweled reflection in the mirror with a frown. "I can't imagine why."

Rosalyn clamped her lips to keep from laughing as she came down from her inversion. "It's a mystery, Lettie." As for the idea of Cade truly being into her, well . . . the thought brought butterflies.

And a giant red flag.

Make that butterflies waving giant red flags.

Across the studio, Lettie shut the closet door. Rosalyn unzipped her bag and pulled out her warm-up tee.

"How long has that knee been bothering you?"

Rosalyn tugged the shirt over her head and checked her watch. Almost time for the six-o'clock class. "Is it that obvious I'm not one hundred percent?" She'd taken the bandage off, and thought she'd hidden her slight limp.

"It doesn't take a psychic to see the difference in your work, darlin'." Lettie gestured toward the silks knotted in the center of the room. "I know when one of my students is holding back. Even if you haven't been my student for a few moon cycles."

"A few." Rosalyn grinned back, unwilling—unable?—to tell her the details about her fall. "Thanks for watching out, Lettie."

"Always, my dear." Lettie pursed her burgundy-painted lips. "There's more to this story, though, isn't there?" She squinted, her narrowed eyes reading Rosalyn like a novel.

Rosalyn stilled.

"You've lost something."

Good grief, maybe she was psychic. Rosalyn nodded, unwilling to lie—not anymore than she already had to.

"Well, we don't have to talk about it—now." Lettie tossed Rosalyn an exercise band. "Want to help the kiddos stretch? Show them a move or two?"

Rosalyn caught the pink elastic and stared down at it. Kids could see through people even faster than Lettie. How could she project joy into a demonstration when she hadn't felt any since her tumble?

Since before then, if she were honest. Since Saudi Arabia . . .

The rush of hot desert air swept over her memory and she clamped her eyes shut.

The spinning tent. The roar of the crowd. Her panic, tangible. The scratchy sheets of the hospital bed, the metal rails cold against her restrained arms. The panic in Blaine's eyes as he relayed their limited options.

She wrenched her eyes open. "I, uh—" She inhaled, gulped. "I don't think that would be—"

The studio door opened, and a rush of pink leos and tiny bunheads flooded the room. One of the girls, a little blonde wearing a white tutu, froze on her way to the barre and gaped up at Rosalyn. "Are you *Barbie*?"

Rosalyn choked back a cough, the child's innocent assumption blessedly removing the coming wave of tears. "I'm not, actually."

"You could totally be Ballerina Barbie." A dark-haired girl with a braided bun chimed in, elbowing the red-headed kid next to her.

She sported a temporary tattoo of a unicorn-cat on her arm. "Can we call you that?"

She smiled, giving in and realizing she didn't mind at all. Maybe there was still joy to be found in the studio—vicariously through these kids, at least. "Whatever you want."

"Sit by me, Barbie." Little Blonde tugged at her hand.

The redhead grabbed Rosalyn's other one. "No, me."

"Duh. She has two sides." Braided Bun rolled her eyes.

"Everyone, take your places at the barre." Lettie's deep voice easily overcame the sudden din. "And no fighting over the dolls." She winked at Rosalyn. "Welcome home, darlin'."

The word rolled around Rosalyn's mind as she took her place with the younger girls. *Home.*

Did people who ran away to join the circus ever get that back?

Staring out at the bay reminded Cade what was at stake.

Home. Sun-tinted waves lapped the pier overlooking the sparkling water beneath him. Somewhere in the distance, a seagull let out a squawk, while the familiar, unmistakable scent of salt water filled the air. He breathed in a drag of it. He loved this town, loved this dock. It had long been the guys' favorite fishing spot, only about half a mile from the Blue Pirogue Inn. So far this evening, he'd been the first to show up, which was perfect.

Gave him time to process the day's myriad mistakes.

Cade pulled a drink from the ice chest and caught his reflection in the aluminum. He fixed a piece of wayward hair that blew across his forehead and spoke to his distorted image on the can. "You're an idiot."

His reflection looked back, unfazed. He took the opportunity to check his teeth. He'd made things weird with Rosalyn at the library, and in front of Mama D, no less. And all afternoon in his office, he'd shuffled through his Magnolia Days list and accomplished way more daydreaming than actual tasks.

He needed to get it together. The town was counting on him. But something about Rosalyn intimidated him, much like it had that night at the Lazy Spoon, watching the moonlight paint her face as they'd talked in the alley for what felt like hours.

Maybe Cade had accidentally acquired two dates for senior prom, but Rosalyn was—and would always be—out of his league. She didn't need him. She didn't seem to need anyone.

So why would she want him?

"Your hair is fine." Linc's scowl suddenly appeared in the can beside him. "Geez, I didn't think we'd invited any women."

Cade cracked open the can, taking time to form a wide smile, hide the embarrassment. "And that statement, my friend, is why you're single."

Linc snorted as he dropped his gear on the dock. "I highly doubt it."

Cade quirked an eyebrow. "Well, I could give you a few more reas—"

"Now, children. Let's get along." Noah set his tackle box near the cooler. Owen hurried along the pier behind him, flip-flops slapping the wood. A fishing pole bobbed on his shoulder.

"Cade was giving himself a pep talk." Linc slapped his shoulder, jostling Cade's drink. He held it away from his Rhoback shorts.

"What's up?" Owen set his pole down, then looked around and winced. "Oops. I forgot to bring bait again."

"Help yourself." Linc opened his own tackle box. Owen reached for a lure and Linc lunged. "*Not* that one."

Owen grabbed a green lure from the opposite side of the box and waited for Linc's nod before straightening. "So what exactly are we hyping you up for, Cade?"

"I bet I know." Noah fished a drink from the cooler, then

propped his sandaled foot on the lid. "Did someone decide to ask out a certain blonde aerialist?"

"Aerialist? Like a pilot?" Owen frowned as he fiddled with his line.

Noah shook his head. "No, think circus performer."

"Like they do in Cirque Du Soleil?" Owen gestured above his head. "That's impressive."

"And dangerous." Linc baited his line.

Noah snorted. "Since when do you care about danger? I've seen you standing in the bay during a thunderstorm."

Linc shrugged. "When you gotta work, you gotta work."

"Can't work if you're dead," Owen pointed out.

Linc scowled.

"I sure feel dead." Noah stretched his neck to one side, then the other. "But the upstairs renovations are finally done and the inn is starting to get booked."

"Probably largely due to Elisa's recent social media efforts." Owen joined Linc near the edge of the pier with his pole. "She's making the Blue Pirogue look good."

"She makes everything look good." Noah grinned back before turning up his drink can. "Now if I can get all the rooms booked . . ." He tipped his head toward Cade. "Hint, hint."

"Magnolia Days will bring in plenty of tourists, trust me." Cade relaxed as he rigged his own bait. As always, the guys had talked themselves into a new subject, so maybe he'd be off the hook with the Rosalyn stuff. The last thing he needed was them trying to pressure—

"Back to asking Rosalyn out." Noah cast his line into the water.

Cade suddenly felt a lot like Linc—grumpy. "Don't hold your breath."

"What happened to long tanned legs and country songs?" Linc smirked as he reeled in his empty line.

"Who is Rosalyn?" Owen abruptly turned, forgetting he was

holding his pole, and nearly clocked Linc in the ribs. He corrected and dodged the glower Linc sent his way. "Is she the aerialist?"

"Famous aerialist." Noah arched a brow. "You don't remember her from high school?"

"I home schooled, remember?" Owen shuffled a few feet away from Linc. "If they didn't attend youth group, I didn't know them."

"She didn't. Her family was more Christmas and Easter church-goers." Cade had secured his bait a minute ago, but messing with it again gave him a reason not to look up while he talked. "Then she graduated and went to Harvard."

The rest of the story burned in his throat. Which was silly. Was so long ago.

"Is this week the first time you've seen her since high school?" Owen asked.

"No. I saw her perform a while back, which gave me the idea to invite her." See? Not hard to say. Why couldn't he have been that nonchalant about it with Rosalyn earlier? Cade shook his head. "And I ran into her after a rival game at the Lazy Spoon back in college."

He also said that nonchalantly, as if the memory wasn't burned in long-term storage.

"What happened? Did Rosalyn shoot you down that night?" Linc cast, the lure sparkling in the setting sun as it arched through the sky.

"No." Cade watched the fishing line sink, the bobber start to float. "I never asked."

"So what I'm hearing is that you were as dumb then as you are now?" Noah snorted.

"Easy for you to say, Romeo." Cade glared at his friend. "You've got Elisa."

"Romeo?" Noah shook his head. "Nah. You were the one with two prom dates."

"How did you even know that? You were living in Shreveport

then." Literally no one would let him live that down. "Besides, it's not like I took both girls. I thought one girl had said no, so I asked someone else, and then . . ." Well.

"*Something* happened at the Lazy Spoon." Linc cut his eyes to Cade.

He sighed. Leave it to the hulk with a man-bun to notice what he'd hoped the guys wouldn't. "It's not a big deal. I just saved her from a jerk with the wrong idea."

Owen's eyes bugged. "You got into a fight?"

Cade hesitated. "Sort of." It'd been a little one-sided. His jaw still clicked now and then when a storm was coming. "He wasn't taking no for an answer from Rosalyn. So I politely tried to talk him down. He got in a sucker punch. Then some of my friends jumped in and then *his* friends jumped in . . . I snuck Rosalyn outside, away from it all. Then we talked in the alley, caught up." The words had been on his tongue. *Wanna get out of here?* Or maybe something less cliché than that.

"Talked, huh?" Noah grinned as he reeled in his line.

"Yes. *Talked.* Maybe had a . . . moment, or whatever. But that was it. End of story." The details, though, the ones he wouldn't share with these guys, were permanently seared in his brain. The humid night air and smell of the dumpster—that part maybe he wished he could forget—but mostly the way Rosalyn's hair shimmered under the security light beaming from the side of the building and the feel of her fingers grazing his jaw as she pressed her cold mug against the bruise forming on his cheek.

"Ironic, isn't it?" She'd rolled in her bottom lip but couldn't stop the grin.

"What? This?" He reached his hand up to cover hers, help support the mug.

"Yeah. Us." Green eyes sparkled up at him, a far cry from frustrated and competitive. "I'm used to us always being on the opposite team."

He nodded. "Leave it to a bully in a bar to bond Magnolia High's top students."

Her return smile was contagious. "We were that, weren't we?"

They'd caught up for ten minutes and talked future plans. She'd just been invited to attend a prestigious aerial college and was debating making the transfer. Leaving Harvard wasn't an easy decision, but neither was saying no to a lifelong dream.

Cade could almost forget the throbbing in his jaw with the way she'd looked at him, opened up to him. Viewed him as a friend, an equal—not a rival. Not Mayor Landry's son. Not the butt of her friends' jokes and hate, the guy to roll her eyes at.

Just *Cade.*

He could almost forget the struggle of that past year at Yale, his grades hovering right above failing. Could almost let go of the fear that welled up every time he thought about his father finding out, about failing his entire family tree full of successful Landrys.

The threat of the bar hanging over him.

"Are you ever going to come back to Magnolia Bay?" he'd asked, hoping she couldn't tell how his hands shook.

Her gaze had been downright flirty, and he didn't think it was from her one beer she'd only drank half of. "Would it matter?"

He could flirt too. Even though that night, he felt more tongue-tied and adolescent than smooth and charming. "It might."

The wind had lifted her hair from her neck, cooled the sweat on his back. Breathed hope into a raw spot. "Then I might."

Thump. Owen popped open the cooler lid, interrupting the memory. "What kind of moment?" He cracked open a can of sparkling water.

Cade had almost kissed her, almost got the guts to see what that 'might' tasted like on her lips. But . . .

"Doesn't matter. That wretched Amber girl interrupted, like she always did in high school. Came to drag Rosalyn off with their crew." Cade rolled his eyes. "She even called Rosalyn out for being with me. Like they were freshmen all over again." Dumb. It didn't take much to remember Amber's dark eyes spitting fire at him, as if he were solely responsible for every male mistake since Adam in the garden.

"And that was that?" Noah asked.

"That was that." Rosalyn hadn't stuck up for him. Just shot him an apologetic look and half-smile and let them drag her off. "Didn't see her again until she appeared in my office a few days ago."

Guess that "might" hadn't held a lot of weight.

"Too bad. You seemed like a good fit—even way back when." Noah gestured to Owen still at the cooler. "Toss me one?"

Owen obliged, missed. The can hit the dock and rolled toward the water.

Linc stopped it with his boot. "What do you mean, back when?"

"Sixth grade." Noah braced his pole against the dock and opened his drink.

Cade sighed. "Here we go with the volcano again."

"You guys had sparks." Noah took a swig.

"That was the vinegar."

Noah nearly sprayed his water. "I doubt that."

"So, to clarify, he's not asking Rosalyn out, right?" Owen shut the lid and sat on top of it.

"Unfortunately." Noah lifted his can in a toast. "Though I can guarantee you Elisa won't let up as easy as we are."

He could go for a Snickers right now. Cade took a deep breath. "It's not in the cards. Rosalyn is only here for Magnolia Days and her family, then she'll be back to whatever globe-hopping schedule famous people have."

"Long-distance relationships exist." Owen shrugged.

So did his overflowing plate of responsibility. Cade held up one hand, imitating his father in a press conference. "Right now, I'm focused on getting through Magnolia Days and then my camp—"

Oops. They couldn't know about the campaign. No one knew the position was about to be open.

"Your what?" Owen asked.

Cade pointed to the water on the horizon. "Wow, what was that?"

Shockingly enough, all three of them actually looked.

Cade cracked his neck and took a deep breath. His game was slipping, on all fronts—and too much was at stake. Being friends with Rosalyn was one thing, but the flirty nature of said friendship should stop. People were getting the wrong impression.

Most of all, him.

Cade carefully schooled his features into a puzzled expression as the guys turned back. "Must've been an illusion."

Sort of like the idea of a future with him and Rosalyn.

Eight

SURELY SHE HAD ENOUGH MONEY FOR a veggie omelet.

Rosalyn pulled the sleeves of her cropped hoodie down over her fingers as she traversed the sidewalk leading away from the studio. The morning had grown unseasonably mild with the threat of rain, but Magnolia Blossom was only a few blocks from Lettie's. Hopefully she'd make it before the inevitable downpour hit.

Her shoes scuffed the sidewalk as she strolled. In a million years, she'd never have imagined needing to be paid *before* an event. But she couldn't ask for an advance without raising suspicion. She was supposed to be rich.

And she was, once upon a time.

The wind blew a light mist into Rosalyn's face, whipping at her high ponytail as she picked up her pace. Her stomach growled. What were the odds that Magnolia Blossom would be having a breakfast sale?

A biker wearing a helmet and knee pads coasted by, and she slowed to draw in the deep aroma of the knockout roses blooming between The Spin Shop and Second Story.

She'd heard a scripture on a social media reel recently—something about the flowers being clothed with no effort of their own?

Sounded nice. If God cared about birds and flowers having their needs met, maybe He cared about hers too?

Then again, the flowers hadn't made stupid decisions to put themselves in need in the first place. Somehow she'd gone from being a straight-A student to the most naive person on the planet.

Though apparently in her father's eyes, she was still a superstar. She'd had coffee—well, tea—with him early this morning before he went to the office, and he'd expressed the same sentiment her mother had about looking forward to the circus and seeing her perform. About being proud of her.

If he only knew.

Rosalyn swallowed, shoved the thought aside as she nodded at a passing jogger. She'd had a productive morning on the silks at Lettie's, and now the rest of the day stretched before her. If Cade wasn't still acting strange, maybe they could finish more Magnolia Days prep. Get back their rhythm after that cryptic comment about his seeing her perform.

Rosalyn's phone buzzed from the deep pocket of her yoga pants as the first raindrop hit her scalp. Her chest tightened as she looked at the screen.

He wasn't going to stop calling.

She slowed to a stop, standing off the sidewalk by Magnolia Blossom. If she kept putting it off, he'd know something was up. She tapped the Accept button and cleared her throat. "Hello?"

"Hey." Blaine's warm voice filled her ear. "Finally. You've been impossible to reach, dollface."

She hated that nickname. "Hey, yeah. I've been settling in."

"How long could it possibly take to settle in such a one-hick town?" Blaine laughed, the sound casting images in her mind of dark sunglasses and neon lights, bourbon and expensive cologne. "What's the name of that place again? I can't remember what you said."

She hadn't said. When she signed with Blaine years ago, she was coming off a group act based in Nashville. He'd never needed to know where she grew up.

And while he could find out if he tried, no reason to make it easy. Or risk *others* finding out as well. After his lie, she couldn't trust him not to give the wrong people the wrong info.

Rosalyn glanced at the clouds piling overhead. "I was about to get in the shower." The lie burned her tongue. But how many lies had Blaine told her? "Can I check in with you later?"

Ugh. She hated the verbiage she defaulted to with him. Technically, she was on leave. This particular leave happened to have a gig attached to it, which Blaine couldn't know. If he realized her knee was ready to perform again, he'd have her on a plane back to a theater in no time.

And while her knee was ready, *she* was definitely not.

"I don't like not being able to reach you." His voice hardened a notch.

There went the mood swings again, the ones she'd tried to avoid ever since they landed back on US soil. "You're reaching me now, silly." She infused lightheartedness into her tone, hoping he'd match it. He'd gotten weird lately, stressed. Was he on something?

"Sure, after how many days?" In the background, a pen clicked. She could see him sitting in his sky rise office, staring out the window toward the fog of downtown Los Angeles, jagged lines of blocky skyscrapers disturbing the horizon. "Is everything okay there?"

She looked up. "Right as rain." Thunder rumbled in the distance.

"It sounds like you're outside. I thought you said you were getting in the shower."

She turned away as a group of women in matching T-shirts pushed inside the diner. "I'm—"

"You know I don't like lies, Rosalyn." The pen clicked faster.

Well, that was ironic. But she couldn't confront him now—not when he was the current gatekeeper for her very life. She gripped the phone. "Calm down. I'm outside, but meant I was *about* to head in to get cleaned up."

Blaine's vinegar turned to sugar. "Sorry, doll. You know how I get when I worry."

Didn't she, though.

The sugar melted into molasses. "I miss you."

Ew. Her stomach roiled. "Blaine—"

"Now you calm down." He laughed, as breezy as the wind tugging at Rosalyn's hair. The sprinkles of rain grew bigger, dampening her shirt. But she didn't go inside. If Blaine heard diner chatter in the background, he'd be livid.

His pen resumed clicking. "I know it's just business with us. Doesn't mean I can't appreciate one of my super stars, right?"

"I guess." Rosalyn's tight shoulders refused to relax. He'd always been quick with the compliments. Not that she wanted them from him anymore. Not since he had proved his true colors, put her in danger.

"Of course, if you wanted to change that status . . ." He laughed. "We already have a foot in the door, right? Would be easy."

"Very funny." Rosalyn took a deep breath, trying to convince her body she was on a phone call, not being chased by a tiger.

He'd given her the perfect segue to ask for an update on their legal situation.

But that would still risk an explosion. She hesitated, debating.

His pen abruptly silenced. "Look, I've got another call coming in."

Decision made for her. She couldn't decide if she was relieved.

"Rest up, take care of yourself so I can get you back on stage where you belong."

Was that where she belonged?

"See you soon." Blaine hung up before she could decide.

Rosalyn eyed the diner, appetite all but gone. How had everything in her career gotten so off track so quickly? And when had she gotten so naive? She'd been a straight-A student her entire life, for crying out loud. Valedictorian. Harvard education. She'd been *so* smart.

So how had she been so fooled?

In school, when she felt stupid, she studied harder. Sacrificed more. Proved herself. Now she had no such remedy.

She was stuck, and it was her own fault.

Tears pressed her eyes, and she blinked rapidly, refusing to let them fall. She wanted to be alone, but with her parents at home, Lettie in the studio, and the diner brimming with customers, her options were limited.

Then a familiar, sleek black car pulled up to the curb.

Cade.

She dug her palms into her eyes, but it did little to dam the emotion threatening to pour faster than the rain.

"Hey." Cade slid out of his car, wearing a smile and no sign of yesterday's awkwardness. He glanced at the darkening clouds, then reached back inside the Audi and retrieved an umbrella. "Is standing in the rain some new kind of aerial practice I'm not aware of?" He grinned. Rosalyn tried to return his smile but couldn't force it up her cheeks. She probably looked a mess. She flipped up the hood of her sweatshirt, burrowing inside it. But the cold pressed deep. "Something like that."

"You going inside to eat?" He popped open his umbrella and gestured toward the diner.

She looked over her shoulder at the bustling café, then back at him, unable to voice her answer as her throat clogged with unshed tears. She lifted one shoulder.

Why had she answered? Blaine always made her feel worse.

Cade studied her, his arm braced on the frame of the door, eyes curious but not judging. It made her want to dive into his embrace. Somewhere safe.

But wasn't that what had gotten her into trouble? Assuming safety in the wrong places?

Rosalyn crossed her arms over her chest, hugging herself. Then the dam broke. The tears finally crested, spilling down her cheek and mixing with the rain.

"*Oh.*" Cade's expression flickered. He opened his mouth, closed it. Tilted his head as he seemed to consider his next words, his eyes reflecting his own storm. "Want to go for a drive?"

Rosalyn hesitated. There was no good reason to get in Cade's car. She needed to be enforcing professional boundaries between them, not encouraging close proximity.

But this was Cade.

And she was tired of doing the disciplined thing, the wise thing, to make up for her mistakes. She nodded once, pausing to swipe her eyes.

If climbing into the front of that Audi was wrong, then at the moment, Rosalyn didn't want to be right.

Cade had no idea where he was going, but he would've driven Rosalyn across the entire country if she'd asked.

So much for his resolve to stay professional.

Rain drizzled as he pulled onto Village Lane. He shot Rosalyn a glance, noting her huddled position in the passenger seat, and reached over to flip on her seat warmer. What in the world had happened before he pulled up to the diner? "Have you eaten today?"

She shivered, staring straight ahead toward the windshield wipers sluicing water off the window. "A bite of oatmeal and banana this morning before my workout. I'd planned to get brunch."

"Here." Cade reached into his console and handed her a bag

of white powdered donuts—the gas station variety. "This is all I have . . . unless I can interest you in a Tic Tac."

She snorted back another laugh mixed with tears. "I can't eat these, but thanks for sharing your precious stash."

"There's plenty more where that came from." He grinned, relief at her smile coursing through him. He hated seeing her cry. Seeing anyone cry, for that matter.

But he felt fairly confident that tears on Rosalyn's cheeks tugged at him in a different way than they would've on Zoey's or Elisa's.

She put the bag back in the console as he pulled up to a stop sign. Left or right could take them around the block and back to Magnolia Blossom. Straight would continue their drive. Selfishly, he wanted to keep Rosalyn close. But if she was feeling a little better, she might prefer to get brunch—alone.

He flipped on his blinker. "I can take you back to the diner for some real food, if you want."

Her smile faded. "No, this is good." She gestured vaguely before huddling back into her sweatshirt.

He clicked off the blinker. "Onward." He eased straight ahead as the rain fell a little harder.

"I'm sorry." Her words were so soft Cade almost didn't catch them.

"For rejecting my goodwill donuts?" He winked. Maybe if he didn't let her know how much she affected him, he could keep up the professional charade. Of course, it'd be a lot easier if she didn't look like she needed the world's biggest hug right now.

Rosalyn reached up and tugged her hair tie free of her hair, letting it tumble over her shoulders like a golden waterfall. "For being emotional."

He slowed as the car splashed through a puddle, holding back his response and hoping she'd elaborate further.

"Usually I'm so focused." She sighed. "Disciplined."

"Rigid?" Oops. Hadn't meant to say that.

But she didn't seem offended as she pulled the hair tie onto her wrist. If anything, it brought back that little ghost of a smile. "Probably." Then it faded. "It's so different with him. He . . ."

Seconds ticked by. She wasn't finishing that sentence.

Cade flexed his hands on the steering wheel. "Look, whoever it is you're talking about—you know I'd beat him up for you, right?" He stared straight ahead as they cruised the next block, unsure if she'd take the remark as kidding or serious. He'd play it off whichever way she chose to take it.

But if she looked into his eyes, she'd know the truth.

"Or you'd send Simon LeMoine to beat them up, anyway." She cast him a sidelong look, her small grin visible in his peripheral vision. "Though I seem to remember you held your own at the Lazy Spoon that one night."

"Ah." Funny how she brought that up when he'd told the guys the story yesterday. He looked both ways through the rain-streaked windows as they stopped at the next intersection. "So you do accurately remember that I am, in fact, a superhero."

Her voice softened. "You were that night."

His eyes darted to meet hers, heat flaring in his chest.

She cleared her throat. "I mean, I totally could have taken him. But it was nice to have backup."

"Backup, huh?" Cade rubbed his jaw, then pointedly opened his mouth. *Click.* "Let's just say I knew it was going to rain before you did."

"Yikes. Sorry about that." She reached over and grazed her fingers across his affected cheek.

A shudder rippled down his spine. Thank the Lord they were at a stop sign. He tightened his grip on the wheel. One move of his head, and he could turn his face into her palm.

"It was worth it." His heartbeat skyrocketed, louder in his head than the low hum of the engine and the faint hint of eighties rock from his playlist. Her hand stilled, fingers gently alight on his stubble that never seemed to realize it wasn't yet five o'clock. *Don't move, don't move.*

But he'd never been very good at denying himself a treat.

He turned his face into her hand, her fingers cupping his cheek. Their gazes locked. She didn't move away, and he couldn't have if the car had burst into flames. Though judging by the heat welling in his chest, it might have already.

So much for his goal to end their flirting.

But this wasn't flirting, was it? Her eyes held something unspoken yet tangible, a longing mixed with a promise that set his world on fire.

"Rosalyn . . ." He swallowed. She wasn't looking away. The slightest movement of her fingers on his jaw sent a stampede of bulls thundering through his stomach that would've made Spain proud. "You know I'd do it again, if you needed me to." Because being needed by Rosalyn Dupree gave him all the superpowers he required.

"I know." Her chin dipped in a nod. "You were always there for me when it mattered. Even when we were each other's competition."

Except now whose competition was he?

Her words drummed a painful beat in his head. *It's so different with him.* How long ago was this "him" that she was still worked up about? Enough to cry over after a phone call?

Regardless, he couldn't stand it anymore. As if by its own accord, Cade's hand found her cheek, cupped her face in a matching gesture until his fingers slid into her hair. The long strands felt like silk, exactly as he'd imagined. "I almost asked you out that night at the Lazy Spoon. I missed my chance."

"I thought you were going to." She traced the line of his jaw with one finger and the hair on the back of his neck tingled. "But then my friends interrupted us."

"Yeah. And then you left." He waited a beat. "Ran off and joined the circus."

She pursed her lips, which had eased dangerously closer to his. "I guess I did."

"And now you're leaving again."

She rolled in her lip, then nodded. "I guess I am." Then she snorted a little. "Ironically, after *your* circus."

Definitely ironic. Cade slowly let his hand drop onto the console between them. Rosalyn eased away at the same moment, so smoothly he wasn't certain which of them retreated first.

Reality had come for them both.

He swallowed, unwilling to let the moment fully go but equally unsure what to say. "I . . . that . . ."

"Yeah." Her eyes assured him she felt the same.

But the truth remained an obstacle between them. She was leaving—and her heart didn't appear free to give away.

His stomach fisted into a knot. "We've missed our chance again, haven't we?"

Honk-honk.

Oops, they were still at the stop sign. Cade quickly eased off the brake and continued through the intersection as Rosalyn settled back in her seat.

"You're a good friend, Cade." She adjusted her seat belt. "I really appreciate you."

Oof. Friend. Right.

And that was that.

ROSALYN STABBED HER VEGGIE OMELET with her fork, regretting the fact that she'd let her guard down with Cade. Regretting that the ride back to the diner had been awkward, regretting that he'd paid for her breakfast while she'd escaped into the bathroom and then slipped away before she'd emerged. Always the gentleman. Always the hero.

Even when she didn't deserve it.

She speared a mushroom, the clatter of silverware and the soft buzz of customer conversations fading into the background.

It didn't matter what Cade thought, because as she needed to remind herself *one* more time—she wasn't a free woman. She would be leaving Magnolia Bay after the circus.

Like Cade said, they'd missed their chance.

"You still doing okay over here?" Elisa appeared at Rosalyn's table, holding a steaming mug of tea.

"I'm fine, thank you." She took the offered mug and cupped it between her hands. "This smells amazing."

"It's a new herbal blend my tea-drinking customers love. Mind if I join you?" Elisa slid into the adjacent bench, her gaze landing on the unfinished omelet between them.

"It was good, I promise." Rosalyn pressed one hand against her stomach. "I don't eat well when I'm stressed."

Elisa nodded, eyes flickering with understanding. Had she seen Cade come in with Rosalyn, yet not stay? Elisa seemed like the kind of person who was too kind to pry. What it would be like to have a close friend who *would* ask nosy questions? Cade had, in the car. Maybe she should've told him more. She'd meant it when she'd told Cade he was a good friend—these days, her only one.

But she loved the way Cade looked at her right now, like she was a polished star—all clean and shiny. Someone worthy of protecting. If he knew the truth about the past year, that look would change. Shift into something distant and disappointed.

"I think the sudden storm threw all of us off." Elisa leaned back against the booth, crossing her arms over her apron as she surveyed Rosalyn. "Of course, there are different types of storms."

There it was—her window into deeper friendship.

Rosalyn wrapped her fingers around the mug handle. Could she trust Elisa to keep her secrets? If she and Cade were friends, Elisa's loyalty could be to him first.

Rosalyn couldn't take that risk. Magnolia Bay was too small a town, and if Cade knew everything, her parents wouldn't be far behind. "Trying to get my routine figured out for the circus, that'll all. It's a lot to plan."

"I'm sure it'll be great." Elisa smiled.

Maybe. The omelet sat heavy in Rosalyn's stomach. Her secrets were turning her into someone she didn't recognize. Someone who lied—even if it was for good reason.

She debated a moment longer, watching as a red-headed waitress whose nametag read Trish flirted with a group of guys wearing cowboy hats and eating chicken-n-waffles. Mama D ambled out of the back hallway on her cane, pausing by a booth with a middle-aged man reading his Bible, and rattled off something that made him laugh. Conversations and camaraderie hovered every-where she looked.

Maybe she could have a tiny piece of it. Just while she was here.

"There's more to it." Rosalyn braced her arms against the table-top. "I fell and injured my knee several weeks ago."

"Good gravy." Elisa's eyes widened. "That had to have been scary."

"It wasn't fun. I had bad dreams about it for a few nights. It should've been much worse than it was."

Sympathy filled Elisa's gaze. "But you're okay now?"

"Sort of. I have to be careful what skills I do." Rosalyn took a quick sip of her tea, the hot brew comforting.

"Should you be resting instead of doing the circus?" Elisa held up both hands. "Not that I'm trying to talk you out of it."

And now they were back to the part of the secret Rosalyn couldn't share. No one could know that her injury, while terrify-ing, had allowed her to come home and regroup. But obligations waited for her, people demanding their money. Blaine said he'd covered for her to have leave time, but she couldn't take much longer. It was a miracle she'd convinced him to let her go to her "one-hick town," as she'd downplayed, and rest for free with her family rather than hole up somewhere he could keep an eye on her.

Like, with him.

Elisa watched her, clearly waiting for an answer.

"I really want to do it." Rosalyn drew a deep breath as she set her mug on the table. And she really needed the money. "It's a good cause. And my routine will be more laid back than usual." She'd cut her typical rate in half, knowing it'd be the only way the town could afford her. And with her current limitations, it felt fair.

Elisa's eyes warmed. "I know that helps Cade out a lot." She laughed. "And if what I saw the other day at the studio is laid back, I'd love to see you perform for real."

It wasn't all it appeared.

Before she could answer, the door behind her jingled open, letting in a gust of misty wind. Footsteps sounded beside their booth and she looked up as Cade looked down.

He'd come back.

For her?

She tried not to notice the way water droplets clung to his darkening facial hair. Tried not to remember that same stubble under her fingers an hour before.

She failed at both.

"I've made a decision." Cade shoved into the seat across from her, forcing Elisa to scoot over with a mild protest. He locked eyes with Rosalyn. "We're going on another drive."

"We are, are we?"

"Yes." Then he did a double take at her plate. "You should finish that first."

She raised an eyebrow. "You're sure bossy."

"You need food." He gestured to her plate. "You barely eat enough as it is."

Rosalyn snorted. "While you eat enough for everyone."

Elisa looked between them. "I've missed a step. What do you mean *another* drive?"

Cade ignored her. "We need a do-over."

"You think so?" Rosalyn cupped her hands under her chin, fighting to hide her smile. Their banter was back. "Do tell."

"In front of Elisa?" Cade asked.

"Yes, in front of Elisa!" Elisa slapped the tabletop with both hands.

"Fine." Cade leaned forward, his cologne wafting over her like a favorite memory. "I got to my office and realized—we're friends, right? I mean, that's what you clearly stated in the car."

Elisa's gaze jerked to Rosalyn. "You did?"

"And there's no reason two friends can't have a moment and

not still be, you know—friends." Cade tapped his knuckles on the table. "Right?"

Rosalyn nodded again. "Right."

Elisa's eyebrows threatened to vanish into her hairline. "You had a *what* now?"

"There was this thing." Cade waved his hand toward Rosalyn. "But she set me straight, don't worry."

"You friend-zoned Cade after a *moment*?" Elisa's voice squeaked and she dipped her head to lower her voice. "Why?"

Heat flushed Rosalyn's neck and for a second, she felt as crazy as the look Elisa was giving her. Why had she, again? "I—I'm not . . ."

Cade's smile remained steady, but his eyes softened a little, as if this part of the conversation was more for them than for Elisa. "Bad timing, as I recall."

Rosalyn squared her shoulders. "Right."

Cade continued. "And while Rosalyn here is clearly adorable, I agree it's the best choice."

His words pinched a little, even as her tight shoulders loosened. "So why do we need a do-over, exactly?"

"Because I need to run some errands on the mainland for Magnolia Days, and I thought it'd be more interesting to go with a *friend* than go alone." Cade scooted the plate closer toward him, then winced as the vegetables registered on his radar. He slid it away.

Too easy not to bait him. "You have friends. Why not ask Noah? Or that funny Owen guy."

"Owen would try to convince me he can tightrope walk at the circus. Or Hula-Hoop with fire, and he can't do either of those things any more than he can walk on stilts."

"Fair." Rosalyn struggled to keep a straight face.

"Besides, I can't leave off the way we did between us in the car. Way too awkward." Cade pursed his lips in exaggeration. "I don't need that kind of bad energy."

Her own straight face was starting to fail. "Might wrinkle your clothes."

She would much rather have Cade as a friend than not at all—and he was giving her that gift. Despite her best effort to resist, she found herself leaning forward again. "Sounds like a date."

He squinted at her.

"A friend date, obviously."

"Good thing. You couldn't handle a real date with me." He wiggled his eyebrows and for a second, she wanted to call his bluff.

"This isn't over." Elisa waggled her finger between them. "One of you two are telling me this whole story later."

Cade smirked as he slid out of the booth. "Don't bet on it. I'm a gentleman, Elisa. I don't *almost* kiss and tell."

Elisa looked up at him with a pout. "That's something Noah would say."

"That's something Noah *did* say once—about you." Cade gestured for Rosalyn to slide out of the booth and join him. "Ready?"

Elisa gripped Cade's wrist. "I'll make you cookies."

He tilted his head. "Chocolate chip?"

"Double chocolate chip."

He shot Rosalyn a wink as she stood. "I'll go ahead and apologize to you now for ruining your reputation."

"Ha. Cute." He wouldn't have to try hard. She'd done that for herself already.

Cade pointed out the front window. "Now what do you say we get in my car without crying buckets this time?"

"There was crying?" Elisa gaped up at them from the bench seat. "You guys are killing me."

Rosalyn called over her shoulder. "I'll tell you my point of view if you find a way to make a high-protein, low-calorie bread pudding."

Elisa abruptly stood and knotted her apron. "Deal."

Rosalyn looked up at Cade to find him already smiling down at her—that same smirk he'd shot her when he knew he was about to win the mathletes competition junior year.

Uh-oh.

AFTERNOON SUN DOTTED THE SIDEWALK in front of Rosalyn, streaming through the tree branches bordering the crowded streets of the French Quarter. Clearly, the rain hadn't reached New Orleans—she should've grabbed her sunglasses like the ones Cade had tucked into the neck of his shirt. At least her clothes had finally dried.

Cade crumpled wax paper in his hand as they ambled through the French Quarter. "I can't believe you turned down homemade fudge."

"I can't believe you ate three pieces of homemade fudge." Should she tell Cade about the chocolate still dotting the corner of his mouth?

Cade shoved the paper back into the pastry bag. "I could have gone for four, but didn't want to seem greedy." On the corner up ahead in Jackson Square, a man fully painted as a bronze statue posed, unmoving, as tourists tossed bills into the coffee can near his feet. The faint sounds of a saxophone drifted on the wind.

Rosalyn drew a deep breath, convinced the scent of chocolate lingered in her nose. "You said this was supposed to be sampling of the chocolate fountain for Magnolia Days, not second lunch." The specialty chocolate shop smelled divine, like the Garden of

Eden had saved a little something back. But breaking her strict performance diet after several weeks of limited training would've been the worst timing. Resisting had been delightful torture.

Sort of like the entire hour-long car ride to New Orleans with Cade, where he'd played early 2000 hits and they swapped more stories from high school.

"You don't know what our next stop is." Cade offered an exaggerated grimace as he tossed the bag into a nearby trash receptacle. "Just remember I tried to give you chocolate first and you refused."

She held back a grin as they neared the towering St. Louis Cathedral. Children shrieked as they chased each other around the splashing fountain in Jackson Square. The strains of jazz music grew louder, and the scent of cinnamon pecans wafted from a street vendor. "I'm not afraid."

And she wasn't—of Cade's next errand or anything else at the moment. Funny that she felt safer here, despite the city boasting a significantly higher amount of crime than Magnolia Bay. For the first time in weeks, she could walk freely without wondering if she was being watched from parked cars or corners of buildings. A carefree needle in a haystack.

Cade tossed a coin into the fountain as they passed it. "Maybe you should be a little nervous. I know I am."

"Me, nervous?" Well, maybe her high-alert status never fully went away. But it was definitely lowered—not that that was what Cade meant. "You obviously forgot what I do for a living. Silks, ten feet in the air?" Rosalyn teasingly knocked her hip into Cade's to punctuate her point. He stumbled a step.

"Careful. You almost made me take out that tarot card stand." He leaned closer to her ear in an exaggerated whisper. "And then how will we know the future?"

She chuckled, glancing over her shoulder at the red umbrella offering shade for a folding table littered with cards. "I already knew my immediate future post-circus." She sobered slightly. Barring a miracle, anyway.

And since she hadn't even prayed for one, it seemed that much more unlikely to happen.

"Hang on." Cade led her off the busy pavement, around a family in matching We Heart NOLA T-shirts, toward the cathedral entry. The giant church rose above them, three imposing spires stretching toward the cloud-dotted, cerulean sky. A sign stating Closed for Nuptials stood beside the sturdy wooden door. "That didn't sound good. What's up, Ace?"

She shouldn't have said anything. Secrets were getting harder to keep from Cade.

She waved a dismissive hand in the air. "I just have some commitments I've got to fulfill after the circus."

"Commitments I take it you'd rather *not* fulfill?" Cade crossed his arms over his chest, studying her.

"Something like that." More like she'd prefer to get a root canal than keep working on this debt that had turned her from a free-flying aerialist to a bird in a cage.

"At least you get to see cool places, right?"

"Right." Desert sand and white hospital sheets filled her mind. She blinked them away. Cade didn't understand, and she couldn't make him.

"I always loved traveling, but these past several years, I don't know . . ." Cade shrugged a little. "I guess I'm turning into Dorothy."

Rosalyn frowned. "Dorothy?"

"You know . . . there's no place like home." He clicked the heels of his loafers together and flashed a wide grin.

"Ha." Rosalyn tilted her head back, squinting against the afternoon sun as she looked up at Cade. His stubble had grown since lunch. How could one man look equally handsome with a shadowed beard and clean-shaven? "I guess that makes me the Wicked Witch then—living in a foreign land?"

"That depends, Ace." He removed the sunglasses from his shirt and carefully slid them onto her face. "Own any flying monkeys?"

Rosalyn smirked. "You're the one trying to hire dancing poodles, right? That's pretty close."

"Guess that makes you a munchkin, then." He draped an arm around her shoulders and abruptly turned her toward the cathedral doors. "Better go spend some time talking to the big guy behind the curtain."

"Cade!" She snorted as she protested entering the church, pushing back against his grip and laughing. An elderly couple holding hands looked over at them and smiled. She lowered her voice, spinning around in his arms. "They're having a *wedding* in there."

He hadn't let go of her, and she'd placed herself right up against him, her folded arms sandwiched against his chest. Heat surged between them, a wave that had nothing to do with the June sun trekking toward the horizon. Her stomach flipped.

"See?" Cade's grin sobered a little as his palms slid free of her arms. She immediately missed the contact as he shoved his hands in his pockets and eased a step back. "It's not so bad—being friends with me."

She licked her suddenly dry lips, grateful her eyes were hidden behind his dark shades still perched on her face. "That's the problem."

"Eh, problems." Emotion flitted through his gaze, too fast for her to identify. He cocked his head to the side. "I'm way more interested in solutions."

Rosalyn raised her eyebrows as her heart pounded an unsteady rhythm. "You flirting with me, Landry?" She mimicked the question he'd asked her, back in Lettie's studio her first night in town.

"Me?" He tugged the glasses off her face and slid them back

onto his own before he answered. "I wouldn't even know what that looked like."

Everything was hotter in New Orleans. The pavement under Cade's loafers. The humidity in the air, which lacked the gulf breezes of Magnolia Bay.

The chemistry between him and Rosalyn.

He shook the remaining ice in his water glass as they sat at Backwater Bruno's outdoor patio, people-watching and attempting small talk that did little to defuse their close encounter at the cathedral. Or the attraction in their banter as they strolled around town, ducking in tourist shops for Magnolia Days door prizes, stopping by the rental company to confirm their massive order for tables and chairs, calling to check on the dancing poodle status.

Rather, Rosalyn had made the call. Cade had been too busy trying not to keep his eyes from shooting red hearts every time she laughingly tried on a purple sequined hat . . . or when she dropped change into a homeless man's coffee can . . . or when she lit up watching a street artist paint a couples' portrait.

At this point, Cade was terrified to take off his sunglasses and let Rosalyn see his eyes—hence his offer to sit outside even though the temps had climbed and sweat dripped down his back.

Would it be more effective to dump the melting cubes directly over his head?

He leaned down in the iron chair and pretended to straighten the cuff of his pants, taking the opportunity to drop the just-friends smile he'd attempted to hold the past half hour and relieve his tired jaw. His quest to kill two birds with one stone today—knocking out Magnolia Days errands and putting his friendship with Rosalyn back on solid ground—had utterly failed. He definitely hadn't accepted friendship as their fate. If anything, he'd discovered the portal to falling for Rosalyn and all but jumped through.

Fortunately, as a politician's son, he had a lifetime of experience at masking the obvious.

He sat up.

"Why are we here again? I have a feeling it's not for the tea." Rosalyn stirred a straw in her glass of unsweetened iced tea.

"Wait and see." Cade checked his watch. Was it merely hours ago he'd caught her crying in the rain outside Magnolia Blossom and nearly kissed her in his car? Nearly kissed her at the cathedral too, when she'd spun into him that way.

Cade flexed his fingers. His arms still felt the curve of her waist, the press of her hands against his chest. He'd tamped down the urge to flex under her touch. To be strong for her.

To be what she needed.

He must *not* be what she needed, even when it came to friendship, because Rosalyn clearly wasn't telling him everything. It seemed she owned more secrets than athletic wear right now.

Were they about the guy on the phone who made her cry?

"You're making me nervous, Landry. Spill it already." She'd ditched her cropped hoodie earlier, leaving a sleeveless leotard that showed off her toned arms and jogger-style yoga pants. Her hair had been coaxed into a ponytail so high it made him think of Saved by the Bell reruns and geometric neon patterns.

He rested his arms on the table. "You like Cajun food, right?"

"Crawfish, of course. Shrimp." She tilted her head. "Are you about to feed me gumbo?"

He grinned. "Something like that." At least he wouldn't have to do this part alone. Adventuring with Rosalyn made everything better.

As if on cue, a waiter bustled up to their table, allowing a rush of AC to drift after him through the slow-closing swinging door.

"Here we are. Frog legs for two!" A steaming dish appeared on the table between them.

Rosalyn went slightly pale, then flushed pink as she leaned forward and inspected the fried delicacy. A cup of orangey-red sauce sat to the side. "Frog *what*?"

"Legs, ma'am." The server, wearing a backward cap and jeans under his waist apron, nodded. "Bruno's specialty. Y'all need anything else?"

"A different lunch?" Rosalyn whispered.

Cade bit back his laugh. "We'll be fine." Maybe. He unrolled his paper napkin, motioned to the one near Rosalyn's hand as the waiter rushed off. "Try one?"

Her flush deepened. "Am I being punished?"

Cade leaned forward. "Bruno wants to bring his frogs to Magnolia Days. I told him I didn't think that would fly with our customers, but he insisted I try some first. On the house. So . . ." He spread his hands over the plate. "Here we are."

Rosalyn eyed him, then the splayed frogs, warily. "You go first."

"Fine." He drew a breath and cut off a bite, trying not to think too hard about it. Popped it in his mouth, grateful for the crispy batter hiding the rest of the texture. He chewed. Squinted. "Tastes like chicken, honestly."

She snorted. "It does *not*."

"You tell me." He nudged her fork closer to her.

Rosalyn eased back, clutching her tea glass. "I'm vegetarian."

"You just admitted you liked shrimp and crawfish."

She took a sip. "Pescatarian, then."

"Lucky for you, these guys swim. Close enough." Cade nudged the plate closer and she all but squealed.

"That doesn't count." Rosalyn curled her lip.

How was she cute even while disgusted? Cade distracted himself with the Cajun sauce on the side. Mmm, tangy. "Here, try it with this."

She narrowed her eyes. "If I have to mask the flavor with a stronger flavor, what's the point of eating it?"

Okay, that was actually valid. Cade leaned back, wiping his fingers on his napkin. "What is your favorite food, then?"

"It doesn't swim, I can tell you that." She still looked wary, as if at any moment one of the frogs might don a top hat and start singing. "I like margherita pizza. And cheesecake, on the rare occasions I break my macros to have any."

Cade took another bite, but this time, the sauce did little to compensate. "Okay, this can't happen." He dropped the remaining leg on the plate. "I don't think anyone will want to buy these at the festival."

"You tried." Rosalyn inched the plate a little farther away from her. "And I provided excellent moral support."

"You're a big chicken, is what you are." Cade tossed a straw wrapper at her.

"So pizza, huh? What about your favorite color?"

"Um, pastel pink. Or lavender. You?"

Your eyes. He cleared his throat. "Green."

"Don't think playing twenty questions is going to make me try any of those frogs."

"I wouldn't dream of it."

She quirked her lips at him, looking way too much like she had their junior year, when she'd hold her report card in his face, tapping the GPA in the bottom corner, and taunt him about their race to valedictorian. "My turn. Favorite genre of music?"

He folded his hands behind his head, elbows braced wide. "Hip-hop."

Rosalyn grimaced.

"Don't judge—you should try it when you're working out." He grinned. "Think of it like an audible energy drink."

She scrunched her face. "I'll keep that in mind."

"What's yours?"

"I listen to a lot of classical."

"Of course you do." Cade snorted.

She sat up straighter. "Now who's judging?"

"Well, I suppose no one's perfect," he joked. But good grief if she didn't come incredibly close. "Okay, here's one. What about your earliest memory?"

"Earliest?" Her brow furrowed as she took another sip of tea. Two motorcyclists roared down Decatur Street, their exhaust lingering over the patio. "I'm not sure. What about you?"

"When I think back to childhood, I see all these fragile things I was never allowed to touch. Tea sets and porcelain dolls." He wrinkled his nose. "And a bunch of suits and fancy dresses crowding the living room after I was supposed to be in bed."

"Let me guess." Rosalyn grinned. "You weren't in bed."

"I usually waited up, hoping our housekeeper would sneak me some of the leftover cookies." Cade laughed.

"Let me guess again. She did."

"So I was *maybe* a little spoiled. Though not in the way Amber always made me seem."

"Oh, Amber." Rosalyn shook her head and sighed. "Don't let her get to you."

He didn't anymore—usually. "You sure always listened to her."

"Amber was . . . infectious." Rosalyn sighed. "She's so passionate about what she believes, she makes you start to think you believe it too."

Yeah. Like about what kind of guy he was. But high school was so long ago—it didn't matter now, right? He was here.

With Rosalyn.

He cleared his throat. "Your turn."

"Let's see." Rosalyn rolled in her lower lip. "Maybe this isn't my *first* memory, but I do remember completely ignoring the swing in the backyard tree my dad had been excited about. I tried to climb the rope it hung from, instead, and touch the top branch." She shook her head. "Mom freaked out, told me that was dangerous."

"And here you are now, climbing things for a living." Cade liked this game. "What about your happiest memory?"

"My first aerial lesson when I was eleven." She didn't hesitate. "I sat in the hammock—that's the apparatus everyone starts on—and spun circle after circle." The sun was still out, but Rosalyn's grin could have lit the night. "I inverted on my second lesson and was hooked."

Cade rocked his chair back on two legs. "I don't know what that means, but it sounds impressive."

"Hammock is a continuous loop of fabric, rather than two individual silks. Each of the silks are called poles." She held up a finger. "Not to be confused with pole dancing. That's a different sport."

He chuckled. "And inverting is just going upside down?"

She nodded. "You could take a lesson sometime. Learn firsthand."

"I'd love to, except I hear there's no aerial studio in Magnolia Bay." He *tsked*. "Maybe one day, a beautiful, famous aerialist will happen upon the Bay and teach me."

"Ha." She stirred her tea faster. "Flattery will get you nowhere, Landry."

And he was trying to get somewhere, wasn't he? Bad idea.

"So what's your happiest memory?"

He should've expected the return question. And no, he couldn't answer with "seeing you walk into my office the other day."

A server showed up to bus their table and Cade nodded his thanks, taking the opportunity to consider.

Then as the guy ambled away with a tub of plates, Cade knew. "I think I was maybe thirteen? I went fishing with my dad. He let me take a sip of beer if I promised not to tell Mom." Cade chuckled. "It was disgusting and I immediately spat it in the bay. Dad laughed so loud."

Rosalyn smiled softly. "That sounds fun."

The memory washed over him, bringing the scent of salt water and sunscreen. "I didn't have to try to be 'on' that afternoon, and I didn't feel like he wanted me to. It was just us. No reputation to protect, no family name or legacy to safeguard." Cade's tone dropped. "We fished and hung out, no work allowed." It'd been a rare afternoon—one that never got repeated, unfortunately.

"That's nice." Rosalyn's voice trailed off, and she stared at something over his shoulder he knew wasn't there. She was looking into time, and he desperately wanted to go with her.

"What is it?"

Rosalyn blinked, her gaze registering back on him. Cade held her gaze, waiting. Hoping she'd realized he could be trusted.

Just when he'd about given up, she spoke. "Like you, I was loved *and* spoiled . . . but I was also taught to 'hide my crazy.' Going into aerial was a big deal for my mom—she hoped it was a stage that would pass, but she got proven wrong immediately."

"Well, sure." Cade settled back in his chair. "After all those rope climbs and inversions."

"Exactly." Rosalyn smiled, then it faded. "Listening to you talk about your dad made me remember this one day . . . I'd been doing aerial about six months. I came downstairs to show Mom my sparkly leo for my upcoming recital. She was outside with her garden club friends. I didn't realize and burst out onto the patio. The women asked about my costume, and as I excitedly started to explain about the hip key skill I'd mastered, I saw the look on my mom's face." Rosalyn's expression sank, and for a moment, Cade glimpsed the young girl she'd been.

"One of the ladies—I only remember she had bright red hair—said, 'Rose, I thought you said she was taking ballet.'"

Cade grimaced. "Uh-oh."

"Mom had to spin a quick tale about how aerial has elements of ballet in it and this lady must be confused. When the women cast each other these amused glances and made these behind-the-hand whispers, I realized Mom hadn't told them. I think she was embarrassed about my choice to quit ballet and start aerial instead." Rosalyn bit her lower lip. "Maybe embarrassed about me too."

Cade reached out, took her hand. Her fingers closed into his. "I'm sure that wasn't it."

"Trust me, that's only one entry from my teenage journal." Rosalyn laughed. "I decided I had to get good, fast, to make her proud. And I did." She pursed her lips. "But I'm not sure she ever was."

Her fingers were soft and chilled against his warmer ones. He squeezed a little tighter. "But she supported you, right? You said she drove you into New Orleans for lessons for years until you got your license."

"Well, yeah. But she had to." Rosalyn shrugged. "I'm sure it was mostly obligation at that point."

Cade hated the lost look in her eyes. "What made you start ballet in the first place? Was that something your mom wanted you to do?"

"Yeah, I was introverted as a kid. Content to stay in my room and read to my stuffed animals." She shook her head with a laugh. "Mom was a social butterfly, with all her garden clubs and fundraising committees. I think she thought I needed to be like that . . . needed 'real friends.'"

"So she dragged you to ballet?"

"Kickin' and screamin'—internally, at least. But I wanted to please her, so I didn't actually put up a fight." A small smile claimed her lips. "Then I met Lettie and I really tried to like ballet, because I liked *her* so much."

"But it still didn't stick." Cade nodded.

"I told you I wasn't good at it. We had a recital, and my mom was so excited—gosh, she spent so much money on my hair and makeup, new slippers, the works." Rosalyn winced. "And I totally bombed."

"I find that hard to believe."

"There's video evidence somewhere, if my mom bothered to save it." Rosalyn snorted. "Trust me, it wasn't pretty. I had horrible balance. I pirouetted right into another girl. I was the worst in the class."

"So you quit because you weren't the best?" He tilted his head.

"I didn't think of it like that." She rolled in her lip. "But yeah, I guess so. I was used to being good at school, and then one day that didn't seem like enough anymore."

Interesting. "You must have been immediately good at aerial, then?"

"It was a better fit." She lifted one shoulder. "Maybe I was more motivated to fly."

"Certainly seems that way." Cade leaned back in his chair. "So we covered favorite music, career choices—what about faith? I don't think you went to Magnolia Grace much growing up, huh?"

"On holidays, mostly." Rosalyn nodded. "Sundays were about resting from whatever society events we had over the weekend. Most of my Sundays were spent practicing aerial or reading outside."

"We didn't go every week growing up either, though more often than not. I think my parents were going through the motions back then." Cade shrugged. "You know, making appearances as a politician. But I sense in recent years their faith has become more genuine."

Rosalyn hesitated. "I'm still trying to figure all that out. Lately I want to pray more but feel like I need to get my life in better order first."

His chest warmed at her honesty. "I get it, trust me. But I don't think that's how that works, Ace."

She raised her eyebrows.

He should be honest too. It was only fair. "I struggled for years to not equate God with my father—you know, needing to be capable, impress him. To represent my namesake well." Cade swallowed. Should he tell her? Aw, might as well. "For example—I still haven't told my dad I failed the Louisiana bar. He thinks I never took it, just changed career paths on my own." He winced.

"You failed the bar?" Rosalyn's eyes widened. "I'd have thought you'd pass that in your sleep."

"My score was about as good as if I'd been asleep, that's for sure." He snorted. "I might try again one day, but . . ."

She nodded firmly. "You totally should."

Or not. He shifted in his seat. "My point is, I've come a long way, and I *still* struggle with the whole 'works' thing. Pastor Dubois preaches on the topic a lot, which helps."

"I should come to a service." Rosalyn's eyes softened. "That sounds nice."

It did. Really nice.

"So, what'd you think?" A Cajun accent suddenly sounded over their table, shattering the moment.

Cade forced his gaze away from Rosalyn to the pot-bellied man with sun-darkened skin, a hair net, and a full-body length apron standing over them with a smile. "Think?"

"Of the frog legs, of course." He clapped his hands together so big, Rosalyn jumped.

"Oh, I'm sorry 'bout that. Bruno Guidry." He shook Cade's hand, then Rosalyn's. "Pleasure, *sha*."

"Great place you got here." Cade nodded, hoping Bruno wouldn't see the unfinished frogs on their table. Then again, if he did, maybe he'd get the hint without Cade having to spell it out.

"Thank ya. Worked hard, for sure." The burly man nodded once. "So what was the verdict?"

"Um." Cade looked back at the plate still on the table, then at Rosalyn, who widened her eyes slightly in silent encouragement to tell him the truth. "They were . . . they were something, all right."

"I knew it! What'd I tell you?" Bruno clamped a beefy hand on Cade's shoulder and patted him twice. "Best in the state."

"Can't argue with that." Because he'd never had any others, but . . . details.

Rosalyn glared at him.

"So I'm in, then?" Hope shone from Bruno's eyes as he backed away a step, big fists clenched at his chest. "We can have a spot in Magnolia Days?"

How could Cade say no? If Bruno didn't sell many frog legs, that wouldn't be Cade's fault. Of course, if he came, that meant taking up a spot another vendor wouldn't be able to fill . . .

He glanced at Rosalyn, then back at Bruno's fist-clenched anticipation, and released a sigh. "You're in."

Bruno let out a whoop. "*Mais, yeah*. You'll not be regretting it."

Cade already regretted the look Rosalyn was still giving him. He watched as Bruno gathered their dirty dishes. "How did you hear about Magnolia Days, anyway, up here in New Orleans?" Maybe some of his advertising had actually paid off.

"Oh, that comedian that comes in. *Sha*, she's a funny one." He shook his head with a *tsk*. "Can't get her to try the frogs, but she'll nab a beignet now and then before a show."

"Comedian?" Cade tilted his head. "I'm not familiar. But hey, I'm glad word is spreading in different circuits about our festival."

"She's got a show going now, if I'm not mistaken." Bruno pointed down Decatur. "Right down the way, few blocks. Came in for a tea and dessert a bit ago, before you folks arrived. Go check her out."

"I'll have to do that." Cade stood, and Rosalyn did the same, adjusting her ponytail. "Nice to meet you in person."

"See you at the festival." With another hearty clap on Cade's back, Bruno took the dishes and whisked back inside.

"Why didn't tell you him no?" Rosalyn immediately asked.

"It's not that easy. Did you see how happy he was?"

Rosalyn pushed her chair under the table. "But you know he won't sell much. That's not doing him any favors."

"Probably not. But . . ." Cade shrugged, checking his back pocket to make sure he still had his wallet. "Maybe the good people of Magnolia Bay will surprise us."

"I hope so."

Thunder boomed. Cade jerked. He and Rosalyn both looked up as the gathered clouds parted and giant raindrops began to pelt their empty table. "Looks like that storm from the bay made it here after all. Want to make a run for it? Or wait it out inside?"

Rosalyn glanced over her shoulder at the restaurant, then back up at the sky. She shot him a grin. "Race you."

Cade watched as she took off through the patio gate, ponytail flopping. Man, he hated running. Yet, as he futilely attempted to stop the smile stretching across his cheeks, he realized something perhaps even more detrimental than unsold frog platters.

Bruno Guidry wasn't the only person Cade couldn't tell no.

Eleven

CADE SPRINTED DOWN DECATUR, LAUGH-ing as Rosalyn's lithe figure moved like a gazelle past the rows of stores, easily staying out of his reach. Shop owners hurried outside to move tables and chairs under their entryways and out of the rain. Cars splashed through rapidly forming puddles.

He finally caught up to her and they jogged past the French Market Inn. "You trying to show me up, Ace?" Cade paused to bend and brace his hands on his knees. Linc would never let him live it down if he knew Rosalyn had trounced him at something fitness related.

"Don't have to try, do I?" She was barely out of breath. Not fair.

"I thought your knee was an issue."

Her grin faded and she looked down at it, flexed her leg, as if surprised. "Huh. That didn't bother it at all." Then her grin returned and she tugged his arm, leading him across St. Louis Street. "Come on, slowpoke. I think the comedy club is down this way. I saw a sign back there."

"Oh, you mean back when you Olympic-sprinted past it?" But losing to Rosalyn didn't bother him now like it had in school. Not if meant she smiled like that.

Then a jagged bolt of lightning cracked the sky.

"Whoops. Over here." Cade ducked for cover under a nearby shop's awning, his chest still heaving from their run. Water dripped off the ends of his hair, tickling his cheeks. The rain roared harder.

Rosalyn tucked into the narrow alcove next to him, soaking wet. Her ponytail clung to her bare arms, and she untied her hoodie from around her waist. She started to push her arms into the sleeves, but the material was already sopping. She shivered.

Before he could consider the ramifications, Cade pulled Rosalyn closer and rubbed her arms. Water sluiced off his palms. "Want me to run over there and buy us a towel?" He gestured toward the store across the street, only half-joking.

"Might need to make it a beach towel at this point." She grinned, mascara forming dark smears under her eyes. He reached over and wiped one of the smudges away. His fingers lingered on her cheek, and he forced his hand back to his side. She'd drawn the line earlier that morning with her friend declaration, and as much as he wanted to cross it—or rather, broad-jump it—he wouldn't.

"Cade?"

"Mmm?" Uh-oh. Had she been reading his thoughts?

She looked into his eyes, making him wish he had an excuse to slide his shades back on. "When did you see me perform?"

Oh boy. He ran a hand through his damp hair, now sticky with wet gel. "You weren't supposed to ask that again."

"I kind of feel like this entire day has had a lot of 'not supposed to's."

"Fair." Besides—at this point, what could it hurt? He took a deep breath. "It was a several months back, in Dallas. I was going to surprise you after the show, but . . ."

She frowned. "But?"

Now for the hard part. "I went to find you backstage, and saw you kiss this guy. I'd brought you flowers, and sort of figured that would be awkward for everyone. So I . . . left." He shrugged, like it was no big deal. Like it hadn't weighed on his chest for weeks after.

Like he couldn't still picture those mangled rose petals lying in the bottom of the trashcan outside the theater.

Her eyes softened with compassion. "You brought me flowers."

"I did." He winced. "I also threw them away."

She nibbled her lower lip. "You were going to ask me out, weren't you?"

Full confession time. "I hadn't stopped thinking about you since that night at the Lazy Spoon."

Her brows shot up.

Too far. He backpedaled. "I mean, I dated other women over those years, of course. But you were always in my head as this what-if. What if I had asked you out that night the alley, before your friends took you away? Before you ran off to join the circus." He laughed. "It's stupid."

She frowned. "It's sweet."

"It's pointless . . . *friend*." There. It was out.

She straightened her shoulders, turning slightly to face the rain. "For the record, I regret that kiss."

"Why?"

She kept staring forward. "A lot of reasons." Then she abruptly turned to face him, her eyes teasing. "Mostly because it was a pretty bad kiss."

Her smile untied the knot in Cade's stomach. "It looked pretty bad, honestly." Back to banter—their friendship safety net. Security flirting. Also, he had to admit—hearing the guy wasn't a good kisser was a nice way to end their shared day together.

Rosalyn smirked at him, looking way too cute for her own good with her rain-slicked hair. "Like you could do any better."

He lifted his chin, pretended to brush something off the shoulder of his shirt. "I haven't had any complaints so far."

The wind picked up, blowing rain into their private alcove. She inched toward him, close enough again to send citrus waves of torture his way. "You know something?" she asked. "Maybe I don't even remember that kiss."

He should step back, give her more room to get away from the rain. But her eyes held him hostage. "You just said—"

She looked up, pretending to think. "No, I've definitely forgotten about it."

She'd moved closer. That, or the magnetic pull between them had finally activated and taken matters into its own hands. And speaking of hands, his were back on her shivering arms, fully by instinct, wanting to keep her warm.

Even though their cozy little spot by the door suddenly felt like a furnace.

He rubbed her shoulders, her skin cool under his palms. "You forgot, huh?"

"You'll have to remind me what the kiss looked like." Something flirty and uncertain flickered in her eyes. She tilted her chin up in invitation.

Despite the gray rain drenching everything in sight, the city streets flared in vivid Technicolor as Cade's senses spiked. This wasn't real. It was a dream. The splashing of puddles and the low rumble of thunder echoed as if through a faraway tunnel. His heartbeat thudded in his ears.

Then Rosalyn's whisper broke through the hollow noise. "Was it like this?" And she reached up on tiptoe and pressed her lips to his.

Dream and reality merged into one. He kissed her in return, his hands finding her waist and holding lightly, as if she might crack. As if *they* might shatter.

Her fingers clenched his shoulders, her breath warm against his neck as she eased back, cautious, lines of uncertainty etched across her face. She was waiting. For approval? Permission?

She had it all.

Cade pressed his forehead to hers, his pulse racing. "I think you've made a mistake."

Rosalyn wilted. "Oh."

"It was more like *this*." He tugged her into him, and she crashed against his chest as his lips found hers again with confidence. She whimpered, returning the kiss with equal fervor.

Time seemed to slow. The rain flowed faster, providing a sheet of privacy around their awning as her arms snaked up around his neck. Her delicious scent took him back to high school, when her hair would brush against his arm every time she leaned across their shared table in the library. To those late-night debate team sessions, when she'd often save the seat next to her despite their being on opposite teams.

Maybe he'd been too intimidated by her and her friends back in those school days. Too easily dismissed at the Lazy Spoon.

Today, he was none of those things.

It was only him and Rosalyn. And the steady downpour of rain finally giving him the opportunity to make up for lost time.

Cade deepened their kiss, feeling Rosalyn press into him as if she couldn't get close enough. His hands on her back, tugging her closer, acknowledged the struggle. She was shaking, and he didn't think it was from the cold anymore.

That made two of them.

He lifted her slightly off the ground, turning her back to the brick wall of the shop as the kiss continued. Her fingers brushed the ends of his hair, setting his neck alight with nerves. His body hummed as the fervency of their kiss slowed, becoming more and more intentional.

It was getting difficult to breathe. But he'd collapse to the pavement before he pulled away first.

As if reading his mind, Rosalyn turned her face to the side, gulping for air. His heart pounded like they'd run ten miles instead of two blocks.

"This time you're mistaken." Rosalyn leaned back, palming his chest with both hands. Her eyes were glassy, her cheeks flushed.

"Because I can assure you, the kiss in the theater was *nothing* like that."

That was a relief. "And for the record, you can now consider that valedictorian bet paid off." Cade closed the slight distance between them, wrapping her into a hug. "I should've made good on that a long time ago."

He could feel her smile into his shoulder.

Cade rested his cheek on the top of her head, willing his heart to slow. To not thunder in her ear.

But she didn't seem to mind as she looped her arms around him and relaxed. The rain began to let up, as quickly as it'd begun. As if it's entire purpose had been for them. Maybe it had.

Then slowly, Rosalyn began to stiffen.

"Don't do that." Cade tightened his grip, as if she might vanish with the storm. "I can tell you're already over-thinking."

"Cade . . ." Her voice pitched.

"I know, we had the whole friends talk. But . . . give it a minute." He pulled away, but only far enough to smile down at her. "We're a gumbo. We need to simmer."

But she didn't smile back. "Cade."

And just like that, reality replaced the dream. He let his arms fall to his sides. "I told myself I wasn't going to cross your line."

Her shaking hands adjusted her ponytail. "You didn't. I kissed you."

"We kissed each other."

She grimaced. "I started it."

He crossed his arms over his chest, warring against the temptation to pull her back against him. "That you did. So why fight this?"

Her eyes darted to the side, then to their feet. "I have my reasons."

"Which are?" He ducked down, trying to catch her gaze.

"It's getting harder to remember them, I can assure you." She ripped the ponytail holder from her hair and twisted it between her fingers.

Was she tearing up?

Cade gestured between them. "We can go as slow as you want. I promise—I make an excellent tortoise."

"You don't understand." She wrapped the tie around her wrist, then appeared at a loss for what to do with her hands. "I know it's confusing."

"Very." Frustration rose in his chest and he fought to tamp it down. But the sudden crash back into reality—her version of it, anyway—was more jolting than he could handle. He wanted to go back to the dream world. The world where it was them and everything made a lot more sense. A world where Rosalyn confided in him and needed him. "I'm not seeing these reasons you keep talking about."

"I can't do this." Her voice cracked. "I'm not—I'm . . ."

"What? You're *what*?"

She shoved her hair behind her ears and met his gaze directly. "I'm married."

Cade stilled. His heart stopped pounding, the rain stopped falling, and the wind stopped blowing. The world stood silent, all color bleeding to gray. His stomach dropped out from under him and he swallowed. Then nodded once. "I'd say that's a pretty good reason."

He wasn't supposed to find out that way.

Or at all.

Rosalyn shoved her hands through her hair, now rapidly frizzing in the post-rain humidity, as she followed Cade through the

French Quarter. Her stomach cramped with nerves. That hadn't gone the way it should have. "Cade, wait."

Without looking, he continued pushing through the crowds, heading for the parking lot where they'd left his Audi. "We've got to get back."

Rosalyn struggled to keep up. Oh, why had she told him? That amazing kiss had thrown her off. Made her wish for things even a genie couldn't grant. Then the guilt had slammed, stealing her breath. Cade didn't deserve this. She'd wanted so badly to back-pedal into friendship, but there was no going back after a kiss like that, was there?

They'd played with fire today, and she'd burned them both.

"Cade, please." He'd pushed for a reason as to why she'd changed course suddenly . . . which was understandable but had also forced her premature confession out.

But he didn't understand the whole picture. *She* barely understood the whole picture.

She trotted faster, weaving around a baby stroller and a man walking a bulldog on a diamond-encrusted leash. "Let me explain."

Cade spun around on the sidewalk. "I don't know that you can."

She rocked backward. There it was. The expression she'd never wanted to see on Cade's face when he looked at her—eyes cold and distant, jaw hard and set.

She'd lost him.

Rosalyn forced her hands to stop shaking, wishing she could throw herself back in his arms and forget the rest. She opened her mouth, but her words stuck. Now that she had his attention, she wished she didn't. Zydeco music drifted from a nearby patio—the sound of tourists having a good time after the storm.

Except she'd launched herself and Cade straight into a new one.

His Adam's apple bobbed in his throat. "Are you married, or aren't you?"

So much story to tell—and it was hard to form coherent sentences when he was staring at her like that. She squeezed her hands into fists. "Technically."

Sadness replaced the anger in his eyes. "Then that's all I need to know." He started to turn back around.

"Cade." She grabbed his arm.

His face flushed. "Rosalyn, you're off-limits. That kiss never should have happened."

"You still don't get it." She pulled him off the sidewalk, around a corner into a gated, paid parking lot. Surprisingly, he let her.

"I need to tell you what happened." Rosalyn tried to ignore the angst in his eyes, focus on the words she owed him. Yet another person she'd hurt with her bad decisions. "About four months ago, my agent Blaine came to me with a huge opportunity—a spot on an international troupe."

"Blaine." Cade crossed his arms. "Is he the guy I saw you kiss that night after your show?"

"Yes, but we never dated. I was so relieved that night to be back in America, that my first show back was a success." She waved her hands. "Wait. I'm getting ahead of myself."

He raised his eyebrows, his silence somehow more intimidating than his interruption.

Rosalyn took a ragged breath, shifting her weight to let a group of tourists with fanny packs push past them. This wasn't where she'd intended to have this conversation—not that she'd ever intended to have it. "The only catch with the troupe was I had to pay up front for my spot, but that's how these things usually go. You earn the investment back and way more while you're touring. Blaine promised me a fortune if I stuck out the tour."

Cade squinted. "I take it that didn't happen."

She shook her head. "He got the loan for me, figured everything out. I signed the papers, and we were good to go. First performance was in Greece, then Turkey. Then our third show was in Saudi Arabia." She tried to control the tremor the mere words sent into her hands but failed. "That's when everything fell apart." She swallowed. "I guess *I* fell apart."

Cade kept listening, arms folded, face stoic. Waiting for the marriage part, she was sure, but he had to—*had to*—understand along the way.

"The stress of my first world tour caught up to me. I'd been sick right before we left, and not up to my usual stamina at our first show. But I couldn't scale back for this troupe. I had to prove myself."

She knew that part he'd get, at least. She hurried to get past the rest. "I pushed too hard and started having anxiety symptoms. My body wasn't healed, and now my mind was in constant overdrive. I was surviving on not enough food and too much caffeine and, well, I had breakdown, I guess you'd say, right there in the outdoor arena."

His eyes softened.

"I fell but caught myself at the last second. Sitting there on the ground under the fabric, stunned, all those people . . . it was too much. They whisked me away to the hospital, but I think it was mostly our troupe manager was embarrassed—he needed it to look like a physical issue and not a mental one. I guess it was both."

She hadn't said this to anyone yet, and recounting it made her taste sand all over again. Feel the desert heat on her arms. The roar of her heartbeat in her ears. "Blaine tried to cover for me, but he didn't understand what was happening either. I couldn't get control of my tears, my words, my racing heart. It was awful. And the hospital didn't know what to do with me because I didn't have any illness they could easily diagnose. So they transferred me to the mental ward."

Cade briefly shut his eyes. "I'm sorry. That had to be . . . wow."

"You have no idea."

Her temples throbbed. "Scariest two days of my life. I wanted to go home—I knew I was fine, I needed a break. Rest. My bed. But

I'd paid into this troupe and couldn't stay. Now I was in debt. And the troupe manager wouldn't speak up for me. I think he wanted me to stay out of the way. Blaine . . ." She swallowed. "He came to me, scared. Had to sneak in the ward, they wouldn't let him in my room since I was a single woman. He said I had no rights there as a woman to release myself." She hesitated. "Unless I was married."

Cade grimaced. "I think I see where this is going."

"Blaine said we could annul it, that it wouldn't be a big deal and we needed to get me home. Lying in that hospital bed, with barred windows and no one speaking English . . . it felt like the only way."

Tears burned Rosalyn's throat. "I was desperate. So he made some calls and paid for some favors, and we legally got married. He handled everything and got me out of there. Got me home."

"And now he's your husband, but on a technicality." Cade frowned. "Still? Didn't you say all this was six months ago?"

"Apparently, it's not easy to annul a marriage. He went to file it and learned we have to actually get a divorce. That's the holdup now, wading through all that paperwork and waiting on the courts. It's more complicated being international."

A muscle jumped in Cade's jaw. "I see." He scrubbed his palm over his chin. "That's a lot."

"I know." She hesitated. "It is for me too, trust me."

His eyes locked on hers. "Do you care about him?"

"About Blaine? *No.* Never like that." She adamantly shook her head.

Cade rocked back on his heels. She couldn't tell if he believed her. "The crying earlier today on the phone though . . . that was about Blaine."

She nodded. "But not in the way you think."

"And the kiss?"

"I was happy to be back. Blaine saved me from that hospital room in Saudi Arabia, and I was swept up in the performance—my first one where I felt stable again. Like all of that other stuff was behind me."

But it hadn't been. Still wasn't. Could she tell Cade the rest of the repercussions she was fighting? *By the way, the Mafia might be after me . . .*

Or would that make him dismiss all of it as an unbelievable story?

As if confirming her fear, Cade reached up and grasped the back of his neck with both hands. "I don't know *what* to think right now, Rosalyn."

"I understand." She'd made horrible decisions for years, listening to Blaine. Seeking fame and fortune, going along with his wild plan. Giving him so much power over her career.

No wonder she couldn't pray or hear God. She deserved what she'd gotten. She'd made her bed, so to speak, and couldn't expect someone to bail her out of her own irresponsibility. She had to see this through on her own. Then maybe, when it was all over, she could have the clarity to listen to the right voices.

Or Voice.

"All was as well as it could be. Mentally, I was enjoying aerial again and performing stateside, taking big gigs to pay off the loan for the troupe that I never earned back. Blaine was working on the divorce paperwork, which we kept secret, obviously." She sighed. "Then several weeks ago, I fell during a show."

She kicked her injured leg out in front of her. When was the last time it'd actually hurt? Certainly not while she was racing Cade. And hardly at all since being back in Magnolia Bay.

Maybe she hadn't wanted to heal.

She straightened. "I came home to recover, and now I'm in your circus and, well, that's it."

Give or take.

"This whole story feels like a circus." Cade shoved his hands into his hair. "Rosalyn . . ."

"It's the truth." She hated how small her voice sounded. How small she felt with that disappointed look in his eyes.

But again, she'd done this to herself. She trusted the wrong people, took shortcuts, didn't manage her own money or career . . . she knew better.

And she had no one to blame for their storefront kiss except herself. She braced herself. "Look, I know you're mad. I can only imagine how I'd feel if you'd kissed me and then dropped that 'by the way' bomb on me." She winced. "I don't *feel* unavailable, if that makes sense. Except—"

"Except you *are*." Cade lowered his voice. "Because you're not only caught up in a bunch of legal red tape, you're also leaving Magnolia Bay again."

"Right." She nodded, the weight of that reality feeling oddly similar to the moment she'd landed on the crash pad. Maybe worse.

Cade held her gaze, as if he thought if he waited long enough, something could change. She'd stand there forever if that were true.

But it wasn't.

She was not a free woman.

A few shops down, the door to the comedy club opened, and a group of men in ball caps ventured onto the sidewalk. A female voice carried after them, amplified by a microphone.

Cade's frown loosened, and he eased back. "Want to go see who Bruno was talking about? While we're here." Was that an olive branch, or curiosity on his part?

Regardless, Rosalyn nodded, reached up to retie her damp ponytail. If there was ever a time to do like Mom had taught her, hide her crazy, pull herself together . . . "Sure." They fell into step toward the club, tension still radiating from Cade's taut shoulders, but not as much censure in his expression.

She wanted to fall back into his arms. That wouldn't— couldn't—happen. But at least now Cade knew. Most of her secret was out there.

The mic'd voice grew louder as they neared the door. "... don't have kids. I mean, I'm not that far removed from the teen years myself. But I know one thing coffee beans and teenagers have in common . . . they're always getting grounded."

Chuckles erupted.

Cade's eyes grew round. "No way."

She paused, not recognizing the voice. "What?"

Without answering, he tugged Rosalyn toward the venue and caught the heavy red door before it closed. Rosalyn blinked against the dim lighting, waiting for her eyes to adjust. A woman stood silhouetted on stage under bright lights.

"I told you I was a barista, right? I've got stories, man. People are weird." She waved her hand in the air.

The crowd murmured in agreement.

The familiar-looking figure continued. "Like the other day, a bunch of customers started getting rowdy." The comedian paused. "It was a total *brew* haha."

A young hostess approached the vacant stand next to Rosalyn. "I'm sorry, we're no longer selling tickets. This show is almost over."

"Oh, we got what we needed, don't worry." Cade looked at the stage, then at Rosalyn, and grinned. For a moment, the drama of her exposed secret seemed suspended in another time.

She glanced between him and the stage, then clamped her hand over her mouth as the comedian stepped further into the spotlight. "Is that—"

"Thank you, thank you." The dry voice deadpanned on as the crowd applauded. "I would say I'll be here all night, but that's a lie. My segment ends in about five minutes." Then she shaded her eyes with one hand and peered toward the door.

Cade offered a casual wave and a grin.

A mild expletive fell into the microphone.

He laughed. "Yep, that's Miley."

Twelve

ALL RIGHT, WHAT'S THIS GOING TO COST me?" Miley cracked a bubble with her gum as she leaned forward from the backseat of Cade's Audi. The cloudy afternoon transitioned into dusk as they sped down the highway toward Magnolia Bay.

"I told you we'd give you a ride for free. I can't believe you were planning to take an Uber an hour each way." Not to mention Cade would've gladly paid Miley to ride back with them and be a buffer between him and Rosalyn.

He wasn't ready for more conversation yet.

He risked a look at the passenger seat where Rosalyn sat, gazing out the window. Her ponytail was up again, hoodie back on, makeup smudges wiped clean. She'd tried to put herself back together.

Currently, he possessed no such ability for himself.

And their kiss . . . his chest heated.

Miley was still talking. "An Uber is expensive, but my car broke down and this gig was worth it." *Crack.* Another bubble. "But I meant what's it going to cost to keep my secret?"

Cade glanced in the rearview. "We're good at doing that, don't worry." He felt Rosalyn's eyes boring into his profile. "Professionals, really." Maybe a cheap shot, but his mood kept flipping from frustrated to sad and back.

But mostly frustrated at himself. What had he expected? Well—admittedly—not *that*. But he should've known better than to start to fall for Rosalyn Dupree. After two *almost*s now—the Lazy Spoon encounter and that kiss—he should take the hint.

Rosalyn Dupree was meant for the circus.

"I'm serious." Miley's voice took a panicked note. "I can't let anyone in Magnolia Bay know I'm a stand-up comedian."

"But you're funny." Rosalyn twisted in her seat, turning to face Miley. "You had that place cracking up. Why don't you want anyone at home to know?"

Cade looked in the rearview at her. Good question. Everyone in town had noticed Miley's better mood lately—this had to be the reason why.

Miley looked away. *Crack*. "It doesn't exactly fit my vibe."

"Vibes can change." Rosalyn's gaze drifted over to Cade. "A lot of things can change."

What exactly about her situation did she think she could change that would matter right now? He clenched the steering wheel. "Change, huh? You mean, like people being friends one minute and kissing the next?"

Rosalyn sucked in a sharp breath.

"Weird example, but yeah, I guess." Miley leaned forward again, bracing her arms on the middle console. "More like, I have a reputation I like and want to keep."

"That's fair." Rosalyn's voice grew quiet. "Reputations are hard to build and easy to lose."

Cade let out his breath and sped up as he neared the exit for the causeway to Magnolia Bay. "Don't worry, Miley, your secret is safe."

Rosalyn stiffened beside him, and he gave her a sidelong glance before reluctantly mouthing the words *yours too.*

Her shoulders relaxed. But tension still creased her brows, probably the same tension that shot up his neck and into his temples.

How had they gotten here? Seemed like five minutes ago they were making out, the future bright, the concept of a "them" finally in reach, and now . . . Rosalyn was in the passenger seat but might as well be a million miles away.

Worst part was, he couldn't even stay mad.

Because he already missed her.

"I can offer you both free coffee as a return favor for the secret." Miley hesitated, rapidly spinning the black bracelets on her arm. "As long as my dad isn't there, of course. He doesn't like me giving discounts."

"I don't mind buying my own coffee. But do me a different favor?" Cade met Miley's gaze in the mirror, taking in the smoky eye shadow, the shiny nose ring. "Think about the fact secrets cause more problems in the long run. It's not worth it."

She squinted. "How so?"

"Because secrets make you have to hide." He held her gaze, fought the urge to look at Rosalyn. "Or worse, run away."

Both women in the car fell silent.

They cleared the bridge and wound their way toward Village Lane. Cade cracked his neck to one side, but the tightness in his upper body remained.

He was such a fool, thinking Rosalyn had been into him. She didn't need him. Oh sure, she—and apparently every other female in the Bay—needed him to keep their secrets. But something wasn't adding up with her story, which led Cade to believe there were more secrets still.

Which meant whatever the other secrets were had to be worse than being secretly *married*.

Which meant Cade had been a distraction for Rosalyn, at best. A placeholder or rebound, at worst.

He glanced in the rearview, at his own flushed face and pinched expression.

At this point all he needed was a big red nose, and he'd be the perfect addition to his own circus.

Thirteen

"T HERE'S A POTHOLE IN MY FRONT OF MY diner."

Cade spun in his chair to face Delia, who stood framed in his office doorway. Her posture seemed straighter above her cane today, her purse hitched on the shoulder pad of her floral blouse.

He let out a sigh. Talk about a Monday. He'd been working for hours on fundraising details and hadn't had enough coffee yet to deal with more bad news—even if Miley had upsized his latte with a zipping of her lips, like she'd done every morning since she got busted in New Orleans last week. "It's not your diner anymore, Mama D."

"Magnolia Blossom will always be mine in spirit, dear." Delia sank into the chair across from his desk. "And speaking of spirits, I'm afraid some are going to float up from the depths of that hole if it isn't fixed soon."

"It's from the hurricane flood waters." Cade scrubbed his palm over his cheek, then winced at the rough texture under his hand. He probably should've sprung for that designer men's lotion he'd seen advertised last night. If this fundraiser gave him one more wrinkle or gray hair . . .

"I don't care if it's from a séance gone wrong." Delia pursed her ruby-red lips and fanned herself with a paper she'd snagged off Cade's desk. "It's a liability. They're popping up all over. Have you seen the one in front of Chug a Mug? It looks like it could—"

"House a family of four?"

Delia shrugged, tossing the paper back into the tray it'd come from. "I was going to say operate as a small B&B, but your description fits too."

He reached for a pen. "I'll add it to the list, Mama D." What was one more entry, at this point?

"I appreciate it." She started to stand, then gave him one look and settled back in her chair. "What's wrong?"

"Oh, nothing I can't handle." He scribbled *pothole* on a sticky note and deliberately added it to the stack of invoices, vendor lists, and projection spreadsheets covering his desk. "There. Happy?"

"Ecstatic." She folded her hands over her stomach and leveled him with a glare. "And lucky for you, I don't have anywhere else I have to be. I can wait you out."

He could already tell this was a battle he wasn't going to win.

"Fine." Cade leaned back in his chair, intentionally ignoring his desk drawer containing Skittles. He hadn't been able to make it to the gym with Linc the past few weeks, and reckoning day would come. "I'm a *tad* behind on Magnolia Days, but I'm getting there." He pointed to the pile of papers. "The poodles are confirmed, so there's that." Thanks to Rosalyn's calls from NOLA.

His stomach knotted. They hadn't talked since. He'd kept busy with the festival, only glimpsing her through the window on his way past Madame Paulette's studio once or twice over the weekend. At some point, he'd have to break the ice with her.

But at the moment, there didn't seem to be a big enough pick. It was easier to focus on preparing for the movie scout to come. To assure Mrs. Peters the Friends of the Library booth would have peak accessibility at the festival. To dodge Trish and her insistence on hosting a kissing booth. To create graphics for the newspaper to print featuring Rosalyn's performance.

Ok, maybe that part hadn't been easier.

The AC unit kicked on, blowing a reprieve of air into his office space. "Everything will be ready to go soon."

"I know I've offered before, but I'm happy to help with anything you need." Delia tilted her gray head. "My great-nephew in Metairie has bouncy houses. That might be fun—"

He held up both hands. "I've got it covered, Mama D. I promise." Bouncy houses required space to put them, and the festival grounds were going to be full at it was—not to mention working in parking for what he hoped would be a big crowd.

She nodded, her brow furrowed as if unconvinced. "Then why don't you delegate something to me? I've got free time on my hands since selling the diner."

"There's nothing to delegate, but I appreciate it." And he did. But delegating things out meant he'd have to follow up on them, and that added extra work to his to-do list. It was easier in that sense to handle it himself.

"I'll take your word for it." Delia braced both hands on her cane. Her gray eyebrows hiked up her forehead. "What else is going on to make that face?"

"Is this not enough?" Cade plucked the sticky note from the stack and teasingly shook it at her.

"Oh, knock it off. I've watched you grow up. All you boys." Delia waved one arm as if gesturing to the entire male population of Magnolia Bay. "I can tell when all isn't well." She smiled. "That's my favorite hymn, you know. 'It Is Well with My Soul.'" Then her eyes narrowed. "And it's not with yours. What's troubling you?"

He hesitated. Maybe Delia would have some advice . . . if he kept it vague. After all, he promised Rosalyn her secret was safe.

He picked up a paperclip and rolled it between his fingers.

"Have you ever had someone you were close to turn out to be someone different . . . not who you thought they were?"

Delia nodded knowingly. "Like a murderer?"

"*What*? No!" Cade made a face at her. "Who exactly are you friends with?"

She adjusted the hem of her shirt over her pants. "You were very serious just now. So I assumed it was a serious allegation."

"Fine. Less serious than murder, but still . . . startling."

"So criminal in another way? Bank robber?"

Cade shot her a look. "You need help."

"I'm about to make a point."

"I can't wait." He bit back a groan.

"If it's not criminal . . ." Delia tapped her chin. "Then that would mean—for this to be *so* upsetting to you—that this person went through a major character change?"

"Not exactly." Cade stared at the paper clip. Rosalyn was still who she was. "More like they kept a secret."

"I see. And was there a good reason for this secret?"

"Well . . . yeah."

Delia's expression took on that of a wise old owl. "Did the secret hurt anyone outright?"

"Not . . . sort of. Yes. I mean—"

"So, a person you care about had a secret, but they didn't commit a crime or even change who they are. And you're riled up?" She snorted. "You should get to work on my pothole, boy."

"It's not that simple."

"Seems like a bit of concrete would do the trick."

Cade tossed the paperclip on his desk. "Mama D."

"I'm kidding. Cade, honey, listen." She tapped her cane on the ground for emphasis. "I'm giving you a hard time because I want you to see the need for grace. Your feelings obviously got hurt. And you're disappointed. All of that is valid. But is this something that's unforgiveable?"

He paused. "No."

"Is it worth losing the friendship?"

"No." The bigger problem was how he and Rosalyn kept skipping right over friendship and then trying to go back to it.

"Think back over the details." Delia's voice gentled. "Is it even as bad as you heard it the first time?"

I'm married. Yeah, it was pretty bad.

But then the details surfaced, like bubbles to the top of the bay. Rosalyn had been alone. Scared. Trapped. She hadn't impulsively rushed down an aisle with the intent for anyone to get hurt.

She hadn't even lied to him—outright, anyway. More like she'd withheld sensitive information. Which was fair, because she hadn't owed Cade anything . . . until after the kiss. And she could have still kept her secret then but had done the right thing, even though she must have assumed he'd be upset.

All while *she* was the one whose entire life had derailed of late.

Maybe he'd been a jerk.

"I see the wheels turning. I'll take that as my cue to leave." Delia stood with a groan. "Never get old, darlin'."

"Who's old?" He stood and walked her to the door.

"You should be a politician with all that nonsense."

Cade forced his smile to stay steady. Rosalyn wasn't the only one with secrets. But no sense in diving into his upcoming campaign with Mama D. He'd managed to put it out of his mind for the weekend, his thoughts fully occupied with Rosalyn. But now . . . his chest tightened and he reached up to massage it. "Thanks for your wisdom."

"Anytime, hon." She hugged him before nudging his leg with her cane. "Now get to work on my pothole."

His chest twinged again. "Yes, ma'am." He stepped aside so Delia could leave.

"And Cade? Forgive that sweet girl." Delia turned in the hallway and nodded her chin at him. "She seems like she's been through more than we know."

Cade froze, one hand on the doorknob. "How did you know who I was talking—"

"This entire town underestimates me." She rolled her eyes. "Remember now—do what it takes to make it well with your soul."

There was nothing to say but another, "Yes, ma'am." Not that he had a clue how to do that.

As Delia ambled away, Cade shut the door and sagged against it. The drooping potted plant near his window matched his own posture. When had he watered it last? The stack of papers on his desk looked twice as tall. His landline jangled, sending another zap of adrenaline through his veins.

His chest fluttered again.

No. He didn't have time for an attack.

But reality piled up anyway. Rosalyn. Their kiss and his misplaced hope. His endless to-do lists. The pressure that none of his efforts would be enough. The scout that was coming . . . at this point, would he fall into a pothole and sue? How would they ever be impressed with a town that was sinking into the earth's core?

But Magnolia Bay *had* to impress this guy. Cade needed the attention put back on the town if he and his father stood a chance at keeping things running without detrimental changes like layoffs and shop closings.

Well, he *and* his father for now.

Soon to be just Cade.

His vision blurred. He tried to find three items to focus on, but anxiety rushed in full force, clawing at his throat until he couldn't breathe. The mayoral campaign meant more pressure. More responsibility. This pace was never going to let up. And he had to do it all or fail.

Which wasn't an option.

He drew a tight breath with little success as he looked away from his overflowing pile of responsibilities. He tried to focus on the individual fibers of the carpet beneath his Sperrys. *One, two, three.* He sucked in a full breath of air. *Four, five, six.*

He reached fifteen, waited a few minutes to be sure, then brushed off the knees of his slacks. He knew what he needed to do. Clearly, there would be no focusing on any of his multiplying tasks until it was well.

With his soul . . .

And with Rosalyn.

The late morning sun streamed through the studio windows, warming Rosalyn's bare arms. She inverted on the silks, her movements rote and without any of her usual artistic grace as she ran through the routine she'd prepared over the weekend. She'd had to do something to keep the image of Cade's disappointed face out of her mind . . . not that it'd helped.

Rosalyn wrapped the silks to prepare for a double star drop. Pouring herself into her workouts had slightly aggravated her knee, but the rest of her body felt good after so much movement. Since coming home, she'd been more lax with her exercise regimen—which apparently had been good for her knee but bad for her emotional health.

Or maybe her secrets were bad for her emotional health.

She rolled into the double star drop, wincing as the fabric caught her harder than she'd anticipated. Thank goodness Blaine hadn't seen that. Not that he was an aerial coach, but he knew how good she was—and had no problem berating her into being better. She glanced toward her purse by the door, where her phone was turned to silent, imagined him blowing it up with endless texts. The fact he'd left her alone as long as he had after their brief conversation the other day was a miracle.

But was *everyone* leaving her alone? Had he been successful in asking for an extension on her loan payments because of her injury? She couldn't know without asking.

She wrapped her feet and moved into a split balance, usually one of her strongest skills. But today, she wobbled. Holding one of the poles with one hand for extra support, Rosalyn fought for balance, tightening her core, squeezing her thighs. She slowly released the fabric. Still wobbly, but better.

"Wow." An awed female voice sounded below.

Rosalyn glanced down. Zoey. "Oh, hey." Gripping the poles in both hands, she unwrapped her feet and slid carefully down the silks to the ground. "I didn't see you come in."

"Sorry to interrupt. I came to bring Madame Paulette her weekly order of beignets." Zoey held up a rectangular bakery box. "She says they're for her students but sometimes I wonder how many she shares." She grinned as she tossed her shock of dark bangs out of her eyes. "Is Madame here?"

"She stepped out. Something about a 'handsome devil of a man' being spotted over at Chug a Mug." Rosalyn smiled back as she clapped chalk off her hands. "I guess Magnolia Bay doesn't get a lot of strangers lately."

"Tourism has slowed. I know that's part of what Cade is working to correct with Magnolia Days." Zoey set the box on the shoe cubby by the front door.

"Will you have a beignet booth at the festival?"

"You bet." Zoey hiked one yoga-pant-clad leg on the barre near the door and stretched. "We need all the sales we can get." She gestured with her chin toward the ceiling. "Could you teach me how to do that sometime?"

"A split balance?" Rosalyn raised her eyebrows. "That's a little advanced—"

"No way. I can't even do the splits on the ground!" Zoey laughed as she traded legs on the barre to stretch the other one. "I meant some basic tricks. Basically cool enough to shut Linc up when he brags about weightlifting."

"Of course." Rosalyn started to knot her silks up off the floor. Her knee was done for the day—maybe so were her spirits. "I think Elisa was interested in learning too. I could show you guys a few beginner skills."

Zoey's face lit. "I'm sensing a girl's night."

"That'd be fun." Rosalyn was only slightly surprised to realize she meant it.

"I bet you're a great teacher." Zoey screwed up her nose as she sank into a grand plié at the barre. "I'd be *so* bad with kids."

"It's fun to watch them learn." Rosalyn gestured to the studio around them. "I helped with the girls' ballet class last week—they're sweet." She hesitated, then grinned. "Most of them, anyway."

"I guess I only see them when they're sugared up at my shop." Zoey laughed.

"Hopefully one day I'll be able to open a studio for kids. I wish I'd started even younger than I did." The statement slipped out before Rosalyn fully processed the cost of it. But since she'd been holding in so much for so long, it felt nice to talk about something vulnerable that wasn't dangerous.

"I would've loved something like that when I was younger." Zoey leaned against the barre, folding her arms over her petite frame. "You should go for it. Maybe Madame would even let you share her studio space here."

"Maybe." Something to consider in the future.

If her future ever came. It all felt so far away right now. She had to leave. And who knew when—and in what condition—she'd be back?

"I heard one of the ballet students in my shop Saturday talking about how Barbie helped her learn first position." Zoey shook her head with a smile. "I should've figured that was you."

"I enjoy ballet now—it helps with learning grace and floor routines for my aerial performances." Rosalyn looked up at her silks, could almost see herself inverting as an eleven-year-old. "As a child, though, I wasn't conventional enough to stick with it." Or maybe she hadn't been good at it. She frowned.

"All of these sports are beyond me." Zoey waved one hand in the air. "I'm flexible but have the grace of a monkey in quicksand. You'll have your work cut out for you."

"I'll talk to Elisa." Rosalyn went to the makeshift pulley and hoisted the silks back up toward the ceiling, out of the way of the upcoming class. "Maybe after Magnolia Days we could set something up."

Zoey peered at Rosalyn from under her bangs, blue eyes wide with hope. "Will you still be here after the circus?"

"I'm, um . . . not entirely sure of my timeline yet." Rosalyn tied off the pulley rope. "But I'm sure we could fit something in." Maybe.

"I'm glad I ran into you." Zoey lifted one hand in a wave as she opened the studio door. "And hey, whenever you need a sweet treat, stop by the shop. On the house."

Rosalyn smiled her appreciation, waving as Zoey slipped into the morning sunlight. The dark-haired woman painted an appealing picture—girls' night outs, teaching kids, eating beignets. A "normal" life. One without the flash of cameras and pressure of performing. Without fame and obligations to the wrong kinds of people.

She definitely didn't want to go back to performing Blaine's gigs, but more than that—she didn't know if she wanted to go back to performing at *all*. Eventually, her loan would be paid back. The divorce would go through. She'd be free to make her own choices again—to perform because she *wanted* to, not because she had to.

And then what?

What did she want?

Rosalyn glanced up at her silks, bittersweet longing flooding her heart. When had the fabric that used to symbolize freedom—freedom from convention, from propriety and rules and clichés—become her cage?

After a moment, she slipped out of the studio and stood under the awning, poised to lock the door behind her. Unusual that Madame Paulette would be gone this long—the guy must have been more handsome than she'd anticipated. Only Lettie.

Rosalyn looked up and down the street, but there was no sign of Madame's flowing caftan, no hint of patchouli wafting through the air. Oh well.

She twisted the key in the lock, double-checked the knob, and dropped the ring into her purse. She'd started up the sidewalk toward home when a siren sounded.

A police car veered down Bayou Boulevard, lights flashing.

Fourteen

I CAN'T BELIEVE MAMA D CALLED YOU." Cade dropped his duffel on the bench in the corner of the gym as Linc scowled beside him. The musty scent of sweat mixed with body spray met Cade's nose as he plopped down next to his bag.

Noah grinned as he sat on the other end and leaned over to retie his training shoe. "I can't believe Linc answered."

"And I can't believe she ordered me to hang out with Cade." Linc stood over them, crossing his arms over his black muscle tank. "Like I have time for babysitting at the end of crawfish season."

"You obviously have time to work out." Noah sat up and gestured to the rows of dumbbells, elliptical machines, and weight racks spanning the black and red painted room.

Linc scowled harder, shooting a glance at the wall clock at the back of the gym, half-hidden behind a CrossFit competition banner. "I make time for what matters."

"So your next personal record matters, but not your friends?" Cade shook his head in mock disgust as he pulled a pair of wristbands from his bag. "Pity."

Linc flexed his biceps. "Is it?"

Noah winced as he stood. "All right, I'm convinced. Show me what you've been doing."

They followed Linc to the rack, where he'd already loaded several weights on the bar for bench press. "You'll want to take some of those off."

"Let me try." Cade pulled one arm across his chest in a stretch, then the other, before straddling the bench. "I've been out of the gym the last several weeks, but I'm not a stranger to it."

Noah and Linc shot each other looks, which Cade ignored. He lay back and wiggled into position. "So why did Mama D ask you to babysit?"

"She said you needed guy time." Linc growled. "Whatever that means."

It meant the older woman saw way more than Cade had wanted her to earlier. After she'd left his office, he'd started for the studio to try and find Rosalyn when he'd been ambushed by two Magnolia Days craft vendors and a food truck owner with myriad questions. By the time he'd calmed the rift between the two vendors, who unnecessarily thought the other was competition, and assured the mobile restaurant owner he'd be able to set up as the first truck in the lot, he'd received a text from Linc.

Linc

Meet me at the gym.

Cade

After work?

Linc

Now.

Cade

I'm in the middle of something.

Linc

Fine. But don't complain next time I call you out
for skipping leg day.

Cade

____
Be there in ten.

It probably was for the best that his mission to find Rosalyn had been thwarted. He still had no idea what he'd say when he saw her, or if his feeling of betrayal would rush back and cloud his senses as it had last week. At least here in the gym, he could work out any leftover emotion without making anything worse.

For either of them.

Cade grabbed the metal bar, arched his back, and pushed. Nothing happened.

He cleared his throat, adjusted his grip, and tried again. Nope. "Maybe take off thirty pounds."

Linc grumbled some version of *told you so*. Weights clanked as the guys pulled two plates from the bar. Cade waited, staring at the ceiling. "Did she say why she thought I needed guy time?" Best to figure out what the guys knew before he said too much. Hopefully Delia had left Rosalyn out of it.

"Probably because you're stressed to the max and won't admit it." Noah's voice floated from behind his shoulder. Cade really hoped Linc was spotting him and not Noah.

It'd probably take *both* of them to spot Linc.

"She said you were going through something." Linc sighed, as if the statement alone was too big a burden. "Whatever it was, I figured the gym would knock it out of you." His voice turned into a coach's bark. "Now push."

Cade pressed again. Nothing. He shifted his feet on the ground and repositioned his grip.

Linc's face appeared upside down in Cade's field of vision. "You gonna lift that bar or buy it dinner first?"

Cade tried again. The bar didn't move. "How much *is* this?"

"It started at three-fifteen. Now it's two-eighty-five."

As Elisa said, *good gravy*. He was working out with an Avenger.

Cade eased into a sitting position and faced his friends, sweat already dripping down his temple. "How much are you both going to make fun of me if I put it at one-fifty?"

"A decent amount, I'd wager." Noah began removing weights from the side nearest him. "Not that I could bench almost three hundred either. Difference is, I *know* I can't."

Cade stood to help. "I think I prefer fishing."

"I prefer *anything* to the girl talk Delia wants us to have." Linc grabbed three plates at once and set them on the mat. "Are we going to get it over with or what?"

Noah followed suit with a twenty-five-pound weight. "Does this forced intervention have anything to do with the fundraiser?"

"Not exactly." Cade debated his options. He couldn't tell them about Rosalyn—not without breaking his word. But if he took the easy way out and blamed his stress on Magnolia Days and the circus, they'd butt in and try to help again.

That left one other reason that was still true. He took a breath. "This is still confidential, but . . . my dad is retiring from office this year and he wants me to run for mayor."

"Wow." Noah tilted his head. "And you're having second thoughts?"

Cade scoffed. "I wasn't given first thoughts."

"I assumed you'd always take his place one day."

"That seems to be the trend." Cade forced a laugh. "I guess I didn't think 'one day' would arrive so soon."

"We're wasting time." Linc frowned. "If you don't want to be mayor, don't run." He jammed the last plate on the rack and stepped aside. "Now try again."

Cade resumed his place on the bench. "You don't understand. I don't have a choice—I owe it to my dad."

"Mayor Landry doesn't seem the type to make his son do something he hates." Noah's voice sounded behind him.

"That's exactly his type, if it's for a greater good." Cade gripped the bar. "I was always in trouble growing up. You remember how often I pranked people?"

Noah laughed. "I remember the Jell-O."

"That was you!"

"*One* time. Not the others."

True. "Ninth grade was the worst." Cade adjusted his grip, knocked out three reps. "I got suspended."

Noah peered over at him. "I was already in Shreveport then. I don't know that I ever heard that story."

"Well, that's partly because Dad worked hard to hide it." Cade reached up to the bar again. "I was caught fighting."

"Slap fight?" Linc snorted.

"Funny. Can you add ten pounds back on?" Cade sat up and waited. "It was over Rosalyn." Which made two bullies he'd saved her from so far. "And I didn't get busted for fighting, I got busted for paying a football player to fight."

"That makes more sense." Linc chuckled.

Noah ignored him. "Who was the punk?"

"Justin Davies." Cade cracked his neck. "Who happened to be the principal's son."

Linc winced. "That probably didn't go over well."

"Dad pulled a lot of strings to bail me out. Then he told me that wasn't the way a Landry acted." Cade lay back on the bench. "He said we use words to solve problems, not fists—whether hired or our own." Even now Dad's words echoed in his memory. A fair lesson, but the look on his face . . .

"I can't even imagine this scenario." Above Cade, Linc shook his head, man-bun wobbling.

"Justin was talking trash about taking advantage of Rosalyn after a dance. At the time, it felt like the right move to defend her." Cade lowered the bar into position. "I asked Simon, the massive linebacker, to scare Justin. I didn't mean for him to *actually* beat him." Even if the jerk had deserved it.

And then the irony of the situation slammed into his chest. He'd put himself on the line to defend Rosalyn from sleazy guys twice now—once in school, and once at the Lazy Spoon.

So why hadn't he responded the same way when she told him her story about Blaine? Rather than giving sympathy for a horrible situation, he'd doubted her.

He was turning out to be the third bully.

Cade lifted the bar for a rep. Mama D was right. Her leading him on—intentionally or unintentionally—wasn't unforgivable or even worth losing a friendship over. If he was really her friend, he'd support her and help any way he could.

Like he had in ninth grade, and like he had at the Lazy Spoon.

The weight of his guilt sank into him—along with the bar on his second rep. He struggled with it against his chest, the metal hard and unyielding.

Linc grabbed the bar with one hand and re-racked. "You good?"

Cade wiped sweat from his face. "Just thinking." Earlier, he knew he needed to make things right with Rosalyn.

But now, he finally knew what he needed to say.

"My turn." Noah gestured for Cade to move. "For the record, *I* think you need to talk to your dad about the campaign. Be honest."

Ha. Cade stood, making room for Noah. One tough conversation at a time, and the one with Rosalyn took precedence. "I don't know. Bad timing."

"Seems like good timing to me. No one knows about his retiring yet, so how big of a disappointment would it be? Someone else can run." Linc shrugged like it was that simple.

Cade shook his head. "That's not going to be an option for my father."

Noah wiped the bench with a towel before assuming position. "So what you're saying is, you owe this campaign to your dad because he bailed you out of trouble? Fifteen years ago?"

"Seems like an odd reason to make a career change." Linc stepped behind the bar to spot Noah.

"I promised myself that I'd never give him reason to look at me or talk to me that way again." Cade pulled his arm in front of him, stretching his shoulder. He was going to regret all of this tomorrow. "Besides, you didn't hear what his campaign manager told me that night."

"What?" Noah huffed as he cranked out reps.

The words echoed in Cade's head as if they'd been spoken yesterday and not over a decade ago. "You owe your dad after this one, Sport. You have no idea how much you threaten his image."

Linc helped Noah re-rack. "Ouch."

He didn't tell the guys the rest. *You want to mess up your dad's entire career because of your immaturity? Time to grow up. Your father needs you.*

"It was enough for me to clean up my act." Cade handed Noah his water bottle. If Cade was needed, he'd show up. Like he had the first half of his life. "You've seen me in the back of a cop car once, bro. It wasn't a good look."

Cade's phone buzzed from his pocket before he could question him. Rosalyn? He pulled it free, pausing to swipe his forehead with his sleeve. Then the screen display registered. Not Rosalyn. "That's weird. Elisa texted me."

"She texted me too." Noah looked down at his own cell.

"What's the problem?" Linc leaned over their shoulders as they all read the identical messages.

Elisa
____

Commotion at Chug a Mug You're going to
want to see this.

Magnolia Bay had lost its mind. There was a circus carrying on in front of Chug a Mug—and not of the red-striped tent variety.

Cade stared at the throng of people gathered outside the front doors of the coffee shop and gaped. "What in the world?" Teenagers, families. Men and women. They all stood clumped in a crowd just off the sidewalk, while a cacophony of music, shouts, and laughter filled the air.

A police car, lights flashing, parked across the street on Village Lane. A uniformed officer shouted commands through a bull horn. "Please clear the sidewalks at once. No loitering, people."

Everyone ignored him.

Madame Paulette performed a tap dance number on the sidewalk, gold bracelets jingling as she swung her arms and huffed. *Tap-tap, tappity-tap.* Next to her, Zoey juggled three beignets— she was surprisingly good, judging by the fact there were only a few powdered white spots on the sidewalk at her feet. Trish, the waitress from Magnolia Blossom, had donned a sparkly costume with a matching top hat and spun a baton, while two other young adults harmonized off-key with their hands clasped in front of their chests. Sadie half-shouted a poem from a worn copy of *Sonnets from the Portuguese*, gesturing wildly with her free hand.

Linc and Noah flanked Cade on each side. "I guess Elisa wasn't kidding." Noah crossed his arms over his chest, his hair falling across his forehead as he stared. "This definitely qualifies as a commotion."

Understatement of the century.

Next to Sadie, a college-aged guy blaring a hip-hop song on his phone started break-dancing. Beside him, another kid performed skateboarding tricks.

"What's gotten into everyone?" Cade looked over his shoulder toward the café, nearly losing his balance as two girls in tutus pushed past him and pirouetted down the street. Something moving across the grass off to the side of Chug a Mug caught his attention. "Is that Owen?"

"Oh, for crying out loud." Noah sighed. "He's tightrope walking."

Sure enough, Owen had tied a rope between two stakes, only about a foot off the ground. He wobbled across the line holding an umbrella, stepping down to regain his balance every two to three steps.

"Zoey!" Linc suddenly barked, making both Cade and Noah jump. "What are you doing?"

Unwavering, Zoey kept her eyes up as she continued juggling, side-stepping to stay under the pastries. "What does it look like?" She shook her bangs out of her eyes and attempted to execute a spin.

Three beignets rained down on her head.

Linc growled.

Elisa broke through the crowd and rushed to join them, wearing her Magnolia Blossom apron and a stricken expression. "There you are!"

Rosalyn was right behind her.

Cade's throat dried at the sight of her blonde ponytail and wide eyes. He flexed his hands at his sides.

Rosalyn hurried to stand next to them, then stepped back as Noah pulled Elisa into his side. She turned toward the drama unfolding on the streets, angling her face away from Cade.

Cade swallowed. He wanted to tell her how ashamed he was of his reaction last week, but in the middle of this chaos wasn't the place.

Noah planted a kiss on the top of Elisa's head, oblivious to the tension lingering next to him on each side. "You don't want to throw yourself in there, babe? Do a trick?"

"Yeah, right. It's been like this for twenty minutes and the crowd keeps growing." Elisa tucked her hair behind her ears and grimaced. "It's like a really bad talent show."

"Where's Simon Cowell when you need him?" Linc muttered, shifting his weight.

"I will say the Blossom is doing great business." Elisa shrugged. "We sold out of blueberry scones and Cajun muffins. I left Lucius baking a third batch so I could come see if you'd made it out here yet."

Cade craned his head to see around the group clustered between them and the action taking place down the street—and give his eyes an excuse to land anywhere other than on Rosalyn. "Who is everyone gathered around over there?"

Linc, the tallest of them, stood on tiptoe to check. He scowled. "Some dude in a blazer."

Cade took several steps down the road toward the cluster, his friends following. The crowd parted, and sure enough, standing in the middle of the hubbub was a middle-aged man wearing sunglasses, a blazer, and dark jeans. His temples were streaked with silver.

The group around them fell silent as Delia hobbled toward the man on her cane, chin lifted in the air. Several pink and teal shopping bags dangled from her free hand. "Do you remember me?"

The man frowned, tilting his head. "I'm sorry, I—"

"No, *I'm* sorry." Trish breezed from behind the stranger, her tone cool as she stared down her nose at Delia.

Delia glared back at her. "I was here yesterday. You wouldn't wait on me?"

The man's eyes widened as he looked between the two women. He took a step back.

Trish moved closer to Delia, shouldering past the man. Her bored tone continued as she swept her gaze over Delia. "Oh . . ."

"You work on commission, right?" Delia inched closer to Miley, her expression haughty.

Trish offered a bored eye roll. "Yeah . . ."

Delia gestured wildly with her shopping bags. "Big mistake. Big!" She thrust the packages into the redhead's face and shook them. Her cane toppled to the street with a clatter. "Huge!"

The crowd began to clap. Rosalyn's eyes grew big and Elisa pressed her hands to her cheeks. "Was that the script from Pretty Woman?"

Delia and Trish took a quick bow. With an uncertain laugh, the well-dressed stranger started a slow retreat. A tight smile spanned his silver-sprinkled goatee. "Um, very nice, ladies."

Cade flinched. Surely that wasn't . . .

Then the man removed his sunglasses, revealing a tanned face Cade had recently seen on social media.

The scout had come early.

Fifteen

"WHAT DO YOU MEAN THAT HANDSOME man isn't a talent scout?" Madame Paulette crossed her arms over her ample chest and glared at Cade. The noon sunlight cutting through windows caught the bangles on her wrists and nearly blinded everyone gathered in the dance studio. "That's what Trish said!"

"Yeah, he's clearly from Hollywood." Owen, still holding his tightrope and umbrella, gestured to his own head. "You can tell by his hair."

Madame's studio had been turned into a temporary town hall, since the number of scorned potential actors wouldn't fit in Cade's office and Sheriff Rubart had kicked them off the street. People lined the walls on both sides of the crowded space, earning muttered reprimands from Madame for leaning on the mirrors.

Cade pinched the bridge of his nose. Janie, the movie studio exec., had sent Trent Lawson to scout as promised—almost a week early. After recognizing the man, Cade had sprinted toward him, hoping to usher Trent out of the chaos somewhere private where they could talk. He couldn't tell at first if Trent had been amused or irritated by the bombardment.

Two sentences into the conversation, it became clear.

"Yeah, it's totally him! Why are you lying to us?" A voice he couldn't identify shouted from the back of the room.

Cade hurried to find his "politician's smile," which he offered to the rows of people both standing and sitting cross-legged on the wooden floor. "If you'll all quiet down for a moment, I'd be happy to explain." Well, *happy* might not be the most accurate word.

Not that it mattered, as the noise—and accusations—continued. The hyped-up teenagers chatted loudly among themselves, while Sadie and Delia talked over each other to identify all the reasons they believed Cade was wrong about the man. Elisa and Noah spoke quietly to each other, gesturing around the room, while Zoey stood beside Linc, arms crossed and rolling her eyes at whatever he said.

Trish pointed her baton at Cade and shouted something he couldn't make out. Even Farmer Branson joined the melee, pacing the back of the room with thumbs hitched in his overall straps, and he hadn't even been part of the impulsive talent show.

Rosalyn was nowhere to be seen.

And somehow, her absence felt even more overwhelming than the presence of the mob.

"Um, guys?" Cade tried to keep his tone pleasant, despite his desire to run out of the building, down Bayou Boulevard, and straight into the nearest pothole. His stomach twisted at the thought of his father hearing about how Cade couldn't command a room.

He wasn't mayor potential, and this further proved it.

Cade's anxiety grew in direct proportion to the din around him. He tried again, louder this time. At this point, he'd give a month's worth of his drawer snacks for a microphone. "*Guys?*"

Linc slipped two fingers into his mouth and whistled. The sudden blast echoed off the walls and the entire room was instantly blanketed in silence.

"Thanks." Cade rubbed his ear. "I think."

The annoyed voices morphed into annoyed expressions. But at

least they were quiet. Cade cleared his throat. "To clarify, Trent—Mr. Lawson—*is* a scout."

"See!" Owen shouted triumphantly.

Cade shot him a look. "I asked the film company that shot here a few years ago to consider coming back to the area, and they agreed. So they sent a *location* scout."

Owen winced. "Oh."

"Yeah, *oh*." Cade pointed behind him to the street outside the studio. "Mr. Lawson has nothing to do with hiring actors."

Delia's gray brows furrowed. "Then why did he watch us so carefully?"

Elisa snorted. "What would you do if the entire town put on an impromptu show right in your face?"

"Exactly." Sadie nodded briskly. "He's polite."

Owen frowned. "I thought people from Hollywood were rude."

Several hands swatted him.

Madame Paulette bumped Owen with one hip, sending him stumbling forward a step. "He might be nearby."

"I'm sure he's aware of the stereotypes." Owen crossed his arms, accidentally jabbing Linc in the back with his umbrella. Linc glared down at him.

Cade sighed. "Mr. Lawson is aware of too many things already, trust me." *Your town here definitely knows how to put on a show.* Trent's laugh had carried more disdain than amusement. *I didn't realize I was walking onto the set of a bad sitcom.*

"Next order of business." Cade planted his hands on his hips and let his gaze drift over the room. "Mr. Lawson came several days early—I didn't even know he'd show up when he did. So how did this happen?"

The entire crowd took a step back and pointed to Trish.

She offered a sheepish grin as she reached up to adjust her top hat. "I heard him introduce himself at the café when he came in for brunch. I might have Googled him, and, uh, spread the word."

The chaos escalated again as everyone started either accusing or defending Trish.

Cade clapped his hands together before a brawl broke out. "Look, I think you guys definitely made an impression." Not the one he'd been hoping for, but it was too late now. "We should all head home, before Sheriff Rubart reminds us of the fire code."

"We've exceeded the legal limit by ten." Madame Paulette jerked her thumb toward the sign posted on the wall.

Great. Sheriff Rubart on his back was the last thing Cade needed.

"Okay, everyone out." Cade pointed to the door. He had zero energy left to put into this. All that begging, and his one chance at getting the movie company interested in a post-hurricane Magnolia Bay had been blown by fifty people seeking their fifteen minutes of fame.

The mob filed past him out the front doors. Didn't they realize he was doing all of this for them? For the town? How was he supposed to meet all their requests without the money to do so? And how was he supposed to raise said money if they were getting in the way of his efforts?

Elisa shot him sympathetic eyes as she made her way past, her fingers laced through Noah's. The sight sent a fresh pang through Cade's stomach. He still hadn't made things right with Rosalyn, and now he had this mistake to deal with—and to explain to his father.

"Sorry, sugar," Elisa said with a wince. "Pie on the house, whenever you want to swing by the Blossom."

Noah palmed Cade's shoulder with his free hand. "It'll all work out. Don't give up yet."

Easy for him to say. Noah had gone on a treasure hunt last spring organized by his recently deceased grandfather and had saved the inn he worked so hard for. Cade worked hard for the entire town, and all he got in return was what—anxiety attacks? Humiliation?

He looked at Madame Paulette, who was now the only other person left inside the studio.

She regarded him with a wary expression. "You think we messed up, huh?"

"I don't know. I tried to talk with Mr. Lawson, but he wanted to go back to Chug a Mug and finish his latte in peace." Cade ran his hands down his cheeks. "Maybe there's still a way to help Trent see Magnolia Bay isn't crazy and is worthy of further consideration."

Though with all that drama, at least the man probably hadn't noticed the potholes and half-finished repairs.

"Oh, we're crazy, honey." Madame laughed. "Anyone wanting to shoot a movie here better learn that quick." Her bracelets jingled as she grabbed a push-broom out of the storage closet. "Now, off you go. I can't have my dancers plié-ing on all this dirt y'all brought in." She started sweeping before Cade could even make it to the porch.

He coughed against the cloud Madame swept his way and quickly shut the door behind him. Then he rubbed his eyes. For a moment, he was a child again. Playing hide-and-seek with his grandmother, who finally—gently—had to explain that just because he closed his eyes didn't mean people couldn't see him.

Maybe this time, if he stood there and kept his eyes shut, he could disappear. Then Magnolia Days would be over, the campaign would be over, Rosalyn would go wherever she was booked next, and his life would be—

His phone buzzed with a text. He looked down.

Rosalyn.

Rosalyn

Come to Chug a Mug, quick.

All Rosalyn thought since the moment she saw Cade standing

on the sidewalk in front of Chug a Mug, hands shoved helplessly in his pockets as he watched the entire town make fools of themselves, was how much she wished she could give him a hug. The stress lines on his forehead had bothered her, and she'd felt responsible for at least two of them.

So when she saw the middle-aged scout duck his head and beeline inside the coffee shop after the energetic, costumed crowd dispersed to Lettie's studio, she'd seen her chance to make things right. The surprised look on Cade's face now, as they crowded around Trent's meant-for-two table by the window at Chug a Mug, made all her fast-talking a few minutes ago worth it. And okay, yeah, maybe she'd name-dropped herself to get the guy's attention. But it worked, and here they were.

"Thanks for agreeing to see us, Mr. Lawson." Rosalyn clutched her cup of herbal tea between both hands. She had to keep her voice steady despite the nerves flushing her body as she made eye contact with Cade—the closest she'd been to him since he dropped her off at her car after their trip to New Orleans last weekend. "Cade, you sure got here fast."

Honestly, she'd wondered if he'd even see her text or if he'd maybe blocked her number. The scent of his cologne wafted over her, mixing with the aroma of freshly ground beans as Miley whipped something in a blender behind the front counter.

He returned her gaze, and man, she wanted to touch the stubble on his face, smooth the frown lines around his brow. Be snuggled back in his arms under a rain-soaked awning. But wanting that had led to her *doing* that, and look what that had gotten them? Disaster.

One day she'd stop making bad decisions.

But now—now, the air was ripe with cocoa and fresh baked scones and . . . hope? The midday sun streamed through the coffee shop windows, glinting off the hanging brass light fixtures overhead. Down the street, a dog barked, and children shouted as they went about their summer day. Everything felt peaceful again on Village Lane—just in time to try to change Trent's mind.

She had to remember this meeting was about Magnolia Bay— not her and Cade.

"Thanks for ordering me a coffee." Cade shot her an appreciative smile before twisting to face Mr. Lawson. "And I'm so glad Rosalyn caught you. I think we have some explaining to do."

"It's Trent, please. And no, I apologize for my abrupt dismissal earlier. This young lady convinced me I had the wrong idea." Trent flashed white teeth as he tugged the front of his blazer into place. "We didn't get to officially meet in the melee. I understand you're the one who requested I come?"

"I did, yes." Cade shook the man's tanned hand. "Welcome to Magnolia Bay. I'm the town director and was involved in a movie that was shot here several years ago. I had the idea to see if you guys wanted to come back." He blasted them with a grin Rosalyn knew the camera would love. "Maybe take advantage of those Louisiana tax breaks."

"Ha. Good pitch." Trent leaned back and patted the sunglasses that hung in his shirt collar, as if suddenly remembering where they were. He grinned. "I thought I came to scout a location, but Rosalyn here assured me the people of this town *are* the location."

"Is that so?" Cade's eyes darted to Rosalyn and she offered a quick smile. He looked away, his expression pleasant but his eyes neutral. She hated not being able to tell what he was thinking. Had she done the right thing in rushing after Trent, talking up the town? Cade didn't seem to want much help with anything lately, but she couldn't pass the chance when she saw it. If she could use her bit of fame to help Cade . . . help the Bay . . . she had to.

Even if that did increase her risk of Blaine knowing she was performing. She ran her finger around the edge of the teacup.

The sun drifted behind some clouds, casting a shadow over their table. Rosalyn cleared her throat. "I told Mr. Lawson—*Trent*—

that Magnolia Bay is pretty special. And that I think we got off to a . . . confusing start." She darted another glance at Cade. Would he hear what she meant? "Maybe accidentally misled you."

Cade nodded. "I agree—on both fronts."

Her stomach dropped. He'd missed her subtext.

But then he paused, his gaze tangling with hers. "Sometimes you just need more information before reacting. Time to process."

Her shoulders relaxed and she released a slow breath. Maybe they could move forward, after all. "I agree on that too."

Trent looked between the two of them, his brow pinched. "Um, right. Great. So we're all in agreement . . ."

Oops. She'd almost forgotten what they were *actually* talking about. Rosalyn raised her eyebrows at the scout, found her smile. "So does that mean you'll give Magnolia Bay another shot?"

Trent hesitated. "I have to say, in my decade of scouting, I've never seen anything like . . . that." He gestured toward the window, where the impromptu talent show had gone on. "I was intrigued."

"That's one word for it, I'm sure." Cade offered a little laugh. "I've got to echo Rosalyn and assure you Magnolia Bay is a very special town. That's why I was so adamant about getting someone out here. We have a lot to offer, especially in the summer, and tourist season has officially begun. It's a great time to get something going."

"Obviously there's a lot to consider when scouting for a set." Trent tapped the side of his cup with one finger, his wide-banded ring thumping against the lid. "Proximity to highways, the cultural connotations of the area, and so forth. But one thing I personally consider is the people. That's the pool they fish from for extras, so there's that factor, for one."

"I *did* do a mean Crowd Scene Guy Number Three in that last flick." Cade saluted Trent with his coffee.

Rosalyn snorted. "I've really got to see that movie at some point." She took a sip of tea.

"See?" Cade grinned at Trent and pointed at Rosalyn. "I'm raising the ratings as we speak. Magnolia Bay is definitely the place to shoot."

Trent chuckled. "Oh, I can see, trust me." He wagged a finger between them. "How long have you two been together?"

Rosalyn sprayed her tea.

Cade's eyes widened. "No."

She gulped, coughed. "We're friends."

"We're old rivals."

She and Cade spoke over each other, frowned. Tried again at the same time.

"He almost beat me for valedictorian."

"Her friends hated me—"

"He was always with the jocks—"

"I mean, not that we've *not* thought about—"

"There was this volcano—"

"*Whoa.*" Trent lifted both hands in apology. "Sounds like there's a story there. Might have to get the writers out here for that one."

Rosalyn's chest heated under her shirt and she sought a sip of tea she could actually swallow this time. She pasted on a composed smile, trying not to read too much into Cade's fumbled words. *Not that we've not thought about . . .*

Did he mean last weekend or in the years before? Not that it mattered.

Except it sort of did.

Cade's Adam's apple bobbed as he nodded at Trent. Definitely avoiding eye contact with her. "Please, continue."

"As I was saying, I also consider the overall vibe of the locals. Do they want to be involved? Will they be supportive? Some aren't, if you can imagine." Trent winced. "They don't like progress or blocked roads or anything getting in the way of their daily routine. It can get nasty."

"I'm sure as you saw earlier, the people of Magnolia Bay are *very* invested in their hometown and whatever it takes to help it thrive." Cade hesitated, then glanced at Rosalyn. He raised an eyebrow. "Hopefully you consider passion a plus and not a negative."

Now who was using subtext? Rosalyn licked her suddenly dry lips. "Cade's right. The people here are very passionate. But sometimes passion can get carried away."

She fought to keep her gaze on Trent despite the feel of Cade's gaze on her profile. "But I think if you guys set up shop in the Bay, everyone would put that eagerness aside and adhere to the rules that were set . . . and *not* cause a problem."

Like she had. With her—*ahem*—passion.

Cade held her gaze. "But wouldn't you say sometimes rules cause more harm than good?"

Oh boy. Her stomach fluttered. "Sometimes. But usually rules are there for *everyone's* safety."

"Safety?" Cade grinned, sending her flutters into a full-fledged swarm. "Don't you work without a net?"

Felt like it right now, actually. "Yes . . . and I've got the bruises to prove it."

"Okay, are you sure you two aren't dating?" Trent tilted his head, eyes narrowing. "You have more chemistry than that last rom-com I scouted for."

Cade's eyes widened, then he leaned forward, covering the reaction with a cough. "I think what we're trying to express is that the people of Magnolia Bay will be on board with whatever is expected of them." He kept his eyes on Trent. "Because they'll have to be."

Rosalyn's heart thundered. Was he still talking about them? Or the town? She couldn't tell and honestly, did it matter? They had to find a way to work together through this festival and circus.

Not give in to the chemistry.

"To that point, I have to admit, I purposefully came earlier than I'd told Janie so the town couldn't prep for me. I like to come on scene and see things exactly as they are." Trent spread his hands wide. "Which was a bit of my annoyance. I assumed word leaked and I was being manipulated."

"Well, you were," Cade admitted. "But it was innocent. Someone heard who you were in the diner and word spread quick."

"That's part of the charm around here though." Rosalyn shrugged, grateful for the rush of the AC kicking on overhead and cooling her cheeks that she knew had to still be hot pink. "Everyone is very genuine—what you see is what you get." Except for maybe her and her secrets. She shifted in her chair. The urge to tell Cade the rest of her situation burned on her tongue.

But that could put him in danger. Not to mention—what would he think of her then?

"Of course, the downside to the whole 'what you see is what you get' thing is you might see a waitress in a top hat or a banker on a tightrope." Cade snorted. "But regardless, it's genuine."

"I understand." Trent waved one hand. "I'd hoped to stay under the radar, but then I wouldn't have had the honor of meeting your star here." He smiled at Rosalyn. "I've always been very impressed with aerialists—it's a unique talent."

The praise washed over her, warm at first, then slowly icing over. More expectation. More pressure to make the show go well as a headliner.

A headliner trying to stay out of the news.

"Any town hosting a top-notch circus with professional aerialists is something to notice." Trent took a last sip from his mug. Through the window, the sun reemerged from behind the clouds, warming Rosalyn's hands clutching her nearly empty cup of tea. "A circus is a very creative idea for a fundraiser, by the way."

"Thank you." Cade nodded. "The entire week-long festival should be entertaining. Food trucks, vendor booths, carnival rides, face-painting . . . plus the three nights of the circus at the end."

Rosalyn's stomach tightened. She'd almost forgotten there were *three* separate performances. Three attempts to shine, but not *too* much. Three attempts to help save her hometown, but in a low-key way that wouldn't bring nationwide attention.

Three attempts to *not* fall from the silks—or fall for Cade.

"You guys have sold me. I'll be back next week and do my best to make sure my boss tags along. Could mean good things." Trent brushed off the sleeve of his blazer, then included them both in his grin as he started to stand. "At the end of the day, we're all on the same team, looking for a win, right?"

"Right." Cade nodded, shook his hand again. He shot Rosalyn a victory smile when Trent turned to pick up his cup.

Same team. Rosalyn smiled back, stood more slowly. Maybe that's why things kept getting out of whack. She and Cade were used to being on *opposite* teams. There was clearly a measure of safety in competing against each other, keeping that distance. Look what had happened when she'd crossed that invisible boundary line.

She lingered at their table, taking her time gathering her trash. Eyed Cade's broad back following Trent toward the front door, absorbed his charming smile and charismatic laughter as he clapped the scout on the back and said goodbye. Watched as he turned and scanned the coffee shop with a slight frown, as if looking for where she'd gone.

Acknowledged the way his smile returned when he saw her—and what that smile did to her stomach.

For better or for worse, it looked like for the next few weeks she'd be working without a net once again.

S TANDING ON VILLAGE LANE, CADE UN-
folded the printed map of Magnolia Bay from his pocket and
smoothed the wrinkles. The afternoon sun streamed over
the sheet, and he squinted. Birds chirped overhead, and the scent of
coffee still lingered in his nose. After their successful talk at Chug a
Mug—thanks to Rosalyn—he'd finally felt inspired enough to quit
putting off the inevitable.

Marking these blasted potholes.

"Mind some company?"

Cade turned, tucking his Sharpie behind one ear. Rosalyn stood
on the sidewalk in front of him with her arms crossed self-con-
sciously. She'd changed since Chug a Mug a few hours ago, trading
workout clothes for linen shorts and a sleeveless top that highlighted her toned upper body. After the coffee meeting with Trent,
they'd shared an awkward side-hug and went their separate ways—
him to his office, and her, he assumed, to her home or the studio.

But the sight of her standing there wanting to help brought
more joy than it should, considering her current situation.

Their current situation.

Cade held up his map, risking a smile. "Only if you want to be
put to work."

"Physical or mental?" She raised her eyebrows.

"Bit of both." He tried not to drink in the sight of her, despite his eyes feeling more than a little dehydrated. It seemed like she'd forgiven him for his overreaction in New Orleans, considering how she'd helped lasso Trent back into the game.

But why—for Cade's sake? Or for the sake of the town in general? He knew better than to assume. And without Trent sitting at the table as a buffer, he had no idea how to interpret her body language. Her tone.

Rosalyn held out her open palm. The wind teased loose tendrils of her hair, ever escaping her ponytail. "Got another Sharpie?"

"Oh no. You have to earn Sharpie privileges." He tapped the marker behind his ear, ignoring the way his heard thudded overtime in his chest. They could be friends. This would work. "I have to warn you, I have a very sophisticated rating system."

"I'd expect nothing less." She fell into step beside him as they ambled down the sidewalk. Two kids zoomed around them on bicycles. Down the street, the sprinkler system in front of the library kicked on, sending arcs of water across the lawn. Prisms of light sparkled in the drops.

He dared to relax. See, he could walk beside her without thinking about taking her into his arms again and—okay, maybe not yet. But he was trying.

"So, what are we rating?" Rosalyn asked.

"Potholes."

She snorted, shoving her hands into the front pockets of her shorts. Then her eyes widened at his silence. "Wait. Are you serious?"

"Unfortunately." Cade lifted one hand in a wave as Pastor Dubois cruised Village Lane in his SUV, windows down.

She chuckled. "I assumed we'd be going on a Magnolia Days task when I invited myself along."

"It's connected. I mean, if they might film a movie here, we've got to deal with the potholes sooner rather than later—not to mention I suspect there are multiple bounties on my head until I do." Miley being the top of that list. Although, she was trusting him with her secret, so maybe she'd let up.

Mama D wouldn't though.

He pointed to the map. "This is an aerial view of all the streets in Magnolia Bay, so I plan to mark where the holes are, then rate them in order of which needs the most attention. Then I can start putting pressure on the public works department to get it scheduled." He grimaced. "Assuming Magnolia Days is successful enough that I can."

"Ah." Rosalyn leaned in to see the map straight-on, her ponytail swishing over her shoulder. Good grief, she smelled good. "And we've only got, what? Two weeks or so until the first day of the festival?"

"Right." So much to do still. But he needed to be able to tell the townspeople—Miley, Mama D, Miley's dad, grumpy Mrs. Peters—that he was working on their concerns. That he heard them.

Cade couldn't risk them doubting his competence and not voting for him.

Rosalyn looked up from the map. "This rating system. Is it, like, one through ten? Ten being the biggest hole in need of prioritizing?"

"I'm disappointed in you, Ace." He fought to urge to ease a half-step away from her and instead smiled like she wasn't wreaking havoc on his neuro paths. "I said it was sophisticated."

"Oh, I'm sorry." She laughed as they continued strolling down Village Lane. "Let's see. Roman numerals?"

He held up one finger to tell her to wait, then turned away as he drew a quick circle on the paper where the pothole in front of Magnolia Blossom resided. He scribbled something next to it, then turned back and presented the map with a flourish.

"Starter home." Rosalyn read out loud, frowned, then smirked. "In other words, too small to house a family of four?"

"Exactly." He fluttered the paper. "Chug a Mug was already rated, so I figured I'd keep it going. Brilliant, right?"

"And to think I beat you for valedictorian."

"The world's an unfair place." Cade handed her the marker. "But at least now you've earned your Sharpie privileges."

"I'll be sure to give this mission the respect it deserves." She tucked the marker behind her own ear, and for a moment, he wondered if they could do this—be friends. Work together. Have fun.

Not make out in the rain.

But only if they completely cleared the air.

"Listen, Rosalyn." He kept his gaze on the beds of tulips bordering the sidewalks, the passing cars on the sun-speckled road, the missing shingles on the roof of Cajun Cuts salon. "Thanks for helping with Trent."

Though he hated that she had to. Hated that for once he couldn't convince someone to do something. Cade was losing his edge, and at the worst time possible. Was it because of the distraction Rosalyn presented? Or the stress of the upcoming mayoral campaign and the sudden accompanying anxiety attacks? Or was it from carrying the entire town on his shoulders?

Okay, maybe he had good reasons for losing it.

Rosalyn kept pace beside him. "I figured it was the least I could do after I handled . . ." She swallowed. ". . . New Orleans so poorly."

"No, *I* handled that poorly." He stopped and faced her now, the map crinkling in his grip. "You didn't—and *don't*—owe me anything. We're not, you know. Dating, or whatever."

Did she wince, or was it wishful thinking?

"Maybe not." Rosalyn hesitated. "But I still feel like I led you on."

"Did you?" Oops. Hadn't meant to be blunt.

She pulled in her lower lip. "More like I got caught up in the moment."

That made two of them. A moment he'd relive for the next several weeks if he wasn't careful.

Still, he had to know. "I understand a technicality is still a technicality, but there's more to all this than just a marriage certificate, isn't there?" Cade asked.

She nodded, brow pinched. A shadow of regret clouded her expression. "It's . . . complicated."

Man, he wanted to push that further. Crack that word open, see what lived inside. There was clearly *still* more to this story. But if she wasn't volunteering the details, it wasn't his place to ask.

So he inhaled instead, shoved aside the rest of the what-ifs, and gently touched her arm. "I guess we've never had great timing, have we?"

A semi-sad smile twisted her lips. "I guess not." She took his hand in hers, squeezed, and then let go.

He should do the same.

They walked in a silence, the sun warm overhead. Cade opened his mouth, unsure what to say next, but feeling it was all still so unfinished.

He was about to crack a joke about the potholes when Rosalyn spoke first. "Thanks for keeping my secret, by the way. No one else knows about this, not even my parents." She looked at her feet as they walked. "I can't disappoint my mom that way."

"I won't tell, but . . ." Cade frowned. "I'm sure they'd try to help if they knew."

"You don't understand. There's no way I can tell my mom her daughter is getting divorced before she even has a wedding." Rosalyn shook her head. "It's not easy being Rose Dupree's daughter."

"Oh, I get family pressure side, trust me." Cade's chest tightened. He considered telling her about the political shoes he was expected to fill soon, but it didn't feel right. This was about her. "What do you think will happen if she finds out?"

"Nothing outwardly. She's too poised for that." Rosalyn took a breath. "Basically, my mom warned me about Blaine before I signed with him, but she could only source 'mother's intuition' as her reason. I thought it was another control attempt, a way for her to say 'told you so' about my choosing aerial, so I disregarded it. But now . . . I guess she was right."

Cade wanted to take her hand again, encourage her to keep talking. But he forced his hand sat his sides. "Right, how? Didn't you say Blaine helped you get out of Saudi Arabia?"

"Yeah, but he's gotten me into a pretty big jam, and I went with it." Rosalyn squeezed her eyes shut. "It was dumb. *I* was dumb. But you've got enough on your plate without me adding to it with all that."

"Never too busy to listen." He'd stop right now and sit criss-cross applesauce on the sidewalk if she'd tell him everything. But that'd be an odd look for a mayor-elect. "Look, I know this isn't my business, but it sounds like a big enough to deal to tell your parents. Maybe they'll surprise you."

"You don't get it." Rosalyn's expression tightened. "I can't disappoint her again over being a bad judge of character."

"Again?"

"It's a whole story. But basically, Mom married into money. I never knew that until we went to my grandmother's funeral when I was . . . I guess nine years old. Grandma's house—the one my mom grew up in—was in this low-income neighborhood. Bars on the windows, overgrown weeds, high crime stats. Mom acted weird, but I didn't care. I was just excited to see my cousins I never knew about."

"Seems right for a nine-year-old." Cade gently guided her off the sidewalk and onto the grass as another bicyclist pedaled by, a cat riding in the front basket. "Go on."

"My cousins were older than me. Preteens and young teenagers. I thought we'd all play games while the adults did the post-funeral lunch prep, but they wanted to walk to the gas station down the street." She scrunched her nose. "In hindsight, I don't think I even asked permission. I assumed it'd be okay because I was with my cousins, and they were 'old enough.'"

Cade slowed his pace, turning to give her his full attention.

"I wondered how we were going to pay for anything, but once we got there, they started stuffing candy bars in their pockets. Soda cans in their jackets. Gum, keychains, you name it. We probably stole a hundred dollars or more of junk." Rosalyn shook her head, her brow pinched. "I didn't say anything. I turned down their offer of a snack, but I didn't try to stop them."

He softened his tone. "You were a kid. It's understandable."

"I knew better. When we got back to the house and got caught with all the stuff, Mom said I'd humiliated her." Rosalyn's cheeks flushed. "I realized later, after eavesdropping on her and my dad, that she was embarrassed over her roots. She took a lot of pride in escaping that town and making a better life for herself, so she panicked when she thought I'd been pulled into that world. I was supposed to be different."

Cade frowned. "Did you ever tell her you didn't steal?"

"I tried, but my cousins lied and said it was my idea." Rosalyn started walking again, giving him no choice but to follow. "Regardless, I stayed silent in that store when I should have spoken up *then*. Mom told me I had bad discernment." She shrugged. "And she was right—Blaine being Exhibit B. I shouldn't trust myself."

They walked in silence as Cade tried to process her story. "Is that why you were so driven in school? So determined to beat me, to be the best?" He could see it. "You were trying to prove you weren't a bad person."

"Maybe so. I already was the oddball in the family, having traded ballet for aerial." She fiddled with the strings on her hoodie. "I guess I figured since I didn't want to conform to something more traditional, then I needed to be perfect at everything else."

"Perfect at the things your mom would be proud of. Would brag about." He got it now. "Grades. Scholarships. College."

Rosalyn stopped in front of a pothole on the corner of Village Lane. "What do you think about this one? Studio apartment?"

He snorted. "I knew you'd be good at this."

Cade watched as Rosalyn filled in the map. "So—that's it? The whole story?"

Rosalyn glanced over her shoulder, then nodded, avoiding his eyes. "The important parts."

He wondered. But she'd trusted him with this much of her story—if there was more, she'd tell him eventually. "Are you sure there's nothing I can do to help? You know, legally with your paperwork? Maybe Blaine isn't familiar with how to get it dissolved quickly."

Rosalyn quickly shook her head. "No, he'll get it done. It's just the international red tape."

Convenient, but—he wouldn't push his opinion.

He cleared his throat and pointed to the pothole to her right. "So, what do you think?"

Relief filled her eyes, and she tapped one finger on her chin and pretended to study the shallow divot. "Pup tent?"

"Nailed it." He scribbled the words on the map, making sure his hand didn't shake in front of her. Making sure the plan cooking in his mind wasn't obvious.

Whether she wanted help or not, what *was* obvious was she needed it. And if she wasn't going to confide in her parents, then the least he could do was check out the red flags waving in his Yale-educated subconscious about the legalities of it.

Secretly, of course. Because they'd finally seemed to find their way back to a fledgling friendship, and he wouldn't screw it up again.

No matter how much he wanted more with her.

Seventeen

THE NEXT WEEK FLEW BY IN A TANGLE of silks, spreadsheets, and veggie burgers.

Rosalyn waited at the front desk in the Magnolia Library for Harper, who had gone to get the final schedule for the Friends of the Library booth that Mrs. Peters insisted on Cade having. A cluster of kids giggled from the children's area, and the scent of lemon cleaner hovered over the polished counter. The bank of computers across the far wall were empty, save for a man in a fedora hunched over the desktop keyboard. He looked up, made eye contact, then looked back to the screen. To her left, a janitor ran a push-broom over the foyer floor.

Rosalyn soaked in the quiet, the peace, the scent of old novels. Since her confession during the mapping, she'd seen Cade every day and, thankfully, they'd found their old—or maybe new?—rhythm. She'd brought him lunch that Elisa supplied from the diner, helped update spreadsheets on her way back from training, and trotted with him around town, checking on vendors and responding to a dozen phone calls. She'd even snuck him a veggie patty once or twice and he hadn't noticed it wasn't beef, which only proved how stressed he was.

He thought he was hiding it, but she recognized the crinkles in the corner of his eyes, the forced edges to his smile, from senior year study hall. When Mrs. Peters insisted Cade come get the schedule that he absolutely did *not* need, she'd immediately volunteered in his stead.

The midday walk—and the brief respite from the proximity to Cade in his office—had done wonders to clear her own head. Forgetting their kiss and remembering all the new boundaries hadn't been easy the past week. Neither had trying to figure out if the chemistry she still felt was only on her side, or if maybe he was that talented an actor after all.

Of course, checking over her shoulder every few hours reminded her why she was making the choices she was making.

She and Cade hadn't spoken of her issues with Blaine again, save for Cade asking once more if there was anything he could do to help on the legal side. To which she'd adamantly assured him no. The last thing she needed was Cade discovering the truth about her loan, the Mafia. She couldn't put anyone else in her danger—hence her ultimate reason for not wanting her parents to know. If the wrong people realized how wealthy Dad was, they could come after her family for what Rosalyn owed.

She'd much rather grit her teeth and pay off her debt and put it all behind her. But that meant trusting Blaine to do what he'd said he was going to do . . . and somehow keeping him happy *and* at bay until he did.

"Here it is!" Harper returned to the counter, sliding the laminated schedule across the desk. She winked. "I hope Cade is paying you extra to be his assistant."

"Ha." Rosalyn took the list, still warm from the laminator. "I think you're the one going over and above." She wiggled the sheet of paper.

Harper rolled her eyes with a smile. "I don't mind. It could be worse." She peeked over her shoulder and lowered her voice.

"That's one plus of having been friends with Amber for all of high school—she prepared us for difficult bosses."

"She'd probably be mad at me now if she knew I was helping Cade this much for free." Rosalyn grinned. "I can almost hear her giving me a lecture on women's rights and wages."

Harper straightened a stack of bookmarks. "To be fair, she probably kept us from unnecessary heartache. Getting past her to go on a date wasn't worth the fight, was it?"

Well, Cade might have been worth it. But he hadn't ever asked.

And Rosalyn sure wasn't going to have been prom date number three.

She shrugged, hoping to appear unaffected. Old habits died hard when it came to talking about boys with this group of girls. "Maybe."

"You do realize why she hated Cade so much, right?" Harper asked.

Rosalyn stilled. "What do you mean?"

Harper's eyes sparkled with a conspiratorial wink. "She had a crush on him, obviously."

"What?" No way. "Amber didn't like *anyone*. Especially not Cade."

"Gabby told me. Amber got drunk one night, right after starting her freshman year at Harvard. She called Gabby, all in her feels about 'the one that got away' and started telling stories about Cade. That's why she was always so hard on him—she knew he'd never go for her." Harper shrugged. "Gabby told me all that a long time ago."

Wow. No wonder Amber was always so dead set on keeping Rosalyn and Cade apart. She shook her head. "I guess we all have our secrets, don't we?"

"That's for sure." Harper winced. "Hopefully most of them got left behind in our teenaged years."

Wouldn't that be nice? Rosalyn tilted her head. "Speaking of dating, are you seeing anyone these days?"

"I'm sure Amber would be thrilled to know I'm not." Harper wrinkled her nose. "Mrs. Peters too. She was fussing about one of our part-timers leaving early for an anniversary date." She looked up at the ceiling. "I believe the words 'irresponsible' and 'frivolous' were both used."

"Surprising. I remember Mrs. Peters being a romantic. Hanging all those valentine decorations up when we were younger." Rosalyn smiled. "The paper hearts would rain glitter during story hour, and my mom would have a heck of a time brushing my hair later."

"I think her snub toward romance is new." Harper shrugged. "Or at least, that's what my coworkers say. I haven't worked here long."

"There's a story there, I'm sure."

"Who knows? Maybe I'll write it one day." Harper shook back her long red hair.

"You should!" Rosalyn checked her watch. "I better get back to the office, but I'll be sure to come see your booth next week during the festival." She skimmed the schedule and pointed to a bullet point halfway down the list. "Preferably during the story hour when you're dressed like a princess?" She grinned.

"I get paid very well here." Harper laughed. "Plus, it's all fodder for that future book, right?"

They said their goodbyes, and Rosalyn left the library, clutching the list Cade didn't need. Should she even show it to him, or ditch it before she got back? She headed down the street toward Cade's office, tucking the list under her arm.

She tilted her head back as she walked, eyes closed, face to the sunshine pouring over Village Lane. The scent of flowers lingered in the air, and despite the beads of sweat forming on her back in the summer humidity, it was a good day. Warmth seeped into her muscles, loosening the tension in her upper back. Her knee felt fine today too, which was good news for the festival—and bad news for her future. Her days of stalling before returning to Blaine and her performance circuit were nearing an end.

The hair on the back of Rosalyn's neck stood on end.

She turned, but her vision was still temporarily affected by the residual brightness of the sun. She blinked, fighting the distorted shadows. But nothing was there, just an empty sidewalk covered in chalk drawings and a squirrel darting up a pine tree.

Weird. She'd definitely sensed . . . something.

She turned toward the other side of the street and there—Sadie was checking the mailbox in front of Second Story. The middle-aged woman, dressed in a flowing dress, waved, and Rosalyn waved back, her heart rate slowing to normal. That had to have been it.

But she should probably walk with her eyes open all the same.

Rosalyn kept on down Village Lane, which seemed oddly deserted when compared to her previous walks with Cade. Then again, it was almost noon. The Magnolia Blossom was probably hopping—which sounded good today—but she couldn't justify yet *another* veggie burger on her limited funds. She shook her head. Weird that months ago she was on a world tour, dining on champagne and caviar, and now she was avoiding daily diner specials because they were too expensive.

But after her debt was paid, she could work long enough to rebuild her savings. And then . . . well, then, who knew? She'd be free—and that was all that mattered.

A shadow darted across the street.

Rosalyn jerked to a stop, pulse thudding in her ears. Was that . . . No. Just the sun going behind a cloud. She rolled her eyes. What did she think was going to happen? No one knew where she was that wasn't supposed to know, and Blaine hadn't even tried to call the past few days.

She was safe.

So why the chills prickling her neck?

Rosalyn glanced back, wondering if she could keep going to Cade's office or backtrack to Sadie. And say . . . what? *Don't look now, but the Mafia might be after me?* Right.

She resumed walking.

A branch cracked.

She spun again, squinting to see the source. Someone had definitely ducked behind that oak on the corner.

Her heart stopped, then lunged back against her chest as she peered harder into the foliage. A person. A *man*.

She gasped. The man with the fedora.

From the library.

Now walking straight toward her.

Cade leaned back in his office chair, grateful that Rosalyn had gone to the library for him because, A—Mrs. Peters's demand that he have a printed schedule of the Friends of the Library booth was a ridiculous waste of time, and mostly B—it gave him a chance to finish the sleuthing he'd started and not been able to finish yet on Rosalyn's situation.

Keeping one eye on the door for her return, he tapped a few more keys, pulling up a third browser tab and waiting as the icon spun. A small tower of books he'd brought back from Yale were stacked, the top one flipped open, next to his pencil cup and a half-eaten bag of Doritos. His computer hummed. *Come on, load.*

With every spin, his confidence sank. This was a long shot. He'd failed the bar—what business did he have thinking he'd find a needle in a legal haystack?

He'd already called and sweet-talked Liz over at the courthouse to give him access to the digital files, normally only available via an account and monthly fee. No one had time for that. So he'd played the mayor's son card he despised yet kept up his sleeve for a time such as this.

Because Rosalyn was worth it.

That access led him to a few dead-ends and more eye-spiraling technical jargon than he'd read in years but eventually proved what he'd thought he'd remembered about marriage license clauses from law school.

He hit a few more keys.

Aha. Further proof filled his monitor.

Cade pulled back up the second tab he'd saved and re-read the fine print. Hope filled his chest—which was silly. This changed nothing between him and Rosalyn, necessarily.

But it could change a lot for her.

He stared at the blinking cursor and frowned, tapping one finger against the mouse. One problem remained.

He had to tell her.

Which meant he had to admit to doing exactly what she'd asked him *not* to do.

Cade stood abruptly, pocketed his keys, and headed to the office foyer. A rush of cool AC blasted him in the hall. Maybe he could start walking and meet Rosalyn on her way back from the library. Try along the way to figure out the right words to let her know the good news.

His heart thudded. "I'll be back, Pearl." He waved at his secretary, who quickly exited her solitaire game.

"I'll hold down the fort." Pearl offered a salute. "Feel free to bring back some Bayou Beignets."

Those did sound good. Cade rode the elevator down to the first floor. The door chimed and opened, and he stepped out as a blonde figure burst inside.

They collided hard.

He steadied the woman bouncing off his chest, grabbing her arms to keep them upright. The scent of citrus filled his nose.

Rosalyn.

"Ace—what are you doing?" He cupped her cheek, scanning her face for injuries. "Are you okay?"

Crimson flushed both cheeks. Her chest heaved as if she'd been running. "I don't know." Panic lingered in her eyes as she struggled out of his grip and turned around, looking behind her.

His arm automatically wrapped around her, protecting her, and he tugged her out of the way of the elevator. "What happened?" He looked over her head and skimmed the lobby, empty except for three potted ferns and a tired coffee pot gurgling next to a sleeve of Styrofoam cups.

Not a threat in sight.

"He was right behind me." Rosalyn faced Cade, her shoulders tense beneath his hands.

"Who?" He slid his hands down her arms, catching her fingers. She held on. "Who was?"

"This man, in a hat." She drew a shuddered breath. "I think he followed me from the library."

A man? Cade pushed past her to the glass front doors of the complex. He stepped outside. No one.

He turned back to Rosalyn, searching her face. Trying to understand what she wasn't saying. "He's gone." But was he ever there? Maybe Cade wasn't the only one stressing lately, fighting panic attacks.

Rosalyn nibbled her lip, wrapping her arms around herself as she slowly joined him outside. "Maybe I was paranoid."

Cade feigned seriousness. "Must have been a really bad hat."

She didn't smile. "He was in the library, and then he was behind a tree, watching me. When I saw him, he came toward me, but I ran the last block here." Her gaze searched the streets, mostly empty during the lunch hour save for a few dog-walkers.

"Come on. Let's talk." Cade took her elbow, led her to a bench nestled in a grove of trees near the office complex. She didn't protest, and it was then he realized she still clutched the paper she'd gone to the library for under her arm.

He tugged it free. "I see this made it unscathed."

She smiled, finally, and his heart cheered. Victory. She surrendered the laminated paper. "Like a roach in a nuclear bomb."

He tossed it on the bench next to them, draped one arm behind her. "Spill it, Ace. Why did a man in a hat scare you so badly?"

She pressed her fingers against her temples, took a deep breath. "This is embarrassing."

"Probably not as embarrassing as his hat."

Score. Another smile.

She met his eyes then, spotty shadows speckling her face as the tree branches overhead interrupted the sun. "I think I overreacted."

"That's okay. But something is making you scared. Suspicious."

Her emerald gaze left his and moved past him, looking at something behind him. She washed pale. "There he is."

He turned in time to see a man—yes, in a really bad fedora—quick-stepping down the sidewalk toward them.

Cade quickly stood, positioning himself in front of Rosalyn. "Can I help you?" He didn't even need Simon LeMoine. The adrenaline, topped with the desire to help Rosalyn, to be what she needed, gave him enough confidence to take down the entire Magnolia High football team.

Plus, the guy was scrawny.

The man drew close enough for Cade to see he was maybe ten years older than them. He wore a wrinkled button-down and a sheepish expression and carried a camera. "I'm so sorry. I think I frightened you, Miss Dupree."

Rosalyn's hand landed on Cade's back as she stood, moving to his side but not fully away from his protection. "Do I know you?"

He stopped a respectful distance away, took off the fedora. "Name's Albert Wally. I work for the Pelican in Jefferson Parish."

Gestured with his camera. "Heard you were performing in the Cajun Circus and wanted a photo."

Paparazzi.

"Oh." Rosalyn's sigh escaped, slowly, like a leak from a balloon. "The newspaper."

Well, maybe she was relieved, but Cade was annoyed. "Dude, you followed her? Then came out of the bushes at her?" He took a step forward—Simon LeMoine would've been proud—and glared. "That's nuts, man."

Albert backed up, hands raised "I'm sorry. Candids get better page time. But she saw me, so I thought I'd explain who I was. Not a creeper or anything." He shrugged, pink swiping his pale cheeks. "I haven't worked this job long. Not very good at it yet."

"Maybe consider a different profession." Cade crossed his arms over his chest. "Like one where people give you permission to take their picture."

"I'll prove I don't have any saved." Albert extended his camera, fiddled with the buttons. The lens cap fell off and hit the ground, and he groaned.

"No, it's fine." Rosalyn shook her head. "Please . . . go." She sank back to the bench.

Albert grabbed the cap, fumbling to replace it as he dipped his hat and left.

Cade waited until his figure was all but out of sight before he sat back next to Rosalyn, flexing his fingers that he hadn't realized were curled in fists. "I always wondered how famous you really were. Guess that answers my question."

Her face was still pale, her chuckle forced. Something wasn't right. And she didn't even know his news. Would she clam up when he told her what he'd learned about her marriage? The pressure to have her tell him whatever this secret was first, before he risked shutting her down, fisted in his chest.

He let his arm rest behind her on the back of the bench, his fingers lightly grazing her shoulder. Providing a point of contact, something concrete. For both of them. "Rosalyn, who did you think Albert was?"

She stared at the clover growing near their feet.

"Come on, it's me." Nerves bunched in Cade's stomach. "Just tell me."

"Fine." She swallowed, let out a half-choked laugh. "I thought he was with the Mafia."

One day she was going to stop shocking Cade every time she opened her mouth.

To his credit, when she dropped this bomb, he didn't so much as flinch. Instead, he went still on the bench, to the point that she stared at him until he finally blinked and she became certain he was breathing.

"Okay." A muscle jumped in his jaw and he nodded. Didn't laugh. Didn't panic. Didn't doubt her.

That was the greatest gift he could have given.

She released a sigh, her pulse still struggling to slow after the false alarm. Birds chirped, killing the silence that landed between her and Cade.

Cade's arm pulled free from around her on the bench, and it wasn't until that moment she realized how much that light graze on her shoulder had comforted her. He leaned forward, bracing his arms on his knees. "Is there more about that you want to tell me?"

She hesitated, and he held up one hand. "On second thought…" He angled to face her, still bent forward, chin propped on his fingers. "Let me go first. I have a confession."

Uh-oh. Though honestly, after her last two, how bad could his be?

She crossed one leg over the other, settling in. "I'm listening."

"Something I remembered from law school niggled at me after you told me about Blaine." He winced, looked at the ground. Scuffed his shoe through the grass. "So I did some digging."

Even though she'd asked him not to? Her chest tightened. "Go on."

"I have all the proof on my computer upstairs, if you want to see the proof, but Rosalyn . . ." His voice trailed off, and he held her gaze. "I don't think you're married."

Even the birds quieted for that one.

She waited. Afraid to hope. Annoyed he'd ignored her request, but also—what if he was right? He spoke with such confidence. "Can you explain?"

"Of course." His shoulders relaxed, and he sat up, an easiness filling his countenance now. "First, I saw that Blaine hadn't filed for an annulment in the US. He filed for a marriage certificate."

"Right." Rosalyn frowned. "He said he had to do that step before we could file for the divorce. Something to do with the international complication."

Cade's eyes softened. "I think he lied."

She started to defend him, then realized Blaine *would* lie. The only reason she wanted to defend Blaine was to defend herself and the bad decisions she kept making.

Cade continued. "What *is* true is that there's a clause on marriage certificates that reference whether the marriage was entered into under duress."

She sucked in a breath. Duress. Why hadn't she thought of that?

"You can file to contest the marriage. And with the origin of the marriage happening overseas, *and* with the fact that you and Blaine have never co-habited, I'd imagine it wouldn't take much to get it approved. Any decent lawyer could help with that." Cade frowned. "If you want to have it approved, that is."

"Of course I do." Her thoughts raced. Blaine had lied, that much was certain—and at this point, not surprising. Not after the way he'd changed since they'd come back to the US. But this seemed a bit much, even for him. Maybe he really didn't know how the law worked.

Her stomach clenched. Or maybe he didn't want to annul it.

As if reading her mind, Cade quirked an eyebrow at her. "Can you think of any reason that Blaine would be trying to cement your marriage further rather than annul it?" He hesitated. "Did you two ever—"

Rosalyn shuddered. "*No.*"

"Making sure. That could complicate the process."

"Is that the only reason you'd care?" The words she'd never intended to speak rode the last of her adrenaline right out of her lips. She pressed them together, but it was too late. They were out there, between them.

Cade's eyes widened. He leaned back against the bench. "No."

Oh. He'd actually answered. Her stomach cartwheeled. "Sorry. That wasn't fair."

"Agreed."

Silence pulsed again. She wanted to sink into the bench, then below it. Straight down to the core of the earth. Where she could quit making a mess of things. Quit listening to the wrong voices—namely, her own.

"Look, Ace. I've taken punches for you before." He snorted. "Thought I might have to again today."

"Nah, you totally had that guy." She smiled, the compliment the least she could offer.

"I'm serious. I want to help you." He held both of his hands up in a sign of surrender. "No more, no less."

"I appreciate it." She did. Even if she wanted it to be "more." This was too complicated, too much.

Always the timing, with them.

Cade's Adam's apple bobbed. "So you're not mad I sleuthed?"

"If that means this whole marriage issue can be put behind me sooner, then no. I'm grateful." Confused, maybe, about Blaine and his motives. But grateful.

"Do you want me to file the dissolution request for you?" A different question lingered in Cade's eyes, one she couldn't quite put words to and wasn't sure she wanted to try.

"Yes, please." Blaine might get notice that she'd taken that legal step, but hopefully not until *after* the circus. She could smooth things over, then, once she was back performing professionally. And then once her debt was paid, she could be free of Blaine forever.

Maybe free of all of it.

Cade nodded. "I'll handle it first thing in the morning. Whatever paperwork is involved, I'll print and bring for you to sign."

"Thank you. I know you're busy."

"Not too busy for this." He tucked his hands behind his neck. "Which brings us back to—the Mafia?"

"That brings us back to Blaine, still."

Cade squinted, clearly trying to follow. "So what's his angle?"

"I don't know, other than maybe control of some kind? That's Blaine's specialty." She used to find it endearing, the way he handled everything for her. Protective.

Just another thing she'd been wrong about.

"Well, if this marriage procrastination isn't about s—" Cade cleared his throat, gestured toward Rosalyn. "—um, you, *personally*, then I'd wager it's probably about money."

"He makes a great living off all his clients, including me." Rosalyn tilted his head. "He even got his manager's cut of my world tour money in advance, so I don't know why that would be a factor."

"So, let me get this straight. Is Blaine *in* the Mafia?"

"No." Rosalyn snorted. "That's who loaned me the money for the tour I had to pay upfront. Blaine has connections everywhere, but I never assumed like that. He told me the loan was from a bank."

Cade nodded slowly. "And you had no reason to assume otherwise."

"Exactly." A leaf drifted into Rosalyn's lap, and she picked it up, spun it between her fingers. "After I fell and got hurt, he got weird. Anxious, which is not like him. Said we were on a strict payment plan, and if I didn't keep up my shows, we'd never make enough to keep current on the loan."

"Which wouldn't have been a big deal if the loan had been through a traditional bank."

"Right. That's what made him confess where the money was from." She told Cade about the panic on Blaine's face, the urgency beneath the surface as he tried to play it off and finally told her the whole story. "I've been watching over my shoulder ever since, unsure how big a deal this is. Or if anyone knows where to find me."

"And you don't have the money to pay it off, to be free of it?"

"No. I thought I had more money saved than I do, but Blaine handles my business accounts and travel expenses. Last he said, my balance was pretty low."

Cade frowned. "Blaine handles that?"

"Just the business accounts—he does for several clients. I didn't have enough cash to fund the whole tour, so I paid part of it from my personal savings and funded the rest." She pinched the bridge of her nose. "Apparently, funded it through the Mafia. What kind of low-budget movie is my life right now?"

"Trent did say he could send writers to script us out." Cade smiled and reached over again, wrapped his arm around her. His side was warm from the sun, and she soaked in the comfort. He smelled like designer cologne and hope. "Don't worry—we'll get this figured out. I'll file those contest forms, and you'll get unmarried as fast as you were married."

The birds were chirping again, the sun peeking around a cloud.

Rosalyn closed her eyes, laid her head on his shoulder. "You make it sound so easy."

"We just have to go through the steps." Cade's frame stiffened, as if he were suddenly holding his breath. "I still think there's something shady though. Do you mind letting me snoop further?"

"Go ahead. You've already helped this much." She'd be a fool to turn down Cade's expertise. If she'd let him help sooner, maybe she could have been legally clear by now.

"I'll need access to your accounts."

She paused, nodded. Cade, she could trust. "No problem. I'll get you everything."

"Good." Cade dipped his head to rest his cheek against her hair. His voice rumbled low in her ear. "Now, in the meantime—there's this mild issue of an entire circus to put on, a town to save, and a week in which to do it."

She smiled into his shoulder. "I'm prepared to give my best performance yet."

Starting with pretending she didn't want to tilt her head up, press her lips against Cade's cheek, and start a fire sure to burn them both.

Eighteen

For better or for worse, Magnolia Days had arrived.

Cade strolled the roped off festival grounds, roughly a quarter mile from Village Lane on the south side of town and narrowly dodged a stray puddle. After several days of rain, the sun had come out and almost everything had dried. It now shone brightly in a crisp blue sky, while puffs of clouds drifted lazily across the expanse, casting the occasional shadow over rows of decorated booths arranged across the grounds.

The red and white striped circus tent stood tall in the back of the field, ready to house components of the circus as they arrived during the week. A raised stage had been constructed in the middle of the lot, complete with sound system and risers for musical performances, and the Ferris wheel was partially constructed, set to be completed by Wednesday. Vendors were putting final touches on their booths, and the food trucks—judging by the various heavenly aromas wafting from the parking lot—were prepping for the coming rush once Magnolia Days opened in half an hour.

He'd pulled it off.

Cade lifted one hand to Farmer Branson, who carefully stacked an array of fresh vegetables on a stand. Two tents down, Miley scowled as she arranged logo mugs on a table next to pre-packaged coffee.

Cade checked his watch. Almost noon—odd that Rosalyn wasn't here. She'd promised to come early and help vendors with last minute needs, plus she'd been eager to see inside the circus tent to figure out her rigging for her first performance Wednesday night. They'd worked together this past week on the final preparations for the festival, and he'd filed the contest paperwork for her as promised. He'd also gotten information from his deep dive into her accounts, and she wasn't going to like it. Now it was a matter of when to tell her without scaring her further. She'd finally stopped looking over her shoulder this past week.

Though he'd started looking over his.

"Cade!" Sadie waved him over from her secondhand books booth, a light wind blowing the hem of her maxi skirt. "Can you give me a hand with this banner?"

He hurried over and took the end of the banner Sadie had created using book pages and twine and held it to the corner of the canopy. "About here?"

"Perfect." She handed him the hook and he stood on tiptoe to secure it in place. "And don't worry—no books were harmed in the making of this banner. These pages are from books that came to my shop already destroyed."

"I would never assume otherwise." No one loved books like Sadie—not even Mrs. Peters. "Need anything else?"

"I think that's it." She craned her neck to look at the banner and gave him a nod. "I appreciate it."

"No problem." He surveyed the tables full of novels sorted by genre, the wooden rack containing pressed-flower bookmarks, and the kitchen towels offering quotes from Austen and Brontë. "Looks like you're ready."

Worry lines creased her brow. "Business has been down, so I'm hoping it's a good turnout." Then a soft smile relit her face. "But you've done a great job putting everything together, so I'm sure it'll go well."

"Thanks, Sadie." He followed her gaze, taking in the grounds. They were all set, weren't they?

"Oh, there is one thing I forgot to ask." Sadie adjusted a bookmark that had slipped out of place. "Where are the porta-potties? I usually avoid them, but my niece will be helping me with the booth this evening, and she's only six. It's inevitable."

"Totally understand." Cade turned and pointed. "They're lined up right over by the food trucks and picnic—"

He blinked.

Where *were* the porta-potties?

He lowered his arm and turned a full circle, but the twelve yellow structures he'd ordered weeks ago were nowhere to be seen.

His heart crashed to his Sperrys the same time Zoey ran toward him from her beignet booth, three spots down. "Cade!" Her eyes were wide, cheeks dusted with powdered sugar. "We're missing the porta—"

"I know." His gut twisted. Of all the things to forget. How many times had he started to confirm the delivery and gotten distracted? He'd much rather have forgotten those blasted poodles than the toilets.

Farmer Branson ambled toward them, thumbs hooked in his suspenders. "What's the ruckus?"

"Is everything okay?" Miley joined them, carrying a coffee cup.

Sadie hugged a book to her chest. "There's no toilets."

Miley's frown deepened as she turned accusing eyes to Cade. "I'm not a wood frog, Cade. People need bathrooms."

"I realize that." Cade looked between all their worried expressions and tried to hide his own. Right now, he had to try to save face. "I'm sure they're running late on the delivery. I bet they'll be here any minute."

He backed away and lifted his cell phone, as if that were proof. "I'll make a quick call to be sure."

Their hiked brows and pursed lips looked as wary as he felt.

"Be right back." He left the group whispering as he turned—and planted his foot directly in the puddle he'd avoided. Biting back a word his mother would have called Pastor Dubois about when he was younger, Cade shook muddy water off his shoe and scrolled his contacts for the number. *Please just be late.*

The phone rang three times, four.

He winced, pacing the other direction as the sun beamed down on his head.

Five rings.

Voicemail. Cade shoved his phone back in his pocket. Did that mean they weren't in the office because they were on their way? It could be a good sign.

But his sinking heart predicted otherwise. Cade stared across the grounds to the empty spot where the porta-potties should have been. The smell of seasoned taco meat wafted on the breeze, and his stomach growled.

He had to figure out a new plan. If there were no bathrooms, people wouldn't stay. Which meant less money spent at the food trucks, fewer people attending the musical performances, fewer wares sold at all the booths . . .

Less income for the town in general and less spreading of the word to friends and family.

Technically, the fault lay with the company he'd ordered from, right? They'd charged his credit card but didn't deliver. Unless, of course, they hadn't actually charged his card. Then it was on him for not confirming.

He pulled up the banking account linked to the card he and his father used for the town and typed in his credentials. The page spun briefly, refusing to load. "Come on." He held his phone up for better connection.

"We have a problem."

He thought about not looking toward the stricken female voice. Thought about yelling "One disaster at a time!" Thought about sprinting toward the food trucks and not stopping until he had a breakfast burrito safely in hand.

But that's not what a future mayor would do, was it? Or a Landry.

He slapped on the smile and turned to see Mrs. Peters bustling toward him as fast as she could over the uneven ground. She expertly dodged the puddle he'd stepped in, giving it a look down her nose.

"How can I help you, Mrs. Peters?" He glanced at the phone in his hand. The loading icon still spun.

The librarian patted the top of her white hair. "As I'm sure you know, I'm part of Magnolia Grace's choir that's performing at the festival this week."

He didn't know. "Yes ma'am?"

"I came to check out the stage situation, report back to the music minister." She curled her arms around her navy pantsuit, the shoulder pads of which stretched wider than her hips. "And thank heavens I did."

"What's wrong, Mrs. Peters?" He snuck another glance at his phone. The app had loaded, and he subtly clicked the account button to scan the transactions. Another spinning wheel filled the screen.

"A senior choir can't stand on risers like that." Her lips pursed as if Cade shown have already known. "We'll break our arthritic knees."

"I'm sure we can adjust the risers for your performance. But you'll need varying heights somehow, or no one will be able to see you."

"Are you calling me short, young Landry?" She lifted her chin—

and her five-foot frame—as high as she could while holding her glare.

"I . . ." He looked down again. "I'm, uh—" The website had loaded. "Yes!"

"Excuse me!" Mrs. Peter's eyes flashed.

"No! Not you." Cade held up his phone. "I was waiting on something."

She scowled. "Back in my day, young professionals had manners."

"I know. And they returned their library books on time too." Cade gestured with his cell again. "I'm sorry, this is an emergency." But now he couldn't look at the data in his hand without proving her point.

She bristled. "So is the stage situation."

"I'll make sure the risers—" Cade sniffed. Why did the air suddenly smell like essential oils?

"Cade, darling." Madame Paulette swept up behind him, brandishing a pink feather boa. Loose feathers fluttered behind her, trailing the ground like a molting flamingo.

Cade reached and checked his own forehead. Cool and dry, despite the sweat forming on his back. So he didn't have fever.

He kept his smile steady. "Hey, Madame Paulette. Let me guess—you have a problem?" He looked behind her, searching for context. But all he could see was Zoey, talking frantically into her phone. Miley stood beside her, also on her cell, one finger plugging her free ear as she paced in front of the book booth. He frowned. Everyone was on their phones. Sadie. Farmer Branson . . . He *had* a phone?

"Honey, you're much too handsome to be so negative." Madame draped the boa around his neck. "I was going to let you know the stage looks perfect for my little dancers to perform this week."

That was a relief. He nodded, fingers itching to check the bank account. "I'm glad to hear it."

She tugged the boa back. "After you make it bigger, of course."

His smile faltered. "I'm sorry?"

"Don't apologize honey, I'm sure it's not your fault." She patted his arm.

"I wasn't—"

"Oh!" She pointed to the food trucks. "I'm glad I came a little early. I swear I could smell those breakfast burritos from Village Lane." She rushed away before Cade could figure out what happened.

At least someone would be getting a burrito this morning.

He looked back at Mrs. Peters, who watched him with a hawkish expression, as if he was supposed to say something else.

But he couldn't wait any longer. "If you'll give me a moment…" Cade held up one finger, then ducked his head as he scrolled the contents of the bank page. He held his breath, ignoring Mrs. Peter's pointed tapping of her orthopedic shoe and willed a charge to appear from the porta-potty company.

Unfortunately, no matter how many times he scrolled, it didn't appear.

This was his fault. He'd gotten too swept up in festival planning, in dreading the upcoming campaign, in Rosalyn, that he'd let the confirmation slide—despite multiple sticky-note reminders scattered across his desk.

Which begged the question—what else had he forgotten?

He pocketed his phone, ready to try to appease Mrs. Peters. But she'd already headed toward the stage as if she might remove the risers herself, arthritic knees and all. Meanwhile, Madame Paulette flirted through the service window of the nearby taco truck.

At least they were both entertaining themselves. Cade just needed to think.

Dad would know what to do.

The thought landed like a chigger, irritating and itchy. Cade walked back toward the vendor booths where he'd left Zoey and the others. Dad would have a connection with someone that could get this resolved—or at least, get a rush order prioritized. He always came up with solutions.

Not that he'd have messed up in the first place—Dad was a true Landry.

Would Cade ever have what it took?

Nineteen

CADE WAS GOING TO BE SO RELIEVED. Wherever he was.

"Thank you so much. You're a life saver." Rosalyn hung up with the manager of Southern Jewelry Co. and grinned at Zoey, who sat in a lawn chair behind her Bayou Beignets table. The smell of powdered sugar and cinnamon hung heavy in the air under the tent. "Southern is in for bathroom traffic."

Then Rosalyn did a double take. "Wow, did you sell all those while I was on the phone?" Zoey's sample platter of treats was half-empty, and there were significantly fewer boxes than there'd been half an hour ago. To that point, the festival grounds already bustled with activity and they'd only been open a short time.

Zoey marked her hand-drawn spreadsheet, bangs draping in front of her eyes. "Yep. Business is booming."

"How many volunteers now, counting Southern?" Rosalyn sank into the lawn chair next to her.

"Let's see…" Zoey counted down the list with her finger. "Bayou Beignets, Southern Jewelry, Chug a Mug, Magnolia Blossom, and Magnolia Grace Church. That's five establishments in walking distance willing to let attendees use their restrooms."

"Make that six!" Sadie waved from her booth down the row.

228

"My part-time girl is working at Second Story today and has been instructed to let anyone in who needs the bathroom."

"Great! Thanks Sadie." Rosalyn turned to Zoey. "I almost had the bank manager convinced too, but they only have a single stall for public use, and he sounded like he regretted having even *that* policy in place."

"That's fair. And I'm sure Lettie would have let us, but her studio is farther away." Zoey tapped her pencil against the list.

"I'll put the studio on an overflow list—in case Cade can't get the porta-potties here tonight." Rosalyn drew a star next to the studio. "We'll need all toilets on deck." It felt good to help. Kept her mind off her own upcoming performance. She checked her phone, but Cade hadn't read her text asking where he'd gone.

"Oh, Pastor Dubois called me back and volunteered his golf cart for anyone who doesn't want to walk all the way to Village Lane for restrooms."

"Of course he did." Zoey laughed as she set her clipboard on the table. "I love that guy."

"He's very generous."

"You should check out a church service with us." Zoey's smile faded. "Wait. I keep forgetting you won't be here much longer."

"I know." Every day put her one closer to being back in under Blaine's watchful eye. Had he gotten wind of the paperwork Cade filed on her behalf? Would he be notified? Cade hadn't updated her on anything with her accounts, so she assumed everything was on the up and up.

Unless he hadn't had time to investigate yet.

She leaned forward in her chair. "I could probably come to church this Sunday before I leave town." It'd be a good opportunity to see everyone before she left Monday.

Including Cade.

"You're such a natural part of Magnolia Bay . . . I'm sorry we didn't know each other back in school." Zoey reached for one of the few sample beignets left on the plate. "You could have taught me aerial."

"I still can, you know. Maybe we can squeeze in that girl's night before I leave."

"Your solution to the toilet problem was a great idea, by the way. I know Cade will be grateful." Zoey gestured to her sugary wares. "I'd offer you a complimentary beignet, but I have a guess what your answer would be."

"That answer might change after my performances are over this week, so ask me again." Rosalyn shielded her eyes with one hand and scanned the festival grounds. Cade still hadn't answered her text, which was odd. She had yet to talk to him today at all. After she'd parked her car an hour ago and hurried over to meet Zoey, he'd vanished, presumably, according to Zoey, to try to make arrangements with another porta-potty company ASAP.

She wanted to tell him he could relax, could focus on other fires for a bit that were sure to ignite. Wanted to make sure he wasn't beating himself up and tell him she'd helped find a temporary solution. That everything would be okay.

But where was he?

Enough was enough.

Cade flexed his fingers at his sides as he paced his father's office, waiting on his return. Dad wasn't usually out of office this time of the afternoon, and Cade desperately needed to get back to the festival.

But this conversation was long overdue.

The air conditioner hummed overhead, and he couldn't help but notice how the fern in Dad's window thrived. Figured.

He had to tell his father the truth—it was a horrible time to run for mayor, even if he could wait several more weeks to start the actual campaign. A few weeks weren't going to solve Cade's focus issues, his anxiety struggles, or how thin he was spread.

Bilbo Baggins had nailed it—*butter scraped over too much bread.*

Cade would never be able to fully focus on the festival if he didn't get this off his chest and out of his head. It had to be said before Dad became even more convinced of his idea of passing the torch. The porta-potty fiasco had been the last straw.

He couldn't do it all.

Cade paused in front of the big window overlooking the park. The afternoon sun beamed through the trees, sending golden stripes of light across people enjoying the day. Hopefully, some of them would head to the festival that evening. Dog-walkers strolled the winding concrete path, while children played in the grass. A beach ball soared through the air, and a kid eagerly chased it down before it rolled into the pond.

Cade loved this place. And he was doing it a disservice because he wasn't fully invested in his goals. Maybe Dad could wait one more term before retiring. Or bail mid-term and give Cade a year or so to prepare between now and then. Get counseling for the anxiety flare-ups.

And get the town in the black before filling his proverbial plate with even more food.

Speaking of. He pulled a pack of Skittles from his pocket and ripped open the bag before checking his phone. He'd silenced it on the way over because the less he knew about what was happening at Magnolia Days, the better.

Several texts had come in, including a few from Rosalyn. He opened the thread.

"Cade! Excellent timing." Dad pushed into his office, shutting the door with a click.

Cade pocketed his cell. He'd have to read them later.

His father checked his Cartier watch, then settled in his chair and picked up the TV remote. He'd gotten a haircut, and his goatee was trimmed short. "I have something I want to show you."

Cade mumbled around his mouthful of candy. "Could we talk first?" He swallowed.

"If this is about the porta-potty issue, don't worry. I handled it." Dad waved his hand through the air and then aimed the remote at the television.

Great. Cade shoved the package back in his pocket. Word was already spreading of his incapability. "How'd you hear?"

"Everyone was talking about it at Chug a Mug when I stopped for coffee."

Perfect.

"I never would've used that particular company in the first place." Dad clicked on the TV and flipped channels. "Honestly, the mistake is on them."

Except Dad knew *not* to use them, further proving Cade's point—his father's shoes didn't fit him.

"Regardless, they should be delivering the pods shortly." Dad scrolled the channel list, his tone unconcerned.

Cade took a breath. That was one load off, though the fact his dad had to bail him out left a different one in its place. He sank onto the chair opposite the desk. "That's not why I'm here."

Dad pointed to the TV, which aired a local news report. "Let's talk in a minute. I don't want to miss this."

Cade leaned against the seat as the news reporter droned about the weather. He wanted to get the conversation over with, but at least this gave him a moment to figure out exactly what he wanted to say.

Maybe he should ease into it. *Dad, I've been thinking . . . there's been a lot going on lately, and I feel like taking on your job would be a bit much right now . . .*

Or maybe the blunt approach. *Dad, I'm not qualified to be mayor.*

Or maybe he needed to think about something else and let the conversation happen organically. He pulled his phone free from his pocket and went back to Rosalyn's string of texts.

Rosalyn

Good news! 😃

You're supposed to ask what 😳

Whenever you get this, call me. I think Toiletgate has been solved.

Cade stared at the words, rocking his chair back. His chest flushed as conflicting emotions roiled. Rosalyn had somehow fixed his problem too? Was *everyone* better at being in charge than he was?

"...an unexpected announcement from Mayor Landry." A local reporter's voice on the TV pitched with excitement. "Thanks for joining us. I'll let you tell the news yourself, Mayor."

Cade stilled his chair, balancing it on two legs.

Dad's face filled the TV screen. He wore the same shirt he had on now—a pinstriped button-down under a navy blazer. "Thank you, Laura. It's an exciting time here in Magnolia Bay."

Oh no. Had he *just* filmed this? Cade rocked again. "Dad. We really need to—"

"Shh."

"I know change can be intimidating." TV Dad lifted his chin toward the camera.

The brunette reporter nodded, eyes laser focused as if his father was a superstar. In a lot of ways, he was—all part of the problem.

A grin broke across Dad's salt-and-pepper goatee on the screen. "But I'm very pleased to announce that my son, Cade Landry, will be running for mayor this upcoming election."

Cade's chair crashed backward onto the floor. He lay unmoving, staring up at the ceiling tiles. His head spun. This wasn't happening.

"This is obviously bittersweet for me and the end of an era." From the television, Dad's voice filled the air. "But it's also the beginning of a new one for Magnolia Bay."

Cade's heart thundered in his ears and drowned out the reporter's perky response. He closed his eyes. He was too late. The entire town knew. He couldn't back out now.

The TV muted.

Cade opened his eyes.

His father peered down at him. "Did you hear that? You're official!"

Officially in trouble, yes. Cade had the sudden urge to laugh. He snorted. Then he chuckled.

"You okay?"

"Yeah, yeah." Cade coughed as he stood. "Skittle went down the wrong pipe." He righted his chair, hysteria past. Nothing about this was funny. Were the walls closing in? He collapsed in the seat, keeping both feet planted on the carpet. What was he going to do?

"Don't worry—this doesn't change anything regarding our campaign timeline." Dad returned to his own chair and clicked off the TV. "You can get past Magnolia Days before you switch gears."

Switch gears? Cade wanted to slam on the brakes. He pressed his fingers into his temples. "That's . . . good. But why the announcement? Why today?"

"I thought it best for the town to have a heads-up. And I've already booked your campaign party at Magnolia Blossom for two weeks from Saturday, after the festival." Dad beamed. "We'll get everyone celebrating early, and then your race will be a shoo-in."

Cade stared straight ahead. A party. His head throbbed faster.

"I didn't mean to spring this on you, but I knew you'd be swamped today and the news spot came available last minute. Obviously, I had to jump on it." Dad picked up his designer gold pen, a gift from the town during his fourth term as mayor. "So, what did you want to talk about earlier?"

"Um." Cade cracked his neck to one side. This was it—his last window to say what he came to say. He opened his mouth, shut it. The past ricocheted around his head. *You really owe your dad after this one, sport.*

"Let me guess." Dad raised his eyebrows. "Is it about Rosalyn Dupree?"

His face must have answered for him.

Dad pointed. "I'm not blind, son. You like her."

He swallowed. "Yeah, I do." It felt good to admit the truth. "But she's not available right now, nor is she planning to stay in Magnolia Bay, so . . ."

"Available?" Dad frowned. "She seeing someone else?"

"Sort of." He couldn't tell her secret. "It's complicated." Not to mention, despite her protests, he wasn't fully convinced she didn't still harbor some lingering feelings toward Blaine. At some point, she'd trusted him enough to give him access to her finances, even go so far as to marry the guy to escape a hospital.

And there had been that kiss he'd witnessed in Dallas . . .

Maybe that was the part he had trouble getting past. Afraid to believe there wasn't *another* secret still hanging out there she didn't want to share.

Dad cleared his throat. "If she chooses to go elsewhere, that's her loss. You remember that." His smile reappeared. "She could have been with the future mayor of Magnolia Bay."

So much wrong with that statement he didn't know where to start. "Uh, thanks, Dad. But—"

"I'm proud of you, by the way." Dad's eager smile sealed Cade's fate. "Not sure if I mentioned that part." He rubbed his goatee. "I haven't told you the whole story, I suppose."

There was more? Cade bounced one leg.

"Part of why I'm retiring early is doctor's orders." Dad tapped his pen against his open palm.

Cade's leg stilled. "What's wrong?"

"Nothing serious." Dad released the pen. "Apparently my blood pressure is high. And I need to eat more salads." He gestured to the paperwork on his desk. "Doc thinks some changes would be good, prevention-wise. Meaning less stress. Of course, once your mother heard that, the gavel slammed."

He winked, but for the first time, Cade noticed the thin lines etched across his face. The grooves on his forehead. The sunspots on his receding hairline.

His dad was getting older.

Cade shifted, hooking one ankle over the other. He widened his eyes, forcing the walls back into their place in the room. "It's okay, Dad." He drew a deep breath and released it with a smile. "I've got this."

Somehow, he'd find a way to make that statement true.

S HE'D DONE IT.

Rosalyn sat on the packed floor in the quiet circus tent that evening, gazing up through the dim lighting at the red and white striped ceiling the way someone might gaze at a sky full of stars.

She'd actually run away to the circus.

She drew a deep breath of slightly musty air that offered a faint hint of peanuts and popcorns from the machines lining the side of the tent and pulled her knees up to her chest.

Outside, muted activity bustled around the grounds as Magnolia Days carried on, but the tent wasn't open to the public until later in the week. She'd come in to rig her silks, learn the layout, make a plan for where she'd enter and begin her floor work before mounting the fabric.

But her first performance wasn't until Wednesday night, and now, she wanted to stop. Take a moment. Soak it all in.

See what was left when it all dried up.

She twisted the scrunchie around her wrist. Talking to Zoey about leaving Magnolia Bay had left an ache in Rosalyn's chest that wouldn't quit. And as much as she liked the dark-haired, wide-eyed baker, it wasn't because of her. Or because of Elisa, or Harper, or any of the townspeople she'd connected with. It wasn't even because of her parents, or her niggling interest at getting back into church, learning how to pray again. All those factors contributed to the ache, but when Rosalyn got very still and honest, it all came down to one.

She was scared of falling.

Falling from her silks, if she went back to performing regularly.

And falling for Cade, if she found a way to stay.

Both potentials felt equally terrifying.

So she sat. Stared at the tent ceiling, lit right now only by rows of string lights, and relived her greatest moments in the spotlight over the years. Complicated inversions. Roll-ups that tested her strength. Flashing camera lights and medals looped around her neck. Invitations and champagne glasses and autographs. Kamikaze drops to the delighted gasps and applause of a packed house.

But there were also gasps of terror that time she unrolled, hit the ground. There was the blinding pain that shot through her knee, the fear that grasped her heart. The clang of ambulance doors and the set line of the doctor's mouth as he shook his head. Declared her lucky.

Lucky. Was she? Or had God protected her—even from her own agenda and pride? Even though she'd never asked.

Rosalyn blinked up at the striped ceiling overhead, wishing she could peel back the canvas layers, peel back the evening sky dusted with stars, and see what was happening in the heavens.

See where her rusty prayers landed.

She rested her chin on her knees. God certainly didn't owe her anything. She'd made a mess of things all by herself. And therefore, *she* needed to fix them.

Fix herself.

Then maybe she could finally feel the approval she sought.

The tent flap suddenly opened behind Rosalyn, scattering

beams of fluorescent light across the ground and over her form. "There you are."

Cade. She twisted around and blinked, held up one hand to shade her eyes and peer up at him. "There *you* are."

He wore dark jeans and a black polo, looking as sharp and put together as always. Though, to be honest, her stomach probably would have dropped the same way even if he'd been in a clown costume. "I haven't seen you all day."

The flap dropped back, shielding them again in the dimmer light as he made his way toward her. "Sorry I didn't respond to your texts earlier. It's been a little hectic." He didn't hesitate or inspect the dirt-packed ground like she'd have expected. Instead, he dropped to the ground next to her, right there in the center of the empty tent, and drew his own legs up. Hooked his wrists around his bent knees.

She studied his profile next to her in the shadows, the line of his jaw. The dimple in his chin. He hadn't been ignoring her. She'd assumed he was busy all day, but . . . it was nice to know that's all it was. "So you heard about the porta-potties?"

"I did. And good thing, or I'd have been really confused when I saw Pastor Dubois toting a family full speed across the parking lot on a golf cart." He smirked. "Thanks for arranging all that, by the way. My dad called in a request with a different company too, so we should be set soon."

"That's good news."

He nodded. "Better late than never, I suppose."

"Spill it. What else is wrong?"

"You don't know?" He didn't even try to deny it. "You might be the only person in Magnolia Bay who hasn't seen the news."

Rosalyn frowned. "What news?" She didn't like the defeated slump in his shoulders, the forward pull of his brow. He'd been there through all of her issues the past few weeks—listening, forgiving, protecting her from her fears. The least she could do was return the favor.

He gazed upward toward the ceiling, like she'd been doing when he walked in. "Well, I have to admit—its small potatoes compared to the Mafia being after you."

Rosalyn snorted. "I would love to only have a small potato right now."

A grin flickered as he cocked his head toward her. "They're serving cheesy Tater Tots in one of the food trucks. Does that count?"

"Sold. But after you tell me about *your* potato."

He inhaled. Released it. "I'm running for mayor."

Rosalyn frowned. "But you told me weeks ago when I first got here that you weren't ready for that. You said, 'Maybe one day.'"

He winced. "Apparently, my father has a different calendar than me."

"I see." Cade for mayor. She *totally* could see it. But . . . "You still aren't ready, are you?"

"No. I went to Dad's office today to tell him that, but he'd already announced it on the news." This sigh was longer, deeper. "I'm also having a campaign party in a few weeks to start 'winning over the town.'" He air-quoted with his fingers.

Rosalyn touched his arm, then immediately let go as her fingers fairly sparked on contact. "Don't worry about the town voting for you. Everyone really seems to like you." She grinned. "Except maybe Mrs. Peters. But hey, if you flex a little, I bet Madame Paulette will vote for you twice."

"Ha." He positioned his arms around his legs. Had he felt it too? "Liking me as a face for Magnolia Bay, as someone to run events and raise the money and bug about filling potholes, is a lot different from finding me capable of running the entire townlike my dad. I couldn't even get this festival going without crises."

"I never liked that word." Rosalyn tilted her head. "*Crises.* Seems like it should just be crisis-es."

"Correcting that will be my first act as mayor."

Finally, a smile from him. Rosalyn grinned back, but it only lasted as long as his—not very.

He continued, brow furrowing. "I don't have a choice. Dad needs me to do this, so I will." He cracked his neck to one side. "I'm a Landry."

"You said that back in high school." And she'd always hated it. Like he was rubbing in his family's position and power, drawing lines between them. He was better, even when she won.

"I'm sure I did." He stared at the ceiling. "Dad drilled it into me every time I got in trouble . . . so, a lot."

Rosalyn waited a beat. "But you know it's okay to just be *Cade*. Why are you so bent on self-sacrificing?"

He shot her a side-eye look. "What do you mean?"

"Why are you running for mayor when you don't want to?" She matched his posture, hooking her arms around her knees.

"Technically, I never said I didn't want to."

She rolled her eyes. "You definitely did, if not with words."

"Reading me like a book, huh, Ace? What is that, thirty-two now?" He winked.

Her stomach flipped. "Don't start flirting with me to get out of this conversation."

His grin inched higher. "It's more fun that way."

Good grief, this tent was getting warm. "I'm not arguing that." She shifted into a more comfortable position, angling toward him, folding her legs to lean closer. "I'm just saying your opinion matters too. You shouldn't have to do something you don't want to because of some misplaced obligation to your dad."

"Misplaced, huh?" Cade raised an eyebrow. "If I say something about pots and kettles, will you get mad?"

Her back stiffened. "My situation is different. I owe people— scary people—money."

"But you're determined to handle it on your own. Not talk to your parents, not get help."

"Because it's *my* problem to solve."

He exhaled. "Like with the volcano, huh?"

"What do you mean?" She narrowed her eyes.

"Sixth grade. You wouldn't let me help." He waved a hand through the air. "Then got mad at me when I helped anyway, tried to make it more interesting to get us a better grade."

She sorted. "More like you were goofing off. Trying to prove you were better than me."

"No, I wasn't."

"But you thought you were."

A muscle flexed in his jaw. "Did you ever think maybe I was trying to impress you?"

She sobered. No, she hadn't. And that still didn't make sense. "Why would you ever want to impress me? You were *the* Cade Landry. You had the football team doing your bidding and two prom dates. Everyone loved you. I was a nerd with safety goggles who could do splits in the air."

"Or maybe they only loved me *because* of my family name and connections." Cade pushed forward before she could form a response. "Regardless, you're only making this money thing your problem now because you're so bent on keeping secrets."

Her chest heated. "I've told you more of my secrets than I've ever told anyone else."

He leveled his gaze at her. "And why is that? Why me?"

"I don't know." No fair, him being so calm when she was so annoyed. Also no fair him looking so attractive when she was this annoyed.

"Think about it, Ace."

Somehow, they'd inched closer to each other during the argument, and now, the tent shrunk until her senses could only absorb the fire lighting in her chest, the spark in Cade's brown eyes, the spicy cedar scent of his cologne.

"I guess you seemed . . . trustworthy."

He cocked his jaw. "Past tense?"

"Present." She licked her dry lips, trying not to let her gaze fall to his mouth. He'd always challenged her, but this was new. This made her want to believe him.

Believe in them.

Silence pulsed between them. Comforting, like a quilt on a cozy night. One Rosalyn wanted to sink into.

Then—"I liked you in high school, you know."

A sudden wash of cold shocked her body. "What?" Rosalyn's eyes widened. "You never let on."

"Why would I? Amber was always in your head." He shrugged. "I guess I assumed you thought the same way about me that she did, so I eventually stopped trying to impress you."

"I did let her influence me." Rosalyn grimaced. "But Amber was wrong about you." Should she tell Cade what she'd found out Harper?

His gaze fell to her mouth, then, and the last thing she wanted to do was talk about another woman.

But Cade didn't lean in. He stayed steady, reclaiming her gaze with a new challenge. "Maybe I can tell my dad my secret about running for mayor if you tell your parents your secret."

That, too, wasn't fair. She shifted away. "You know I can't tell my parents everything. Not yet. Some of it, not ever."

"I understand, but . . ." Cade took her hand, his palm pure fire against hers. "Give people a chance to decide how they feel about you, Ace."

She stared at their entwined fingers. "Are we still talking about my mom?"

"Did you ever think maybe your mom is proud of you and wants you to stick around?" He squeezed her hand. "I know I do."

Her stomach twisted. "My future is a question mark. And you're about to be mayor, or at the least, keep being the face of Magnolia Bay."

"I know." He grazed her fingers with his. "We've been around this loop a few times now, but it doesn't change the fact I want to kiss you again."

She swallowed hard. "I want you to kiss me too." There went her stomach again. The air hummed.

He reached over with his free hand, tucked her loose hair behind her ear. His face lingered close to hers, and he squeezed his eyes shut as if in agony. "You understand why I can't yet, right? Not until the dissolution is accepted."

Her skin tingled, disappointment mixed with electricity. "I understand." Pretty honorable stuff. Heroic.

Made her even more scared of falling.

But maybe some fears were good.

They held each other's gazes, temptation thrumming. Her resolve weakened. How important was paperwork, really? A simple legality . . .

"Look, Ace, eventually, this will all be over." His eyes held a promise, one that wasn't moving to his lips but she heard loud and clear. "And then . . ." He tugged her forward, dropped a kiss on her forehead. "We'll see what *then* looks like."

It seemed like it was going to look like long-distance struggles and mayoral campaigns and endless aerial performances. But if he was holding out hope for a different story, maybe she could too. At the least, maybe they could live in denial a little longer.

Run away in the meantime to a circus of their own.

Cade leaned back, a spark lighting his eyes that made her think of freshman-year pranks and debate team wars. "Hey, there's a whole festival going on out there, remember? Wanna go ride the Cajun carousel?"

Instead of kissing him? No. Rosalyn squinted, trying to let her emotions catch up, regulate. "That depends on what exactly makes it Cajun."

"The animals." Cade hopped up and tugged her to her feet. "There's an alligator, a pelican . . . I call dibs on the crawfish though."

"Of course." She followed him out of the tent and into the festival.

Who needed a carousel when Cade had strapped them into a roller coaster?

Twenty-one

T HIS IS EMBARRASSING." LINC SHOUL-dered the handle of the mallet and scowled at the crowd forming around the high striker game outside the circus tent Wednesday evening. The scent of Cajun tacos and tangy barbeque wafted from the food trucks parked across the lot. "I feel like a show pony."

"Well, you *do* have a mane tied up in that bun." Cade took a slurp of sweet tea as he looked up at the towering red and gold strength test. This wasn't the time to tell Linc what his own score had been when he'd attempted the game earlier in the day—less than brag-worthy, for sure.

Noah, wearing a backward baseball cap, snorted as he pinched off cotton candy. "I can't believe you let Cade talk you into this."

"Hey, slow down. I want a piece." Elisa looked like a teenager in her denim overalls and pink tee. Noah extended the cone of blue sugar toward her, the look of adoration in his eyes the same one Cade feared showed up in his own every time he caught a glimpse of Rosalyn.

"Everyone started piling up outside the tent before we were ready for the first performance. I figured Linc would make a good side show to buy some time." Cade shook the remaining ice in his cup and grinned. "Besides, you know he loves being the muscle of the group."

Linc grunted but didn't argue as he switched the mallet to his other hand.

"Seriously you guys . . ." Zoey pulled off a clump of Noah's cotton candy despite his protest and shoved it in her mouth. ". . . that giant tent won't be big enough to hold his ego if you all don't hush."

Good point. Cade shifted his weight as he looked toward the tent, closed up before the first performance. He was more than relieved Rosalyn was warming up in the backstage area and not here to see this one-man muscle show.

He, however, could not wait to see *her*. Magnolia Days had sailed by without too many issues, though navigating the event took all his time. He was only able to steal moments with Rosalyn throughout the festival, and rarely alone. Which was depressing, seeing how—against his better judgment—he wanted to soak in as much time as possible before she left the Bay.

After the initial porta-potty disaster and one temporary malfunction with the Ferris wheel, things had gone relatively well. Attendance stayed high and sales seemed solid, especially on the food truck side. Magnolia Bay sure liked to eat. But with its admission fee and exclusive merchandise sales, the bulk of their fundraising profit was sure to come from the three nights of the one-ring Cajun Circus.

Which was almost ready to start. Hopefully Rosalyn was too. And the dancing poodles and the magician and the Hula-Hoopers . . .

Cade checked his watch, then turned to the crowd behind him. "Ten minutes until the tent opens! Have your tickets ready."

Excited murmurs rippled through the group as they pushed closer to the red velvet ropes Cade had borrowed from the movie theater. It seemed like good news to Cade that there were a lot of people he didn't recognize—tourists? Noah had mentioned the Blue Pirogue was fully booked this week, something that hadn't happened all year.

And if Trent and his executive liked what they saw and wanted to film here in the near future, well . . . maybe Cade was actually going to pull this off.

Maybe he couldn't pass the bar, but maybe he *could* run the town.

Three small kids pushed through the wall of adult legs in front of them and looked wide-eyed up at Linc. "You're huge."

He glared at them.

The smallest kid ducked behind a taller one. Then another little boy, his cheeks stained with red sno-cone, held up his scrawny, sunburned arm. "Will you flex?"

Linc shifted the mallet. His eyes darted to Zoey, then back to the boy. "I definitely will not."

"Boo." Zoey called around her mouthful of candy, eyes sparkling. "Come on, Hercules."

Cade snorted. "And you were worried about *us* making his head big?"

Linc released a long-suffering sigh. "You do realize I'm not a Disney character."

"Um, you do realize Hercules was a mythological Greek hero before Disney made him a cartoon," Zoey shot back.

Elisa scrunched her brow. "You *both* realize he's not actually real, right?"

Down the row of nearby game booths, someone threw a dart at a wall of balloons. *Pop.* The huddle of kids jumped. The smell of slightly burnt popcorn wafted on the evening breeze. Cade looked at his watch again. "Eight minutes, everyone!"

"Come on, hit it, already!" Zoey started clapping her hands and chanting Linc's name. She was quickly joined by Mama D,

Noah, Elisa, Miley, Sadie, and a dozen others waiting to go inside the circus tent. "*Linc . . . Linc . . . Linc . . .*"

"Aye!" With a scowl, Linc steadied the mallet, aimed once, and then hefted it onto the buzzer. The puck flew up the runner and slammed into the top with a loud clang.

Cade's eyes widened. Noah's hand went still on his cotton candy. Zoey's mouth gaped. The standing crowd hushed in awe.

"There." Linc tossed the mallet onto the hard-packed dirt. It reverberated with a thud Cade felt up into his shins. "Happy?"

"I'm not sure yet." Noah surrendered the rest of his cotton candy to Elisa. "Surprised, maybe. Jealous, for sure."

Cade clapped Linc on the shoulder as they turned away from the high striker. Now he was really glad Rosalyn had missed that. "Are you *trying* to make the rest of us look bad, or does it come naturally?"

Linc narrowed his eyes. "I believe you promised me a free corndog in exchange for flaunting me around."

"Right." Cade pulled a wad of red carnival tickets from the pocket of his slacks. "*Bon appetite.*"

"Wait up." Zoey, still nibbling a handful of cotton candy, called after Linc. "I like corn dogs too." She ran behind him and jumped on him piggyback style. "You sure you won't flex?"

Without looking back, Linc shook her off like a gnat and kept walking. She landed lightly on her feet, trotting after him and chanting *Hercules* over and over as he stoically made his way toward the food truck.

Noah caught Cade's gaze and knowingly lifted his chin. "We just gonna let that ride?"

"Did you like us bugging you about her?" Cade nodded toward Elisa.

"He's got a point, Noah." Elisa snorted as she pulled off the last piece of spun candy from the cone. "Besides, Zoey swears they're just friends. It goes both ways."

"Whatever." Noah crossed his arms over his plaid shirt. "Cade and I are friends, and I never jump on his back."

"I know, sugar." Elisa patted his arm and winked. "But that's only because he'd be mad that you wrinkled his shirt."

"Hey now—" The alarm on Cade's watch dinged. He sucked in his breath. "It's time."

Nerves flooded his stomach. This was it. His to-do list flashed and he could only hope everything had been checked off. So many thoughts running rampant, yet somehow, under all the pressure and expectation, one rose above them all.

He was going to get to see Rosalyn perform again.

And maybe convince her to stick around afterward.

Cade inhaled and turned to make the announcement as the tent flaps burst open.

Owen stepped out in a black top hat and red tailcoat, brandishing a riding crop. Gold brocade danced down the legs of his pants. "Ladies and gentlemen!"

Everyone fell into anticipation. Children stared with wide eyes, until the only sound was the crunching of caramel corn and the whir of the Ferris wheel.

Cade held his breath. After all Owen's begging to perform on stilts and tightrope walking, Cade had caved and given him the role of ringmaster. Would everyone buy it?

Fully in character, Owen adjusted his gold cravat and lifted his chin with an expression Cade would bet he'd practiced in front of the mirror. He expertly spun his crop and paced in front of the velvet ropes, a mischievous smile filling his face. Between his impish grin and black eyeliner, he looked like a cross between Edward Scissorhands and Willy Wonka.

Cade risked a glance at the crowd, who stared at Owen, mesmerized. Cade's shoulders eased a notch. They loved it.

When the silence had stretched as long as possible, Owen

dipped into a bow. "Let the circus"—he stood abruptly and released a cloud of gold glitter into the air—"begin!"

Heart pounding, Rosalyn peeked from behind the stage curtain that separated the wings of the tent from the eager audience sitting beneath its roof. The smell of peanuts and crawfish hung in the air like Cajun cologne. In the center of the arena, the trained poodles line-danced on cue to Sweet Home Alabama—an instant crowd pleaser.

Trying to focus on anything but her upcoming performance, Rosalyn watched as the dogs sat, rolled over, and then took a bow as the last strains of the song ended. The crowd erupted into applause—almost as much as they'd given the silver-haired magician. He was scheduled to go back for an encore toward the end of the show—after Rosalyn's routine and before the singing jugglers and fiery Hula-Hoops.

It was almost her turn.

She let the curtain slip back into place and flexed her fingers, pacing, testing her knee. Sweat dampened the back of her glittery white leotard.

Her first show back since falling.

She'd tweaked her more recent routine to accommodate any stiffness that might show up. She'd thoroughly stretched and hydrated. She'd mentally reviewed her routine, imagining perfection. She was prepared. There was no reason to worry.

She needed more rosin.

"Have you seen a purple bag?" Rosalyn asked the magician who stood scrolling social media. A pair of fake handcuffs dangled from his wrist.

Without looking up, he pointed to her duffel sitting on the sword-trick box next to him. "I didn't stab it, don't worry."

Rosalyn headed toward it, dodging three costumed Hula-Hoopers and one unicyclist as they rushed toward the curtain.

Owen approached as she dug for her trusty bottle of spray-rosin. "You ready?"

She sprayed her hands, then flexed her fingers again. "Ready." She nodded with what she hoped looked like confidence at the local banker, whom she'd met earlier at Magnolia Days with Cade. He'd made an excellent ringmaster so far.

She followed him toward the curtain. At least tonight, she didn't have to worry about Blaine watching, critiquing. He'd most likely hear about the circus eventually from media coverage, but not until she was back on her regularly scheduled performance circuit, where he couldn't complain. Hopefully by then, the paperwork for the annulment would have been accepted, and she could write off that bad chapter. Focus on paying her debt with this last round of performances and then be free to figure out the rest of her story.

So why did staring up at the silks rigged in the center of the rink make her feel like her story was already over?

"Don't tell me you're nervous." Owen adjusted his top hat. "You're practically famous. Isn't this what you do?"

"You'd be surprised." Rosalyn rotated her shoulders, stretching the tension from her neck, slipping into the splits.

"Ouch." Owen blanched. "How do you do that?"

"Practice—more than most people want to do." She smiled but it still felt shaky. So did her hands, for that matter. She needed to get it together or her fear of falling would become a reality. And too much was riding on this performance.

For her and the town.

"You're up after the hoops of fire. I'll announce you." Owen flicked her a thumbs-up, then ducked behind the curtain.

Rosalyn closed her eyes, leaning deeper into the stretch. She tuned out the TikTok video streaming from the magician's phone, Owen's voice announcing the next act, and the musty odor of rosin emitting from her hands.

She slowly stood from her splits, wishing Cade had been able to make it backstage to tease her and call her Ace and settle her nerves with his quick wit and adorable smile. With his promise of future kisses and his hope for their stories to merge.

Her phone buzzed from her bag, and she dug it out, holding it carefully with two fingers to avoid getting rosin on the screen. Ugh, two missed calls from Blaine. She'd handle that later.

And yay. A text from Cade. Was he reading her mind now?

Cade
____

You're going to do amazing. I'll see you after the show.

She'd needed that. She slid her phone back into her bag, and her smile sobered.

Needing him was scary. After all, last time she'd needed a man, it'd ended in a disaster of lies and international red tape.

Cade was different though. She had to remember that, not be afraid. He wasn't Blaine, and he wasn't Mr. Popular from high school anymore, intent on showing off and showing her up. He could be trustworthy.

She rotated her ankles, her wrists. From inside the ring, the crowd applauded the Hula-Hoopers. Fresh tension radiated down her back. Almost time.

When was the last time she'd done aerial for *fun*? With no stakes . . . no one depending on her to carry a show or make a certain score or impress an audience that grew increasingly harder to impress?

Owen started talking into the microphone again, his announcer voice booming through the tent.

She missed the days when simply performing was enough.

"... with graceful acts defying gravity ..."

She missed the days when aerial wasn't a cage.

"... as she literally flies through the air with the greatest of ease ..."

And she missed Cade. What if she *could* stay? Right *now*. Not in the speculative future.

What if she could actually fly again?

"I give you our very own ... Rosalyn Dupree!"

Rosalyn sucked in her breath. Pulled back the curtain. Lowered her shoulders.

Here went everything.

Something was wrong.

Cade stopped mid-chew of popcorn and watched Rosalyn as the spotlight turned her hair golden. The sparkles in her leotard shimmered and danced under the beam, but her normally rosy complexion looked pasty. And it had nothing to do with the canned lights.

He stood from his aisle seat in the first section of risers, almost forgetting to catch the single red rose he'd bought to give her after the show that had been balancing on his lap. Clutching the rose and the popcorn, he watched as Rosalyn approached her red silks, reaching up and giving them a tentative tug. Then she dipped into a curtsy, which he knew from her tech instructions was the cue to start her song. Still in mid-bow, her eyes flitted around the tent, jumping from section to section.

Like she was looking for someone.

His heart stammered.

She stood upright, her smile wobbly, as the first note of music sounded through the speakers.

Cade waved one arm wide through the air. Popcorn scattered onto the row of people sitting below him, and he winced. "Sorry." But he didn't take his eyes off Rosalyn, willing her to find him in the crowd. He waved bigger.

Then her searching eyes locked on him, and her smile grew. Her shoulders lowered. Her cheeks flushed.

He held her gaze, knowing there was no way she could see his face clearly or hear his words, but he muttered "You got it, Ace" anyway. He kept standing until she nodded, then with a smile, mounted her silks.

"Down in front," a voice from behind hissed.

Oops. He sat, scrunching low and resting the rose across his lap. "Sorry." But not really. Rosalyn Dupree, needing anything from *him*? Made him believe maybe he could fly too.

And with the news he'd figured out late last night, maybe they both could. He'd looked into her financials after the opening dust of Magnolia Days had settled and followed the trails to discover two truths. 1. Rosalyn wasn't as broke as she seemed to believe, and 2. Blaine had been moving her money into investments that Cade would bet Rosalyn had never approved. Under Rosalyn's master settings, Cade restricted Blaine's log-in to keep him out of the accounts until Rosalyn could decide what to do with the information. Even set it to send a notification to his and Rosalyn's email addresses if Blaine attempted access.

Maybe, *maybe* this meant she could pay off her loan and not have to go straight back to performing.

Unless she wanted to.

He watched her on the silks, his hopes soaring as high as she balanced. Maybe it'd been selfish not to text her immediately last night with his discovery, but it'd been late, and he wanted to tell her in person. See the relief and joy on her face as she realized the truth.

She had options.

Rosalyn twisted next into the move she'd told him was a hip key rollup, and it was as if she'd transferred all her nervous energy directly to him. She was beauty and grace, while his stomach knotted like a sailor's practice rope. *God, protect her.* He prayed as if the fervency of his pleas was the sole thing keeping gravity at bay.

He bounced his leg, scattering popcorn as she flew through her next skill, something that resembled an archer holding a bow and arrow. Then she flipped and expertly wrapped the silks around her legs in time to the music, moving into different positions, each more graceful than the one before.

His leg stilled its bouncing as the hauntingly beautiful song continued, forgetting to be nervous for her as his stare fixed on her soulful expression. She easily translated the melody through the long lines of her body. Her leotard, cut low in the back, showcased the definition of her muscles as she worked. Every time she reached out with one lean arm to beckon the audience, Cade found himself leaning forward. Every time she closed her eyes and reveled in the song, he felt tempted to do the same.

Though not at the expense of taking his gaze from her.

Rosalyn climbed higher as the tempo built, wrapping herself in a fluid whirl of fabric, until she reached the top portion of her silks. The music beat a steady rhythm and she paused. Then as the song reached its big crescendo, she released the silks, dropping several feet to a soundtrack of the audience's gasps.

The fabric caught her as it was supposed to, as Cade knew it would, but that didn't stop his heart from fleeing into his throat anyway.

A teenager sitting in front of Cade leaned toward the woman next to her. "I want to learn how to do that!"

The woman twisted around. "Think you can get her back here for a workshop or something?"

Cade swallowed. "I hope to do better than that." Convince her to never leave.

The rest of her routine passed in a blur of various skills and jaw-dropping flexibility. Cade's adrenaline raced. If this was considered holding back, well . . . he only wished he'd bought tickets to see her perform all over the world.

And next time, he would *not* throw away her flowers after the show.

As the final notes played, Rosalyn slid down her silks onto the ground and into the splits, arms stretched high. The audience leaped to their feet in a standing ovation. She stood, waved, and bowed. Then she met Cade's eyes before she smiled and disappeared behind the stage curtain.

His heart raced as he shouldered past the throngs of people still clapping. Time to get backstage and deliver this rose.

And some news he hoped was worth a thousand bouquets.

TWENTY MINUTES LATER, AFTER THE FINAL parade of acts, Rosalyn could still hear the applause ringing in her ears.

Backstage, she pulled shorts over her leotard and zipped her hoodie before shouldering her duffel. Energy flowed, despite her trembling legs and achy knee. She'd done it—and she hadn't fallen. Now to find Cade and get that good news. This was turning out to be a pretty great night after all.

All that worrying for nothing.

She pushed her way out of the tent and into the crowd, who lingered on the festival grounds, holding leftover boxes of caramel corn and candy. Twilight had faded into dusk, and the carnivals lights blazed brightly against the growing shadows.

Linc, Miley, and Owen, still wearing his ringmaster's hat, stood with Noah and Elisa at a balloon dart booth several yards away, where it appeared Noah was trying to win Elisa a teddy bear. Rosalyn's parents should be around here somewhere, though Dad was probably hitting up the beignet booth before Zoey sold out.

Where was Cade? They should have determined a meeting

point, but now her phone was dead. He'd mentioned Zoey would be opening her shop that night for their friend group to hang out while she put away leftover inventory . . . she could catch up with him there, but didn't want to wait. Maybe he'd gotten tied up in a festival emergency.

She continued to scan the crowd, smirking at the long line stretching out from Backwater Bruno's frog leg truck. Funny that had turned out to be a hit.

"Hey, doll."

Rosalyn stilled, ice pricking her veins. The laughter of children and *ping* of arcade games faded around her. Her shoulders tightened. *No.* A rush of warm evening wind tugged her hair, still stiff with glittered gel, but she barely felt it graze her neck. She turned slowly. *Not here.*

But there was Blaine, wearing a designer polo and pressed chinos, holding a bouquet of mixed flowers. His ever-present leather satchel hung from one shoulder, and he seemed more big-city out of place than ever, posed against the backdrop of small-town festivities.

He smiled, all charm. "Saw the show. You were amazing."

Rosalyn licked her dry lips, her performance lipstick long gone. "What are you doing here?"

"I came to see you. I tried calling." Blaine stepped closer, his musky cologne familiar and overpowering.

She swallowed. "But how did you know where—"

"It's my job to know, doll." He gestured with the bouquet. "The real question is, why are you secretly performing?"

His gaze held steady, despite her rapid blinking. He didn't look mad—why didn't he look mad? But hadn't he been unpredictable since Saudi Arabia? Maybe he was just holding it together to not cause a scene.

Regardless, she needed to downplay—she couldn't trust him.

Rosalyn fought the urge to retreat and lifted her chin. "Performing? Come on, this hardly counts." She waved one hand at the striped tent behind him. "It's a silly fundraiser I agreed to when I got here. I felt bad for them."

She couldn't read his gaze, but he seemed to be buying it. She added the final touch. "Besides, it gave me a way to test my knee before I got back to my real shows."

"Ah." Understanding lit his eyes. "I gotcha."

Rosalyn's shoulders relaxed.

Was he coming in for a hug? She instinctively moved back, right onto someone's shoe in the crowd.

"I'm sorry—" Rosalyn's distracted apology died as she looked over her shoulder, into the face of her old classmate. "*Amber*?"

This was a night of surprises and none of them good. The only surprise she wanted was the one Cade had yet to tell her.

"Rosalyn!" Amber grabbed her arm, her chin-length bob swinging across her sharp jaw. "Wow, look at you. It's been years." She pulled a brunette woman closer. "Gabby, can you believe our girl here?"

Rosalyn's old friend from school turned, carrying a cone of pink cotton candy. "*Totally* can't." Gabby shook her head, hair flowing over the shoulders of her sundress. "You were fabulous tonight, Rosalyn. But I'm not surprised at all."

"Um, thanks." Worlds colliding. This was too much. And what did Blaine want? He hovered nearby, near her elbow, impossible to ignore. "What are you two doing here?"

Gabby grinned. "We realized on social media we were both going to be home visiting family, so we planned to meet up for the festival."

Half listening, Rosalyn cast a look over their heads at the throng of college-aged kids attempting to win goldfish, at the huddles of middle-aged parents eating foot-long corndogs and children downing lemonade slushes.

No Cade.

"So what else is new? Are you still single?" Gabby asked as she pinched off another bite of pink fluff.

Rosalyn hesitated. How to answer that? Technically married, but crushing hard on Cade, yet not officially in a relationship . . . nope. Couldn't explain, especially in front of Blaine.

"Of course she's single." Amber crossed her arms over her black T-shirt and smirked. "See what happens when women go for their dreams without being distracted by men? They become *successful*. I told you for years it's the superior way. We're far more evolved, so we can accomplish more without—"

"But what about him?" Gabby pointed her cone at Blaine.

He stepped closer, wrapped his arm around Rosalyn's shoulders. She stiffened.

"Who is this?" Amber's steely gaze registered on the bouquet in Blaine's hands, and her brow furrowed into anarch. "Who are you?"

"Me?" Blaine pointed to his chest before grinning at both women. "I'm her husband, of course."

"*Husband*?" Amber's brows arched into her hairline.

Her tone sounded as shocked as Rosalyn felt. "Blaine, what are—"

Cade's face suddenly registered in Rosalyn's peripheral vision. *Finally.* Her heart surged and she tried to duck out from under Blaine's grip. Cade was so close but seemed to be stuck in the crowd behind two kids and a slow-moving man on crutches. Was Cade carrying a rose? *Aww.* Joy pulsed.

Wait.

He was frowning.

Her joy stuttered. *Ugh, Blaine.* He wasn't taking the hint to release her. Rosalyn turned her face up, forcing another smile to temper her curt whisper. "Let me *go*—"

Then Blaine kissed her.

Full on the lips.

Her pulse roared in her ears. Gabby's delighted cheer collided with Amber's snort of disgust.

Rosalyn's mind reeled and she wrenched away from Blaine. She sucked in a breath and looked again in time to see Cade.

Tossing her rose in a nearby trashcan.

He'd turned into a circus clown.

Cade's throat knotted as he pushed through the nighttime Magnolia Days crowd, away from Rosalyn. But no matter how fast he maneuvered through the throngs of people, he couldn't outrun the image of that kiss. Of all the moments in history to have to repeat themselves.

His stomach burned, his fist clenching at his side. All the times he'd held back from kissing Rosalyn the past week, all those efforts to do this the right way. To wait until she was legally free. To be noble. He'd thought she'd wanted that too.

But what had it gotten him?

A big red nose.

Out of breath, he paused near the row of food trucks, the lingering scent of turkey legs and cinnamon nuts doing nothing to tempt his appetite, for once.

The truth turned his stomach—Rosalyn was kissing exactly who she wanted to.

Cade leaned against the side of the Friends of the Library booth, turning his back to the line of kids waiting their turn for Harper to paint their faces, cheeks. Stars twinkled above, breaking the night sky. He crossed his arms, watched the horde of people lining up for funnel cakes, and tried to control his breathing.

It wasn't just the kiss but the words she'd uttered before that wrung his heart. He'd located Rosalyn in the crowd, after having apparently missed her backstage. He'd seen Blaine approach, then got tripped up by a kid stopped to tie his shoe. By the time Cade had made it toward them, he'd heard the whole story. *Silly fundraiser. Felt bad for them. Going back to my real shows . . .*

And then the grand finale that connected all the dots—the kiss. Rosalyn clearly wasn't over Blaine. The access she'd allowed him into her life and finances, the blind trust she'd given him in the hospital—*if* that whole Saudi Arabia story was even true—made sense now. Cade's instincts had told him all along that something wasn't adding up, that someone had a different motivation in play.

He'd assumed it was Blaine, but maybe it'd actually been Rosalyn.

"Cade *Landry*?"

The voice he'd hoped never to hear again after that night at the Lazy Spoon registered over the din of his heartbeat. He drew a breath, then turned and painted on a smile that should have won an Oscar. "Amber . . . uh . . ." He couldn't remember her last name and didn't care to try harder.

"Stockwell." Amber's eyes narrowed.

"Of course." He nodded at her, then at the taller, thinner woman standing next to her. "Gabby, isn't it? I saw you guys across the grounds earlier." With Rosalyn. Before his heart had cracked wide open. He kept his smile though. "Glad you ladies could make it to the festival."

"It's so . . . quaint." Amber lifted her chin, lips pursed. "Well done for a small town, anyway."

Well, she hadn't changed. "The cotton candy is amazing." Gabby's eyes widened with sincerity.

"Even if Magnolia Days isn't big-city worthy, I hope you're enjoying yourselves." Cade slid his gaze to the food trucks, wondering if he could get away with pretending to hear someone call his name. "I've got to—"

"We're running into *so* many people from high school, like Rosalyn." Amber stood with her arms folded over her cross-body bag. "*And* meeting new ones."

His smile tightened. "That's what a festival is for."

"Like Rosalyn's husband." Amber's grin stretched to catty. "Have you had the pleasure?"

"Pleasure? I thought you hated—never mind." Cade shook his head. It wasn't worth it. The aroma of cheese fries turned his stomach, and he started to step away. "I've got festival business to attend to, so I'll see you ladies around."

"Wait." Amber stepped forward, unfolding her arms. "I think you left something behind." She held out a rose.

The rose he'd thrown away, now crumpled. Was that mustard on the petals?

He didn't take it. Or reward Amber's tight-lipped, knowing grin with a response.

His heart thudded, and he was right back in the alley of the Lazy Spoon, being made to look a fool as Rosalyn chose to go with Amber and her friends instead of staying to catch up with him. Right back in freshman year, when Amber spread the word about Cade's father saving him from being expelled about the Justin Davies situation.

Right back in sixth grade, volcano goo dripping off his shirt, Amber and her friends cheering as Rosalyn accused him of being a show-off and ruining everything.

Amber twirled the stem between her fingers. "You probably thought you had a chance with her, didn't you?"

Gabby elbowed her friend in the side. "*Amber.*"

Amber ignored her, her gaze shooting fire. "Daddy might have gotten you the grades and the popularity, but I guess he can't get you *everything* you want, huh?"

"Okay, that's it. We're leaving." Gabby tugged at Amber's arm. "You're not in high school anymore."

She shook Gabby off. "Rosalyn's husband looks like he's loaded too."

Cade tightened his jaw. Ironically, Blaine *was* loaded—just not with his own money.

"Did I strike a nerve? *The* Cade Landry, finally taken down by a woman?" Satisfaction gleamed in Amber's face. "Imagine how you made so many of us feel back then."

Us? He narrowed his eyes. "You have no idea what you're talking about, Amber."

She scoffed. "Or maybe I do. Maybe *you* don't want to admit that, for once, being a Landry isn't enough."

"Come *on*." Gabby shoved Amber in front of her, pushing her down the walkway. They nearly collided with a teenager on a skateboard, but Amber barely seemed to notice.

She turned, walking backward, tripping over Gabby. "The Landry name wasn't enough to pass the bar either, was it?"

Her parting words hit their mark. How did she even know that? Cade's eye twitched and he pressed his lips together to avoid causing a scene as Gabby propelled her friend forward, turning around to mouth *I'm sorry* at Cade.

He waited until they were out of sight, then leaned his head against the library booth and closed his eyes. Amber's words ricocheted in his mind. He didn't really care what she thought, did he? Man, but they'd hit a target.

Because being a Landry *wasn't* enough. Or maybe, he wasn't enough to be a Landry.

Was the entire town about to find out when he tried to become mayor? Would he be the laughingstock, falling short of his family name? Maybe Rosalyn and Blaine were laughing together about his attempts to save the day right now.

What a night. "Cade, come quick!"

Are you kidding me?

He opened his eyes as Miley rushed up to him, the hem of her flannel shirt hanging long against frayed shorts. "What now?"

"The porta-potties are full."

That wasn't an emergency. He scrubbed his hand down his cheek. "I'm sure people are used to lines, Miley. It'll be fine."

"No, everyone is *sick*." Her eyes grew wide in her flushed face and she tugged at his sleeve. "Come on."

Okay, *that* might be an emergency. He started to follow her, matching her quick stride toward the line of food trucks. "What do you mean *everyone*?"

"Everyone who ate at Backwater Bruno's."

Of course. How else would he expect this night to end?

Twenty-three

INTERIOR LIGHTS GLOWED FROM THE front window of Bayou Beignet, a welcome haven in Rosalyn's tumultuous night.

She parked in front of the shop, her stomach knotted as she fumbled for her keys and bag. Her phone had charged on the short drive there—enough to show Cade hadn't tried calling or texting since he'd seen her with Blaine. Maybe he wouldn't be there, but she wasn't sure where else to try, and he hadn't even read the text she'd pounded out at the last stop sign.

She'd figured he would know that kiss was not her doing. After everything they'd shared the past few weeks, *surely* he'd know.

But her quiet phone suggested otherwise.

She slid out of the car, hesitating before walking toward the fleur-de-lis painted front door. The moon shone in full force, bright enough to light the street. Shadows lurked under shop awnings and she once again was overcome with the urge to look over her shoulder. Hopefully Blaine had taken her suggestion, gone to his hotel, and would give her space until tomorrow.

After his surprising—and unwelcome—kiss, she'd excused herself from Amber and Gabby. "I can't believe you did that." She led Blaine to a spot away from the crowd.

"Come on, you're still my wife a bit longer." Blaine grinned, not realizing what he'd done. And probably wouldn't care if he did. "Just having fun."

"We're not married. Or at least we won't be for long, no thanks to you." She told him of the clause and the filed paperwork, watched the storm gather in his eyes. But she didn't care—she felt a bit like a tornado herself. "Go back to your hotel. I've got to sort a few things out."

"But we need to talk about your loan payments—"

"Tomorrow, Blaine. You've done enough tonight." Then she'd stalked away, her heart threatening to burst from her chest, half in disbelief she'd actually had the nerve to do that.

But Blaine hadn't protested or tried to come after her. Also somewhat unbelievable. Maybe, like a quintessential bully, he'd just needed someone to stand up to him. Maybe she should've tried a long time ago.

Add that to her growing list of bad judgment calls.

Through the window of the shop door, the whole gang was gathered around two black iron tables—Linc, Zoey, Noah, and Elisa. No Cade.

Her hope that Cade wasn't avoiding her plummeted, and she pulled open the door, trying to find a smile.

"There's our star!" Zoey gestured Rosalyn inside. Strings of fairy lights glowed above the counter and the display case, empty of beignets tonight. The sage-colored walls were as welcoming as Zoey's smile. "Come sit. We've got festival leftovers I'll have to throw away if they don't get eaten."

"Pretty sure Linc won't let that happen." Sitting with one arm draped around Elisa's shoulders, Noah saluted Linc with his coffee cup and a grin.

Across the table, Linc scowled as he brushed powdered sugar

off his black T-shirt. "I burn more calories in a day than you do in a week."

"But who's counting?" Zoey popped a bite of pastry in her mouth as she reclaimed the chair next to Linc. "I'm sure not."

"Sit by me, Rosalyn." Elisa pulled out one of the chairs near her, close to the platter of beignets. "Cade should be here soon. There was an emergency after the festival."

"There was? Oh that's *great*." Rosalyn's hopes shot high again, like the bell on the strongman game outside the tent, and she scooted her chair up to the table.

Just in time to look up and find everyone staring at her, heads cocked.

"I mean, *not* great about the emergency." More like great that Cade wasn't ignoring her. She reached for a beignet. If she'd ever deserved one . . . "I mean, what happened?"

"Apparently the frog legs vendor gave a bunch of people food poisoning." Zoey winced. "Last I saw, Cade was asking Bruno to pack up and go home. But Bruno was upset about his contract being broken—I heard the word *lawsuit* thrown around."

Oh no. Cade would be taking that one personally. Rosalyn winced. "Hopefully they'll get it sorted."

The bell on the door chimed, and they turned as Cade strode inside. "Hey." His normally gelled hair was mussed, his eyes tired. He nodded at the guys, then took a chair across from Elisa and diagonally from Rosalyn.

Oh.

She waited, but he didn't look at her.

"How'd it go?" Noah asked. "Was the frog guy reasonable?"

Cade rubbed a hand over his jaw. "I've got to talk to August Bowman tomorrow, so, let's leave it at that."

Uh-oh. The town's oldest, and best, lawyer. That couldn't be a good sign. Neither was the stiffness in Cade's back as he reached for a beignet, still avoiding Rosalyn's eyes.

She swallowed.

"Oh, Rosalyn—I never got to tell you that you did *amazing* tonight." Elisa flashed a bright smile. "Don't you think so, Cade?"

Rosalyn wasn't positive, but she was fairly sure Elisa kicked him under the table.

"Absolutely." Cade finally looked up, met her gaze, broad smile in place. "Great job. Now do it two more times for me, and that's a wrap."

Um, what?

She shot Elisa a quick look, who shrugged. Zoey frowned, while Noah's brows lifted. Okay, so not just her. This felt like a Twilight Zone version of Cade. No, it felt like high school Cade, the one who used to push past Rosalyn in the hallways, ignore her unless he was trying to beat her. The one who laughed with the jocks about the nerds. Got by on charm and reputation.

The one who gave a little bit of merit to Amber's jadedness.

Rosalyn picked at the beignet she no longer wanted. "What do you mean, *that's a wrap?*"

Cade rocked his chair back on two legs, hooked his hands behind his neck. "I'll cut your check Friday night and then you'll be free and clear." He cleared his throat. "You know, for your *real* shows."

Oh no. He'd heard her conversation with Blaine. She closed her eyes.

A muffled slap sounded, as if someone might have popped Cade on the shoulder—probably Zoey—followed by furtive whispers. Probably Noah and Elisa.

This was bad.

Rosalyn opened her eyes and folded her arms across her middle, holding herself together. "You know I didn't mean that."

"Mean what?" Noah asked.

"Heard you say it." Cade shrugged. "Saw you kiss him too. That's twice now, so it's okay. I get the hint, trust me."

"Kiss *who*?" Noah persisted.

Rosalyn's heart sank and she brushed back a piece of hair that had slipped free of its glittery prison. "There is no *hint*, Cade. I said what I had to, to get rid of him."

He scoffed. "Convenient."

Linc's mouth hung open. "Bro."

"What?" Cade rocked the chair back again. "There's a reason you won't stand up to him, Rosalyn. A reason you keep him in your life."

"You don't get it." Rosalyn's voice shook despite her efforts. Her chest burned beneath her hoodie. "You're not the one whose life or family could be in danger if you upset the guy holding all the cards. Besides, tonight I—"

"Is there even any danger, Rosalyn?" Cade squinted at her. His cocky expression made her want to slap him—and maybe cry. "You're so quick to believe all of this guy's lies. There's a reason for that too." He shook his head. "Probably because you don't actually want to get divorced."

"*Divorced*?" Elisa and Zoey echoed this time.

Noah scooted his chair back with a screech against the tile. "Look, maybe we should let these two talk in priv—"

"There's only been one lie." Substantial though it was. "Blaine tried to help me, granted, with a bad idea, and yeah, he lied about where the money came from, but he's not a *complete* monster." Because that would make her a complete idiot. And she'd shut Blaine down tonight, hadn't she? She was handling this on her own. "Regardless, that doesn't mean I want to *date* him."

Cade's eyes flickered in challenge. "No, just marry him."

Ouch. Her nails dug into her palm. "Well, I'm sorry I can't make a call and have my dad fix everything for me. Some people try to handle their own messes."

The shop fell silent, the tension pulsing in Rosalyn's ears. She sucked in a tight breath. "Cade, listen . . ."

"No, I think it's time you listen to yourself, Rosalyn. Because I hear you loud and clear." Cade's chair landed hard on the floor and he stood. "I've lost my appetite, Zoey. Thanks anyway."

Rosalyn's heart twisted. He had it all wrong. But the fact he could even believe all this about her told her what she needed to know.

She still wasn't good enough for Cade Landry.

Her stomach knotted as he walked toward the door, away from her. Away from them.

"By the way." He paused, turned, one hand on the knob. "I checked your accounts. Pretty sure that not-a-monster husband of yours has been stealing all your money."

The glass rattled as the door slammed behind him.

"You're telling me Cade was right?" Rosalyn stared at her parents across the table at Chug a Mug the next morning, the scent of Dad's black coffee mingling with the lemon scone on Mom's plate.

Rosalyn had tossed and turned all night after Cade's cryptic comment. Was he saying that to get back at her for her own hurtful comment? Or was he serious? How could she even find out? Financials were beyond her—she'd never had to deal with money. There'd always been plenty of it—until recently, anyway—and someone else managing it for her.

She'd finally landed on the only option she had left.

Ask for help.

Dad adjusted his glasses, turned the laptop to show her. They'd secured a booth in the corner of the coffee shop for privacy, and she'd never been so glad to have her back to a wall. Or so surprised at her parents' eagerness to help when she'd approached them at home an hour ago, still in their robes, and asked if they could talk.

"Yep. This guy's been moving your money around. Taking liberties you didn't know about." Dad pointed to the screen. "Looks like there's been some investments made too. That's where a lot of your money has been tied up."

Her stomach rolled. "That's horrible." Mom's manicured nails drummed a rhythm next to her plate, a concerned frown marring her otherwise youthful face. "Are you certain?"

"Very." Dad tapped a few more keys, pulled up a different account. "The good news is you're not nearly as broke as you assumed." He shrugged as he peered over the top of his glasses. "Looks like a lot of it has been moved to a different account, but still in your name."

"I don't have the log-in info for anything else." Rosalyn groaned. "I'll have to get that from him, somehow." That would be interesting. Then she hesitated, almost afraid to ask. "Do I have enough to repay my loan?"

Dad tilted his head, squinted. His mustache had gone full gray over the last few years, giving him an even more distinguished look. "How much do you owe?"

She told him and his gaze darted about the screen, mouth moving silently as he did the math in his head.

This was too much. Rosalyn pressed her fingertips against her flushed cheeks. She wasn't broke . . . which was good news. And Cade was right . . . which was bad news. Blaine had lied about *way* more than the loan.

And she'd all but defended him.

No wonder Cade had been so upset last night. He'd seen them kiss—twice—and knew all this about her finances, while she sat there annoyed and said right to his face that Blaine wasn't a monster.

She'd be suspicious at that point too.

Dad finished counting and picked up his coffee cup. "Looks like it'll be close. Maybe some of those investments will come back lucrative." He leveled her with his gaze. "But if it's important, I can make up the difference. Consider it an interest-free loan until you're set up again."

Interest was not the problem. "I couldn't let you do that." Although, granted, neither could she remain in debt to the Mafia. A detail her parents still didn't know. Nor did they know about the marriage complication.

"We don't mind." Mom took a bite of her scone, wiped her mouth with her napkin. "Though I'm sure the bank would be accommodating, especially if you're making a lump payment against the rest."

In a traditional situation, sure. But she couldn't give the rest of those details. Mom was handling all of this well, but it was only scratching the surface of the whole situation.

She'd already taken a career path her mother didn't like and had to listen to her say she was disappointed that day with her cousins.

The whole truth today would feel like three strikes.

"What do I do?" Rosalyn pointed to the laptop. "How do I stop Blaine from taking more money? Do I call the police?"

"Cade put a block on the account, restricting Blaine's access. I think for now, you should focus on the circus—you've got two shows left. We'll handle the legal side after that." Dad pulled the laptop toward him, signing out of her accounts one by one. "Who knows? Maybe your manager will come forward, do the right thing."

And maybe those dancing poodles would learn to fly. "Honey." Her father tapped her arm. "The bigger question is, why didn't you come to me with this sooner? I'm an *accountant*."

She shrugged. "I thought it was pretty clear-cut. I was in debt from leaving the world tour early." And hadn't realized Blaine had lied about more than simply *who* she was in debt to.

Her parents watched her. She had to give them more. "And I was embarrassed." That was the truth.

Dad shook his head. "No reason to feel that way. You trusted your manager—that's not unreasonable."

But she should have had the red flags sooner. Cade saw them immediately. Rosalyn swallowed. "I guess not."

"We're proud of you." Mom patted her arm next. "You're handling this bump with a lot of grace, and look—it's not even as bad you thought!" Her face was all sunshine and roses.

While Rosalyn sat there with her secret stash of rainclouds and thorns.

She forced a smile. "Right." Maybe she had more money than she thought, but she didn't have a way to pay her loan off without Blaine—and no way to tell him to do so without admitting she knew what he'd been doing in her financials.

That wasn't a conversation she was looking forward to having, but it had to be done or she'd never be free. Maybe she should bring someone with her—not Cade. Obviously.

Should she tell her parents the rest?

Rosalyn rolled in her lip, debating. If she did, this was the moment. It wouldn't take much . . . just one more surrender. One more white flag thrown on the table.

She drew a breath and—

Dad shut the laptop with a snap. "I have to say, it's pretty impressive Cade figured all this out so quickly."

She closed her mouth. Cade had actually figured out a lot more than that, and she hadn't listened. Her throat knotted.

"He's always been a smart cookie." Mom nodded her approval, eyes shining. "And now he's running for mayor."

They continued chatting about the campaign angles Cade might take as they finished their coffee.

Rosalyn's window had shut.

She released a sigh, struggling to participate in the political conversation. It was for the better. She needed to focus on her show that evening and didn't want to see the look on her parents' faces once they heard the whole story.

The same disappointment Cade had when he looked at her last night.

Twenty -four

CADE TOSSED A PEANUT IN THE AIR, tried to catch it with his mouth. It bounced off his nose, landed on the floor of the risers among discarded popcorn kernels and candy wrappers. From the stands around him, families sat in groups, adults scrolling their phones while kids tossed popcorn at each other and giggled. The second performance of the Cajun Circus was about to start, evident from the jaunty music streaming through the overhead speakers. Hopefully tonight would bring fewer disasters—no more overcrowded porta-potties and pending lawsuits.

Guilt nudged. Maybe this was his fault. After all, he'd wanted to tell Bruno no but went along with it. And look what happened.

Couldn't tell his father *no*, couldn't tell a stranger *no*.

He wasn't cut out to be a leader.

Rosalyn's words echoed from that afternoon in New Orleans when he'd looked into Bruno's hopeful face. *You aren't doing him any favors.* She'd been right. Was the same about to happen as a result of this election?

Cade tossed another peanut. Missed. Speaking of Rosalyn, he

hadn't talked to her since last night, and why should he? He hadn't talked to any of his other contract circus employees since last night.

And with Blaine in town, wasn't that all she wanted to be?

He'd changed his seat for tonight's performance, not wanting to risk Rosalyn finding him in the crowd. He'd considered staying home, but—this circus was *his* baby. Plus, Trent and his boss were due to show up either tonight or tomorrow night, and he needed do be available. Duty called, even if his heart still ached.

And if Blaine showed up again, well, Cade was mature enough to look the other way. He tipped his head back, tossed another peanut.

"You're being a jerk."

He caught this one, straight down his throat. Cade coughed, sputtering as Linc rolled his eyes from the seat next to him. "Give me those." He snatched the bag from Cade's hand, poured a few in his mouth.

Cade brushed peanut dust off his hands. "What do you mean? I'm sitting here minding my own business."

"Last night." Linc's gaze landed on him with the force of Thor's hammer. "To Rosalyn."

"You don't understand." The lights dimmed, then the music shifted as the fan-favorite poodles paraded into the ring. Children scooted to the edge of their seats to watch, mesmerized as the dogs started their tricks. Teens stopped scrolling their phones to snap pics.

Linc remained unimpressed, the flickering lights casting colored orbs across his corded arms. "Enlighten me."

Cade snorted. "Since when are you an expert in romance? Or any relationship, for that matter?"

Linc's dark eyes flashed. "Just because I choose to be single doesn't mean I don't know when someone is being treated poorly. And you treated Rosalyn poorly."

"Dude. She kissed another guy."

"Didn't she try to explain?"

Cade shifted positions on the riser. "Well, yeah, but—"

"Then quit being a jerk. Man up, apologize. She's a good woman—doing you a favor by being in this circus in the first place, right?"

True. Cade cleared his throat, watched as two dogs jumped through hoops. Off to one side, another set of poodles climbed a ladder and caught a ball from the top of a stand. "It's not that simple."

"Swallowing one's pride never is." Linc clapped him on the back—hard. "Choke it down with that peanut and do the right thing."

"It's complicated."

"You already said that. Less talk, more action. That's what women want."

"Again, how would you—" Cade bit back his own protest at Linc's growl. "Never mind."

"Look, you obviously like her. So, as I said . . ." Linc shoved the nearly empty bag of peanuts against Cade's chest. "Go make it right. Maybe she was actually telling you the truth all along."

Cade shook his head. "Right, like the Mafia is *actually* after her? And she *actually* legally married someone under duress and she *actually* likes me instead of her husband, even though I personally witnessed her insulting Magnolia Days and kissing said husband?"

"*Actually* . . ." Linc paused. "Yeah."

It was hard for Cade to wrap his mind around that possibility, even harder to hope for it. After all, hadn't he and Rosalyn agreed their timing was always awful? What made this any different?

Owen, in full ringmaster gear, swung his mic like a rock star to the applause of the crowd. "Next up, our very own world-famous aerialist—Rosalyn Dupree!"

His chest tightened as he waited for Rosalyn to take the ring. Longed for—and dreaded—seeing her. But maybe Linc was right.

Maybe Cade had let his past grievances keep him from hearing Rosalyn out, believing her. Sure, it looked bad—but what if she *was* telling the truth?

What if he was telling the wrong person no this time?

Owen turned toward the backstage area, clearing his throat before dragging her name out again. "Rosalyn Duuupreeee!"

Where was she? She wouldn't miss a cue, would she?

Linc frowned. "Better go find her."

Cade was already standing before Linc's suggestion. "On it. And don't get a big head that I'm listening to you."

His own head had been big enough for the both of them—one of the many things he needed to remedy when he found Rosalyn.

She'd missed her cue. And now Blaine stood between her and the back entrance into the circus tent.

Holding another blasted bouquet of flowers.

Rosalyn fought back panic. She had yet to talk to Cade or get anything settled between them. What if he thought she was sabotaging the show on purpose?

"Blaine, I'm late." She tried for the second time to push past him, but he sidestepped her, eyes wide and not a little affected. Alcohol? He'd never been a big drinker, but then again—she clearly didn't know him well.

"Come on. Take them." He shoved the flowers at her and she automatically caught them.

What in the world was he up to? Had he actually fallen in love with her? Was this a stalker move?

She glanced over her shoulder, but short of scaling a fence or climbing a tree, there weren't a lot of places to skirt around him. The wind whistled through the oak branches overhead, the moon high and bright. This end of the parking lot behind the tent was dim and vacant, except for one porta-potty meant for the circus performers.

Unfortunately, none of the other performers were in sight, since the show had already started. Even now, she could hear Owen calling her name over the speakers.

"I told you yesterday we needed to talk, and you blew me off." Blaine stepped toward her, and she swallowed, fought the urge to retreat. Standing up to him, being firm, had worked last night.

Maybe lightning would strike twice.

"Good grief, don't look so nervous." He rolled his eyes, glassy as they were. "I want to talk, and you keep avoiding me. Not answering my calls or texts all day."

She shot him a look, one that suggested he take the hint.

"I know you're mad about the whole loan thing, but it's just business." Blaine shrugged, his trendy V-neck shirt and navy blazer a stark contrast to the porta-potty next to him. "You never would've gotten approved for a traditional loan, and you were supposed to make everything back in triplicate." His brow furrowed. "Obviously no one could have predicted your little freak out in Saudi Arabia."

"My freak out?" She crossed her arms, suddenly chilly in her rhinestone-studded leo and leggings despite the warm summer air. "That's what you think that was? That all of this is *my* fault?"

"Freak out, episode—whatever you want to call it." He shrugged. "And yeah. You got yourself into that situation. I got us out."

His words burrowed, spread, like a parasite. This was her fault, but not in the way he was implying. She *had* made the decision to hire Blaine as her manager. Had trusted him, let him "rescue" her with marriage in a foreign country, believed he wasn't capable of the very things he was doing. Had defended Blaine to the man she was falling for, all in the name of pride. Afraid of being found out.

She really *wasn't* good enough for Cade.

"The point is you're okay now." Blaine's tone gentled and he touched her arm. "And we're doing everything we can to get you back in business. I'm here for you."

She jerked away, angry at him. At herself. "You want to talk? Why don't we *talk* about how you've been stealing my money?"

His show smile appeared, the one he used to negotiate deals with stubborn industry leaders. "*Doll.* I have no idea what you're talking about. You wanted me to handle your money when you signed with me—so I made some investments." He laughed. "You should be thanking me."

She lifted her chin, grateful for the flowers that hid her trembling hands. "Investments I didn't approve? In accounts I can't access?"

Blaine waved one hand in the air. "I have all of that information, obviously. I'll get it to you."

"I'm sure. Like you were going to get our marriage handled?"

His confident expression flickered. "I told you, it takes time for—"

"You filed a marriage *certificate*, Blaine. Not an annulment request."

"I know. That's required for international—"

"No, actually, it's not." She held his gaze, called his bluff.

His smile faltered. "How did you figure that out?"

"Is *that* what's important?" She raised her eyebrows. "Because I think it's more important that I'm onto you. You've been lying to me for months. Maybe longer."

He shook his head. The wind shifted, bringing the scent of burnt popcorn and corn dog batter wafting over them. "You have all of this wrong. I'm on your side."

"No, I'm pretty sure I'm seeing it clearly for the first time." Rosalyn tossed the bouquet on the ground. The breeze scattered broken petals across his loafers. "I know you never tried to get our marriage dissolved. I know you're a liar. And I know you're mishandling my money and making decisions for things I never authorized."

His eyes narrowed. "Is that what you think?"

"That's what I *know*." She held his gaze, trying to ignore her throbbing pulse, her panic that Blaine might be even more unpredictable than she imagined. But bullies always backed down, didn't they?

She squared her shoulders, ignoring the rushing in her ears. The fear threatening to claw her throat. "I want you to pay off my debt to whatever mob boss you borrowed it from, and then I'm out. You and I are done."

His jaw set. "I'm afraid it's not that easy."

"It is for me." She pointed to the broken flowers. "I know you came here to try to get back in my good graces. But that's not going to happen."

"Fine. Have it your way." Blaine's lips pressed into a thin line and he backed up, clearing her path to the tent. "But I'm actually here to save your life."

Cade craned his neck to check the ring for Rosalyn as he rushed toward the steps. But the red silks, dangling from the rig in the center of the ring, remained vacant.

Okay, now he was getting worried.

He hurried toward the backstage area. Maybe Rosalyn had been listening to warm-up music in headphones and hadn't heard Owen? Or maybe she'd had a wardrobe emergency or couldn't find her rosin.

Or maybe she was upset because he'd been a jerk. No, she was a professional. It wouldn't be that.

People in the stands whispered to each other, until the arena seemed abuzz with impatience. Two teens started a food fight with nachos. The din grew as voices raised and the confusion increased.

"Is it over?" A kid shouted loudly. "What about the girl who flies?"

And then—oh no. Trent, eating cotton candy and sitting next to a well-dressed, middle-aged man with silver highlights who could only be from Hollywood. Of all the nights . . .

Time for damage control.

Cade changed routes and hustled away from backstage and toward Owen. They needed a distraction until he could find Rosalyn. But what? They'd not planned any backup performances. Maybe the magician could go next?

As he rounded a tent pole behind the ring, Cade nearly plowed into someone wearing a dark T-shirt and baggy jeans. "Sorry." Then he did a double take. Miley. An idea registered. He gasped. "Miley!"

"What? I'm right here." She cracked a bubble with gum and peered at him, her nose ring glistening under the overhead lights. "Which is more than I can say for Rosalyn. Where is she, anyway?"

"I'm not sure." Cade winced as the food fight grew larger. Kids shrieked. Parents yelled. He raised his voice over the growing chaos. "I need your help."

Owen cleared his throat as he stood framed in the spotlight in the center of the ring. "Our aerialist must be detained." His nervous chuckle filled the mic. "Um, how about those poodles though, huh? Pretty groovy."

Cade scrubbed his hand down his cheek and shook his head. "Guess I owe you anyway, Mr. Secret Keeper. Want me to go backstage?" Miley looked over her shoulder.

"Actually, no." Cade gathered all the charm he could muster and channeled it into his smile. "I need you to go *on* stage."

Miley blinked. "I'm sorry, it's so loud in here." She blew another bubble. Two kids raced past them at full speed, throwing caramel corn into the air like confetti. "You won't believe what I thought you said."

"I mean it, Miley." He rested his hands on her shoulders. "I need you to do your comedy routine."

"You've lost it. All this circus dust is getting to your brain." She tapped his forehead with a black-painted nail. "It's the only explanation."

Cade shook her a little. "You're so good! You're a legit act."

She wobbled under his hands. "And I legit can't perform in front of people I know. That's the whole point of doing shows in New Orleans."

Frustration clawed at his chest. "I'm not asking you to take a ring to Mordor. Just tell some jokes."

She visibly swallowed. "I'd rather take the ring."

They locked eyes in a silent showdown. Caramel corn rained over them as the food fight ensued.

From the stage, Owen paced as the tech operator fought to keep the spotlight on his erratic movements. "Um . . . maybe if we all call Rosalyn's name at the same time, she'll hear us?"

Oh man. This was not the impression they were supposed to be giving of their town.

Cade turned back to Miley. "I'm officially begging."

"Fine." She huffed as she pushed away from him. "But only because that"—she jabbed her finger toward the arena—"is getting painful."

"Bless you." One of the many knots in his shoulder loosened. "And look on the bright side. At least now I don't have to keep your secret anymore."

Miley headed toward the ring, walking backward as she pointed at him. "You owe me."

He saluted. "Lifetime supply of Skittles."

"I'm thinking more of an IOU once you're mayor." She saluted back.

He'd created a monster. But as long as the monster was funny . . . "Deal. Go!" Cade texted the schedule change to Owen. Hopefully his ringmaster would be desperate enough to check his phone.

He slipped his cell back into his pocket. Then . . . oops. "Miley!" He trotted after her, reaching into his other pants pocket.

She turned, her dark eyes narrowed. "What *now*? I need to babysit some hobbits too?"

"Gum." Cade held out a tissue.

She leaned forward and spat her gum into his hand. "Happy?"

He folded the tissue. "Break a leg."

She glared. "I could only hope." Then she strode into the ring.

At least they'd bought a little bit of time. As Cade tossed the tissue, Owen announced Miley over the speaker.

Miley snatched the mic. "What a night, huh? I imagine you're confused. First there were pink poodles. Then a Tim Burton character appeared." She patted Owen's shoulder, who had yet to walk away. She gently pushed him along, raising a chuckle from the audience. "And now you expected to see an amazing performer fly through the air on beautiful silks, but instead, you're getting some weird girl with a nose ring making fun of people. It can only mean one thing."

She paused and the audience quieted to hear.

"That's right. You're in a fever dream."

A few chuckles spread through the crowd.

Miley paced slowly in the spotlight, one hand shoved in her back pocket. "Actually, you're in Magnolia Bay, but that's basically the same thing."

More laughter, louder this time. Those who had been standing took their seats again. Cade released his breath. Maybe this would work.

"I can't believe I'm here either, trust me." Miley switched the mic to her other hand. "Did you know statistically, people are more afraid of public speaking than dying?"

The crowd murmured.

"Yeah, I'm glad giving the eulogy at your own funeral isn't possible. I mean, talk about the worst day *ever*."

The audience roared.

Cade brushed a piece of popcorn off his shoulder. Crisis averted.

Now to find Rosalyn and hope there wasn't a new one.

Twenty -five

I'M HERE." ROSALYN HURRIED INTO THE back of the ring and stood next to Owen, her heart rate skyrocketing. Her hands shook. Save her life? What had Blaine meant?

The colored stripes on the tent blurred into a solid sheet of red. Was Miley doing stand-up comedy? Or maybe she was hallucinating. She blinked and swayed a little.

"Rosalyn!" Owen turned and gestured for Miley to wrap it up. He touched Rosalyn's arm, slick with sweat. Oh no. She needed more rosin.

He peered into her eyes with his overly made-up ones. "Are you okay?"

She tried to nod in the affirmative. *No.* Blaine had gotten in her head. *If they can't find you, they'll find someone you care about.* He'd snorted. *At least now I know that won't be me.*

Then he'd walked away. A power move meant to make her run after him. And she'd wanted to. Was the Mafia *here*? Had he not cleared it for her to have more time on her payments?

Had he set her up again?

Her stomach roiled. What if they found her parents? Put them in danger . . . or Cade. Or any of her friends here she'd been seen around the Bay with the past few weeks.

Cade . . . they still hadn't talked. Her heart hurt. She was mad. Scared. Ashamed.

And Blaine was right. She'd brought all this on herself.

Rosalyn struggled for a sufficient breath. She had to pull it together, get through the next two nights, then she could go . . . away. The fewer people involved now, the better.

She cast a look across the stands, but who was she even looking for? Not like she would recognize anyone out to harm her.

"Do you need another minute?" Owen frowned at her.

There was no more time. The scout was waiting, she had to be perfect. She shook her head in reply and the tent spun. Oh no. This was just like before.

Like in Saudi Arabia.

". . . with no further ado . . . Rosalyn Dupree!"

Wait. Owen had already announced her again? She blinked. The audience began to clap and cheer.

She started for her silks, her heart hammering as she grasped the fabric and positioned herself for the opening notes. She fought to focus as she waited for the music to begin. But her thoughts raced along with her erratic heartbeat. Flashes from Saudi Arabia.

This was different. She was on US soil. She was safe.

Was Cade even *here*?

The music sounded and Rosalyn mounted the silks. She flipped into a hip key rollup, then began a strategic climb for her split balance. Her arms shook.

She'd never gotten a fresh coat of rosin.

The song soared and she maneuvered into the splits, squeezing her core as she pointed her toes. Just in time, she remembered to be graceful. To smile.

To pretend like her world wasn't crashing around her.

As the music shifted in tempo, she started setting up an S-wrap, inverting before tucking the fabric around her waist and behind her back. She flipped the other direction and gripped her silks, arching her back and stretching her legs. She hadn't performed the wheel down drop last night, but it'd be easier on her sore muscles than the other drop from yesterday.

Her palms sweated as she completed the last wrap. Her vision blurred.

No. Not now.

Rosalyn held steady toward the top of the rig and waited for the song to reach its crescendo, trying to ignore the myriad thoughts running rampant. Trying to channel the adrenaline, make it work for her instead of against her.

Trying not to let the fear take control. History didn't have to repeat itself. She would be fine.

Then suddenly, there was Cade. Standing near the first row of risers to her left, looking up at her, his brow furrowed. He was here.

But what was he thinking? Was he mad at her? Mad about throwing off the show schedule in front of the scout?

His presence had brought her comfort last night, but now, she had none. She couldn't read him, could barely even *see* him through the panic taking control. She blinked.

The chord she'd been waiting for sounded. Rosalyn released the fabric on cue and spun like a pinwheel down the length of the silks, unwrapping a layer with every turn.

Too many layers.

Something was wrong.

Her heart thudded.

The fabric should have grabbed her by now, hitching around her waist and jerking her back with an intensity that often left a bruise.

But there was no more fabric.

She was falling.

Again.

The music distorted in her ears. The tent blurred. Someone screamed.

Rosalyn reached out and grasped the air, fingers clawing as they finally hooked onto one of the poles. She clung, digging in her fingers as gravity took over. Which way was up? She rotated another full spin and caught the second pole as she braced for impact.

She collapsed onto the mat.

Cade leaped over the short wall separating the ring from the first section. He landed on the ring floor, charging toward Rosalyn before fully regaining his balance. His thoughts churned with his feet, fears keeping rhythm with the pounding of his heart. *No. No. No.*

"Rosalyn!" He pushed past Owen, who shouted into the crowd to call an ambulance. Linc and Miley immediately went to work holding back the curious audience from surging forward. Someone shouted for a nurse.

"Are you okay?" Cade dropped to his knees beside Rosalyn, taking her hand. He was afraid to touch anything else. Her eyes fluttered open.

More shouts sounded behind him, but he refused to take his gaze off her face. Her eyes closed again, her complexion pale against her black leotard. Glitter shimmered in her hair. But her chest rose and fell with each ragged breath. *Thank You, God.*

He squeezed her palm. "Can you hear me?"

She pulled in a deeper breath and fully opened her eyes. They blinked, then widened with panic, and she tried to sit up.

"No, don't move!" Cade gently pressed against her shoulders. "You fell. We're waiting on the paramedics." Thank God again he'd insisted on the crash mat. Worry weighed him down, until all he wanted was to collapse next to her.

That'd been close. Too close.

"I think I'm okay." Rosalyn gingerly rotated her neck, then shook each of her arms. "You're here."

"Of course I'm here." Cade eased back to give her space as she sat up, cast a look over his shoulder. August Bowman and Noah had joined Linc and Miley's efforts in crowd control, alongside Elisa's father, Isaac Bergeron. Even Mama D stood guard, waving her cane in warning. It seemed to be working. The ring was empty, save for Owen still pacing on his cell phone and barking a demand for an ambulance.

He twisted back to Rosalyn. "I think you should wait for a professional before you get up."

"I caught a lot of my weight before I hit the ground." Rosalyn flexed her feet and winced as she slowly stood. He grasped her arms, supporting her. "My knee is a little tight."

Why did she keep staring past him into the stands? Was she looking for Blaine?

Regardless—"Rosalyn . . . I'm so sorry."

"I'll be okay, I promise." She hadn't let go of his arms, which was good, because he didn't want to let go of her either.

His eyes roamed her tear-streaked face. If something had happened to her, with this mess still between them . . . He swallowed. "No, I mean, for last night—"

"Miss, are you okay?" Captain Sanders from the fire department stepped toward Rosalyn. A paramedic carrying a black medical bag followed close behind. "They said you fell."

Rosalyn wiped her eyes, stepping away from Cade. "I'm fine."

His arms immediately felt empty, the air between them, still charged. Had she heard his apology? Accepted it?

"With all due respect, ma'am, you don't look fine." Captain gestured toward the bag. "Let me run some vitals, okay?"

Before she could protest, Sanders ushered Rosalyn toward the stands to sit down. Cade cast a look over their heads, up the risers to the seats where Trent had been sitting. Empty. Not surprising, seeing how people cleared out upon realizing the show was definitely *not* going to go on.

Of all the nights. He watched as the captain examined Rosalyn's eyes with a small flashlight. Maybe she would be ready to talk after the exam, finally hear him. Forgive him. Maybe Trent and his boss would be outside waiting to talk, and they would be impressed with what they did see.

Maybe this night could still turn around.

"Hey." Noah crossed the ring to Cade, his face grave beneath the rim of his ball cap. "Is she okay?"

"I think so." Cade looked back at Rosalyn, who was clearly protesting the rest of the exam. The paramedic standing next to Sanders planted his hands on his hips and pointed out something Cade couldn't fully catch about "falling ten feet."

"She was just shaken."

"I would be too. I think we all are, watching that." Noah shook his head. "I'll have nightmares."

"No kidding." Cade's heart still throbbed with residual panic.

And worry that they still hadn't resolved things between them. He watched as Captain Sanders snatched his walkie-talkie from his belt and held it to his ear. Then he dropped the oxygen meter back into the medical bag and exchanged quick words with the paramedic. They grabbed their gear and rushed off, leaving Rosalyn alone on the risers.

Strange. Cade stepped forward. Maybe now that she'd had a short break and time to catch her breath, she'd listen to him. He could tell her the whole story about her financials, convince her to stay in town a few more weeks. Rest.

Reconnect.

"Cade." Owen huffed up behind him, bending over and bracing

his hands on his knees. His theater makeup had smeared dark circles under his eyes. "You've got to come right now." His mouth pinched into a grim line. "There's an emergency."

Twenty -six

ORANGE FLAMES LICKED THE NIGHT SKY. Cade stared at Bayou Beignets, completely engulfed in fire. Streams of water shot onto the blaze, which greedily consumed everything in the charred building. Clouds of black smoke billowed away from the residue, drifting toward the starless sky as the fire truck's strobe lights flashed.

Cade drew a deep breath of smoky air and immediately regretted it. He turned his face into his elbow and coughed. Firemen soaked the roofs of the shops next door with more hoses, calling caution to the crowd pressing against the barriers constructed on the road.

"What happened?" He didn't expect Noah or Owen to have an answer—they'd been there as long as he had—but the question begged to be asked. They'd just been there the night before.

Noah's face was drawn, arms crossed as he stood beside Cade on the sidewalk, apart from the crowd. "They don't know. Chief said it started during the circus." He exhaled. "Thankfully, no one was there."

Cade released another cough. "Does Zoey know?"

Noah pointed. Cade followed his gesture to a spot in the shadows, where Zoey stood silhouetted against the fire truck headlights with Linc. Her face was burrowed into his wide shoulder, and he cupped the back of her head, as if to prevent her from turning around to watch. Smoke cut through the air around them.

Cade's heart twisted. Poor Zoey—watching her shop burn while the entire town lingered. Even now, Madame Paulette tried to question Captain Sanders while the man balanced a hose on his shoulder. Mrs. Peters and Trish also pressed against the roadblocks, though he suspected, judging by Mrs. Peter's bossy frown and Trish's flirty smile, it was for two very different reasons.

"I'm gonna go attempt to help with crowd control." Noah rolled his eyes in the direction of Madame Paulette. "And I'll let you know if I hear anything on the cause. Do you need to get back to Rosalyn?"

He should. But would it look bad to the town if he abandoned the emergency, as mayor-elect? Did Rosalyn even want to see him? "I'll stick around for a bit, see if I can do anything."

She wouldn't just leave, right?

"I'm sure Dad will be here any minute if he's not already." But he didn't see his father in the lingering crowd.

Cade shoved his hands in his pockets as a new worry occurred— were people going to want refunds? Rosalyn had been a featured performance and had barely had a chance to do a single skill before the entire event shut down.

And would she be able to perform tomorrow night for the final show?

Not that she owed it to him to stay. He'd been a jerk, as Linc had candidly pointed out.

Someone tapped his shoulder. "Excuse me."

Cade turned.

The middle-aged man who had been sitting with Trent stood before him, sympathetic eyes peering beneath thick brows. He had to be six-foot-three. Trent stood to the man's right, wearing his trademark sunglasses and blazer.

"This a horrible time for introductions, but I'm Marc Oliver from WiseNet Productions." The taller man extended his hand. "You know Trent."

"Yes, of course." Cade shook his hand. "I appreciate you coming." He gestured to what remained of Bayou Beignets. "I'm sorry your visit worked out like this. This isn't our best night." Though it was certainly going worse for others. His gaze darted back to Zoey, heart dropping.

"Things happen. This is a shame, for sure." Marc stepped back as a chunk of burnt roof fell into the building. Heat surged and fresh ash rose into the sky. "I will say, I think Magnolia Bay has a lot of potential."

Cade heard the unspoken conjunction hovering in the air. "But?"

"But you guys aren't there yet." Marc gestured toward the smoke. "Between this new eyesore and all the repairs still needed around town . . . unfortunately, it's not film-ready. And I can tell it won't be for some time."

Cade's stomach knotted. He fought to keep his smile and professionalism. "I understand. Maybe you'll give us another try in a few years."

Assuming there was still a town by then. Assuming the Blue Pirogue didn't close and the shops didn't start slowing dropping like flies as tourism slowed . . .

The knot tightened.

"You put on quite a production earlier—we were impressed with what we got to see." Marc's smile dropped into concern. "And I sincerely hope your aerialist is okay."

He nodded. "Me too." Rosalyn wasn't his though, was she?

"We'll get out of your hair. You obviously have your hands full." Marc nodded toward Trent. "I'm sorry we don't have better news."

"Yeah, sorry, man." Trent clapped him on the shoulder as Marc started down the sidewalk. "I really wanted this to happen."

So did he. "I know." Cade cleared his throat. "We'll keep in touch."

"You got it." Trent shot him a thumbs-up before hurrying to catch up to his boss.

Smoke curled around him. Cade coughed as he stared at the steaming structure. Firemen hoisted long hoses. Ash drifted lazily from the sky. The acrid scent of defeat hung heavy in the air.

He had to tell his father he wasn't running. He clearly wasn't fit for a leadership role. So many people depending on him to make Magnolia Days the most profitable one ever, and he'd failed.

But if he didn't run, he put his father in a bind and would fail his family name.

His lungs constricted. Cade was tired of no-win situations. He didn't have what it took to pass the bar. He didn't have what it took to run his hometown.

He didn't have what Rosalyn needed. And could he blame her after last night?

Cade checked his phone on the off chance she'd texted him back. He'd let her know when he left with Owen that he wanted to talk as soon as she was ready, and he'd keep her posted on the fire.

No responses.

A surprised gasp sounded to his left, as Sadie, Harper, and several new onlookers joined the group. "What happened?" Sadie's face was stricken as she looked at Cade for answers. He looked down at his cell, then at the fire, and shook his head.

He had none.

She was so tired of falling.

Rosalyn cautiously re-entered the deserted circus tent, one hand on the gear bag she'd forgotten backstage. She'd driven almost all the way to Bayou Beignets to find Cade before realizing and turning back to go grab it. Now, everyone was gone—gathered at the fire, most likely.

The emergency had gotten the paramedics off Rosalyn's back, who had wanted her to go to the hospital as a precaution, but that was hardly worth the despair her new friend must be going through. Poor Zoey.

Seemed like nothing about this night had gone as anticipated.

Cade's apologies rang in her ears, hovering, making her unsure what to do with it. She

eyed her silks, still rigged in the center of the ring.

Funny how quickly things changed.

She shouldn't be here alone, not with all the what-ifs circling her mind, but something held her in the ring, kept her eyes fixed on her silks. Her knee twinged. A nasty bruise was forming on arm. Her head pulsed, but nothing a dose of Tylenol couldn't help. The paramedics had been cautious, as expected, but she really was okay.

Physically, at least.

Thankfully, her parents hadn't seen her freefall. They'd planned to come tomorrow night for her final show, but now . . .

Would the show go on?

So many unknowns.

The portable lights were turned off, the moon shining from the open flaps and the multiples strings of fairy lights providing the only glow in the tent.

As if beckoned by an unknown force, Rosalyn dropped her bag on the packed floor and walked back to her silks, trailing her hands over the glossy fabric. It'd been way too long since she performed for herself. For joy. For love of the sport.

After everything that happened—would she get that back? Or would she always be afraid of falling now?

She swallowed. But it wasn't just about the accidents. She stared up at the long strips of material. She'd been losing her edge way before the falls. Before Blaine's lies, before Saudi Arabia. When had it started?

When had she lost herself?

Her knee trembled. She shuddered as the replay of her fall flashed through her mind. Figured—she'd needed the best performance of her life tonight. For Cade. For the scout, for the town.

And yet when the stakes were the highest, she'd given the worst performance possible. There was something almost poetic in that.

Rosalyn took a breath. Her pride throbbed a lot harder than her knee, though it didn't feel great. And yet, she had to do this.

Needed to.

A prayer formed on her lips, one she couldn't quite put to words. Then before she could change her mind, she inverted onto her silks, wrapping each pole around her foot. There was no music. No audience.

Well, maybe an audience of One. If she hadn't disappointed him too.

She channeled her grief into the fabric. Rolling, wrapping, climbing. Her breath came in even gasps as she expelled the energy and adrenaline flowing through her weary body.

Man, she'd messed up. Big time. Trusting Blaine, being naive, letting herself get taken advantage of. Denying what was obvious out of pride.

Cade had tried to tell her the truth. But now she was stuck. The Mafia was out there—somewhere. Blaine was gone, her only link to paying off her debts. He'd have to get in touch with her eventually to handle that, but it'd be like him to leave her hanging until the last minute. Let her be scared for the way she stood up to him.

She flipped upside down into the splits, extending her leg above her head. It was her fault. Blaine held all the cards because *she'd* let him. Rosalyn shook out of the split wrap and climbed again, arching into a perfect pendant. Then she began to wrap for a star drop. The crash mat was no longer under her silks, but she didn't care.

She needed Something way bigger to catch her this time.

Rosalyn wrapped the silks around her leg. Blood pounded in her temples from the upside-down pose. It wasn't just Blaine who had her in chains. It was expectations—her mother's, her own. A lifetime of trying to be the best.

Maybe achieving perfection all those years at school had been the issue. Maybe that's what made Rosalyn spiral into panic when faced with the idea that she might not be perfect after all. If she wasn't, what did she have to offer?

Maybe that's why she clung to her pride with both hands.

She was afraid of falling from it too.

She wrapped the fabric tighter.

Held the star position, arms and legs extended, one hand grasping her silks. All she had to do was let go. This time, unlike earlier in the evening, she knew she'd wrapped correctly. But her hand felt glued to the fabric.

What if she fell?

Tears dripped off her face to the ground below. What if she never got free of Blaine or this debt? What if she never felt like she was enough for Mom? What if she never got to perform for *herself* again?

And Cade . . . her heart ached. She needed him. His very presence comforted her, challenged her. Brought out the best in her.

Made her laugh. Feel safe.

She gulped. He'd apologized, but . . . did he want her to stay? *Could* she? It seemed best to tie all this up on her own. Get away from Magnolia Bay and settle her debts, finish this paperwork nightmare of a marriage, and stand on her own two feet awhile.

Hadn't she and Cade always been on opposing teams anyway?

She stared at the ground below her, so far away.

Surrender.

The word bubbled from her heart and echoed in her brain. Tears pricked Rosalyn's eyes and she gripped the silks harder. No. She couldn't surrender. Surrender meant telling her parents the truth. Letting go of pride and perfectionism. Opening her heart to Cade, taking a risk. None of that was safe.

It'd be falling all over again.

Surrender.

It came again, like a voice this time, firm but gentle.

Was God finally speaking to her?

"Help me." The prayer slipped through her lips as more tears fell. Then a piece of fear slipped off and joined them. She swallowed. "I'm scared." Speaking the truth out loud loosened another piece.

Maybe that'd been the secret. Simply speaking up.

And being heard by the One who had been whispering all along.

"I'm scared of rejection." She forced boldness into her voice. "I'm scared the worst about me is true."

The statements fell off her lips and mingled with her tears on the arena floor, each one lightening her load, loosening the knot in her chest.

"And if the worst *is* true . . . if I'm not perfect . . . will anyone want me?"

Rosalyn took a breath, hands shaking against the fabric.

Cade's words from that fateful day in New Orleans, at Bruno's, filled her mind. *I don't think that's how that works, Ace.*

She'd believed so many lies for so long, stating truths out loud suddenly felt marvelously clear. And she didn't have to have it all together first.

She really didn't have to be perfect.

A measure of peace slowly wedged in her heart. She couldn't predict the future, or what Mom would think, or if Cade would stick by her through her imperfect mess.

She couldn't control any of those things. But she *could* make good decisions—starting with telling her parents the whole truth.

And she could tell Cade how she felt. She could squash her pride once and for all.

And fly. Rosalyn let go. Unrolled.

Soared.

Joy bubbled. The fabric caught her—or maybe love?—and Rosalyn smiled as she stood, back on solid ground. The urge to whistle overcame her, and she laughed. Yep. She could do this. She could tell the truth, could reveal her imperfection.

She could surrender.

Rosalyn let go of the fabric and turned to grab her bag. Movement fluttered across the ring as she stood upright. She looked over and froze.

A man's silhouette blocked the tent exit.

 Twenty -seven

ARE YOU *SURE* YOU DON'T WANT A coffee?" Cade's mom hovered in the doorway of his parents' elegantly decorated living room, still wearing a neatly pressed pantsuit despite the late hour. "I can make decaf. We have the pods."

Cade stretched back on their white leather couch, careful not to let the soot-covered soles of his shoes touch the material as he hooked one ankle over his knee. He was sure he didn't want any coffee, as he'd already stated twice. He was too jittery to consume anything.

For the first time in his life, he wasn't hungry.

He had to tell his dad he wasn't running for mayor.

Before he could refuse the coffee again, Dad leaned over from his perch in his favorite recliner. He wore his reading glasses, and his dress slacks hung over the top of his padded gray house shoes. He'd ditched his loafers the minute they had returned from the fire. "For Pete's sake, son, she's gonna levitate off the floor if you don't give her a task."

"Does she even know how to make it?" Cade whispered with a

wince. Penny Landry was great at table settings, event planning, and hosting—not so much at anything related to the kitchen.

Dad shrugged as he leaned back in his chair. "The housekeeper taught her how to use the Keurig a few weeks ago. Hard to mess that up."

Guess they'd find out. "Sure, Mom." Cade pulled a beige-and-black accent pillow into his lap and tried to get comfortable. His nerves thrummed. Rosalyn wasn't answering his texts—and she'd never shown up at the fire. Had she not forgiven him? Or maybe she went to the hospital to get checked out?

Or had she actually left?

He cleared his throat. "Decaf would be great."

Mom's face lit. "Be right back."

"I think I know why you asked to talk." Dad fiddled with the coaster on the black oak end table. "But first, how's Rosalyn?"

He'd love to know the answer to that too.

Dad continued. "I didn't see it, but I heard about her fall."

Cade briefly closed his eyes, but no, then he saw her accident in vivid replay. "She's fine, I think." Wherever she was. "As she put it, she managed to catch herself to some extent before she hit the mat."

"That had to have been scary—for everyone." Dad lowered his head and gave him *that* look over the top of his glasses, the one that always meant he was saying more than he was saying.

But Cade couldn't handle subtext tonight—or any more discussion about Rosalyn. He simply nodded. "It was."

An awkward pause ensued as the air thickened with expectation. The clock above the custom fireplace mantel ticked a steady rhythm, and cool air rushed over Cade's face via the ceiling fan.

Dad shifted in his chair, the leather squeaking. "Look, son . . ."

Then a sudden clanking of coffee mugs sounded from the kitchen, followed by a muttered "curse substitute," as Mom had always called them growing up.

Cade exchanged an amused look with his father. "I'm glad I didn't actually want coffee."

Dad snorted. "You know you'll have to drink it anyway."

There were a lot of things tonight Cade had to do that he didn't want to. But the sooner he got this conversation over with, the sooner he could go home and prepare to face everything tomorrow would bring. Fielding phone calls from refund requests. Balancing the books on the festival. Helping Zoey navigate her insurance claim. Brainstorming a fresh round of town fundraising ideas.

Adjusting to the idea of Magnolia Bay without Rosalyn in it.

Cade took a deep breath. "You don't want me to run for mayor, Dad."

The clock ticked away several seconds. "I don't?"

"I can't even pull off my current job." Cade scrubbed his palm over his jaw. "The festival is flopping. The circus—well, I don't even know if we're going to have a circus tomorrow. The town is still in the red . . . I failed."

Dad sighed. "I was afraid you were going to say that."

He wasn't even trying to refute it or give him a pep talk? No "You're a Landry, you can do it"?

"I'm not ready for this step of mayor. Just like Magnolia Bay isn't ready for a movie, again."

Dad tilted his head. "I take it the scout said no?"

"Adamantly." Cade wiped at a spot of soot on his sleeve. A new layer of fatigue washed over him. "I don't blame them. Everything is a mess right now. I tried to force too much, too soon."

"I think you're doing the same thing to yourself." Dad's quiet voice calmed the tumultuous tossing of Cade's thoughts.

"What do you mean?"

"You've always had big ideas." Dad smiled, the chair creaking under his weight as he angled toward Cade. "Even when you were a kid. You're a go-getter. A prankster." He laughed. "As evidenced by all the times I bailed you out."

He didn't need reminding. But his dad was smiling. Cade frowned. "You thought that was funny?"

"Creative more than funny." Dad shook his head. "My point is, you always shot for the moon. You love big. You feel big. You put yourself out there, for better or for worse. This is one of those 'worse' times."

Cade stared at his hands, not even realizing he'd clenched them in his lap. He let go, watching his skin flood with color again. "I let you down a lot, growing up. I don't want to do that again."

Dad removed his glasses. "You've most certainly never let me down."

"Come on. You had to practically bribe the principal to keep me from getting expelled."

"That man was a joke." Dad smirked. "He couldn't see past his angel-child's halo to realize there were horns on the kid's head."

Cade stilled. "So you knew Justin was the real issue? Why didn't you let on?"

"It's called diplomacy. I navigated the situation so that it was best for everyone. Besides, I couldn't let you think that was the way to solve your problems—even if I did think that kid deserved a fist in the nose."

Huh. "I always thought you were disappointed in me."

Dad waved his hand through the air. "It was bad timing . . . on election year if I remember right." He met Cade's gaze. "But *never* disappointed."

"But I'm a Landry." Cade hadn't intended to give himself the speech, but someone had to do it. "Doesn't not running make us look bad? I'm not stepping up to fill your shoes. I'm failing the family name."

Mom swept through the room, a red coffee mug in hand. "Here you go." She proudly presented it to Cade, clearly oblivious to the tension in the room.

Cade looked down into the nearly transparent brown liquid and managed to hide his shudder. "Thanks, Mom."

"I'll let you two keep talking." She slipped back into the kitchen.

Dad watched her go, his expression pensive. "Like all parents, I'm sure there are things we could have done differently. I hate that you feel like you have to hide how you feel because of our name. Like with this campaign. Choosing not to run is not failure. It's just a little surprising—I thought that was your ultimate goal all along, when you came home from Yale and didn't pursue law."

Cade stared into his mug. "While we're on that subject . . . you should probably know I didn't change careers by choice." He looked up, determined to say it to his father's face. "I didn't pass the bar."

Dad nodded. "I know."

"You—what?" Cade stared at his father, who looked completely serious. "Why didn't you ever say anything?"

"I figured you didn't want me to know, or you'd have told me yourself."

Cade blinked at him. "Are you serious?"

"That's a hard test." Dad shrugged. "Not everyone passes the first try. Doesn't mean you're a failure. The bigger issue is why you didn't just try again."

Because failing twice felt like tenfold.

Dad's expression sobered. "Look, son. You have choices here. If you want to run for mayor because you're interested in the job, I'll support you. If you want to keep doing what you're doing, that's fine too. We'll find another candidate. But the last thing I want is for you to wake up with your own stress-related health problems in a few years." He winced. "Learn from my mistakes."

"It might be too late for that one." Cade risked a sip of coffee, wincing at the watery texture. "I've had some anxiety flare-ups lately, and I didn't say anything because I didn't want you to think I couldn't handle all of this."

"No one can handle everything." Dad replaced his glasses. "The question is—what do you want?"

Cade's throat tightened along with his grip on his mug. A drop splashed over the side, landed on the couch. "I'm not sure what I want."

No, that wasn't true. He wanted Rosalyn to stay in the Bay. He wanted to help bring the town back to its full potential. He wanted to *help* people. "You know, one of my most vivid memories is when you were inaugurated. I was ten, and I had this red-and-blue striped tie."

"I remember." Dad smiled. "Your mom spent a week picking out your outfit. I think she stressed over it more than mine."

"The high school marching band played and you looked so regal. I remember thinking I wanted to be important too. Like you." Cade shook his head. "I think somewhere along the way, that turned into thinking I had to literally *be* you—the ultimate Landry standard."

"I never meant to create that kind of pressure."

"I know. I didn't blame you." Cade wiped his thumb over the coffee spill on the cushion next to him. "You know, I liked helping Rosalyn with some legal issues the last few days. It felt . . ." He looked up at the ceiling, exhaled. "Rewarding."

"There you go." Dad slapped his thigh. "Maybe that's your sign."

"Maybe." Cade rolled the concept around in his mind. Trying the bar again? But what would happen to the town?

He absently took another sip of coffee-colored water. Huge mistake. He set the mug on the end table. "I know I love Magnolia Bay. I don't know how exactly I want to serve it down the road, but I know I want to. Just not as mayor."

Dad nodded. "I'm sure there's a way to make that happen. But there are a few things we need to clean up. Like canceling the campaign party."

"Right." More humiliation headed his way. But at least this time he could go into it knowing his father was on his side.

"Look, this was on me." Dad scooted to the end of his chair and braced his arms on his knees. "I pushed you to run too soon, and on top of that, I railroaded you with the announcement before you were ready. So I'll be the one to cancel everything."

"No, Dad. I appreciate it, but I want to." Cade pressed his lips together. "In fact, keep the party as planned. I'll make the announcement there, so everyone can hear at the same time. At least they'll get cupcakes out of it."

Dad's brow rose. "I respect that." His voice softened. "And I hope you know I'm proud of you, whether you're the town director, the mayor, or a street-sweeper."

"Is that position available?" Cade joked, even as his throat swelled. *Proud.* The word sank in deep, like a balm. "Thanks, Dad."

He swiped at his eyes. Man, he was tired. And still smelled like smoke. "By the way, I can't believe Mom is letting me sit on this couch right now while I'm this dirty."

"She's getting a new one for her birthday." Dad waved one hand through the air.

Cade snorted as he slid to the edge of the sofa. "Then I guess I can confess to that coffee spill I made."

"Nah. We'll keep that one between us. After thirty-five years of marriage—you pick your battles." Dad winked. "I'll tell her you're leaving."

They stood. Cade checked for a text from Rosalyn, even while knowing it wouldn't be there. He did have several new emails, though they wouldn't be from her. She technically hadn't ever responded to the one he'd sent inviting her to perform at the circus.

Had that only been less than three months ago?

Cade gave the emails a quick scroll as he waited by the front door for his parents to return from the kitchen. Magnolia Days business, a digital receipt, two daily Bible verses he was behind on reading and—an alert from the bank?

He stopped. Blaine had attempted access in Rosalyn's accounts two days ago, but the notice had gone to Cade's spam account. A follow up email had made it to his inbox—along with another, whose subject title read "Thanks for Registering."

Cade squinted as he read the fine print, heart thumping. Oh no. He'd created a new log-in, gotten back in. Already the numbers in the balance were lower than before. He had to tell Rosalyn, ASAP.

He kept scrolling through the fine print. Was that why Blaine had shown up suddenly at the festival yesterday? He must have tried access two days ago and came to see Rosalyn in person.

But why the rush?

Cade frowned. The flowers . . . the charm . . . the kiss. Blaine had obviously been trying to get on her good side. Again, why? To try to regain access? Rosalyn wouldn't have granted it.

So how had Blaine gotten a new log-in?

Something wasn't connecting.

His parents headed toward him from the kitchen, his mother's voice pitching in protest. "I heard you earlier, Ted. You know we've been married thirty-*six* years this fall, not thirty-five."

Dad shot Cade a wink, then smiled at his wife. "Honey, with you, it only feels like ten."

She good-naturedly rolled her eyes. "Well, you're still not going to get to sit on the new couch."

"Yes, dear." Dad pecked her on the cheek. "Always remember, Cade, when it comes to marriage—what's yours is hers, and what's *hers* is hers." He chuckled.

Cade sucked in a breath. That was it.

That's why Blaine wanted to stay married.

He quickly said his goodbyes and jogged to his car, dialing Rosalyn's number on the way. She might not want to forgive him or stick around town for him.

But if his hunch was right, Blaine was much more desperate than either of them would have thought.

Twenty-eight

B LAINE. YOU SCARED ME." ROSALYN pressed her hand over her racing heart as she tugged her gear bag up on her shoulder. Shadows crisscrossed the tent, his form still partially obscured in darkness as he approached. "What are you doing?"

Relief that it wasn't someone else—some unknown gangster—was so potent she almost didn't care why he was there.

Almost.

Blaine came closer, into the glow of the fairy lights, his face flushed, collar unbuttoned. "We've got to go."

Oh man. He'd lost it. Fear flickered, and then she remembered—he was a bully. She lifted her chin. "I'm not going anywhere with you."

Then she pushed past him, out of the tent, into the festival grounds. The balmy night air caressed her sweaty neck, and she drew a steadying breath. The parking lot was to her right, and she strode toward it, heart thrumming. *Don't follow me, don't follow—*

His hand caught her wrist. "Wrong way, doll."

"*Don't* call me that." She whirled around, tugged free. "Let me go."

"That's a little bossy." His eyes flashed. "Seeing how you have zero cards to play here."

"Have you lost your mind?" She backstepped away from him, noting the whites of his eyes, the taut set of his shoulders, his mussed hair. This wasn't the buttoned-up, professional Blaine she knew.

This was a desperate man.

"No, Rosalyn, you're the crazy one if you *don't* come with me." He took her elbow, started hustling her toward the opposite end of the parking lot. "Do you have any idea who we're dealing with?"

She started to resist his propelling her forward, then paused. Maybe if she went along with it, she could catch him off guard, get away long enough to run to her car. Her phone was zipped in her bag, nowhere near reach to send a subtle text.

She steeled her voice, hid her nerves. "You're the one who took out the loan. Why are you worried about it now? I have the money—or most of it. Pay it off and be done with this. Then we can both stop looking over our shoulder."

"You don't get it." His grip tightened on the sensitive skin about her elbow and she flinched. "It's not just your loan . . . and you don't have enough to pay it off, anyway."

"What do you mean? I saw my accounts—"

"You think you got it all figured out, don't you?" Blaine shook her arm, made a *tsk*. "Don't worry, I found a loophole—as I'd planned."

She stopped hard, throwing him off balance. "*What* are you talking about?"

He let go of her, squared off. Parking lot shadows sent sharp angles across his face. A cloud drifted in front of the moon, casting an eerie glow through the haze. "You might be a star, Rosalyn, but you're so gullible. Do you really think marrying me was the only way out of Saudi Arabia?"

Her breath hitched. Surely he didn't—

"I knew you'd eventually wise up to your money being moved around, so I made a backup plan while I had the chance. Foreign country, you having that silly fit. All the puzzle pieces came together like magic." He smirked. "Being Mr. Rosalyn Dupree now gives me all kinds of perks."

It had all been a scam . . . Her stomach clenched. She wanted to throw up. "You lied to me."

"Of course I lied, Rosalyn." Blaine scoffed. He pulled his key fob from his pocket, and headlights from a silver Porsche flashed a few yards away. "Who doesn't lie when they owe the Mafia an insane amount of gambling debt? You're more naive than I thought."

"You used my money—used *me*—as a launch pad for gambling?"

He tilted his head, shrugged. "If that's what you want to call it."

She *wanted* to punch him in the face.

He shifted his weight, eyes darting around the deserted lot. "I came here after you blocked me to try to convince you to see reason, partner up with me to get out of this mess. Which you didn't."

She crossed her arms over her chest. "You really thought a bouquet a flowers was going to make me okay with you stealing my money? Lying to me? Tricking me?" How had she ever trusted this person with her career? Her entire life? She'd been such a fool.

"You were way too lucrative of all my clients to let it go. So I did what I had to do." He shoved his hand through his hair. "For the record, I never meant to get in this deep."

Her heart stammered. So they were both in danger—and it sounded like he'd already spent more of her money. "You're not going to get away with this. I'll get a lawyer and—"

"You better hope I *do* get away with it." Blaine snorted. "You think they won't use you to get to me? What you owe is chump change compared to my debt. And they'll get it all, one way or another. We've got to work together to fix this."

"I will *never* work with you again."

"Come with me. It's safer if we're together. Then they can't use you as collateral."

"You expect me to trust you to keep me safe? When *you* put us in this mess?" She backstepped away. "You're insane."

His eyes darkened. "Rosalyn, get in the car. We'll go somewhere safe, make a plan. We need to book you some bigger gigs now that your knee is—"

"No." She was done with this. She looked him in the eyes, held her ground. "I'm going home, Blaine. I suggest you do the same."

On shaky legs, she turned toward her car.

She'd made it approximately six steps before arms wrapped around her from behind, pinning her own arms to her sides. Her bag fell to the ground.

"I said get in the car, Rosalyn!" Blaine lifted her off the sidewalk, swinging her toward his vehicle.

Her legs windmilled in the air and she shrieked. "Let me go!"

"This is the only way." His arms were a vice around her middle. Adrenaline and panic seemed to be giving him unnatural strength.

But not enough. The second her feet touched the ground again, she kicked back and found traction in his shin.

He cursed and grappled with her as she flailed for freedom. She turned and slapped him and he grabbed her forearms in rough fists, holding tight. "As always, you're making things way more complicated than they need to be." He growled, his cheek flushed red from the contact.

"*Let go!*" She briefly considered head butting him at this close range, but didn't want to risk the injury to herself. She had to stay sharp.

"Just get in the car." Blaine panted, his eyes feral. He shoved her toward the Porsche.

Rosalyn swallowed, gauging her next move. He'd already lied and stolen from her—now physical violence. What was next?

Her mouth went thick and dry. *God, help me.* The prayer tumbled from her anxious mind.

Surrender.

Now? Rosalyn might be new to praying regularly, but that idea seemed like horrible timing.

She struggled against Blaine's iron grip, but her fight only seemed to make him stronger. He was half-dragging, half-carrying her now. Her bad knee throbbed in protest. A few more steps and she'd be tossed inside the car, where escape would be much less likely.

Surrender.

Then the meaning hit her. She stopped fighting and went limp in Blaine's arms. Her dead weight caught him off guard, and he faltered in his forward progress. "What are you doing? Stop!"

Fighting her instincts to struggle, she hung as heavy as she could, offering no resistance for him to use as leverage. He couldn't get a grip on her, and her arms slid out of his sweaty grasp like wet noodles.

She crumbled to the warm pavement.

"Hey!" The word roared from behind, followed by the pounding of footsteps.

Rosalyn looked up in time to see Cade launch himself over the back end of the Porsche.

And slam his fist straight into Blaine's jaw.

Where was Simon LeMoine when you needed him?

Cade shifted on the edge of the uncomfortable ER bed, the smell of antiseptic and sweat permeating the small space. His nose throbbed, along with his shoulder from where he and Blaine had ended up tousling on the ground as the cops arrived.

But he had a feeling he'd be riding the adrenaline wave of seeing Rosalyn taken against her will for hours to come.

He took a deep breath, closing his eyes against the harsh fluorescent lights not helping the pounding in his head. Was Rosalyn still in the waiting room? Sheriff Rubart was taking her statement there, or at least, had been when Cade was ushered through the swinging ER doors a half hour ago, blood dripping all over his favorite shirt and the hospital floor.

Blaine had a surprisingly solid head-butt.

The pale blue curtain surrounding his bed whooshed open and a middle-aged, dark-haired nurse in navy scrubs entered. "Here's your meds and your cold pack, honey. We're waiting on the X-ray results."

He eagerly took the ice pack she handed over, pressed it against his sore face. "Thank you."

She handed him a cup of water and some pain medicine, which he eagerly threw back.

Groaning sounded from the other side of the curtain, along with the clinking of handcuffs against a bedrail. Cade sat up a little straighter.

Maybe he didn't need Simon after all.

The nurse raised her eyebrow at him, pursed her lips knowingly as if hiding a smile. "Let me know if you need anything else. The doctor will come back with the results." She pulled the curtain shut as she left.

Cade swung his dangling feet against the side of the bed. He didn't want to be stuck here. He wanted to find Rosalyn, finish his apology. Maybe she wouldn't trust him again, after he'd treated her so poorly the other night—and she definitely had no reason to stay in Magnolia Bay—but he had to at least make sure she knew how he felt before she left.

The curtain whooshed back open.

He looked up. "That was fast—" Inhaled. Not the doctor. Rosalyn.

"Hey." He cleared his throat, his carefully practiced, profound apology fleeing his memory. "I—I wanted—"

She came straight at him, a blur of citrus and hair spray and desperate warmth, threw her arms around his neck, and kissed him.

Ow.

The best kind of pain.

He dropped the ice pack and cradled her head with the back of his hand—his knuckles hurt too, but man, he'd do it all again for her—and kissed her back, all salty tears and gratitude and longing. They were nearly the same height, him sitting on the high bed and her standing wedged between his legs, and she snuggled in closer, breaking the kiss to briefly rest her forehead against his.

"Thank you," she breathed.

He pulled back to look at her, his fingers trailing down the soft arms of the hoodie she'd thrown on sometime over the past half hour. Her elaborate performance hairstyle was mussed, blonde hairs fraying free from her tousled, glittered braids. Dark makeup was smeared under her eyes, slightly bloodshot.

She'd never looked more beautiful.

Had she forgiven him? "A thank-you note would've been acceptable, but I'm not complaining." He grinned, and she finally did too, her shoulders sagging as if a burden had lifted.

"Seriously." Her smile faded. "I don't know what I would have done if you hadn't shown up."

"I have no doubt you'd have handled it. But I'm glad you didn't have to." He reached out, tucked back a stiff piece of hair-sprayed hair behind her ear. "What did Sheriff Rubart say?"

"That his wife was going to monogram Blaine a pillow for his extended stay in jail." She snorted. "He had some other choice words, but those are the most repeatable."

Good.

"There's a lot to figure out legally. Sheriff is going to make some calls, try to get ahead of this Mafia threat." She jerked her head toward the curtained area to their right, where Blaine still groaned. "Thanks to your right hook, Blaine isn't currently able to get us the information he needs."

"I'd say I'm sorry, but I'm not."

"How did you know I was in trouble?" Rosalyn moved to sit beside him, and he scooted over to give her room. "You showed up out of nowhere."

Cade relayed what he'd realized at his parents' house, with the emails, the new log-in. "I knew there had to be another motivation driving him. It finally clicked. I prayed and felt the urge to go back to the last place you were. I didn't know you'd be there, but God did."

Rosalyn picked at the corner of the thin sheet beneath them. "I prayed a lot tonight too."

"I'm glad to hear it." He pulled in a breath, needing to know for sure. "Listen, I'm sorry about the other night. I assumed the worst, was a complete jerk."

"I said awful things too." She met his gaze, eyes watery with unshed tears. "I should've listened to you about Blaine—you tried to warn me."

Cade shook his head. "You were conned—by someone you should have been able to trust. It's not your fault."

"Some of it is though. My quest for perfection has made me—ironically—take shortcuts. Seek approval and fame in lieu of wisdom." She winced. "I've been prideful. I think that's why I couldn't admit you might be right about Blaine. I was afraid of what that meant about me . . ." She swallowed. "That I wasn't perfect."

"Being perfect—like being beautiful—is subjective anyway." Cade met her gaze, held it. Took a chance. "I personally kind of think you're both."

Her cheeks flushed. "*There's* that Landry charm." She bumped his shoulder this time. "What a night, huh?"

"Yeah, of the two of us, I didn't think *I'd* be the one needing the hospital this evening."

She shook her head. "We're quite the team."

"Hey, I'll gladly take a broken nose if it means we're on the *same* team this time."

Rosalyn picked up the abandoned ice pack from the bed, held it gingerly against his face. The cold seeped into his aches, the warmth in her eyes filling the rest of the cracks. "This seems familiar." She smiled. "Though I have to say an ice pack seems more effective than a cold beer mug."

"Agreed." He met her gaze, eyes dropping to her lips and then back to her eyes. "So you forgive me?"

"Yes. I would have, even if you hadn't taken down a would-be kidnapper." She adjusted the cold pack against his cheek. "Though that certainly helps when it comes to grand gestures." She hesitated. "You know I still have to go back though, right?"

There it was. The pin in the balloon. He swallowed. "I wondered."

"All this legal mess, upcoming scheduled shows . . . there's a lot I need to wrap up before I can start over." Rosalyn's gaze softened. "Before I can think about coming home."

He reached up, covered her hand that was holding the pack with his own. "*Are* you going to come back to Magnolia Bay?"

Her eyes turned flirty. "Would it matter?"

He searched her gaze, feeling like he could take down a dozen monsters for her. Feeling like he could live in their banter and memories and *teamwork* for the rest of his life. "It might."

"Then I might."

Her lips curved into a smile before she pressed them back against his.

Twenty -nine

H E MIGHT BE THE FIRST MAYORAL CAN-didate in history to quit a race at his own campaign party.

Cade stood in front of the Magnolia Blossom's yellow door two weeks later and took a deep breath. As soon as he opened it, he had to be professional. Had to pretend like he hadn't gotten only three hours of sleep last night, tossing and turning over Rosalyn not being back. They'd texted over the past few weeks, but the last few days, communication had dwindled. Had she changed her mind about them? Gotten swept back up in the spotlight of her career? Or busy trying to get home? He hadn't wanted to push, but surrendering had been hard—harder even than the task still before him.

But he was a Landry. He would resign with dignity.

Then go home and kill a bag of spicy Cheetos.

Cade opened the door and was immediately welcomed with a rush of cold air, the aroma of freshly baked peach pie . . . and roughly fifty people screaming "Surprise!" in his face.

He reeled back a step and blinked, taking in the smiling faces of his parents, Mama D, Mr. and Mrs. Dupree, Miley, and Pastor

Dubois. He turned, and there was Sawyer and Owen. Sadie and Mrs. Peters and Harper. And Noah, Elisa, her father Isaac, and Linc—well, *he* wasn't smiling. But he was standing next to Zoey, who was beaming enough for them both.

Cade moved slightly farther into the room. "Um, yes. I'm surprised." It wasn't anywhere near his birthday. And the red, white, and blue streamers hanging from the ceiling and the American flag printed centerpieces were most certainly not birthday-related decor.

"He doesn't see it." Delia, wearing a sleeveless blue dress and giant red earrings, pursed her lips.

"Oh, for crying out loud." Madame Paulette stepped to the front counter, her red scarves trailing behind her. "Look up, dear." She rolled her eyes as she stage-whispered to Elisa. "It's a good thing he's so cute, huh?"

Cade looked up at the banner hanging over the barstools and the dessert display, his smile dissipating. The festive red, white, and blue *Happy Campaign Party* wording had been edited with a black marker, to now read *Happy Un-Campaign Party*.

"We're firing you," Madame Paulette loudly announced, as if the sentiment weren't plenty self-explanatory enough. The diner full of people began clapping and cheering.

Well, this was a twist. He was being rejected before he could fail.

"Oh no. Look at his face." Madame pressed her fingers against her cheeks, her heavily made-up eyes growing wide. "Someone, quick. Make him understand."

Delia stepped forward, her hands clasped in front of her chest. For the first time since her surgery, she didn't hold a cane. "We're firing you because we love you."

Feeling slowly returned to Cade's knees. He opened his mouth, then shut it, unsure how to process.

Delia came closer, wrapping her hand around Cade's arm. Her gray head barely came to his shoulder as she smiled up at him. "We all think you're a great town director and we don't want to lose you in that role. So if you run, we all agreed we wouldn't vote for you. It's not the right fit."

Ouch.

"We want the best for you." She squeezed his arm. "Because we know you want the best for our town."

"You do?" He looked around at the smiling, hopeful faces around him. They all contained zero judgment.

This wasn't an insult. It was . . . a gift.

He hesitated. It was also his out, if he wanted it. He could accept their decision and save a bit of face—or be honest and say what he originally came to say.

"You're right, Mama D. It's not a great fit." Cade swallowed. "I actually came here today to tell you all that I'm withdrawing from the race." From the crowd, his father met his gaze. Pride lingered in his eyes.

"Oh, wonderful." Delia slapped Cade's shoulder. "Then tell us already!"

"Yeah. *Speech. Speech.*" Noah started the chanting, which was quickly picked up by Zoey and Elisa. The rest of the town followed.

"Okay, okay." Cade grinned and held up both hands, looking for a place to stand where everyone could hear him.

Elisa dragged a barstool away from the counter and situated it near the windows, facing the crowd. "Here's your stage. I don't have a microphone, sorry."

"Don't worry. Cade's never had a problem running his mouth," Linc ribbed. Zoey elbowed him in the side.

Cade propped on the edge of the high stool, resting one foot on the bottom bar. He looked out at some of his favorite people in town as they all stared back. At least his facial bruising had mostly resided, the hairline fracture healing straight. "Despite Linc's confidence endorsement there, this is actually a little intimidating."

Everyone chuckled.

Cade drew a deep breath. "Like I said, I came here today to withdraw from the race. And while I knew it was the right decision, it still felt like failing."

He blew out his breath as he faced his beloved town. "I owe you all an apology."

Faces crinkled in confusion. He wished he had a microphone, something to do with his hands. "Several of you tried to help me with Magnolia Days, and I rejected your efforts because I was trying to do everything myself."

Murmurs sounded around the room.

"I'm starting to realize that I need to be needed. And if *you're* helping *me*, then I'm not needed." He hesitated. "And somehow in my brain, that meant I wasn't wanted."

"That's ridiculous," Mama D scoffed.

"I agree—now. But in thinking that way, I did this town a disservice—and many of you, personally." He let his gaze encompass the group. Miley, chomping her gum. Owen, eagerly nodding as if he'd support whatever Cade had to say. Farmer Branson, bushy eyebrows hiding most of his stoic expression.

"Magnolia Days took a hit when the circus ended early." Cade grimaced. "And as many of you have probably heard, there won't be any filming here any time soon."

A few disappointed groans sounded through the café. He felt like moaning along with them.

Rosalyn hadn't come.

"About that." Delia stepped toward him, held up a clipboard. "We've got ideas for fundraising."

Cade leaned forward on his stool. "You do?"

"Of course. We care about this town too, Cade Landry." She fisted one hand on her hip. "You're not alone in this restoration project even though you tried to be. If you'll let us, we can put Magnolia Bay back together . . . well, together." She frowned. "I should've practiced that. It sounded more poetic in my head."

"We can *all* put it back together," Madame Paulette suggested.

"Or, you could say, 'together, we can all put it back.'" Elisa twirled a lock of hair around her finger. "No, that's still not right."

"Together is better?" Sadie offered.

Miley popped a bubble. "I have a bedtime, people."

"Miley's right." Delia handed Cade the clipboard. "Several of us met earlier today and wrote out our ideas. Maybe we can't have a circus every weekend, but there's plenty we can do if we band . . . together." She sighed. "Drat."

"I hear you, Mama D." Cade braced the clipboard in his lap and scanned the sheets, filled with ideas that took up the front and back of two pages. Everything from bake sales and car washes to a community-wide rummage sale and silent auction and a state-wide fishing tournament was listed. Yet another page appeared to be a list of names pledging to donate items and time toward the various projects.

Surprise flickered. These ideas were *good*. Cade should have listened to them sooner.

And the best part was—he wouldn't have to pull them off alone.

"You know what? I accept." Cade held up the clipboard with as real a grin as he could muster. "Let's get *together*"—the crowd groaned on cue—"and start scheduling some of these."

Cheers erupted.

"So who's gonna run for mayor now?" Sadie's voice rang above the noise.

"That's a great question." Dad stepped forward, holding his hands up to command the room. It immediately quieted. "I'd love to hear some nominees to get the ball rolling."

"What about Mama D?" Elisa suggested.

Delia reeled back. "I'm way too old for politics, but thanks for the vote of confidence, honey. What about Sadie?"

"Me?" Sadie's eyes widened and she gripped the back of the

chair in front of her. "I'm better with books than people. I think it should be Pastor Dubois."

"Oh, that's so kind of you, Sadie." Pastor smiled as he dipped into a slight bow. "But there's no way my schedule at the church would allow that. My first priority is shepherding all you wayward sheep." Everyone chuckled. He nodded toward his son. "What about Owen?"

Owen gulped, his face washing pale against his red T-shirt. "Um, thanks, Dad. But you've seen how I get in front of a crowd."

"Aw, come on." Elisa, standing under the banner next to Noah, patted Owen's arm. "You did a great job as ringmaster."

"That's because he got to hide behind eyeliner and those coat-tails." Linc scowled at the room at large. "And don't any of you even *think* about saying my name."

The diner fell into a thick silence.

Then . . . "What about Miley?" Owen joked.

Miley coughed hard on her gum, slapping her chest. "You guys are trying to kill me."

"Hang on." Dad came to stand by Cade, held up his hands with a chuckle. "I know this is sudden, so everyone take the weekend and think about it. I'll have a box in my office for you to place your nominee when you're ready."

"All right, then. If that's all on the political front, it's time for cupcakes!" Delia raised her fist to the chorus of cheers. Everyone turned toward the desserts. Cade stood, setting the clipboard on the table as the room lit with excited chatter, and breathed a sigh. He'd done it.

Now he could go home to those Cheetos and agonize over why Rosalyn—

"Wait!" Noah waved his arms to quiet the room. "There's one more order of business."

"Now what?" Madame Paulette planted her hands on her hips. "Politics make people hungry, Noah."

He ignored her and turned to face Elisa, who stood in front of the counter. "I wasn't going to do this here."

Elisa looked back at him with a smile, her brow slightly drawn in confusion. "Do what?"

Noah reached in the pocket of his plaid button-down and bent to one knee.

Elisa's eyes widened. She sucked in her breath. "Oh my gosh."

"Oh my *gosh*." Zoey slapped Linc's arm.

Delia, who stood closest to Cade, clutched his sleeve. "*Oh* my gosh."

Cade steadied her with his free hand, unable to keep a smile from spreading across his face. Maybe nothing else had gone as planned lately, but this—this was better.

The room fell into reverent silence as Noah looked up at Elisa, who had her hands pressed against both cheeks. "I realize this isn't the most romantic setting, but I've been carrying this ring around for weeks hoping for the perfect moment." Noah's Adam's apple bobbed in his throat. "I can't wait any longer to be your husband, Elisa Bergeron."

Tears streamed freely down Elisa's cheeks. "Well that's good, sugar, because I can't wait any longer to say yes."

"I technically haven't asked you anything yet." He grinned, his eyes misty.

"Then hurry up already." Elisa bounced up and down.

Cade cast a quick look toward Zoey and Linc. Zoey had her hands clutched under her chin, her face radiant. "Elisa Bergeron." Noah cleared his throat, then started again, voice thick. "We've been through a lot. I used to just fight with you. Then, somewhere along the way, I started to love fighting with you. But now . . . now I just love you." He held up the ring, a beautiful solitaire. "And I'd love to *not* fight with you for the rest of our days if you'll have me."

"Yes!" She didn't even wait for him to put the ring on her finger before she launched into his arms.

He wrapped her in a tight hug as the room burst into applause. Then they pulled back to kiss, and the whistles started. Blushing, Elisa drew away far enough to let him put the ring on her left hand. "It's perfect. That was perfect."

"You're perfect." Noah dropped a kiss on her nose.

"I'm going to throw up." Miley sighed as she turned away. "Where are those cupcakes?"

The rest of the room flocked to the happy couple's side. Mrs. Peters sidled up to Cade, who hung back from the festivities. Her vintage pantsuit today was a burnt orange.

"A gift for you, young Landry." She sniffed and handed him a book with a red bow on top.

"For me?" He carefully removed the bow to see the title. *If You Give a Mouse a Cookie.* Cade grinned, meeting the older woman's eyes even as gratitude tightened his throat. "You shouldn't have."

He'd won over Mrs. Peters. Who'd have thought?

She lifted her chin. "It's due back in three weeks." Then she winked—*winked*—before heading for the cupcake table.

Delia joined him before he could close his mouth. "See? You're doing better than you realize." She patted his shoulder. "People care about you."

"I'm starting to believe it." He set the book on the table behind him. "Thanks, Mama D."

"I'm happy everything is working out. For everyone." She released a pleased sigh, then shot Cade a sidelong look. "Now . . . what's the plan for these potholes?"

He snorted. "Yours is up first, of course."

"I bet you tell that to all the girls." Delia rolled her eyes.

Cade grinned. "Just the ones I like."

The front door opened with a chime. Cade did a double take as Rosalyn slipped inside, her hair long and loose. His heart spiked. She looked stunning, wearing a simple pink sundress in lieu of her usual workout gear, dainty gold sandals covering tan feet.

Mama D cleared her throat. "Your mouth is open." Then she winked before merging into the crowd.

Cade tried not to stare as Rosalyn wove through the group. But she'd never be able to blend into a crowd. She was a star.

Maybe it was too much to expect her to ever come down.

Then her eyes landed on him and her face lit, shooting sparks straight through his heart.

Or maybe there was always reason to hope.

"Hi." Breathless, she landed at his side. Citrus wafted over him.

"Hi yourself." He edged them over to the side of the room, out of the flow of traffic lining up for cupcakes.

"Sorry I'm late. What'd I miss?" She looked up at him, hair flowing around her shoulders, all beauty and grace.

"Oh, not much. Just my concession speech, which occurred *after* I got lovingly fired from attempting to run in the first place. And a town-wide effort to help save the Bay now that the movie crew isn't coming." He snapped his fingers. "Oh! And Noah proposed to Elisa."

"Is that all?" Rosalyn laughed, holding up a piece of folded paper. "Mom's printer is on the fritz, so I had to run by the library."

He took the paper, wondering if he could take her into his arms too or—

"Read it." She was practically bouncing.

He unfolded the slip. A confirmation letter? He skimmed the words. *Congratulations on signing up for the Louisiana bar exam.* Followed by a paid-in-full receipt.

What?

The question must have been in his eyes, because she tucked her hair behind her ears, words spilling from glossed lips. "This was my first order of business after getting some of my money back."

"Rosalyn—"

She held up one hand. "I worked with a well-known industry lawyer a lot of entertainers in my circuit use, and he was great.

Everything is sorted. I'm safe. The debts are repaid, and Blaine is being held without bail." She met his eyes. "But I realized that moving forward, there's only one man I really trust with my career . . . and my heart."

Cade nodded soberly. "Owen Dubois."

She snorted. "*You*." Her eyes shone with . . . love? "I want you on my team—in every way."

His heart swelled. Oh, he wanted that too. Except—he frowned. "You realize if we're together, then my representing you is a conflict of interest?"

"No, I didn't." She laughed. "See? You're good at this already."

Joy and need and gratitude filled his lungs. "I'm good at something else too. Come here."

And she did, willingly, their lips dancing as he breathed in her scent, his fingers tangling into her hair, his heart full to bursting. She believed in him. She didn't need him—but she wanted him.

She was home.

The room burst into applause, and it took several moments and a quick breath for him to realize they were clapping for them. Still, he didn't want to pull away.

"See?" Noah's triumphant voice rose above the crowd. "*Told* you they were in love back during that whole volcano thing."

Cade grinned against Rosalyn's lips.

Yeah.

He kinda knew it then too.

Thirty

Two weeks later

I CAN'T BELIEVE I LET Y'ALL TALK ME into this." Cade adjusted positions on the dunking booth board, his bare feet dangling into the water beneath.

Rosalyn grinned, sidling up as close as the oversized tank would allow. Cade looked way too cute in swim trunks and a white T-shirt, sunglasses tucked into the neck. "It's for the town, Landry. Get on board."

The Water Day fundraiser Delia planned was going great. The mid-August sun shone bright overhead. Across the park, children squealed their way down the inflatable slide set up near the gazebo.

And she was here with Cade.

For good.

"Yeah, quit complaining." Noah wound up his pitching arm as he stood a few yards from the buzzer mounted on a tarp to Cade's left. "A little water never hurt anyone."

"Just accept now that you won't bring in as much money as Sheriff Rubart or my father did." Elisa stood to Noah's side, where she'd stopped admiring the way her engagement ring shimmered under the sun long enough to have a conversation.

Next to Elisa, wearing a tank top and shorts, Zoey snorted. "I'm pretty sure Noah and Linc will help make up any difference."

"Yeah, I'm pitching until he goes in." Noah tossed the ball from hand to hand. "Take my money." He lined up for the shot.

"Wait!" Rosalyn reached toward Cade and grabbed his sunglasses. "I'll hang on to these for you."

Cade smirked, shifting positions on the bench. "You're assuming he's going to hit the buzzer."

"Okay, that's it." Noah narrowed his eyes. "Step back, Rosalyn, unless you want to get splashed."

"That's a lot of confidence." Linc crossed his arms over his muscle tank.

"I played baseball growing up." Noah squinted at the buzzer. "Just wait." He threw the ball.

It bounced two feet from the buzzer and rolled back toward him.

"I think it's safe to give me my sunglasses back." Cade laughed.

Rosalyn slid them on her own face. "Not a chance. I believe in my friends."

"Cheap shot, Ace." Cade pressed his hand over his heart, his eyes dancing, and for a second, they were eighteen again. Standing on the outdoor platform at graduation as a dozen cannons shot confetti high into the air. Locking eyes across the throng of students as they moved their tassel to the other side of their shiny blue caps.

Completely unaware of all the future held.

Rosalyn's stomach fluttered on cue. Oh, but she liked being back in Magnolia Bay. Liked that she had made new friends and restored a full relationship with not only Cade but her mom.

She'd finally told her parents everything. All the mistakes, the lies, the misplaced trust. The bad decisions and fear of being rejected if she didn't do everything perfectly.

And like in Chug a Mug that day with the laptop, they'd handled it with grace.

"I never wanted you to be perfect at ballet, I just wanted you to have fun," Mom had said.

And wasn't that ironic? "Well, I never had fun because I wasn't perfect at it."

They'd laughed together, teary. "None of us are perfect. Sure, I was disappointed you quit—but not for long." Mom's eyes had glazed over as she took Rosalyn's hand, squeezed. "You were obviously meant to fly."

And looking into Cade's steady gaze now, she realized there were multiple ways to do exactly that.

"Throw again." Zoey plucked a dollar bill from Noah's hand and gave it to Rosalyn. "Here."

"Might as well fork over a ten and save her the trouble of opening that bag a dozen times." Linc grinned, his dark bun shifting.

"He's going in, don't worry." Noah narrowed his eyes in concentration. Threw.

Missed.

Rosalyn tucked the money in the zippered pouch she was guarding. "One more?"

"Ah, whatever." Noah handed over a fiver.

Across the park by the hot dog stand, Mama D screamed as she slid down the water slide in a hot pink swimsuit. Madame Paulette greeted her at the bottom, wearing a swim skirt that hung to her knees. "My turn!" Together, they scrambled up the inflatable stairs.

Near the slide, Miley lay out on a beach towel, wearing a black swimsuit and dark glasses, ignoring the kids running circles around her with water guns. To her right, Sadie and Harper camped out in lounge chairs, a pile of novels stacked next to a cooler between them. Nearby, under an umbrella, Mrs. Peters scowled at a kid playing a handheld video game.

Elisa and Zoey pressed next to Rosalyn as Noah continued his pitching attempts. "Is it true Blaine is in jail?" Elisa asked.

"Yep." Rosalyn nodded. "For a long time—thankfully, not here in town."

"Your life is like made-for-TV movie." Elisa shook her head. "An aerialist in a Cajun Circus, running from the Mafia."

Rosalyn laughed. "I'm happy to change the channel, in that case."

She'd never dared to dream this day could come—and it felt better than she'd imagined.

"Did Bruno move forward with that lawsuit?" Noah paused his next attempt at the buzzer.

Cade shook his head. "He backed down, apologized for the threat." He sighed. "And as part of said apology, gave me a voucher for a lifetime supply of . . . wait for it . . . free frog legs."

"*Eww.*" Zoey, Elisa, and Rosalyn protested in unison.

"I'd try them." Noah shrugged as he wound his arm up.

"You do, and you can keep your kisses to yourself," Elisa warned.

He winked at her before releasing the next shot.

Missed.

A few of the young ballet students from Lettie's studio skipped past, slurping popsicles as purple juice rolled down their arms. "Hi, Barbie!" They waved.

Rosalyn smiled and waved back . . . which reminded her . . .

"Tell them the other good news!" Cade called from his perch, as if reading her mind.

Elisa and Zoey looked at her with raised brows.

She could barely contain her grin. "I'm about to start looking at real estate here in town for an aerial studio."

Zoey squealed and grabbed her arm. "Take my money! I'll be your first student." She wrinkled her nose. "Once I have money again, of course."

"I've got to find a place first, and get a loan secured."

"With a *bank*," Cade added.

She rolled her eyes at him. "There's still a lot of legal stuff to wade through with Blaine's theft, so in the meantime, Dad is going to co-sign for me."

As much as she'd wanted to put things back together herself, she'd realized the beauty in *not* being able to handle everything perfectly—and the gift it gave others to help. She smiled as Cade mocked Noah's next attempt.

Zoey took another bill from Noah and handed it to Rosalyn before turning to Elisa. "Have you guys talked wedding dates yet?"

"Only a zillion times. But we haven't nailed anything down." Elisa's eyes shot hearts as she watched Noah pitch. "He's actually way better at baseball than this, guys. I've seen him play."

"You're blinded by love." Zoey rolled her eyes.

"What about you, Zoey?" Rosalyn zipped the money bag and tucked it under her arm. "What's going to happen with your beignet shop?"

"My insurance company has a lot of questions." Zoey's eyes flitted to Linc, who stood with his arms crossed, surveying the park like a bodyguard. His bun ruffled in the breeze. "I'm still waiting to hear from the fire department on what started the fire, which obviously matters for the claim."

"I'm sure it'll work out." Elisa rubbed her friend's back. "You know we're all here to help you."

"I do. And everything happens when it's supposed to, you know?" Zoey cut her eyes to Noah and she smirked. "Except for maybe Noah hitting that target."

"Oh, for crying out loud." Linc tossed a twenty toward Rosalyn, snagged the ball from Noah's hand, and threw it hard. The ball landed squarely on the buzzer.

The bench gave way beneath Cade and he sank beneath the water, arms flailing. He came up sputtering, shoving his hair back from his head as he stood. His white T-shirt clung to his chest and biceps.

"You're welcome, Rosalyn." Linc shot her a wink.

"I almost had him," Noah protested. Elisa patted his shoulder in consolation.

Cade hoisted himself out of the tank, dripping onto the grass. Then he squished toward Rosalyn, mischief in his eyes.

"Oh no. Don't you dare." Rosalyn held up one finger, heart pounding.

"Come on, Ace. Get on board." Cade mocked her earlier words as he hurried toward her, arms held wide. He grinned as water sluiced off his shorts onto the ground.

Rosalyn squealed and started to make a run for it. He easily caught her, cool water immediately soaking through her tank and shorts. "You can't get away that easily."

She surrendered. Turned and wrapped her arms around his neck. "I wouldn't dare try."

In her peripheral vision, Elisa clutched her hands to her chest. "Aww.'"

"Just precious." Zoey sighed.

Linc rolled his eyes. "There's *way* too many hormones in this park."

Zoey and Elisa both swatted his arm as Cade pulled Rosalyn in for a kiss.

She closed her eyes and kissed him back, breathing in the scent of water and sunscreen and his lingering cologne, memorizing the feel of his broad shoulders beneath her hands. Their timing had turned out perfect after all.

There was no place like home.

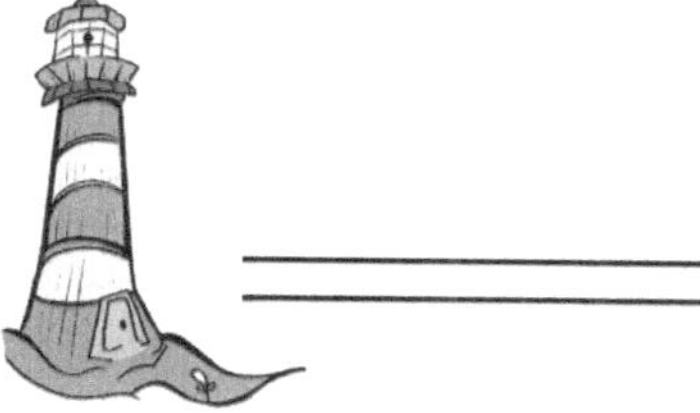

Read on for more from the
Magnolia Bay
series

"A swoon-worthy, deeply satisfying romance."
- USA Today bestselling author Susan May Warren
Meant for Me
BETSY ST. AMANT

He was her best friend. Still is. But when her beloved beignet shop burns down, he'll have to be more if she hopes to start over. But will friendship survive the dangers of a marriage of convenience?

Lincoln "Linc" Fontenot enjoys working out, running his crawfish business, and the company of approximately three people. Zoey Lakewood has been at the top of that short list for years, the only bit of sunshine he ever allows to part his comfortably cloudy sky. But when Linc's steady, quiet world is rocked by the unexpected guardianship of a teen girl, his friendship with Zoey becomes even more crucial. He needs help, bad...but maybe not as bad as Zoey.

Zoey's never had a problem manifesting joy. But having just lost her home and her beignet business to an uninsured fire, for once she struggles to find the silver lining. She and Linc arrange to help each other out—as just friends, of course. She'll provide teen-parenting assistance while he provides a place for her to get back on her feet. But one thing her friendship with Linc has never had to navigate is close proximity.

Tension—and chemistry—mount as they attempt to manage this sudden insta-family. But Zoey just lost everything, and she can't risk losing her best friend, too. Will her friendship with Linc go up in flames like her beignet shop? Or will Linc and Zoey finally realize they were meant for each other?

One

Friday

THERE WERE TOO MANY PEOPLE IN HIS boat. No, there were too many *kids* in his boat.

The evening sun began its lazy late summer descent, casting a golden glow atop the waves of Magnolia Bay. Linc Fontenot held back a scowl as yet another sticky-fingered, freckled-faced child grabbed for the steering column of Linc's twenty-foot pontoon. Of all the nights for Anthony, his college-aged tour guide, to call in sick. Should have told him to pop an Ibuprofen and get to work.

"We'll be off shortly." Linc attempted a less-fake smile at his pontoon full of eight croc-wearing, camera-clutching tourists. He probably sounded as annoyed as he felt, which wasn't great for the five-star reviews he was in desperate need of, but some things, like the weather and this wind stirring up waves, just couldn't be helped. The boat rocked again, and he braced his legs as he stood starboard, arms crossed.

The dock—unlike the boat—sat annoyingly empty as they bobbed. Where was Zoey? She'd sworn she was on her way ten minutes ago. And not that she'd lie, exactly, but it'd be just like her to leave him hanging, stretch him to his max before swooping in to help at the last minute.

"What's this do?" The same freckled, sun-burnt kid reached for one of the levers on the steering column.

Linc swatted his hand away, let his scowl free. "Blows up the boat."

"Really?" The kid lowered his hands to his side, blue eyes wide against red cheeks.

Linc narrowed his eyes. "Wanna find out?"

Freckles adamantly shook his head and cowered into his mother, who wore a buckled life jacket despite the fact they hadn't even set sail yet and vests were optional for participants over twelve. The mom frowned at Linc, wrapping her arm around her son.

Five stars, five stars. "Uh, help yourself to the sodas in the cooler there." Linc stepped away, turned his back. See? This was why Anthony did Boiling Bayou tours in the off season. Linc was better with crawfish than people.

He shaded his eyes and gazed up the dock, toward the boat house and the slightly leaning, boarded bathroom facility and the miniscule concession counter that made them able to pitch this bay-side tour business more legitimately. In the bow seat, a middle-aged couple wearing straw hats started arguing, one of them sounding like they'd already hit up happy hour at the pub before boarding. Great.

He could probably only stall about five more minutes, and then he'd be forced to drive the boat *and* talk, God help him. Maybe they'd get lucky and see a dolphin, despite the last sighting having been weeks ago. No way would Linc be able to create the same energy Anthony did—giving facts about bay life and stats about the gulf beyond, making the tourists laugh and want to come back. Honestly, it was just a bay.

But he'd come back years ago, hadn't he? So maybe it was more.

Two kids started a loud game of rock, paper, scissors, and Linc wondered for the tenth time if he could raise his age limit for tours. But then he'd be turning away families, and exhausted dads with fat wallets looking to sit down for an hour were the only reason he was able to keep things running in the off season. The hurricane last year made this past crawfish and shrimp haul the smallest Linc had ever had. He just had to make up the difference this fall and winter with these side hustles, then hope for a solid season next spring. Problem was, he wasn't generating enough traction on the tours yet, and Eliza, who'd helped market his buddy Noah's inn recently, suggested he focus on getting people to leave reviews.

Positive reviews. He winced. This was all doable, right? No need to worry.

Except for the fact Zoey might not show up and he might have to play the role of fun-loving guide. *That* was reason to worry.

But there she was, finally, jogging over the sun-warped planks, dark hair bouncing over her small, fairy-like frame. Her slouchy, oversized bag slammed her jean-clad hip with each step, her smile wide and knowing as she barreled straight down into the boat.

"Took you long enough." Linc kept his voice low, his stance solid as she braced one hand on his shoulder to soften her abrupt landing. Wasn't that what he always did for her? Had done while she stood and watched her own business burn to the ground several weeks ago?

He wasn't the only one needing to make up profits. At least his status wasn't emergency. Yet, anyway.

She blinked up at him, blue eyes large beneath thick bangs, her smile far from innocent. "Now, did you think I left you here alone with all these—" she dropped to a horrified whisper "—*people* on purpose?"

"Yes. I did." His shoulder tingled under her touch. Been doing that lately. Somewhat bothersome.

"And yet you called me anyway." She winked, moving her hands to plant on her narrow hips. "I sort of like being your only hope."

He scowled again as he made his way to the wheel, shaking off the lingering burn on his arm. "Desperate times."

"Am I getting paid for this?" She unzipped that ridiculous bag and pulled out a black band.

He plopped down on the captain's chair. "No."

She affixed the band over one eye and struck a pose. Good grief, she'd brought an eye patch. "What about now?"

He snorted. "I asked you to lead the tour, not channel your inner Captain Hook."

"Same thing, right?" She pulled a fake goatee from her purse, peeled off an adhesive strip, and affixed it to her cheeks and chin. Then draped a gold chain over her neck, rolled up her shirt sleeve to reveal the fake—*please* be fake—bicep tattoo of a heart reading MOM, and turned to the tourists with a grand gesture. "Ahoy, mateys! Welcome aboard."

Oh, brother. Linc shifted into reverse and the boat puttered away from the dock as Zoey launched into an even thicker accent, sounding more British than pirate. But the kids had quieted down, and even Mrs. Uptight looked relaxed now, leaning back against the seat and smiling as her son stared mesmerized at Zoey.

Same, kid, same. Linc threw the throttle into drive. Hard not to stare at Zoey, lately. Which obviously was just proof Linc needed a vacation. He'd been working too hard the past month, was getting tired. Or something.

Something dangerously close to vulnerable.

He squinted into the sunlight as he navigated them out of the inlet into deeper water, keeping an eye on the wind still sending rogue gusts. Zoey might be goofy, but she'd rack in those five stars for him. He'd pay her for helping today, even though she wouldn't be expecting it. She'd been couch-surfing over Magnolia Bay since her apartment lease ended and the insurance from the fire at Bayou Beignets had yet to pay out. She needed all the money she could get, despite insisting she was fine. He knew better, knew that was why she'd been scrambling to create her own side catering business in the meantime.

She also insisted she couldn't stay with him, even though he had two extra bedrooms. Said she'd cramp his style. And she would. He rather liked his high ceilings and cedar beams and wide windows with a view of a pond, his own private corner of Magnolia Bay. It was peaceful. Quiet.

But maybe some temporary company didn't sound *too* awful.

Zoey leaned in toward her audience, casting one leg straight out to the side like it was a peg. "Who can tell me why one pirate pushed another one overboard?"

The parents exchanged knowing grins while the kids shook their heads.

"Because they got into an *arrgh*-ument, of course!"

Linc rolled his eyes as the adults chuckled. "I thought Miley was the resident comedian around here." The moody young barista had shocked everyone with her comedy skills at the Cajun Circus fundraiser his friend Cade hosted earlier in the summer. "You should probably keep your day job, Zo—"

Oops. She had no day job anymore. He winced.

Zoey narrowed her eyes, the wind brushing back her hair and giving her an even more genuine pirate-like appearance. "If you're going to insult me, commit already. Don't stop mid-sentence like a coward."

"Sorry." He briefly released the wheel and held up both hands in surrender. "I didn't think it through."

"Since when do you care about that?" She turned back to the tourists, thankfully before she saw the grin Linc fought to hide. Maybe that was why he tolerated Zoey. Okay, more than tolerated. She had moxie. Always told him what he needed to hear.

Never seemed to be scared of him, unlike most of the rest of the town.

"I've got one more question for ye, then we'll turn our attention to the murky, treasure-laden waters of Magnolia Bay." Zoey wiggled her fingers toward the freckled kid.

The boy jumped up from his seat and grinned. "I have a question too!"

"Please remain seated at all times," Linc droned.

The kid reluctantly perched on the edge of the bench seat. The engine hummed beneath them. "What's your pirate name?"

"Oh! Um." Zoey cleared her throat, cast a quick look at Linc.

He shook his head, stoic. Nope, not helping. She'd gotten herself into this...

"It's, ah—" She adjusted the eye patch that had slipped. "Captain Z, of course."

Freckles sank back, skinny brows furrowed. "That's *bor-ing*."

"I mean, that *was* my name. Before...the fire." Zoey squared her shoulders.

Freckles blinked and the rest of the crowd grew still. "The fire?"

What was she doing? Linc steered them toward the open water, where two jet skis raced. He scowled. In this wind? Those arrogant idiots better follow the traffic rules...

"Argh, that's right. I'm homeless." Zoey lifted her chin, patted her goatee as if she were making up a simple story and not merging fiction with reality. "Did you not see the burnt building on Village Lane?"

"I did." A younger girl, life jacket securely buckled, raised her hand, eyes wide. "That was yours?"

Anyone else, he'd worry about the story sending them into a PTSD episode. Even his stomach twisted when he remembered the flames, the sweat pooling on his back as Zoey buried his face into his shoulder, hiding as her award-wining business burned to a crisp.

But to Zoey, it was apparently just one more obstacle to pole-jump over onto a sunbeam. One more silver lining to an already gloriously metallic cloud. Did anything *ever* bother the woman?

Though she did refuse refused to walk past the shop in its current shape—the shape on hold while she waited for the claims department to sort the whole mess out.

"Arrgh, it's true. Cannon-fire." She wiggled her fingers again and this time, Freckles' grin returned.

"What's your new name?"

"Did you get a promotion to Captain because you won the pirate war?"

"Did anything else burn down?"

"Where will you live next?"

The kids ignored Linc's stay-seated command and jumped up and down, shooting rapid-fire questions, while the moms exchanged mildly concerned looks—as if they weren't entirely sure how to reconcile the very real, burned building with Zoey's story about very unreal pirates.

Anthony never gave him these kinds of problems.

Linc shook his head, gearing down to keep his distance from the jet skis still racing in a zig-zag. His fingers stuck to the lever, residue from Freckles, no doubt. *Why* were kids so sticky?

"Hang on, guys. You have to answer a question for me, first." Zoey raised her arms for attention, wobbling as Linc turned the boat portside to avoid the worst of the jet skis' wake. She planted her feet. "Why were the kids so restless in pirating class?"

Freckles blinked at her. Life Jacket Girl shrugged. Linc couldn't look away, either, Zoey holding the entire boat captive as she rose on tip toe, face light, eyes sparking with drama and life and sun.

Man, she was pretty.

"Because they were…over-*bored*!" Zoey lunged forward, arms splayed, as the kids jumped and shrieked. Then the wind slammed a wave into the wake of the second jet ski. Linc jerked his attention back to the wheel, two seconds too late. The boat launched. And Freckles went flying.

His mom screamed at the splash. Zoey caught herself, tripping over the younger girl who had fallen to the slippery boat floor. She popped up like a wide-eyed gopher. Two dads jumped up, raced to the edge of the boat, slipping in their crocs. Every other gaping mouthed, wide-eyed head on board turned accusingly to Linc.

He cut the boat to idle and sighed. So much for five stars.

Zoey Lakewood had never fancied herself a betting woman, but if Magnolia Bay ever lowered itself enough to host a wet T-shirt contest, she'd put her life savings on Linc.

Not that there'd be any left, the way she was currently plowing through her savings account after the fire.

Linc's flip-flops squished as he unceremoniously deposited the freckled boy back into his mother's arms. His shirt stretched taut against his broad back and biceps. One of the men—the boy's father?—reached to shake Linc's hand, but Linc brushed it off, returning to his captain's chair as his mane of wet man-bun coursed rivers of water down his thick neck.

He was mad.

Zoey winced as the chaos meter in the boat escalated a notch, everyone swarming the kid with exclamations of concern. Did anyone blame her? Maybe she shouldn't have been so dramatic with her pirate vibes. But how was she supposed to know the boat would lurch at the *exact* wrong moment? Wasn't that Linc's job as captain to know?

She tried to catch Linc's eye, but he only jammed the boat into gear and scowled as he flipped his dripping hair out of his face. "Tour's over."

Oh, dunkin' donuts, he wouldn't look at her. So he was mad. Which wasn't fair, but he'd get over it. Not much had been fair lately, and *she* wasn't complaining. "Well, that over-bored joke sure was timely." Zoey plastered on a bright smile for her damp audience, who didn't smile back as the boat began puttering—slowly, to Linc's credit—back toward the dock. She quickly pulled off her eye patch, blinking against the sunset glinting off the bay. "I guess I should have mentioned swimming was optional at the *end* of the tour only..."

Crickets. Make that soggy crickets. She gulped.

The boy's parents continued fussing over him, while the young girl in a life jacket wrinkled her nose and tried to scoot as far from his spreading water puddle as possible. Linc muttered stuff about "*told* them to remain seated" as they neared the dock. Which was valid. So maybe it was a little of everyone's fault.

Still. She tried to think what else she had in her purse that could help save the tour, the bag her best friend Elisa often referred to as Mary Poppins's. Personally, she'd rather think of it as Hermione Granger's, but same concept—endless supplies.

She began digging. Eye patch, ChapStick, the keys to her tired but trusty Jeep, her Alice in Wonderland coin purse, tissues, a mini screw driver, phone charger, a folded jump rope, pepper spray, emergency stash of candy—*aha*. This sure qualified.

"Who wants Starburst?" She tugged the colored bag free and held it up. The kids cheered and more hair ties sprinkled to the floor like confetti. "Plenty for everyone. Parents too." She handed the candy to the mom of the overboard boy. "Here, enjoy." Maybe this would buy some time to fix this.

She scurried to Linc's side as the others gathered around the Starbursts. Time to test the waters. *Waters*, ha. That was a good one. "Ahoy, Captain."

"They're going to want refunds." A muscle ticked in his jaw, his eyes hidden behind dark sunglasses. Probably calculating how much gas he'd already spent and wouldn't get reimbursed for by the time he gave everyone their money back.

She shuffled her feet, frowned. She hated when he was upset. Ironic, maybe, as she seemed to upset him the most.

"Maybe offer refunds?" Zoey reached up to adjust the strap of her bag around her shoulder. "It's only one tour, and hey, it got cut short so now you can go home. Alone. To be, you know—*alone.*"

As he liked. Which was part of why she kept refusing his offer to stay in one of his guest rooms while she waited on her insurance payout. Linc didn't really want her there—he just felt obligated since he had unused space.

"True." Linc's lower lip tugged to one side, as if fighting a smile. Ahh, a moment of humanity. "There's not *always* a bright side, you know."

"Oh sure there is. Just gotta *look* for it." She pulled his sunglasses off his face and immediately regretted it.

His laser gaze slammed into hers without blinking. Linc. Always steady. Strong.

Annoyed, maybe. But there.

For her.

She'd never really figured out why. He'd certainly never made a move on her, so it wasn't romantic intention. He'd been there when she was younger, too. Like that one day back when she was in middle school and took baking lessons from his aunt and he—

"*Or* maybe some people see things that aren't there." Linc snatched his glasses from her, returned them to his face.

O-kay, then. Mr. Grumpy was back. Zoey stepped back as he secured the boat to the dock. The tourists stood, grumbling and shucking of life vests, one of them mumbling about one-star reviews.

Oh, no. Linc needed *good* reviews. And everyone leaving the tour squishy and annoyed wasn't going to get those. She had to salvage this for him, even if it wasn't technically her fault. At least, not all her fault. *Lord, a little help? Something happy?*

And then, like the parting of the red sea—okay, slightly less dramatic—the sun glinted off a distant wave and revealed...

"Dolphin!" Zoey pointed. Her heart soared.

The kids squealed and the adults whipped around to look. "Where?" Everyone rushed portside, and the boat rocked precariously.

"There it is!"

"I see it!"

The grumbles turned to delighted murmurs. Everyone stood still, watching, as a second dolphin crested the water. The pair bobbed in the setting sun, cruising back out toward the gulf, slicks back shining like—well, like a silver lining. Zoey breathed a sigh of relief. *Thank you.*

Linc joined her, crossing his arms as several people began snapping pictures of the dolphins. His sunglasses were tucked into the collar of his wet shirt. But for once, his brow wasn't furrowed, his jaw wasn't tight. "Good save."

"I prayed."

"Figured."

She shrugged. "Least I could do."

"Was it?" Turning, Linc's eyes lingered on hers, then dropped to her lips.

Um. Huh? Her mouth went dry. Her stomach dropped. "I—"

"You forgot to shave." He ripped the goatee off her chin like a band-aid.

"Ow!" She rubbed her jaw, more surprised than hurt. "I forgot it was there."

Linc smirked. "Then I'll amend my earlier statement to include that some people don't see what *is* right there."

"You're right." She ignored the flutter in her stomach, the slight shake in her hands, and forced her brightest smile. "They sure don't."

She rolled in her lower lip, trying not to watch as he meandered back to the captain's chair.

And maybe they never would.

Thank You!

Thank you so much for reading *No Place Like Home*. We hope you enjoyed the story. If you did, would you be willing to do us a favor and leave a review? It doesn't have to be long—just a few words to help other readers know what they're getting. (But no spoilers! We don't want to wreck the fun!) Thank you again for reading!

We'd love to hear from you—not only about this story, but about any characters or stories you'd like to read in the future. Contact us at www.sunrisepublishing.com/contact.

Acknowledgments

I thank my agent in every book because she's just that wonderful. Big hugs to Tamela Hancock Murray, for hanging in there with me for the last decade and a half. PS. You're never allowed to retire.

Susie Warren – this book almost did me in but your cheerleading and editing genius kept me going. Thanks (again!) for always nudging me to go deeper, try harder, write stronger. You're an inspiration.

Megan – I don't fully understand how you deal with me while I'm on deadline but I'm grateful you always text back! Love you and your encouragement and your prayers. Keep being you.

Roxanne – Grateful for the gift of a heart-sister in Lafayette—and a Cajun one to boot ☺ Love you always!

To the whole talented team at Aerial Expressions – you girls are AMAZING! Truly. Keep soaring. (and no micro bends!)

Hubby – I know you can't keep up with which book I'm writing anymore, and that's okay. You still support me and hey, you can deadlift 400 pounds, so it's all good. I love you!

Allen & Kellye – you guys didn't have anything to do with this novel, but you had a lot to do with my heart while I navigated this particular deadline, so...thank you. When I think of "good gifts from above," I think of y'all.

Jesus – As you well know, this book took a lot out of me. Thanks for filling me back up. #SoliDeogloria

About the Author

Betsy St. Amant Haddox is the author of over twenty romance novels and novellas. She resides in north Louisiana with her hubby, two daughters, an impressive stash of coffee mugs, and one furry Schnauzer-toddler. Betsy has a B.A. in Communications and a deep-rooted passion for seeing women restored to truth. When she's not composing her next book or trying to prove unicorns are real, Betsy can be found somewhere in the vicinity of an iced coffee. She writes frequently for www.ibelieve.com, a devotional site for women.

Learn more about Betsy at www.betsystamant.com.

MAGNOLIA BAY

Where southern charm and romance intertwine...

"Heartwarming, genuine, and utterly captivating."

–SUSAN MAY WARREN
USA Today bestselling author

We solve the problem of what we read next.   Available on Amazon

SUSAN MAY WARREN and TARI FARIS

with Mandy Boerma and Andrea Michelle Wood

We solve the problem of what we read next.

Available on Amazon

YOU MAY ALSO LIKE...

When a blizzard strikes Deep Haven and Megan is overrun with catastrophes, it takes a former Ranger to step in and help. But the more he comes to her rescue, the sooner she'll move out... Come home to Deep Haven in this magical tale about the one who got away... and came back.

Still the One by Susan May Warren and Rachel D. Russell

Working together to keep Fox Bakery from going under, Robin and Sammy find that something more than friendship is simmering between them. But will Robin follow her old dreams back to the glamor of Paris, or will she discover how sweet it is to be loved in Deep Haven?

How Sweet It Is by Andrea Christenson

Back in Hearts Bend for the first time in ten years and thrown together at Haven's Bakery, Chloe and Sam have a second chance at first love. The more time Sam spends selling pastries, the more he sees a new future. But where does Chloe's heart belong? Can they find the recipe for leaving regrets behind and start something new?

One Fine Day by Rachel Hauck and Carrie Padgett

We solve the problem of what we read next.

Available on Amazon

**WHERE EVERY STORY IS A FRIEND,
AND EVERY CHAPTER IS A NEW JOURNEY...**

Subscribe to our newsletter for the latest news, weekly giveaways, exclusive author interviews, and more!

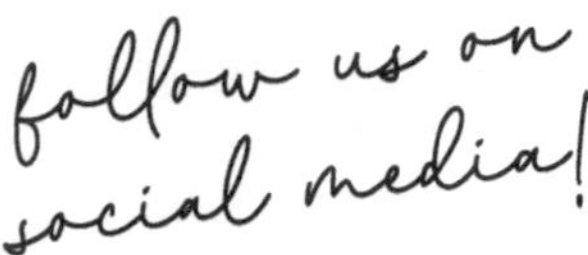

Shop paperbacks, ebooks, audiobooks, and more at
SUNRISEPUBLISHING.MYSHOPIFY.COM